Violent Warriors
of Peace

By

David Kelley

Hidden Manna Publications

DEDICATED

To the men and women who guarded the borders between east and west, making sure that men and women in western Europe were not oppressed by tyranny. They usually served with little thanks or recognition. They also gave up time and sacrificed for the love of freedom. I also want to thank my wife, Norma for sticking with me through the time I served in the military in Europe.

Contents

Book I

8TH INFANTRY DIVISION

LARSON

8-inch gun moving into position

BAUMHOLDER, GERMANY

Chapter 1

ON MANEUVER

Dean put his hands over his ears. "Fire!" the Sergeant yelled. The man pulled the lanyard and the big gun belched out its two-hundred-pound projectile. Smoke and fire engulfed the tube of the gun. The cold January wind sent the smoke back, hiding the M-110 eight-inch howitzer briefly.

Dean loved the smell of burnt gun powder. He had been watching them get the weapon ready for the first fire mission. The hard breeze brought the smoke back his way and he smiled to himself as he breathed in the scent once again.

He adjusted the ear plugs in his ears as he anticipated the next round being fired from the big gun. Sergeant Cassidy, the man in charge of the ammo, grabbed him by the shoulders, gently pushed him directly behind the tube of the howitzer, and told him to watch closely.

Sergeant Thomas, the man in charge of the weapon, had his ear to the phone. Dean could read the man's lips. It was clear he was informing the man on the other end that they were ready.

He yelled out to the crew to "fire". The man holding the lanyard pulled the rope and the round exploded out into the cold foggy air. Dean could see the large mass of steel leave the gun for just a second. It was soon lost in the smoke that surrounded the gun. The gunner and the assistant gunner made adjustments on the deflection and azimuth. The next round was loaded into the breach and was sent downrange.

There were four eight-inch guns lined up in a row which made up Charlie Battery third of the sixteen which was the designation of the unit he was attached to. It was an outfit that was a part of the Eighth Infantry Division. After Thomas had sent his third round down range, the other three guns started firing in unison, adding to the thunder that engulfed the whole area. The ground shook with each explosive salvo and the cannons reared up against the recoil spade. They fired four rounds each, then the battery fell silent.

"Hey Sarge, why did the first gun fire those three rounds and then everyone else joined in?" asked Dean, looking at Cassidy.

"Well, 'cruit', Thomas's gun was getting the range of the target. It's called a bracket. He fired one long then one short and the last one was on target. Then the rest of the battery joined in, destroying the target. When all the guns started firing, they were firing for effect, meaning that they had the right range so they poured it into the area. Those guns can put a round on a dime twenty miles away," reported Cassidy.

PFC [Private First Class] Flanders from the special weapons unit came running up to Dean ordering him back to the duce and half van. They had gotten orders from battalion that they were to put a nuclear round together. Dean needed to stand guard outside to make sure that no one could walk in on the procedure.

He had been in Germany for only a couple of weeks and this was the first time he had gone out to the field. Dean hurried to the van where he was given his M-16 with five live rounds in the clip. Spec. 4 [Specialist 4] Oliver was in charge of the guards. He placed Flanders at one corner of the van. Private Tom Cain went to an area at one of the front corners of the vehicle. Oliver steered Dean to the other back corner of the truck and he would post himself at the last position in front of the van.

Dean adjusted his glasses on his thin face and slung his rifle over his broad shoulders. He stood six-foot one inch with a thin muscular build. It had been a whirlwind of a ride for him. In the process he had gotten a real education. During his time at Fort Ord, California, the DIs [Drill Instructors] had added to his vocabulary by volumes but he was sure his father would not approve of the words he had learned. While on leave in Monterey California, two women offered to be his girlfriend. He told them "No thank you" he already had one. His buddy later had to explain that they were prostitutes. He was sure Natalie, at that time his wife to be, would not have liked that. He was interrupted by Oliver.

"Okay Larson, your mission at this corner of the van is not to allow anyone to enter the imaginary line between any of us guards; shoot them in the butt. I don't care if it's the general of the army. You got that 'cruit'?" Oliver said eyeing Dean suspiciously.

Dean just nodded at him. Oliver turned to leave but Dean caught him by the sleeve of his parka

"What's your problem with me Oliver?"

"Because of what happened down at the shed. Are you some kind of narc or undercover MP [military police]?" asked Oliver?

"Oh, no, I just don't do drugs. I like my beer, but I don't get high so quit your worrying. I'm not going to rat you out," Dean spoke with a smile on his face.

"We'll see if I'm kicked out of the unit and end up on the gun. I will come looking for you," retorted Oliver.

Dean could see why Oliver was concerned. If the brass even thought that Oliver was doing drugs, they could transfer him out of the section. If he was caught with drugs, he would also be given an article fifteen which could be a reduction in rank and loss of pay.

Two officers approached the van looking at the set up and all four guards. Dean could see that one was a two-star general the other was a full-bird colonel. They stopped and discussed something between them. They approached the area that was off limits, angling toward Dean. He was watching them closely. Just before they were going to breech the security area, he told them to halt. They slowed but continued moving forward into the area he was guarding. Dean took his M-16 off his shoulder and put his fingers to the charging handle of the weapon.

The general responded by taking the cigar out of his mouth and ordered Dean to stand down. The two officers backed off a little. Dean had never seen the general before. He was tall, about six-one or two with broad shoulders and penetrating blue eyes. The colonel Dean had seen at the battalion headquarters before. His name was Colonel Gordon and he was the battalion commander. He stood about shoulder high to the general but had a quiet commanding presence.

Dean shouldered his rifle and saluted them and they returned it. "So, soldier, what would you have done if we had penetrated your perimeter?" asked the general.

"I don't know how it would have looked on my next job resume; having to tell them that I shot a general. I'm sure they would have thought twice about hiring me," stated Dean with a smile.

The two officers smiled back. The smiles didn't seem natural on their faces.

"So where do you come from soldier and how long have you been with Charlie Battery?" asked Gordon.

"I come from Idaho, sir and I've been with the battery for about a month now, sir."

"Iowa, that's not far from my stomping grounds, Ohio," Gordon responded.

"Sorry sir, but I said, *Idaho*, 'I-D-A-H-O, not Iowa."

Gordon looked a little shocked and embarrassed.

"Where the hell is Idaho, son?" asked the general.

"It's south of Canada, west of Montana, and Wyoming, east of Oregon and Washington state, and north of Utah and Nevada, sir. Since I came into the service, I've had to give a lot of people a geography lesson on where Idaho is," Dean said with a smile.

"Out west. Is it pretty country?" asked the general.

"Yes, at least I think so, sir."

"Well, young man, you keep up the good work and shoot any fat generals or colonels that intrude in your perimeter," the general ordered.

They exchanged salutes and left the area. Dean looked over at Oliver and Oliver gave him a thumbs up. They continued to guard the van until the test was over.

The inspecting officer was followed out of the van by Sergeant Marks. He was telling Marks the [gigs] or minor mistakes the team had made while being tested. Howe and Campbell, the two Spec 4's that had gone through the test were discussing the inspection as the rest of the team climbed up in the back of the van. They had four gigs and the inspector considered them one of the better teams that he had seen in the last couple of months.

The Special Weapons [SW] section assembled nuclear rounds for the guns. The section was done with their part of the field maneuvers. They broke down the round, putting the parts in the various containers. One of them pulled out a deck of cards and started playing spades with three others. Dean fished through his duffel bag pulling out a book and began reading it.

Leaving Campbell in charge of the section, Marks wandered out to the guns. They were in the midst of another fire mission. He liked the army and was thinking about making it a career. He could not gain any more rank than what he had, which was Buck Sergeant unless he became a part of one of the gun crews.

Late that night, they moved to another position, practiced setting up, and completed two more fire missions. The sudden boom of the big guns woke Dean out of a sound sleep since this was his first field maneuver. He was startled and sat up straight. Marks was awake smiled and assured him that he would get use to it someday.

Dean liked his section chief. He stood about five feet eight inches and was black with curly hair and a bright white smile. He had a calm demeanor about him, taking everything in stride. Campbell was a Spec 4 with the longest time in service. He was just the opposite of Marks. He was about six feet two inches with a pale complexion. His straight hair was parted down the middle. He said very little and was married living on the economy which meant he and his wife lived in the small village of Baumholder, Germany.

They spent two days in the hills that were located in the southern part of Germany. It was lush, green, and fog covered the area, with a light snow, making it miserable and cold for everyone. The last time they set the guns up, Dean saw a World War II pill box a couple hundred yards away. It had pockmarks all over it from rounds hitting it.

After several fire missions in the morning on the second day, all the vehicles lined up and convoyed to the wash rack where the black mud was washed off the olive drab green vehicles. The four eight-inch guns were mounted on a tank-like under carriage. Dean rode with Howe in the two and half ton van as his assistant driver.

They scrubbed the truck down after off loading the dummy nuclear round and the NROSS safe in a secure location. The safe held the coded messages by which authorization came down to use nuclear weapons. They drove the van to the motor pool and locked it up. They had to walk about a mile over the hill to Camp Alenbaug, where the battery was staying while their barracks were being renovated in Baumholder.

"So, Larson when is your wife coming in from the world?"

"She's flying into Frankfort on May 25th. Why do you ask?"

"We need to make arrangements with Top so that he'll let me take you down to Frankfort to pick her up. We all talked it over and decided that you're my 'cruit', I'm going to show you the ropes.

It's going to work out well with you.

The renter in the basement where I live is going back to the world at the end of March. I'll talk to my wife, Dee tonight and see when I can bring you home for dinner. You'll get to meet her and Andy, my son. Then I'll introduce you to the landlord and you can make arrangements to grab up the apartment."

"Thanks man, I can't tell you how much I appreciate it." spoke Dean enthusiastically.

"No problem 'cruit'. You're going to have to get a car, so you need to pass that European driver's test. When the unit gets your background investigation back, you'll have to go on the NROSS duty roster, whenever they get a message down, you have exactly five minutes to get back to the base and decode it." informed Howe.

They walked quietly the rest of the way from the motor pool to the German barracks in Alenbaug. The German army camp was nothing to brag about; the buildings were old, most likely built during World War II. Hitler had trained his army in the area during the conflict and had established the base in the area because of the weather; it was overcast most of the time.

The allied bombers rarely had opportunities to bomb the place because of the low visibility. Dean decided that it was a sound tactic since he had not seen the sun since arriving in the place.

He walked into the billets and instantly smelled the latrine, [bathrooms] it didn't matter how well you cleaned the sinks, toilets, or floors, it stunk. Everyone slept in a big bay on bunk beds and when you moved the beds to mop the floors, the beds left holes in the linoleum where they constantly sat.

Every once in a while, a German soldier came knocking at the window begging for "Vhiskey" as their accent changed the word whiskey. They were willing to trade just about anything for a bottle. Some of the Americans were going home with parts of German uniforms because of the barter system.

The rest of the battalion was back in Baumholder residing in their renovated barracks but Charlie battery was still stuck in Alenbaug waiting for the German construction crews to finish the work. Whenever it was time to eat a meal, the NCOs [non commission officers] would march the whole unit over the hill to the American facilities so they could eat at the mess hall. The coffee was no good: it could curl the hair on a man's toes sometimes. Whoever made it should have been drummed out of the service for destroying taste buds.

The average day started at seven am with the Chief of Smoke calling soldiers out of the barracks and getting them into formation. Chester would make sure everyone was accounted for. Lance Chester, stood about six feet three inches and he had a burn mark on the right side of his face. His size alone made him intimidating.

As the battery stood in formation, a sergeant would go through the barracks to make sure everyone was in formation. He would make sure the bunks were made and the floors were clean. He would check the cleanliness of the latrine and a couple of windows were open. A barracks guard would be placed on duty to keep the German soldiers at bay. Chester would make the unit, do a police call around the area which was picking up the trash and getting rid of it.

He would call the battery to attention and release the sections to the section chiefs. They would march them to the mess hall for breakfast. The men that lived in Baumholder would have to march with them. They would have a cup of coffee while everyone else ate their meal. The meals were set up like a buffet with a wide variety to choose from.

The next hour was filled with PT [physical training], a run of two to three miles with calisthenics. They would do short order drill where they would march in different formations. Marks would also check their appearances to see if their uniforms and haircut measure up to regulations.

After he was satisfied, he would call them to attention and march them to the motor pool where they would pull maintenance on the two vehicles assigned to the section. The five ton that was used to carrying the round was almost brand new while the van was a much older vehicle.

Dean learned to be a gas station attendant, checking oil pressure, the antifreeze, tire pressure and so forth. Cleaning up the insides and any other minor thing that the average soldier could accomplish. Word had come down from battalion that they would have to paint the vehicles camouflage colors this summer and Dean would be doing that little chore.

During the latter part of the day, Dean took some time to study his book on driving in Europe. Thank goodness most of the European nations drove on the right side of the road except Great Britian. Howe helped him with some of the signs and technical things in the book.

Howe stood about five feet eleven inches tall. He wore glasses, had a mustache with curly brown hair. Dean liked him but didn't completely trust him. Howe reminded him of the cartoon character Snidely Whiplash. Snidely was always trying to tie a woman to the train tracks to steal money. He always felt like he should keep his hand on his wallet when they were together.

The days seemed to drag for Dean, he was looking forward to starting his life with his wife Natalie. Her letters cheered him up, but it was nothing like being with her. They had gotten married just before he came to Germany. He enjoyed hugging and kissing her. He dreamed about her at night.

Dean considered her very attractive with nice legs and a great figure. She had long brown hair, wore glasses, had a slightly crooked smile, and beautiful white teeth. She always wore modest outfits, but they always revealed the wonderful curves of her body.

She was a country girl he had met her at a high school basketball game. Dean was going to Minico High School near

Rupert, Idaho. She was a student at Burley. He was on his way to the concession stands when he turned the corner and ran into her. She happened to be carrying a soda, which she spilled all over him. She was shy and very religious. He believed in a God but didn't go to church or even think about God much. From that point on they dated and eventually planned a life together.

In late March, the unit was trucked out to the firing range to zero in their weapons. Dean loved shooting, so he always looked forward to getting on the firing line. It was about ten in the morning and like most mornings in Baumholder, it was overcast with a light drizzle of rain falling. He got in the foxhole position first and was ordered to load the magazine in the rifle. Dean was told to charge the weapon and fire at will. He fingered the safety off and sighted down the barrel.

The first round went downrange. A slight kick from the stock reminded Dean that the M-16 was a lot easier on the shoulder than his 30-30 rifle back home. He took aim and sent another bullet toward the stationary target. After he fired the third round, he adjusted his sights. It was the first time he had used the weapon that supply had assigned him. All the rounds had struck the right shoulder of the silhouette.

He fired the weapon three more times and waited for an indication as to where the rounds were hitting the target. This time all the bullets penetrated the middle of the silhouette. He emptied several magazines into the target, getting the same results each time. Sergeant Thomas gave him two magazines of ten rounds each for automatic fire. It was the first time he had ever been allowed to shoot the rifle on automatic. He aimed a little low and to the left as he was instructed. Sure enough, the weapon would climb slightly and move to the right when fired on auto.

Chapter 2

PERSISTENT FOE

Dean turned the big five-ton truck to the right but he had negotiated the corner badly. The cobble stone street he was on was very narrow and he found himself blocking traffic on both streets. It was his first time driving the truck and he had just gotten his driver's license. He grew red in the face with embarrassment as he put the vehicle in reverse, and backed up to get out of the mess he was in.

"What a s-stupid 'cruit,'" White sneered. "Where did you get your license? Out of a 'Cracker Jack' box?"

Dean took it all in stride, not saying anything. This seemed to energy White who was the company clerk. He started a rant using a lot of four-letter words that was bringing Dean to the end of his patience. He was about to pull the truck over and put a fist in White's big mouth when Campbell stepped in. He was sitting by the door and had been watching Dean drive.

"Shut up White!"

Private Sam White was taken back. "Hey Campbell, buddy we came into the unit about the same time and I'm just trying to teach him the ropes."

"White, I'm a Spec 4 and you're a private. You know why you're a private because you've made some mistakes. He just made a mistake and he is learning, so leave him alone," Campbell said with a determined look on his face.

The barracks for Charlie battery were finally completed, so the unit was packing up and moving back to Baumholder. Everyone was as happy as they could be, the rooms were spacious, some were three or four men to a room. This not only allowed a bunk and footlocker, but a cabinet that each man could use to store private articles such as stereo systems and almost every soldier had a receiver, turn table, cassette player, and a pair of speakers.

While moving, Dean was given orders to haul some loads in the five ton. He was going to be assigned to drive one of the trucks eventually and they wanted him to get some practice. They had loaded up some of the items from first sergeant's and White's office. That is why White was riding with them.

White was one of the men at the shed the night they passed around hashish and handed Dean the pipe. When Dean rejected the invitation to smoke it, he could tell that White had taken an instant dislike to him. Whenever White had the opportunity to make fun of him, to give him a little shove, or try to trip him up, he would. Dean continued to try to avoid him or ignore the insults, but this just seemed to encourage White. White was an old timer with a lot of friends. Dean was sure that he would be outnumbered if he got into it with him.

They unloaded the truck, most of it going into the offices. Marks informed Dean that he would be rooming with Oliver and Fletcher. The last items off the truck were his personal items. He found his room and laid claim to the empty bunk. Oliver and Fletcher were settling in, both of them had cabinets and they were setting up their stereo systems. Campbell had taken the truck back to the motor pool.

Soon Dean was listening to hard rock and watching the other two drink beer. He went in to take a shower. It had been a long week and he was worn out. It was a Friday and though he wanted to sleep, the music was blaring from every room in the building. He finally gave into the noise and wrote a letter to Natalie.

He paused with pen in hand wondering about his young wife. He knew when she joined him that it was going to be some real culture shock. They had been sheltered in Idaho from drugs, ugly language, and actions. He was trying get her ready for all of that but didn't know how to say it and not alarm her.

Finally, the OD called a halt to all the music and lights went out. Dean stayed awake for a while trying to figure out what to say but he finally fell into a fitful sleep without a solution to the problem. The next day he decided that she would have to experience it.

On Sunday evening after Dean had taken his shower, he was followed into his room by White, and George Nelson, a broad-shouldered heavyset man. White was thin, medium height, with wire rim glasses framing green eyes.

"What do you want?" asked Oliver.

"We want your help, Oliver. We want to take Larson here and throw him out in the street without his towel," responded White with a smile.

"Why, what has he done to deserve such embarrassing treatment?" inquired Fletcher.

"One, he's a 'cruit'. Two, he's stupid. Three, I don't like him. And four, I think he's a narc," White said with a touch of hatred mingled with every word he spoke.

Dean decided to draw the line here. He choked back the fear that was causing him to want to run or escape. Instead, he got into a fighting stance, looking at all four men. He was determined to throw as many punches as possible. He was fed up with White and he was going to resist him whenever White gave him any grief.

Oliver was sitting on his bed, but now he stood up getting between White and Dean. He was facing the two intruders but was looking in White's eyes.

"I don't think so, White. For one thing, he's my 'cruit', not yours. Two, I think he's pretty smart because he stays out of trouble. Three, I don't care if you like him or not, I like him and that's what matters. As for the last item on your list if he was a narc, he would already be out of the section and the rest of us would be hounded by the Battery Commander. You two turn around and get out before we call the rest of the section over here from across the hall and kick your tails all the way downstairs where you belong," Oliver said, shaking a finger at White.

Dean could tell by the expression on their faces that they were angry and a little surprised by Oliver's reaction. The two of them left without saying another word.

Fletcher gave Dean a beer. Dean wiped the sweat off his forehead and took the beer in hand. He took a big gulp and thanked them both for their help.

"You know this is not over with, Larson," Oliver stated, turning to Dean.

Dean just nodded, feeling dread in the pit of his stomach. He didn't like fighting and tried hard to get along with everyone. That did not mean he hadn't fought at times. It seemed that no matter what a person did in life sometimes a man had to resist a bully and this looked like one of those situations.

"Keep on your guard, Larson. I will watch your six to make sure Nelson doesn't gang up on you with White, but you're going to have to earn White's respect one way or another on your own. The good thing about all this, is that White is going back to the world in April or May, so you only have to put up with him for a couple more months." Oliver spoke with a quiet knowing smile.

Things stayed quiet for a couple of weeks and Dean was glad. One evening at roll call, White handed out the mail as usual. Dean thought it was strange that he didn't get a letter from Natalie, but he thought that maybe she was busy with a test at school or a big project, so he forgot about it. She was finishing up her senior year in high school.

When everyone was dismissed for dinner, he started walking to the mess hall with the rest of the men. He was surprised to get a tap on the shoulder from Nelson. The man was smiling as he informed Dean that White had missed one of the letters in the pouch and it happened to be for him. A warning bell went off in Dean's head that this was an ambush. When the rest of the battery was dismissed, most of the married personnel left for home and the sergeants that lived in the barracks went for chow.

Oliver, true to his word, showed up with Fletcher at Dean's side. He gave him a knowing look, grabbed Nelson on one side and Fletcher took hold of the other arm. They escorted him to the mess hall.

Dean swallowed hard trying to keep fears from taking over his head. He needed to keep it together to win this battle, and he was planning on winning. Dean was taller and slightly outweighed White but when fighting, the outcome is never certain. He walked slowly into the barracks. It had two entrances and he took the one on the north side of the building. The office to the right was where the Battery Commander worked, the one on the left was the company clerk's office, and the door in the back was the first sergeant's office.

White was sitting at the desk and hardly looked up when Dean walked in. He just stood and reached for a letter on the filing cabinet that was behind him. White talked to him for a few minutes, looking toward the door for Nelson. Dean informed him that Nelson was busy. White held the letter out toward Dean in his left hand.

Dean went for the letter but he kept an eye on White's right arm. Sure enough, White threw a hard roundhouse at Dean's head. Dean ducked low so all White hit was air. Dean threw a hard right punch at White's groin and connected. He heard a loud grunt of pain escape White's lips as he went to the floor on his knees. He cupped his hands over his mid-section and started moaning.

"I don't like to fight but when I do, I don't fight fair, I fight to win," growled Dean.

He stood up and grabbed a hand full of White's hair. He was going to punch him in the nose, hoping to break it and leave a lasting impression with him. Making sure that he knew not to mess with him anymore. White held up a hand, pleading with Dean not to hit him again. Dean's father had told him not to give a foe any mercy in a fight. He thought about what to do next, but was suddenly interrupted by a soft cough from the doorway.

"What's going on here?" questioned First Sergeant England.

"I just came to retrieve a letter that White forgot to give me at roll call," stuttered Dean.

White managed to pick up the letter that had fallen from Dean's hands during the fight. Top England nodded and dismissed Dean with a wave of the hand. England stood about five feet six inches and he was stocky with light blue eyes. He was graying at the temples and had dark brown hair on top.

Dean exited the office and made the sounds of tramping down the hallway. He quietly moved back toward the office and spied through the crack between the door jam and the door that was still open. Everyone called the first sergeant "Top" and the position always demanded respect. Even some of the officers were careful about how they treated him. Top sat heavily in White's chair, he placed a boot on White's shoulder and pushed the kneeling man to the ground.

"Well, White, it looks like you bit off a little more than you can chew. Now listen, you dope smoking dirt bag, you leave Larson alone or you're going to end up in Mannheim spending a few years chopping wood and digging trenches in prison if you don't behave yourself. You know I can do it because you've processed the paperwork on some others that ended up there. Now listen, your company clerk because I knew you were a bully and I knew I needed to keep an eye on you. Larson has the makings of being a good soldier, so hands off. You tell that gorilla, Nelson to leave him alone, do you understand me?" England hissed in a low threatening tone.

Dean had heard enough and quietly left for the mess hall. He never had any more trouble from White, who left the army in April. Nelson even became friendly and hung around a lot with Oliver. It seemed that word got out about what happened because Dean had no problems with anyone for a while.

About the time White left for home, the unit was ordered to pull post guard duty. Since Dean had not gotten his background investigation back yet, he was required to walk a post. Howe advised him to go for the NCO [noncommissioned officers] club post, since it was only two hours of duty. Howe informed Dean that he needed to know the chain of command, the code of conduct, and to have his weapon and uniform in mint condition.

Dean did not want to pull a regular guard duty post, which was two hours on, then four hours off, then two hours on, and another four off. He studied the chain of command and the Code of Conduct. He took one of his uniforms over to the laundry, had it cleaned and starched. He polished his jump boots to a high gloss shine and cleaned his M-16 several times. He had started a mustache since everyone in the section had one. He chopped it very close to his upper lip.

On the day of the inspection, he answered all but one question correctly. He was one of the few given his choice of guard post. He chose the third rotation at the NCO club. He would walk his post from three to five in the morning. He had never been to the club before so he did not know the lay of the land.

Baumholder was a beautiful village built on the highest mountain in southern Germany. The town was constructed on one side of a ravine, but most of the base was established on the other side. The NCO club happened to be built about halfway down in the ravine. It was surrounded by a thick forest and a steep edge on one side that ended at the bottom of a gorge. Rumor had it that they built it that way to curb the drinking.

NCOs stayed sober enough to make sure they didn't fall off the edge and break their necks. The sergeants visited the club often, and it was said that very few of them left real drunk, unless it was in a taxi.

Dean was roughly awakened at two thirty-five in the morning by the Sergeant of the Guards. He slipped his boots on, grabbed up his gear, and was down at the truck within five minutes. His post was the second one that they came to. The guard that he relieved was standing on a loading dock at the rear of the building under a light. It was a cool night so Dean was ready to walk his post just to keep warm. The sergeant in charge gave him some final instructions and within a few minutes Dean was all alone. He was wide awake. The temperature helped, but his surroundings encouraged him to be vigilant. The darkness made the trees and bushes form strange monsters in the shadows.

He started around the right side of facility, the side with the steep ledge, if a man fell, he would end up at the bottom of the ravine. Dean could make out a narrow path that took him near the precipice but was safe to walk on. It was marked every so often by something that glowed in the dark. All of a sudden, some of the mechanical systems turned on at his left side and he almost jumped out of his skin. He veered away from the noise almost falling down the incline. The only thing that saved him was that he grabbed onto a branch of a nearby tree. He pulled himself up, knocking rocks down into the gorge. They seemed to fall for a long time making all kinds of racket until they hit the bottom.

He was sweating, and could barely hold back the fear that gripped every part of his being. He finally turned the corner of the building, where a large parking lot came into view. The adrenalin started to subside, when suddenly three wild boars came romping out from amongst the trees on the other side of the lot. They were grunting and making all kinds of strange noises.

The three charged towards Dean, who instantly started hollering at the top of his lungs. He took his rifle off his shoulder and started waving it overhead. He would have shot them if he had any rounds but the army had not seen fit to supply him with bullets. The boars weighed over two hundred pounds each and could have killed him easily. They veered off to his right suddenly but that was enough for Dean. He hurried back to the dock where the light was and stayed there until he was relieved of duty.

Two days after Post Guard Duty, two M.P.s [military police] showed up at the barracks. They took Private Luke Thorton into custody. Thorton had been assigned to the crew of number three gun. While Dean had been guarding the NCO club Thorton was posted to patrol the motor pool. He had opened the gates, gotten into a Gama Goat [a pug nose vehicle about the size of a large pick-up] and took it joy riding to Idar Oberstein, a small village not far from the base.

The big problem was that he had not gotten back before the next guard came to relieve him. He was tried in a military court and ended up in Mannheim, a city that housed a large military prison. He would be digging ditches and chopping wood for five years.

It was a good lesson for Dean, he not only walked all of his guard posts after that but made sure he was where he was supposed to be at all times.

Chapter 3

NATALIE

Finally, they were on the autobahn traveling at a high rate of speed, weaving through the traffic. At one point a truck pulled out in front of Howe, he had to slam on the brakes so that he didn't rear end it. He tried to pass the truck on the right side of the vehicle once they had passed a slow-moving car but the truck driver honked his horn. He waved Howe to the rear and got into the right-hand lane allowing Howe to pass him according to the law.

Howe and Dean had gotten off from their duties a little late. They were going to be late picking Natalie up at the airport. There were no speed limits on the autobahn, so Howe was putting his car to the test, accelerating around the slower vehicles with great enthusiasm.

They pulled into the airport parking lot ten minutes late. Dean rushed out of the car and into the terminal, forgetting the paperwork concerning the flight and gate number. Howe showed him to the gate that Natalie was supposed to come through. He had looked at the number for days now and was pretty sure they were at the right place. People were exiting but Dean did not spot Natalie. They both knew they were late and it was not unusual for a flight to be late.

Unfortunately, Dean could not remember the flight number so when they checked the arrival times of the flights, Dean could not remember the one Natalie was supposed to be on. They discussed the problem and Howe volunteered to retrieve the paperwork while Dean stayed at the gate in case she showed up. Howe was also going through the baggage area to see if she might be there.

He had gotten a description of her and went downstairs. In the baggage area, he noticed a young lady sitting in one of the chairs, looking concerned and just a little frightened. She also fit Dean's description of his wife. He took a chance and asked her if her name was Natalie Larson. The woman nodded her head looking around to see if she could see someone she recognized.

"Hi my name is Robert Howe and I bet you're looking for Dean?" Howe said smiling.

"Yes, where is he? You're kind of late. I was getting concerned that he had forgotten me."

"Sorry but the army didn't let us go, so we didn't get here on time."

He then waved a hand toward the gate area and led Natalie to Dean. She ran into his arms and he lifted her off the ground, swinging her in the air. He gave her a short kiss since they were in public, he grabbed her by the hand as if he was never going to let her go. He used the other hand to grab her suitcase, and they quickly exited the air terminal toward Howe's car.

Dean and Natalie climbed into the back while Howe slid into the front seat. Dean and Natalie held each other all the way back to Baumholder and he told her about the village they would be living in. Howe understood, being married himself, and quietly kept his attention on the road in front of him.

Howe parked in front of the three-story home on the quiet street that made up the neighborhood that Dean and Natalie would live in for the next couple of years. It was a tan stucco with a private stair leading to the third floor where Howe lived. Their German landlords occupied the ground floor, they were middle aged and had no children.

Dean and Natalie had the daylight basement. It was small with its own entrance, a hall into it with a large closet to the right, next a bathroom. The kitchen was at the end of the hall, it was small with a table for two. The only room to the left from the hall was the bedroom, it was very spacious with a king size bed. The hallway was wide and the apartment was furnished.

It had a small table with two chairs, a stove, refrigerator, and counters. The bedroom had a dresser with the largest bed Dean had ever seen. When Dean was checking out the apartment with the landlord, he had turned around to fall into it to see how soft it was. The German had tried to stop him, but it was too late and Dean had fallen across it, only to be surprised to find a board running down the middle of the bed. His back had been sore for a couple of days after that. He placed Natalies's bags in the bedroom and gave her a quick tour of their apartment. In the bedroom she made a comment on the size of the bed but he informed her of the board down the middle length wise. She raised up on her toes and kissed him on the neck whispering in his ear and nibbling on it, she blew in it and Dean got the message. The bed was comfortable and cozy because of the board and they always slept on the right side.

The next morning was Saturday, and she fixed him eggs, bacon, and toast with coffee.

"Well how do you like Germany, Dean?"

"It's gotten a lot nicer today, babe. It's been kind of dreary ever since I got here. I haven't seen the sun since I left Savannah, Georgia. I do like all the guys in my section and most of the soldiers that make up the battery. I have some bad news, though. They're sending me to Grafenwöhr in about a month for thirty days."

"What is a Grafenwöhr?"

"I guess it's a small town up on the Czechoslovakian border. They have a large training facility up there where we will take our battery test.   They keep so many troops in that area to be a deterrent to the red army. I guess it's one of the few passes that they can use to send tanks into Germany from the east."

"What am I going to do while you're gone Dean? I don't know anyone, and we don't have a car."

"Robert's, wife Dee, will show you the ropes. We are invited to have dinner with them tomorrow night. She knows the base and has an international driver's license. While I'm away, you can study to get your license. I've got mine and when I get back from Grafenwöhr, we'll look for a car. Since you couldn't drive, I decided to wait to get a vehicle until I get home. Tomorrow is Sunday so I will take you around and show you the lay of the land."

Natalie pulled her chair closer to Dean gripping his arm tightly, laying her head on his shoulder. The thought of not having him around for thirty days in a foreign country with no family stirred up a fear in her that she had never felt before.

"Don't worry, 'love.' You'll be fine and Dee seems to be a nice gal."

"Dean, we were only married two weeks and you shipped out to this place. I get here and a little over a month from now you'll be running to where, again?"

"Grafenwöhr, on the Czech border."

"Can't you get out of it somehow Dean?"

"No, it's my job Natalie. I have no choice in the matter." Dean said sternly.

He gave her another long kiss and suggested they start the day. She pulled a robe out of the suitcase and poured another cup of coffee. They sat on the couch and she gave him the latest news from back home. He told her about his job and the men that he worked with in the special weapons section. He did not tell her about his fight with White, thinking it was not something that he wanted to discuss with her. She told him about how her family was doing, and that she had stayed a couple of nights with his father and brother. At lunch time he took her to a guesthouse, having lunch and then they took in a movie.

They woke early the next day, took showers, ate breakfast, and visited awhile before starting their walk to see the rest of Baumholder. The street they lived on was short, with their apartment in the middle. The weather was, as usual, cloudy but no rain. At the end of the block of houses, they came to a crossroad. The one to the left would lead them to the base which included a large theater, the PX [Post Exchange] and the Commissary. The road to the right took one past a large empty field, then to the guesthouse, Arnold's garage and the rest of the village. It was a nice hike, cool because the sun was hidden behind the rolling clouds and a light breeze was weaving itself through the hills.

They shopped in the PX, looking at all the items that they could purchase. Dean had been saving up for a cheap stereo system to buy before he left on the maneuvers to keep Natalie company. They had no television, so they picked a stereo out with a few albums. They purchased the records right away but would wait for Howe's help with the stereo system. It wasn't too expensive, but they planned on getting a more advanced unit later. Next, they went to the Commissary and picked up a few groceries. On the way home they passed a bakery and saw a chocolate cake. They bought it to celebrate their reunion.

After they got home, they had a piece of the dessert only to be greatly disappointed. It was not sweet at all. They later found out that there was a sugar shortage during World War II so all German pastries were lacking the sweetness that Americans were used to. They lounged around until six pm then they went upstairs to have dinner with the Howe family.

Dee answered the door. She was a petite woman with long brown hair. She wore black rim glasses and had a nice face that always had a smile on it. Robert was wrestling with his little son Randy on the floor. The two-year-old had light brown hair, and shore stubby legs that were always in motion. The child was laughing loudly as his father tormented him by tickling him under the arms. Dee scolded them, telling them that they had company and that they needed to behave themselves.

They all sat down to steak dinner. Robert had grilled them with a special sauce. They were good, Dean hadn't had steak in a long time.

The Howes focused on Natalie, asking her how her trip had gone and what she thought of Germany so far? She informed them that the trip had gone well and that she was just glad that she was back with Dean.

"What do you plan on doing when you get out of the service Robert?" asked Natalie.

"I plan on going back to Illinois and going to college for business."

"What kind of business do you want to get into?" Dean inquired.

"I don't know but, I want to make a lot of money, whatever I get into. You know we will be going back to the world about a month after Grafenwöhr so the van will be your problem. What do you want to do when you get out of the army Dean?"

"I'm going to college, and I want to be a teacher back home. There's not much money in it but I'm not interested in becoming rich just helping others to become good people."

"A noble profession Dean, I want to help Robert get through school and then be a full-time mom," remarked Dee.

"Dean I have a mechanic friend by the name of Arnold that has an Opel Cadet station wagon for sale. I could take you over to his place tomorrow after work and you could take a look at it."

"That is fine but I was hoping to stop by the PX and buy a cheap stereo system to keep Natalie entertained while we are gone." Dean was not real interested in a car at the moment. Natalie would not be able to drive it and he was not sure if he had socked enough away for the car and stereo system.

They left the table with coffee in their hands and sat on the couch in their spacious living room. The Howe apartment was nothing like the one that the Larsons were living in. It had a large living room, a nice bath, large kitchen and one large bedroom. Robert suggested that they could have the place after they left. Natalie looked at it with longing in her eyes. Dean caught her expression so he asked Robert how much the rent was. Howe told him and Dean let out a gasp.

"How do you pay the rent on this place Howe?"

"Well, Dean that is another thing I want to talk to you about. I kind of dabble in the black market. You know that cigarette ration that you never use and you give to me? I sell those cartons to the local Germans and make a good profit off of them. There are several guys that don't smoke and I do the same with their cigarettes. I also sell the Germans whiskey at an inflated price. They love the stuff but you can only buy so many bottles from the Commissary before they cut you off. I use very little of my pay to take care of the rent. I'm willing to introduce you to the right people, if you want to take over my business when I leave."

"I don't know Howe, Let me think about it." Dean said, surprised by the revelation.

Dean had been willing to give Howe his cigarette rations since he did not smoke. He thought Robert and Dee puffed on the things way too much, but Robert was the only one that smoked. He turned things over in his mind.

He knew Natalie liked the apartment and they wanted to do a lot of traveling. This could be an answer to obtaining the things they both desired. On the other hand, he would be breaking the law and he had no interest in spending hard time in Mannheim which is where the large military prison was.

"Well think about it Dean, but if nothing else, you can take a portion of your rent off if you give your four cartons to the landlord. This is one way I take care of my bills. If you want to get on the landlord's good side, give him a fifth of whiskey on Christmas. You'll always have both him and his wife as good friends."

Dean nodded and searched Natalie's face, wondering what she was thinking. How was he to know that Howe was a criminal. The thought crossed his mind that many others did the same thing to make ends meet in the service. He didn't feel good about taking over Howe's business. Giving his cigarettes to the landlord! Maybe, but he really didn't want to get involved in Howe's enterprises.

Dee, changed the subject, asking Natalie if she wanted children. Natalie affirmed that she did and as soon as possible. Dean had never thought about it much, he took it for granted that they would have a family someday. He thought they would wait on children so they could travel. Having no children was not set in stone for him but the thought of being a father was scary.

The evening ended pleasantly, and the Larsons went down to their home in the basement. They talked over Howe's proposition.

"Well, Natalie what do you think of the Howe family?"

"Dee seems to be very nice and Randy is a cute little boy but I don't know about Robert. Dean I don't want you to get involved in his black-market scheme."

"I don't know, I'm not willing to go to Mannheim. Now I know why Howe reminds me of Snidely Whiplash," he said with a smile. "We will use our rations to help pay the rent and a good gift to the landlord for Christmas. It can't hurt German and American relations. After all a gift is a gift."

Later he told Howe he wanted nothing to do with his business. It was after he met the men Howe dealt with. They were a mean looking lot that gave Dean shivers down his spine. That meant that they would have to be content with living in the apartment that they were renting now.

The next morning, Dean was back in uniform servicing his vehicle, doing calisthenics, and drills. Natalie visited with Dee and enjoyed little Randy's company. She asked about a local church, but the Howes were not church going people. Dee did inform her of a place on post that could give her information concerning the different fellowships on base.

She told Natalie that her shopping day was on Tuesday and that she would be willing to take her to the PX, the Commissary, and the information center if she wanted to go. Natalie jumped at the chance. After discussing things with Dean, she bought the stereo system, groceries, and picked up the information concerning church services the next day. She also purchased several books.

They spent quiet evenings at home, reading books, listening to great music and having intimate conversations about their hopes and dreams. Natalie brought up children but Dean suggested that maybe they should wait awhile, get some traveling in before they had a child. Natalie wanted three but Dean liked even numbers, so they agreed on four, two boys and two girls. They turned to the subject of church, after some prodding Dean agreed to attend at least a couple of services to see what they were like.

When he was a child, his parents took him to his grandfather's church but after his mother died, they stopped going. He enjoyed it but the thought of going back after seeing the way his father felt about God made him feel uncomfortable. Bud Larson, his father, had become bitter toward God after watching his wife die of cancer.

That Sunday, they walked over to the church which was located in a large home. The pastor seemed like a nice guy. The congregation had only two other women in it. The pastor spoke about King David and his military exploits. There was no music and most of the congregation was unfriendly. The service seemed fine to Dean but Natalie was not impressed, so they never went back.

They tried another church on post twice but again Natalie did not enjoy the services and they never went to the church again. That was enough for Dean, he had given her three shots at different churches. He decided to quit looking for a church while they were stationed in Baumholder.

About two weeks before they went to Grafenwöhr, Howe talked Dean into going to see his mechanic friend, Arnold about the Opel. Arnold was a robust German with graying hair at the temples and a hardy laugh that was infectious.

He showed Dean an Opel Cadet station wagon that he had working in top running condition. It was a faded yellow with decent interior, four cylinders under the hood and a stick shift. Dean took it for a spin and was impressed at how well it ran. He drove it over to the apartment and picked Natalie up. The car reminded her of the old Ford that she had while in her last year of high school. Dean took it back and made an offer on the vehicle, there was some dickering back and forth but eventually they both agreed on a price and worked out a payment plan. He made sure all the paperwork was taken care of before he went to Grafenwöhr.

One morning, late in June, Robert Howe drove his car to the billets. He bailed out with Dee close behind him. Randy was in her arms, Dean exited from the other end with Natalie close behind. Robert gave Dee a long kiss and told her that it would have to last for thirty days. He picked up Randy, hugged him and tickled him until he laughed, then gave him to his mother.

Dean also gave Natalie a long deep kiss and whispered how much he loved her before releasing her. While this was happening, several men were giving catcalls and whistles towards the two couples.

The ladies left in the car and the battery was marched to the motor pool. The trucks were already loaded up. The driver and assistant driver took their positions in their assigned vehicles. Dean was going to drive the two and half ton van while Howe would act as his assistant driver.

All the vehicles had governors on them which allowed them to get up to a speed of about fifty-five miles an hour but not much past that. The eight-inch guns had been driven on flat bed rail cars and ferried to Grafenwöhr by train. Their drivers had been shipped with them. They were already up there with some of the NCOs. It was a six-hour trip on the autobahn by convoy, so Dean would be driving most of the day.

Chapter 4

GRAFENWÖHR

Dean was amazed to finally see sunny skies in Germany as they came off the mountain that Baumholder was located on. Dean and Howe arrived in Grafenwöhr with the rest of the convoy at about three-thirty in the afternoon. It had been about a six-hour drive with some nice scenery. The fields of green and the villages that dotted them kept his attention for the two hours that Howe slept in the passenger seat.

They unloaded the NROSS at battalion headquarters. He parked the deuce and a half ton van next to the section's five ton in a large temporary motor pool. They pulled their personal gear out of the back and followed the rest of the battery down a dusty road to their new living quarters. A large tent city had been erected in a huge clearing surrounded by trees. The tents were erected above thick concrete slabs with twelve cots in each tent.

Dean took a cot near the one that Howe laid claim to. He placed his sleeping bag out on his new bed and stored his duffel bag and combat gear under the cot. They were ordered outside for formation to make sure everyone was accounted for. The battery was released to the mess tent, where they were given a hot meal.

After dinner, Dean brought out a book and started reading where he had left off. Several card games broke out and a radio was tuned into a nearby station. Several men had snuck beer into their vehicles and were consuming their treasures.

The liquid was quickly hidden when Sergeant Marks entered the tent. "Larson, you have guard duty tomorrow at the motor pool. You will be posted at twenty hundred hours to midnight. Any questions?"

"Yes, what is the uniform and do I report to our command tent or to battalion?"

"Sorry, you will report to our command tent and the NCO on duty will post you. Your uniform will be fatigues, web gear, a full canteen and flashlight. No M-16, just a club. If you have any trouble, you can use the club liberally. There will be no landline for the phone so if you have any questions, you will either have to run back to the CP [Command Post] or use your own common sense. Any more questions Larson?"

"No Sarge, I get the drift,"

"By the way you guys take it easy on the beer I don't want any problems, you know what I mean?"

"I'll make sure they behave themselves," Campbell remarked.

The next evening, Dean started walking his post at the motor pool at eight pm. It was a warm night with a bright full moon. It didn't take him long for his eyes to adjust to his surroundings. Around nine that evening, it became really quiet and Dean was left with his thoughts.

He wished he was back with Natalie and yet he was looking forward to being out in the field doing his job. Besides that, he was set to take leave after they got back and was taking Natalie to Paris for a second honeymoon.

His thoughts sometimes went back home to Idaho and his father. His father was a farmer and he would be busy out in the fields this time of year with Jack, Dean's brother. As the hour struck nine-thirty, he heard several voices. He went to investigate and found three men surrounding a jeep.

"What are you fellers doing?" he asked.

The large man fumbled with a lock on a jeep that kept the steering wheel secured in place, he turned to look at Dean. He had a surprised look on his face. He gaped for a few minutes answering the question with a slightly slurred voice.

"I'm Spec Four Stone, the colonel's driver, and he ordered me to go to the post headquarters for some paperwork that they need before tomorrow."

"It doesn't take three of you to get a bunch of papers. Who are these two riding with you?"

"They're just two of my buddies wanting to go for a ride. I asked the colonel and he said it was alright," declared Stone.

"Fine but you better have the key to that lock or I'm going to bust a few heads," Dean said, lifting the club in the air.

Stone turned his flashlight beam on focusing back on the lock and chain that held the steering wheel in place. He finally inserted the key and turned the tumblers setting the vehicle free. He got into the jeep with his two friends and with a wave to Dean, drove the vehicle out of the area. At midnight the sergeant of the guard brought Dean's replacement.

Dean didn't know the sergeant or his relief. On the way back to tent city, the sergeant quizzed him about the events that occurred at the motor pool. Dean reported what happened and that Stone and the other two had not returned. The sergeant grilled him on why he had not reported it to him earlier. Dean informed him that he would have been in trouble for leaving his post, so he remained guarding the motor pool. Besides, Stone had a key to the jeep and his story made sense. The sergeant released him back to his bunk where he was soon slumbering in his sleeping bag.

At 0700 Dean was rousted out of his cot and told to report to Top right away. He dressed and trudged over to the battery's command tent. He found England and Captain Cabot standing near a table, talking quietly. He saluted Cabot who returned it. He suggested that Dean take a seat. He waved him over to an uncomfortable folding chair in front of the table. They questioned him about Stone and asked him why he had not reported the incident right away to the CP.

"Well sir, I was the only guard on duty. When Stone produced a key, I figured he was authorized to take the jeep. I was instructed by Marks not to leave my post unless I was under grave threat. They did not threaten me or act like they were going to take it by force. I was also told that if I felt threatened or I couldn't handle the situation, I was to run back to the command post for help. There was no telephone line so I couldn't check on his story."

"That is what we thought happened," said England.

"What's the problem Top?"

"Well, it seems that Stone and his buddies were not authorized to take the jeep out last night. Stone is the colonel's driver, but they took it out joy riding and then snuck off the base to Grafenwöhr, where they purchased beer and got even more drunk. They had an accident on the way back here. The MPs got involved and arrested Stone on DWI charges. One of the passengers was badly hurt and they medevacked him to the hospital at Ramstein. The other one ended up at the medic's tent with minor injuries."

"They wanted to give you an article fifteen for dereliction of duty, at least one of the officers was pushing for it. Top and I pushed back with Colonel Gordon listening to both sides of the equation," interjected Cabot.

"Yes. You must have left an impression on the colonel when we were out in the field during the winter because he remembered your name and told the Captain to drop any notion of punishment against you," England said with a smile.

They dismissed Dean for breakfast and back to fulfilling his duties. As he walked to the mess tent, he thought about what he had just heard. How could they even consider bringing him up on charges when he had done all the right things in the first place? The incident gave him an uneasy feeling about the army as a whole.

The next day, the battery was out in the field doing fire missions on targets roughly six miles away. Each time they moved, Dean's job was to park the van in the assigned space and then raise up camouflage netting over the truck. Campbell was short, he was going to start processing out of the army the day that they got back from Grafenwöhr. Howe and Oliver were the number one team at putting the round together. Flanders and Cain became the number two team.

Cain had received his background investigation back just before they left on maneuvers. The section had to use a man from the FDC [Fire Direction Center] to pull guard duty, because they had background clearances and they were the only other section in the battery that was clear for such duty.

The next day, they were inspected on putting the round together. Dean was placed at the right rear of the truck, but no one tried to penetrate their perimeter. The operation went well with only four gigs [minor mistakes] against the team.

The minor infractions did not fail the team, but were suggestions on how things could be done better. If a team failed the inspection, the battery commander could be fired from his position, and transferred to another unit. Marks and the section were patted on the back and given a job well done by Top.

That evening, the battery had a night fire mission and all seemed to go well, but two hours later the unit was told to stand down. A large number of brass came out to Charlie Battery. They inspected the gun sights and the bags of powder in each burn hole.

Dean wandered over to one of the ammo carriers where Sergeant Cassidy was standing, watching them labor over the guns. Cassidy was a little round man with a pleasant face, freckles dotting the bridge of his nose, and black framed glasses encircling lively blue eyes.

"What's up Sarge?" inquired Dean.

"Big trouble Larson," Cassidy responded with the most serious face Dean had ever seen on him.

"Well give me the scoop here, I'm dying with curiosity."

"One of the batteries out here in the field has made a big mistake and fired a round short. It landed in tent city, hitting one of those big concrete slabs, and killing eight soldiers and wounding five others. Someone is going to jail for that one."

"Did one of our guns do it?"

"We don't know, they called a cease fire on all the batteries out on field maneuvers. There will be a team like this one checking every battery until they get to the bottom of it. The minute they told everyone to form up at the rear of the guns, I knew someone had fouled up. That way no one can adjust the settings on their sights. I saw it one other time at Fort Hood, Texas. Those guys were lucky, no one was killed but it was close.

A sergeant ran up to a captain, saluted, and reported something to the officer. The captain nodded and called everyone on the inspection team over to him. They loaded up in their jeeps and disappeared into the night. An hour later the battery was ordered out of the field back to tent city. It was very late when they finally parked the vehicles and hauled their equipment back to their cots.

They were called to formation at ten the next morning. The roll call was called, accounting for everyone, then they were released to the mess tent. Everyone took showers and cleaned up the equipment. Colonel Gordon called the gun crews out to speak to them about what had occurred the day before. He informed them that one of the one five-five guns had shot short and eight grunts had been killed from the explosion. The gunnery sergeant and the powder man would be charged with man slaughter because they had failed to make sure of the charge. All the units at Grafenwöhr would stop whatever they were doing at 1900 hours and give the dead infantry men ten minutes of silence.

The unit stayed in tent city for a couple more days. They showed a few movies, and set up a beer tent for some recreation. They organized a few football games and baseball competitions. Dean played some ball and got a couple of homeruns but the time seemed to drag for Dean. He wanted to get done with the field and get home to Natalie but he could not rush it.

The unit was slated to stay in Grafenwöhr for thirty days, no matter what. Drinking some beer did help dull the senses a little and helped him fall asleep easily. They were not allowed to go into the village of Grafenwöhr itself, it took special permission and it was rarely given.

They were sent to the field several times, usually three to four days at a time. On one occasion, while convoying from one position to another, Dean observed a Cobra helicopter swoop down out of the sky, making a run. It was late at night and when the ship opened up on the target, it was like releasing a steady stream of fire towards the ground. It was an awe-inspiring sight and Dean was glad the pilot didn't have a bead on him.

A week before their thirty days were up, they convoyed out to the field to do their battery tests. The SW section was tested on the second day. They received a NROSS message to put the round together. Again, Howe and Oliver went through the inspection, this time they came out with only two gigs which made Cabot very pleased with their efforts.

The four guns also did a superb job of hitting their targets in a quick and efficient manner that gave them a high rating. The FDC broadcasted the data for the fire missions to the guns quickly, calculating the deflection or pitch and azimuth, the direction the guns were pointed.

The maneuvering of the unit in the dark went well without anyone getting lost. When the battery came out of the field two days before leaving for Baumholder, everyone was tired and dirty, yet excited about having a little beer and resting up and sleeping in a little.

The Grafenwöhr dust was white and light, it caked on everything and made it a pasty white. The men of the section made fun of Marks after each road march. He looked like an old man, since the dust would make his black curls gray. He wore goggles and when he lifted them, he looked like someone had gave him two black eyes. The rest of his skin was the color of a dead man—a gray pigment.

Tent city never looked so good, offering hot showers, hot meals, a cot, and a tent to sleep in. They loaded the eight-inch guns on the train a day before the convoy left on the autobahn. The next morning, Howe and Dean packed their gear in the van and headed back home. They got back to Baumholder late in the afternoon. Dee brought Natalie over to the billets after Robert called her. Dean got a smothering hug and kiss which revived him from the long drive.

After Grafenwöhr, you were not considered a 'cruit'. You had earned some respect for getting through the thirty days of constant strain under battle conditions.

Chapter 5

NEVER AGAIN

Dean white knuckled the steering wheel as he maneuvered the little Opel through the traffic that was pressing in on him on every side. He and Natalie were going around the Arc de Triomphe in Paris, France. There were about twelve lanes going in and out of the circle, and all the drivers were acting insane.

Natalie was trying to guide him to the avenue that they needed to turn down to get to their hotel. The sweat dripped off his forehead as he continued swerving to miss cars that suddenly appeared in front of him.

Natalie finally spotted the street that they needed to turn down to get out of the madness that swirled all a-round them. She pointed it out to him, but it was too late, they had to traverse the monument one more time.

Dean swore under his breath and told her to keep her eye on the avenue and warn him when they started getting close. He noticed several obscene gestures and fists directed his way, but they made it to safety. They found a parking spot and he pulled into it, stopping the car. They both starred out the window and took in deep breaths of air to calm themselves.

"Damn, that was the worst traffic I have ever been in, but we made it," whispered Dean.

"Why don't we leave the car here and fly back to Baumholder?" Natalie said shaking her head.

"Good idea," Dean nodded with a smile. "How far is our hotel from here?"

Natalie looked at the information concerning their reservations, then looked at the street addresses. She pointed at a large building that thankfully was their hotel. They both exited the vehicle and walked to their hotel. They went in and asked the desk clerk if he spoke English? He answered in the affirmative and they asked him if they could get into their room. He informed them that the cleaning ladies were still going through the accommodations. He suggested bringing their luggage in and store it in their room. They accepted his invitation and he supplied them with a map of the city. He also made a suggestion on the route they should go to catch the sights.

They quickly stored their things in the room and were off to the Eiffel Tower which was a few blocks away. Dean had brought his new 35mm camera, so they took pictures of the Arc de Triomphe on the way over to the tower.

The Eiffel Tower was constructed on a large park which was immaculate, with flowers weaving in and out of the green grass. They rode the elevator to the second story where they photographed the city from different angles. It was an exciting time for both of them, they had always wanted to see Paris. The tower was an awe inspiring, structure that they both had seen in books but it was grander in reality.

They realized that they had not eaten lunch, so they looked for a restaurant on the way to their next destination which was Champ de Mars. They found a McDonald's so they went in and ordered two meals. The hamburger sauce had a strange flavor to it, otherwise the meals were like back home. It was nice to sit and relax in familiar surrounds for an hour.

The Champ de Mars was another large park in the middle of Paris. It was a family park, also immaculate, with flowers and trees planted in well-defined patterns. They stopped at an outdoor cafe on the way back to the hotel. Both of them ordered dishes that had lamb as the main course.

The night clerk was not as friendly as the one from that morning. He abruptly gave them the key to the room, saying very little, and waved them toward the staircase. The room was nice with a little balcony that faced a side street or an alley. The view was not spectacular, just a building across from them, but there was very little traffic and it was quiet.

As they were about to fall asleep, they were brought wide awake by a man walking down the street singing and playing an accordion. They went out on the balcony and listened to the music. Dean threw a couple of Francs down and they applauded him as he walked away. They nestled back into the bed and were soon asleep.

A continental breakfast awaited them the next morning in the hotel dining area. As they walked out the door of the hotel and down the street, they spied a tan envelope on the Opel. They retrieved it and took it into the desk clerk. He informed them that it was a parking ticket and that they were being fined twenty Francs for leaving the vehicle on the street. He suggested that they drive the Opel to the guest parking lot, which they did.

They proceeded to the Louvre Museum where they gawked at the European art that was on display. It was like a full-size review of art history in school. Of course, the art was more beautiful and larger than what they had observed in the books in high school.

They rested, then took the shortest route to Notre Dame and the Holy Chapel. Notre Dame was awe-inspiring, the Gothic architecture with spires pointing to the sky and the steep roof that swept down toward the ground. The windows were drab, but there were some stained-glass windows inside, toward the front of the great cathedral.

It was the many archways and pillars that held up the great ceiling that amazed the traveling pilgrim. The gargoyles that watched over the facility and the stone carvings of the saints also caught the eyes of the tourist. They spent three hours at Notre Dame and the Holy Chapel taking in everything they could.

They left the grounds and followed the Seine River until they came to a little cafe where they had a late lunch. They slowly wandered back to the hotel, where they relaxed and discussed the events of the last two days. They sat in the hotel dining room drinking coffee and discussing their favorite parts of the trip so far. They both agreed that Notre Dame was the highlight of the trip. They decided that they were just going to wander around Paris the next day.

Dean was an early riser, he quietly sat in the chair next to the bed, watching his wife sleep. Some of her shoulder length hair hid one of her eyes, her pleasant nose twitched every once in a while. One of the thin straps on her nightgown had slid down revealing a sturdy shoulder with milky white skin. She was cute and intelligent and shared his desire for adventure.

He laughed to himself as he thought of how lucky he was to win her hand in marriage. He leaned down and kissed her tenderly on the bare shoulder. She stirred, so he kissed her on the cheek. Her green eyes pooped open and she smiled up at him.

"Hey love, I'm going down to get some coffee in the dining room. I think I'll read some of these pamphlets that we picked up about the many sights here in Paris. Whenever you want to come join me for breakfast. I'll be waiting."

She nodded and stretched her arms and legs out. "Give me a chance to shower and dress and I'll be right down."

He drank a cup of coffee and fingered through the pamphlets, gaining insight into the history of the buildings that they had visited. He was on his second cup of coffee when Natalie showed up with fresh hairdo and new clothes. They had the continental breakfast which consisted of a variety of cheese, meats, and breads with juice or coffee to drink. They decided to walk the Champs Elysee, one of the main streets that came into Paris, and visit some of the shops while they traversed the avenue. They would have lunch and follow the Seine River on the way back. The day was beautiful and, if nothing else, the sun and blue sky was a novelty, considering the gray overcast that surrounded Baumholder most of the time.

Dean was fascinated by the history that was everywhere they walked. Some of the buildings were built before the United State became a nation. They bought several items so they could prove that they had been to Paris. Statues of the Eiffel Tower and Arc de Triomphe were among the collectables that they obtained. They found the American Embassy while they wandered down one of the streets. They entered to talk to someone about what they should do concerning the parking ticket they had been given. The young man that sat at the desk greeted them in perfect English which startled them at first. They rarely heard that, except from someone that was wearing an American military uniform.

"What can I do for you?"

"We got this parking ticket and we were wondering what we should do about it?" Dean asked.

"Have you enjoyed your stay in Paris?"

"We have had a great time seeing the sights of the city such as Notre Dame, the Louvre and so forth, but I have found a lot of the people in Paris to be unfriendly," Dean stated.

"Yes, some of the waiters and waitress have been short with us because we didn't speak French ignoring us at times. The night clerk at the hotel grunts at us and points. He hardly says a word to us. The traffic is scary," Natalie spoke out.

"I hear that from a lot of the people that are in the military. If you get out of Paris and into the country side you'll find that many of the natives are much friendlier. Do you plan on doing that?"

Dean and Natalie looked at each other and both of them spoke at the same time. "We will never come back here again!"

"We have seen what we came to look at but we have no inclination to come back to France," Dean added.

"Then I would suggest that you keep the ticket as a souvenir," the young man suggested with a smile.

Dean and Natalie left the place with broad grins on their faces. Dean stopped at the bottom of the steps. He turned to Natalie and grabbed her hand, Looking in her eyes.

"Well, that's it, Bonnie. We can never come back here; they will most likely put our faces in the post offices and have warrants out for our arrest."

"That's fine with me, Clyde. We are in this together and I'm not interested in seeing any more of France."

They found McDonald's again and ordered two more meals that reminded them of home. They continued wandering near the Seine River, where they encountered several artists painting landscapes, dogs being walked, and children playing. It was a leisure time of exploring various avenues that might lead them to a new discovery. It was late when they got back to the hotel and they were tuckered out. They had dinner, a shower, and were in bed early. If they were serenaded by the man with the accordion that night, they never heard him.

Dean awoke around eight in the morning, it was unusual for him, he rarely slept past six am. They had to be out of the hotel by eleven. He quietly arose, dressed, packed his bags, and roused Natalie out of slumber at nine am. He reminded her that they shut down the breakfast at ten in the morning. She needed to get up and come down to the dining room. He was going down and grab his first cup of coffee. She nodded, informing him that she would be down in a few minutes.

It wasn't long before she had joined him and they consumed their meal. They had one more cup of coffee while they plotted a course on the map to get out of the city. Dean was dreading driving in the Paris traffic. They waited until eleven am to leave, in the hope that it would not be so chaotic on the roads that time of day. As they left the hotel, Dean looked toward the Arc de Triomphe, only to be disappointed.

He observed a menagerie of different vehicles flashing by. In fact, an accident had occurred and instead of slowing some of the drivers, they drove up on the sidewalk, causing pedestrians to scatter in all different directions. They waited an additional fifteen minutes before starting, allowing the accident to clear out.

He started the car, took a deep breath, and maneuvered the little Opel out on to the street. He looked at Natalie as they approached the traffic circle. "Tell me when I'm supposed to get off on our street, I only want to go around this circle two times at the most, babe."

"I'll try Dean, just keep your eyes on the road and watch for the crazies," she said with a loud sigh.

They plunged into the melee, swerving away from near misses with a couple of vehicles. Dean stomped on the brakes to avoid rearending a car that steered into his lane. He said something under his breath that Natalie was glad that she did not hear.

In the process, she had grabbed part of the seat and the door to stay upright in her seat. She lost the map but quickly retrieved it. She looked at the name of the avenue that they were passing and quickly got her bearings. She informed Dean that he had to bypass three streets then take the fourth and they would be on their way home. He started sliding to the right getting into position to go down the avenue that would lead them away from the city. A Frenchman tried to cut him off but Dean held his ground and made the turn in the nick of time.

They did not hear what the driver yelled as he waved his fist at them. They were both glad that they had not taken French in high school. Even the side streets were crowded and hectic as they drove toward Germany but it was a lot calmer than what they had escaped.

They had driven for about twenty minutes when Dean looked off to his left, he couldn't believe it. He came to another intersection gazed toward the left, and he was dumbfounded. He came to another intersection and gazed toward the left, calling Natalies attention to the spectacle. It was the Arc de Triomphe. He parked the car and got out. He was frustrated and angry, not at Natalie, but at the situation. He cussed a few minutes.

Natalie had never seen him so livid and it scared her. She stood back from him, watching and wondering if he was going to hit her. Dean had never cussed that way in front of her, but she had never been around him when he hit his finger with a hammer. He calmed down, took the map out of her hand and looked it over carefully. He came alongside her, both of them looking intently at the streets and names on the paper.

"Do you see what is wrong?" he quietly asked her. She looked intently at the map, carefully spying out every detail. She suddenly looked up at him showing a flush of red on her face as she realized she had been looking at the map upside down. "I am so sorry, Dean, I must have picked it up wrong when I dropped it in the traffic circle."

"That's okay, but if you do it again, I'm going to fire you as my navigator," he said with a smile.

The smile eased the tensions and made her feel better although at the time she thought they might end up in a divorce court. He explained to her that he was upset at the situation and not at her.

They walked down the block and got the name of the street that they would have to take to get out of Paris again. This time the traffic was not as bad, and they were soon driving down the right avenue and out of Paris.

"I'm sorry for getting angry back there, I was just really frustrated with the thought of going around that monument one more time. Here, I was thinking that we were finally getting out of dodge only to look over and find the Arc again."

"I was wondering if you were going to send me home, the way you were acting for a minute or two."

"No way, we can't afford that. You are stuck with me. Our parents can't interfere and they can't help us, so we have to learn to live with each other because I'm not interested in getting rid of you."

"I'm going to check on USO tours when we get back home. Let someone else plan things out and drive us around. That sounds less stressful," stated Natalie.

It was late when they got back to their apartment. They just went to bed and Dean was awake at five the next morning. He reported back for duty.

Chapter 6

NEW RECRUITS

Dean was depressed after coming back from sunny Paris. A lot of changes had occurred since his leave had started. Sergeant Marks had transferred to the guns, leaving Oliver in charge for the time being. It was unlikely that Oliver would be put in permanent charge of the section because he was going back to the states, come September.

They had gotten a new recruit for the Special Weapons crew. His name was Jack Reed and he came from New York. He was tall, thick through the chest, with an interesting sense of humor. Dean liked him immediately and they became friends quickly. The battery also got a new second lieutenant. He was as thin as a rail, with black rim glasses that covered most of his face. Dean had his doubts as to how long Lt. Danner would last in the battery. He thought Danner looked kind of wimpy, hardly one that could take the physical stress of a combat unit.

Two new privates went to the gun crews. Private Glen Wilson went to the number three gun and private Drew Blout was assigned to the number one-gun crew. Dean's first impression of Wilson was that he did not have a clue about anything, and he seemed foolish in his actions and his speech. Blout on the other hand, was clever, but not in a good way, a lie was as good as the truth to him and Dean didn't cotton up to either of them.

Sgt. Lonnie Howard came in with the new recruits, he was a Vietnam veteran with cold blue eyes and a stout frame. He rarely smiled but toed the line with his gun crew, doing his job well.

On one of the few sunny, beautiful days that Dean saw in Baumholder, Oliver was ordered to take the section to the motor pool and pull maintenance on the two vehicles. Everyone was in a good mood, laughing and joking. Oliver was trying to act like a good section chief but was caught laughing at some of the antics that everyone was pulling. Reed was constantly trying to get him to lighten up, finally Oliver suggested that they all should try to act like soldiers and take care of the trucks. Oliver was starting up the ladder into the back of the deuce and half van. Reed reached down to the ground and picked up a large stone. "Heads up!' he yelled.

He tossed the rock straight up in the air. The rest of the crew watched the path of the projectile. Oliver did not understand what Reed had done and turned on the ladder to ask him what he meant by the shout. Reed thought Oliver would have been inside the van by the time the rock descended to earth. Gravity being what it is, Oliver became the unsuspecting target of an accident. While every-one else scattered, the rock came down, hitting Oliver in the middle of the head. Oliver's eyes rolled to the back of his head and he crumpled into the van. Dean was to his side first. He grabbed a hand and opened up an eye lid. Oliver was alive but he was out cold.

"Is he alright?" asked Reed.

"Yes, I think he is, but if you want to see tomorrow morning, I suggest that you make yourself scarce until roll call this evening. We will try to calm Oliver down after he comes to," warned Dean.

"Yeah, I'd high tail it out of here, he is going to be peeved," chimed in Flanders.

"I wouldn't show my face to him until I have to. I would also be holding a six pack of beer as a peace offering," suggested Cain.

Oliver stirred a little and that was all Reed needed to start running toward the motor pool gates. Oliver slowly came to shaking his head and moving his limbs around. He finally sat up looking from one face to another. "What the h—l happened? Who hit me in the head?"

"Take it easy Oliver, you have a knot on the top of your head that looks like a goose egg. I would be really careful about how you put your cap on for the next few days," remarked Dean.

Oliver felt the top of his head, allowing his fingers to explore the little hill on his head. He winched several times as he touched a few of the more sensitive spots. "Well, what happened? I suspect that Reed had something to do with it since he's missing."

"It was an accident, Oliver. Reed tossed a rock up in the air, thinking you would be in the van by the time it came down. Have a little mercy toward him Oliver. I'm sure he is never going to do it again," pleaded Flanders.

"Besides that, he is going to bring you a six pack as a peace offering. We all know how you love your beer," commented Cain.

"It depends how long he stays away. I better not see him too soon, even with beer."

That evening, Reed reported back for roll call and gave Oliver his peace offering. Oliver had calmed down, so he allowed Reed to live another day. He wore his hat at a funny angle, trying to keep it off the tender part of his head for a couple of days.

Before Oliver went home to Texas, Reed decided he would cement his friendship with Oliver and to get closer to Dean. He invited them to go on a camping trip wherever they wanted to go. Reed offered to pay for the food and beer. Oliver and Dean agreed, so they made arrangements with a local farmer to stay in one of his pastures. They would set up their tent near a little village called Idar Oberstein. It had a couple of guesthouses and a market where they could buy food if they ran low. Blout invited himself by suggesting that he would gladly add to the beer and food supply. Reed reluctantly gave in. He and Dean didn't care for Blout, but Oliver enjoyed his company.

They left early Friday afternoon with Top's permission. They set the tent up near a stand of trees, they drank a few beers, and started dinner. Reed provided four steaks and they cooked them to perfection, with raw carrots and fried potatoes as sides. They cooked everything on a propane stove because open flames were not allowed.

The three men were soon gazing at the stars and downing the beers that Blout brought for the trip. Reed and Dean sipped at their brews very slowly, Oliver was a little quicker, enjoying the beer and the conversation. He discussed the town in Texas that he was going back to, and the girl that waited for him. They were going to be married. He was going to wed her before he was drafted but they decided to wait in the fear that he might end up in 'Nam.' [Vietnam]

Blout, on the other hand was having a hey day with the beer, guzzling one after another. He said very little, only adding one liners to the conversation that was taking place. The air was cool, so they donned their field jackets to keep warm. Blout soon complained that they were running low on brews.

"You three have been drinking too much," Blout complained.

"Bull, you've been swelling that stuff down like a hog in slop," remarked Oliver.

"Hey I bought the beer and I should be able to drink the way I want," sneered Blout.

"Why don't you shut that trap of yours before I put my fist thorough it. You invited yourself on this little expedition, investing the beer in it was your idea, cruit" Oliver snarled as he stood up. He took a few steps toward Blout.

"Hold it, why don't we go down to the guesthouse and I will buy a few rounds. Then we can come back to the tent and sleep it off," suggested Dean. He didn't like Blout, but he didn't want Oliver to get into trouble.

Blout was unsteady as they traversed the hill through a large stand of trees toward the village. The other three had to help him navigate the ground. Oliver threatened to leave him on the trail several times. They entered the guesthouse about nine in the evening, so the crowd was thinned down to mostly farmers having their final drink before going home to bed. Larson ordered four tall liters of their best beer. Blout took several gulps before informing them that he had to use the facilities.

The bar keeper pointed to the bathrooms and Blout staggered toward the one with the men's sign on it. He accidentally bumped one of the Germans that was seated at a table, spilling his beer in his lap. Blout didn't apologize, just continued toward the men's room. The German stood and said something that Dean was sure should not be repeated in public. The German sat down and Dean gave a sigh of relief. Suddenly the farmer stood up and followed Blout into the bathroom.

"I believe we're about to have trouble," whispered Dean.

A few seconds later, Blout came flying out of the bathroom with a red-faced German on his tail. Blout had been hit in the face and was bleeding from the nose. His glasses were nowhere to be found and he was trying to gather himself off the floor. The big German was about to help him up. He gathered a piece of Blout's field jacket in his large hand, rearing back a big fist at the same time.

Oliver yelled something and flew toward the altercation. One of the men at the table tried to get out of the way of Oliver's bull rush but he was to slow. Oliver helped him by knocking him to the floor. The other four at the table were feed up with the rude Americans. Angry, they all stood up to pursue Oliver, but Reed and Dean understood what was happening.

Dean and Reed wade into the group of Germans swinging landing several blows on the men. Meanwhile, Oliver closed the gap between himself and the German. Bout received another punch, but Oliver swung a round house, connecting with the German's right temple, sending him flying toward the women's room. Oliver was at Blout's side trying to bring him around.

"Big trouble," Dean said in a calm even voice.

"What now?" Oliver said turning his head toward the rest of the room.

The owner of the guesthouse was on the phone, which meant the police would be coming soon. The other farmers were on their feet, moving menacingly towards all four of them. They were barring the exit. Oliver looked into the bathroom and saw a window.

Reed grab Blout up and get him out the window while Dean and I hold off these guys."

"We could just leave him." suggested Reed.

"That is tempting but naw, can't leave him behind. The police will be real nasty with him. So, hurry."

Reed easily hauled Blout into his arms, opened the window, and stuffed him through. Oliver picked up a chair and swung it at the majority of their adversaries. One man came rushing in but Oliver caught him with a right hook, knocking him backwards. Two of the men were on Dean before he could defend himself. Both of them landed blows, knocking him to the ground but Reed suddenly appeared, shoving one of the men into two other men that were advancing toward them.

Dean kicked the other attacker between the legs. The man fell to his knees. Reed helped Oliver to the bathroom, grabbing a chair at the same time. Dean pulled Oliver through the door toward the window. Reed turned swinging the chair, it caught two of their foes, knocking them back. Reed rushed into the bathroom with the chair, locked the door and wedged the chair under the doorknob. He pushed Oliver the rest of the way out the window. Reed helped Dean out the window and then squeezed through to freedom himself. Dean and Reed secured one of Blout's arms and ran up the hill towards the woods with Oliver behind them.

They heard the front door of the guesthouse slam and footsteps running toward the back of the building. They now noticed the wail of police sirens and the blue flashing lights. Not only were local citizens looking for them but the police were now involved. Pure adrenaline forced their bodies to drag Blout up the hill at a rate that they could not explain. They were soon hiding among the trees and brush. Several of their pursuers passed near them, but they remained quiet and in the hiding place.

Blout started coming to, and they had to cover his mouth so they would not be discovered. Eventually, it became quiet. They waited for another half hour or so before getting Blout on his feet and started for camp.

The three of them were fed up with this new 'cruit,' allowing him to stagger behind them. The left side of Blout's face was red and swollen. His glasses were missing, which made it difficult for him to navigate back to camp. The three straddled a four-rail fence which was about fifty yards from their campsite.

Blout was having a lot of trouble getting over the barrier. He tried to squeeze through the rails, but they were too close together. He tried to climb over it, but fell backwards landing hard on the ground a couple of times. He called out to Oliver for help. Oliver told him that he was on his own. Oliver, Dean, and Reed decided that it might be entertaining to watch Blout overcome his present problem.

Blout made it up three rails before he fell again. The fifth time, he made it to the top and leaped for the ground. The fence pole he used to steady himself on snagged his field jacket as he leaped. Instead of landing on the ground, the pole went up the middle of his back and kept him aloft, hanging like a scarecrow. The audience of three laughed so hard that they had tears running down their faces while Blout yelped for help. He wiggled from side to side, but could not free himself from the jacket.

He entreated them to free him from his constraints. They ignored him and went to the tent, where they laid down and were soon asleep, in spite of Blout's cries for help.

Oliver woke first, he went to Blout to make sure that he was alright. He was asleep, still hanging from the fence pole. He suddenly woke and started cussing Oliver out. Oliver cuffed him with an open hand in the face on the swollen side. "You're in no position to use that tone with me, so shut your mouth before we leave you here for the buzzards," hissed Oliver.

"I'm sorry Oliver, just let me down from here," pleaded Blout with a forlorn look on his face.

Oliver grabbed the zipper of the field jacket and pulled it down. Blout slid out of the constraints, falling with a thud to the ground. He suddenly realized that he could have done the same thing, but had been too drunk to do it for himself. He had to massage the feeling back into his arms, laying on the ground. His nose still had blood on it from the fight and bruises all over his face.

They were joined by Reed, and Dean who looked down on Blout with disdain.

"What a mess this guy is. I'm sorry I allowed you to talk me into bringing him along," remarked Reed.

"No lie, this clown is a real jerk. He is as stupid as a summer day is long. He just had to make a mess of things. We could have had a lot more fun but you had to piss off the Germans. By the way, what did you say or do that made that one knock the crap out of you besides spill a little beer on him?" asked Dean.

"I don't know, I don't remember any of the minor details from last night."

"I suggest you don't get so wasted next time," Dean scolded.

They packed up early and went back to the barracks. They did not want any problems with the locals or the police because of what had occurred the night before. Oliver would not associate with Blout after that. All three of them saw him as trouble. Oliver was glad he was short. He was looking forward to getting back to Texas and getting away from meat heads like Blout.

Monday morning brought a changing of the guard. Captain Cabot was being posted back to the states. He was being relieved by Captain LeRoy Law. Chief of Smoke Chester called the battery to attention. Top England marched out with the two captains and a short ceremony took place in which the battery standard was exchanged from Cabot to Law. Cabot was about five feet eleven inches tall, but compared to Law he was short.

The new BC was about six two. He towered over everyone except Chester, who almost looked him in the eye. Captain Law was very thin, wore wire rim glasses, had a crew cut, and a head that seemed too small for his body. Cabot gave a small speech at the end of the ceremony, thanking everyone for the hard work they had given him while he was in command. The new BC spoke about some of his expectations and everyone was released to perform their daily duties.

That evening before everyone was released for the evening, Law inspected the battery. He stopped in front of Oliver telling him that he needed to trim up his mustache and to press his uniform, it looked like he had slept in it.

Campbell had seven more days before he went home and Howe left two weeks after that. Dee and Randy were already back in the states. After the formation both of them commented on how glad they were leaving the unit. Oliver showed up the next day with a trimmed mustache and a pressed uniform but he fumed all the day making abusive comments about the new BC.

Thursday, Chester informed SW that Spec Four Alan Walker from the Communication section would be put in charge. He was a transfer and would be given the rank of an acting E-five sergeant which meant that he would have the authority, but not get paid for the position. Dean had not associated with Walker much and didn't know him well. Oliver whispered under his breath that Walker was a kiss up and wished them all luck.

Walker stood about five eight, had a round happy face, and a stout body. He laughed a lot, but was very serious when it came to getting the job done. Dean asked how a guy that came from commo could have Mike 5 status and work on the nuclear round but they had put him with communication temporary until he had gotten his background check. He now had it and was ready to become a part of SW. He would be in charge starting the coming Monday but Oliver ran things most of the time. It was probably good; it saved the unit from a lot of head butting between Oliver and Walker.

On Friday afternoon, the battery was called to formation to be released for the weekend. Oliver had been in a good mood allowing most of the section to do errands around the base. They worked on the trucks but Oliver had been joking and laughing with the men that had hung around. At the end of the day Chester called the formation to attention with Law at his side.

Chester discussed some items concerning assignments over the weekend. He ended his announcements and the BC took over. He declared that the barracks did not meet his standards and that there would be a GI party starting Saturday at seven am. Even the men that lived off base would have to participate in the exercise.

Everyone moaned and started griping, so Chester called everyone to attention, then released them to go to chow. As the captain and chief of smoke turned to leave, Oliver yelled loud for everyone to give the new BC a left-handed salute. Most of the battery lifted up their left hand with a middle finger pointed skyward.

On Saturday, Oliver had the section sweep out their rooms, dust, fix their footlockers, and make beds. He got his stereo going with his favorite artist and pulled out the beer. Section chiefs were told that they would have to inspect their areas and when it was up to the BC's standards, they could release the men. Oliver looked at the area and suggested that it was all good and they were released. Chester interfered with that assessment. He demanded that the floors be stripped and waxed. This was accomplished and then everyone was released.

Dean did share some good news which took the bite off the ruined day. He handed out cigars to everyone. Natalie had gone to the dispensary and they had informed her that she was pregnant. Dean was caught between two desires. He was excited about becoming a father but how would it affect their travel plans. Of course, he was rooting for a boy. He was also concerned about the kind of father that he would be.

Monday morning formation found Walker at the head of the SW section. He was wearing buck sergeant stripes. As everyone was being released, Campbell stepped out of the formation with his duffel bag on his shoulder and shook everyone else's hand. He spoke kind words to the section and then left for his flight home. A couple of weeks after that Howe would do the same thing.

A month later Oliver would catch his freedom bird to his sweetheart in Texas. When he was saying goodbye to Reed, he took Reed's hand and invited him to come and see him anytime and he would put him up for a couple of nights. He had one stipulation; he would not allow him to carry a rock around in his hands.

It was another sad good-bye for Dean, he not only liked them but they were the some of the last draftees in the battery. They added spice to the section, creating adventures during a lot of dull moments in the motor pool.

Chapter 7

DRUGS AND BEER

Dean entered the barracks on a cold rainy fall morning. Wilson, the new recruit, was sitting at the bottom of the stairs looking dejected and very alone. His nose was bruised, his right eye was black, and his left check was red. Dean was about to ask him what had happened to him when Top England waltzed in and beat Dean to the question.

"What happened to you Wilson? Someone beat the daylights out of you?"

"Huh, I huh, well it's like this," stammered Wilson.

"He fell down stairs, didn't you Wilson?" exclaimed Nelson from the top step.

"Yeah, Top, that's what happened, I slipped at the top and rolled down the steps."

"Do you need to go to the dispensary?" asked England.

"Naw, I'll be alright."

Top went into his office, letting the matter drop. Dean had no intentions of dropping it, he was curious as to how Wilson got all those bruises. He found Flanders mopping the hall in front of his room. He questioned him about what had happened to Wilson. He just shook his head.

"What an idiot he and Blout are. Wilson got a bunch of money from the government; his sign-up bonus, so he went out, bought a bunch of beer, and some hash. He invited Blout to go out with him to the woods and smoke and drink it up."

"So that doesn't explain how he got all those injuries?"

"Well, Nelson and a couple of his buddies found them and invited themselves to the party. Wilson told them to go get their own smoke and beer. Nelson took exception to his rude behavior, so him and his buddies taught them some manners with their fist if you get my drift," Flanders said with a big smile. He didn't like Blout or Wilson.

Blout suddenly appeared in the hallway. He had two black eyes and a cut near his lip. He was wearing his glasses, he looked down and away as he passed them, but Dean decided that he was going to rub it in.

"Blout what happened to you?"

"What's it to you?" He said turning and looking up.

"Nothing, but I would suggest that you and Wilson watch where you're going. Accidents do happen I know, but you two need to be more careful."

"This was no accident."

"Huh. Top asked Wilson how he got all those injuries and Nelson told him that Wilson had fallen down the stairs. Your buddy confirmed that. I just thought you fell down with him. You mean something else happened to him?"

"No, you fell down with Wilson, didn't you Blout?" stated Nelson. He came up the stairs and was looking intently at Blout. Blout wilted under Nelsons's glare and nodded in agreement with his antagonist. He turned and went back to his room. Nelson walked by Dean, and Flanders with a smile on his face.

"Those two are not going to make it. Neither is that butter bar lieutenant, Donner. They are all a bunch of wimps," Nelson said, shaking his head.

It's true Donner was having a lot of problems, coping with the men. They only showed him any kind of respect when a NCO or another officer was with him. Otherwise, they made fun of him, calling him names or making obscene gestures to his face. He complained to Top and the BC but when the men were questioned, they denied doing it. Since there were always at least two of them and no one else seemed to witness the infraction, they were not able to give out any punishment.

Dean and Reed stayed out of it. They figured Donner had enough troubles and eventually a natural process would occur and he would be replaced. Dean felt sorry for him; he figured Donner had joined the army to get some respect. It had backfired and he was getting more grief than he could handle. He was not physically strong enough to handle the rigors of a combat unit in the field. Dean figured that he weighed about 115 pounds and was as thin as a fence post. He most likely had more brains than bronze.

Some of the pranks they pulled on him were pretty funny. Many of the soldiers got a lot of laughs at the expense of poor Donner. Spec four Randall, a member of a gun crew, complained to him that the rest of the gun section was slacking off at the PX and he needed a pipe stretcher from the battalion motor pool.

The lieutenant offered to retrieve the item for him so he could get the job done. He walked the three blocks to battalion maintenance and asked a sergeant for a pipe stretcher. The sergeant stood up saluted and started laughing. He informed Donner that there was no such tool and that the old timers usually pulled that joke on the new recruits.

Donner didn't think it was funny; he went storming back to the gun and Spec four Randall who was now surrounded by the rest of the gun crew. Donner started yelling at them and making threats. When he screamed, it was shrill and sounded more like a girl's voice than a man's. One of the sergeants had to come over and calm him down. Captain Law called everyone together, asking everyone to lay off Donner. That was a mistake; no one liked Law so it just encouraged them all the more.

One of the men working on a truck asked Donner for some help. The lieutenant asked him what the problem was. The PFC got him looking at a wheel bearing and stumbled a little, applying his hand to Donner's back to steady himself. He apologized to the lieutenant but had left a big greasy hand print on Donner's clean fatigue shirt. Several others did the same thing so Donner could not blame it on one man.

He would be walking down the vehicle line and one of the men would pucker up their lips and act like they wanted a kiss from him. He would shake his head and move to the next truck only to get the same kind of treatment. Top finally stepped in, asking everyone to please give Donner a break. England was well liked and respected. They eased off of him a little.

The battery was given Post Duty in the middle of October. This required the men to be assigned various details concerning the common areas on base. The men would have to do police calls [picking up trash] around the air field, the PX, the NCO club and so forth. Some of them would be given the job of spot painting the buildings on the post, any odd job that needed to be done. Sergeant Howard, the new NCO, was allowed to pick a crew to go out to the air field and the wash rack to do a police call on those areas.

The first man he picked was Dean to drive a truck to haul the garbage and men to the areas that they were assigned. He picked Blout and Wilson plus two others to accomplish the missions. Dean was glad he only drove the truck and didn't have to do any labor. He couldn't figure Howard; why would he pick the two dopers? He soon found out.

They ran out to the wash rack and gathered up the garbage, next they stopped at the airfield. Howard directed Dean to an open field and into a stand of trees.

"What's up Sarge?" asked Dean.

"We're going to take a little break. I picked you for a reason Larson; they tell me that you don't do drugs, is that right?"

"Well, I drink but I don't get high, if that's what you mean?"

"That's exactly what I mean. Your job is to make sure no one bothers us while we take a smoke break. You see someone coming, you yell out fast."

Dean nodded, got out of the driver's side, and wandered around the truck. Smoke came bellowing out of every opening in the canvas that covered the bed of the vehicle. If he got a whiff of hashish, he would move further from the five ton. Howard threw open the back curtains of the truck and climbed out, motioning Dean to take his position behind the steering wheel. Dean pulled the truck back on to the road and they policed up the air field. On their way to their next assignment Howard took a good hard look at Dean.

"You know what will happen if you rat on us, don't you?"

"Yeah, you'll kick my tail end, but I'm not a rat so put your concerns behind you."

"It makes me feel much better; that you know the score if you do say something. Why don't you smoke?"

"My mother smoked and died from lung cancer. I did try it one time. I started coughing and hacking, I couldn't figure out what was so great about it. The reason I don't do drugs is that I don't like losing control and doing stupid stuff. Even when I drink, I usually stay coherent enough that I don't get obnoxious."

"Well, I got started on the stuff in 'Nam.' It was the only thing that helps me forget sometimes. I know it's not much of an excuse but it's the only one I have right now."

"You made the choice to start, you can choose to stop, but I know that is easier said than done."

Silence filled the cab, but this seemed to satisfy Howard. They continued to do their assignments. Dean got out to stretch his legs. He was standing by the cab when Wilson got in his face and threatened him if he told anyone about them smoking dope. Dean pushed him back; he was too close to him. A scowl took over Wilson's face.

Howard reached for him but Wilson shoved Dean before the sergeant could stop him. Dean grabbed Wilson's arm, twisted it over his head, and brought it back behind Wilson. He pushed Wilson's face hard against the cab, smashing his nose against the metal. He quickly looked around to see if anyone else was coming. Blout was moving to help Wilson but Howard pushed him back.

"You ever threaten me again Wilson, you'll be walking on your elbows. Do you understand me? I don't like you, so stay away from me," hissed Dean in his ear.

"I already dealt with Larson, so leave him alone. That goes for the rest of you. Dean knows what will happen if he squeals," exclaimed Howard.

"Okay, I'm sorry man, just let go of me," pleaded Wilson.

Dean released him and they all climbed back into the truck. He drove them back to the barracks where he let them off, turned the truck toward the motor pool, and parked it for the evening. Walker was about to walk back to the barracks so he waited to accompany Dean. He asked him how his day had gone. Dean considered Walker not only his section chief but a friend, so he spilled his guts about what had gone on.

Walker assured him that he would tell no one about Howard and his crew. He made Dean a promise that he would try to keep him away from any kind of duties with Sergeant Howard and his two buddies. Dean informed him that he would appreciate that. He was glad to get home to Natalie who gave him a big hug and kiss. He told her about the events of the day. She listened in awkward silence. She could not relate very well; she did not drink and had never tried drugs. She had grown up in a very strict religious home.

Dean had been her first and only boyfriend. He soon learned while he was dating her that he had to abide by strict rules and he respected her and her parents for the boundaries that they had set. He would drink once in a while in front of her, but quickly learned that she would not participate in any alcoholic beverages.

A few weeks after the post duty. Dean came to the barracks to report in for the morning, Walker was standing at the doorway. He told Dean that he wanted to talk to him privately after formation. They had roll call and Dean realized that they did not call out Wilson, Blout or Howard's name. He glanced around and noticed that all of them were missing from roll call. Walker grabbed Dean by the arm and led him towards the mess hall.

"I've got some news for you, but you have to promise me that you won't tell a soul."

"Sure, what is it, Walker?"

"Cassidy was pulling duty this weekend. I happened to be visiting with him when he got a phone call from an official in Frankfurt. It seems that three of our boys got into some serious trouble."

"Was it Howard, Blout and Wilson?" asked Dean with a knowing smile.

"You got it, it seems those three did the most stupid thing you can do in Germany. They robbed a taxi."

"You're kidding me! They tell you in orientation not to mess with the police or taxi drivers up front."

"I know. They don't want the word to get out until the BC gets all the details, so keep this little piece of news under your hat. Just dumb as doorknobs," Walker said shaking his head.

"I agree with that. I never cared for any of them," Dean said coolly.

A couple of days later the BC called the afternoon formation and gave some details concerning the three missing soldiers. It was true that they had robbed a taxi, but as they fled the scene of the crime, another taxi driver had observed them. That driver informed the police who checked all the hotels down the street that they had been running down. It was not hard to find them; the night clerk gave the officers the pass key. The four policemen flew into the room with their nine-millimeter weapons drawn. The three were quickly arrested, subdued, and thrown into a squad car. The three were booked and thrown into prison. The penal system in Germany did not provide jails, just prisons.

Two to three weeks later, the army got back the three missing troopers. The first time Dean and Walker saw the three was in the mess hall. Blout and Wilson were sitting by themselves and they were consuming everything in front of them like they had not eaten for months. Sergeant Howard was at another table stuffing his face as fast as he could.

Walker grabbed a tray, filling it up while Dean grabbed a cup of coffee. Dean pulled up a chair near Howard who hardly looked up as he continued to fork food into his mouth. Walker pulled up a chair across from him and looked directly into his eyes.

"What, didn't they feed you guys in that German prison?"

"You mean that dudgeon they tossed us in? It was hot and nasty in there all the time. All we got to eat was cabbage soup and black bread twice a day."

"No wonder you're eating like your mouth was wired closed for a month. I bet this chow tastes pretty good today," remarked Dean.

"No, it doesn't taste good, it is like having a Thanksgiving dinner in July. It's the best meal I have ever tasted and that is no joke," Howard said as he gulped down another fork full of food.

"Why are your two buddies sitting over at the other table?" inquired Walker.

"I guess you know that they claimed we robbed a taxi. Those two are claiming I pulled the stunt and that they just happened to be riding in the taxi when I grabbed the money from the driver. They are going to testify against me. Those two are real jerks and if I had an opportunity, I'd beat both of them to a pulp. The taxi driver has already identified us so I believe we are all in serious trouble."

"Didn't you listen to the lecture on this nation, they tell you not to mess with the police or taxi drivers? Every taxi has hidden buttons and when they are threatened, all they do is push the button and about a dozen taxis converge on the location." Walker said shaking his head.

"I have to admit, I was high when we sat in on those meetings, I hardly remember any of that."

"Boy, talk about learning things the hard way. Do you remember anything about Mannheim?" asked Dean.

"No, but my lawyer has already informed me how much time we three could be spending there if we lose the case."

Howard excused himself and went through the line for a second helping.

"Wow, those three have fallen in the toilet and someone is going to flush them down the drain. They are going to lock those guys up and throw away the key for a while. I hope Howard can get use to digging ditches and chopping wood," remarked Walker.

At the end of the day Dean went home to Natalie, who met him at the door with a warm hug and a nice long kiss. He told her the story about Howard and his two buddies. She listened intently as she roamed around in their small kitchen, getting dinner ready.

"What will happen to them after Mannheim, will they continue to stay in the army?"

"No, they will all get dishonorable discharges, I'm assuming."

"I think it just goes to show you what happens when you fool around with drugs, it just leads to trouble," she said, smiling as she set a large plate of spaghetti and meatballs in front of him.

He picked up his fork and dug in. She sat across from him and started eating her plate full of noodles and meat sauce. He thought to himself that he was a very lucky man. She was a good cook and she had chosen him to be her husband. The baby was due in February and he was hoping it was going to be a little boy.

The kitchen was warm and they talked about the latest letter they had received from her mother. He later put some music on and grabbed up the latest book he was reading. Dean relaxed sitting on the sofa near Natalie.

Chapter 8

LAST DRAFTEE

Specialist four Clyde Randall was the last draftee in Charlie Battery and he was leaving for home in couple of weeks. The first evening Dean had gotten to Baumholder, Clyde took him to a guesthouse in Idar Oberstein and got him drunk.

Clyde introduced him to a close friend that owned the establishment. His name was John Lindy, a retired Air Force veteran. He had married a beautiful German lady and made his home in the tiny village. The other guesthouse was the one that they had trashed in that big fight. Just for safety, everyone in the battery stayed away from the other establishment so there would be no trouble.

Dean, like most of his classmates in Rupert, Idaho, had been a part of the partying crowd. He would go out with his baseball teammates and have a couple of beers. However, Randall introduced him to German beer, it whipped him good. He had three beers and was feeling the effects.

"What is going on here I'm already feeling drunk Randall?"

"You've been drinking American beer which is three percent. German beer is six percent. That is why you're already drunk."

Dean got sick and they had him drink something that was about seventy-five proof alcohol. This made him sicker still, to the point that he had to rush to the bathroom and throw up. When he came back, they asked him how he was feeling. He told them that he felt a lot better so Randall set up another round.

Dean got pretty plastered that night but Randall took care of him, making sure that he got back to the billets safely. He went to his bunk to turn in, but someone had torn his blankets off and the bed had been pulled apart and left in the shower. Randall led him over to his area and allowed him to sleep things off on his upper bunk. The next day Randall helped him get squared away.

Dean took him back to the guesthouse as a farewell party. John and Randall teased Dean for getting so drunk. They talked about field exercises, and somethings that had occurred on the shooting range. Randall was from New Mexico and Dean liked to listen to his drawl and about the ranch he had grown up on in the desert areas of the state.

Dean limited himself to four beers but he freely bought the rounds for the first friend he made when he got to Baumholder. This time Dean took care of him by taking him back to the barracks and getting him to bed in his room. Randall left two weeks later and the unit seemed to change with his discharge.

The officers and sergeants demanded a more spit and polished outfit. The vehicles were the color of olive drab green but everyone was ordered to paint them camouflage colors, black, sand brown, and a forest green. This helped the vehicles to blend into their surrounds. This little job kept Dean busy for a couple of weeks working on the van. The all-volunteer army became a better-looking army, but Dean thought that the draftees were better field soldiers.

A week after Randall left, they got two new 'cruits' in. One was called Jim Ford who was assigned to the SW section. He had a cheesy mustache, with a build of Frosty the Snowman. He had a good sense of humor and a smile that rarely left his face.

Richie Huff could have been the brother of Lt. Donner; he was thin as a rail, with a weasel looking face; sharp features and a long, pointed nose with a face to match it. The old timers took one look at him and shook their heads. "What are those recruiters thinking of, putting that clown in a combat unit? I'm surprised he can carry his M-16 around without dragging it on the ground," suggested Reed after formation.

"Hi, my name is Jim Ford," the new man declared, holding out his hand.

Dean and Reed shook it, and introduced themselves as they walked toward the mess hall.

"Well, I feel kind of sorry for the guy. He is going to get a real education around here," stated Dean as he looked over at Richie.

"He's a trip," declared Ford.

"How do you know him?" asked Reed.

"I went through basic with him, man. He wouldn't take a shower so some of the guys gave him a blanket party. I wasn't a part of that. He slept several bunks down from me so I didn't have to smell him. They took him into the shower with a wire brush. I guess he was clean when they got done with him but they had to send him to the hospital for that. That's why we are getting here at the same time. He had to recover from that shower and finish basic while I was going through Mike five school. I also got held over after Mike 5 so here we are going to the same unit."

A blanket party occurred when several people in a unit didn't want to be identified. They would throw a blanket over a person's head and they would teach him a lesson the hard way. Often it was a beating to get there point across.

"I wonder who's going to get stuck with him?" Reed spoke thoughtfully.

"I'm just glad he's not in our section," Dean responded, shaking his head.

Richie spoke to someone nearby. His voice was high pitch, almost like a cartoon character. Everyone turned their heads to him and Dean thought, he doesn't stand a chance here.

Chapter 9

FULL ALERT

Dean stepped out of his car near the barracks into the cool moist foggy air. It was October 1973. Something was happening, men were rushing off in every direction. Trucks were pulling up to the armory and supplies were being loaded up. Walker came running out to Dean, stopped in front of him, and caught his breath.

"I tried calling you, but I missed you at home. You need to go back to your place and pack up your gear. All of the American military in Europe has been called on alert. I guess some of the Arab nations have attacked Israel. You need to get your duffle bag packed with clothing, helmet, web gear, and anything else you might need and get back here as soon as you can. We might be deployed to the Middle East very soon. Natalie needs to get packed also; if we get sent, the army will be flying her home. Any questions?"

"What are the chances that we will be going"

"I have no idea Larson, I'm just a sergeant and following orders, so get to it. I'll see you back here in about twenty minutes."

Dean hopped back in his car and rushed back to his apartment. All of Baumholder seemed to be in motion everywhere he looked as he drove through the base. Trucks and Gama Goats were pulling out of motor pools or filling the parking areas near the barracks. The drivers of tanks and self-propelled guns were starting the engines to warm them up.

He burst through the apartment door to find that Natalie had gone back to bed. She was startled by the door opening and Dean rushing in on her. Her hair was a mess and her eyes were big as saucers as he ordered her out of the sack.

"I'm in a big rush so come and help me pack while you listen. Please get my OD's [olive drab utility uniforms] out of the dresser while I pull my duffle bag and gear out of the closet."

He explained to her what was happening and that she was going to have to get packed up in a hurry. He whispered how much he loved her and that he would try to keep in touch with her. He kissed her hard, then her lips, grasped some of her hair, and took a sniff of her perfume before leaving through the door.

Back at base men were in formation, about to be sent to the mess hall. Dean found Walker who directed him to stow his equipment in one of the rooms that the section was assigned to sleep in. He was then ordered to go to the motor pool and get his truck ready for deployment if needed. Flanders was in the five-ton pulling it up behind bravo batteries vehicle.

"Where you heading?" asked Dean.

"Cain and I have been ordered to the nuclear armory site in case they decide to take the real weapons to this little fracas. You better get off the side step. I need to follow the other batteries when they pull out, we're convoying over there under the S-2 captain."

Dean stepped down and waved bye as they left with the rest of the convoy. That gave Dean a very uneasy feeling; the thought that this war could get that ugly. He proceeded back to the van where he found Jack checking fluids and tire pressure.

"What's the word Reed?"

"She's ready, so why don't you start her up. We can pull around front of the barracks and load up the personal gear. Walker doesn't want us wasting any time. He sure was stressed out when he came running into the room this morning announcing the alert."

Dean got into the van and started the diesel engine up. He clutched in, grinding the gear into second and put the vehicle in motion. He navigated from the back of the barracks to the front. Reed and Dean grabbed up the personal gear and stored it in the van and locked up the back door.

Walker showed up and informed them that they needed to make sure they had room for NROSS and they might have to take the dummy round and components with them. The BC was calling a meeting in the classroom at ten hundred hours and everyone was required to be there. Until then, they could hang out near the battery area.

Reed had not had breakfast yet, so he went over to the mess hall to grab up some food. Dean followed him to keep him company and drink a bad cup of coffee. They discussed the current crisis with Dean grilling Reed on any rumors he had heard. They eventually retired to Reed's room, where they played cards until the meeting. Reed was one of the first ones to the classroom located on the third floor of the building. Huff was sitting in one of the desks on the front row.

Reed winked at Dean and went straight up to Huff's seat. "Newbie, don't you know that you're supposed to sit in the back of the classroom?"

He picked up Huff and his desk, took him through the next door to the game room and set him down. Everyone in both rooms were laughing hard and loud except for Huff. He came out of the chair and jumped on Reed's back. He was screaming and hitting Reed with one hand while holding on to him with the other.

Reed just continued to the front of the classroom smiling all the way. He hardly missed a step, this only infuriated Huff all the more. One of the NCOs stepped in and broke up the little tussle. He was smiling all the time he calmed Huff down. He sent him over to the other side of the room and halfheartedly chewed Reed out for causing such a ruckus.

Top England suddenly entered the room and called, "Attention." The men came out of their chairs and stood at attention while Captain Law marched up to the podium.

"Be at ease and sit. This is the word that I got from the top. The U.S. Army in Europe has been put on full alert. This is not a drill, but the real thing. It seems that the Egyptian and Syrian armies have made a surprise attack on Israel.

They made several incursions into Israel's borders and have caught the Jewish nation with their pants down. Israel is an ally, so if they need our help, we will be sent over. I hope all married personal have informed your wives that they could be going home. You will be staying at the barracks tonight. Cots will be provided for you and you will be staying in the rooms with your various sections. Top will be giving out the various training schedules, all activities will be taking place in this area or at the motor pool, no exceptions."

After hearing the BC talk about why they were on alert, Dean had a hard time concentrating on the next things that were stated. All kinds of emotions went dancing through his thinking processes. He thought of taking another life was scary. The question was could he even do it.

He hoped he would not come face to face with that task but that they would be at least twelve miles away if they got involved in this fight. He didn't want Natalie to be a widow or his child to be fatherless. He hoped that things would settle down.

Law nodded at England who called everyone to "Attention." The BC left the room and Top took over the podium. He allowed the captain to get down the stairs before he had everyone sit. He had a very stern look on his face.

"War is a very ugly business, it can be very confusing, but you all need to focus on your jobs and complete what is in front of you. We need to work as a unit, so put aside any problems you might have with another soldier in the battery. You have another enemy and you need to concentrate all your efforts on destroying those men that have started this conflict.

"You have been warriors of peace, making sure that the Soviet Union adhered to the boundaries that were laid down after World War II. Now, you could find yourself in the midst of a shooting war. Keep your heads down and your eyes open. I want all sections to go through the motions as if you are in a battle and that you are doing your jobs. In other words, gun crews do dry fire missions. Special weapons, get the dummy round and practice assembling it using different members of the section. Practice until it becomes second nature. Any questions?"

"What about Flander and Cain, will they be back any time soon?" asked Walker.

"No, they will be at the armory until we either stand down or we go to the Middle East."

Walker had Dean pull the van around behind the barracks and parked it fairly close to the foundation of the building where the battery armory and supplies were located. Spec four Dan Jackson and Ford were the only other members of S.W., and Jackson was a short timer, ready to get out in three months. Walker placed him in back as the guard.

He was an imposing character, weighing in at about two hundred and fifty pounds, standing at about six one. He was well built and very muscular. Jackson was a transfer from another unit.

Walker started Dean and Reed off as the team to practice putting the round together first. He then paired Jackson and Reed, switching to Dean and Ford who had not been cleared to work with the round. He gave up his seat as the reader and tried his hand at helping assemble the weapon himself.

Walker felt like he was at a disadvantage because Flanders and Cain were at the nuclear site and he had always thought of them as his best team. They would get no practice and he could not make comparisons between the six men.

It was apparent that Jackson had a short timer's attitude and was just killing time until he got out of the army. Walker did warn him that if they went to war, the Army could extend his enlistment but this did not change his attitude. At noon Walker put Jackson on as guard again and kept him there.

They took a break for lunch and Walker put them through some physical training and by two p.m. they were back practicing on the round. At five p.m. they were called to formation where Top informed them that they were still on full alert. He did release the married men to go home to have dinner with their wives. They were to be by a phone if they were called to deploy. They had exactly one hour to eat and then they were going to spend the rest of the night with their sections.

Dean jumped in his car and rushed home to Natalie. He surprised her, hurrying to her and giving her a large passionate kiss. She quickly made dinner for him and Natalie drove him back to the battery area so that she could have the car in case the unit was shipped out.

He gave her a long goodbye kiss, not knowing if he would see her again. He told her what the alert was about while they were at their apartment and to show up at the battery area around five pm every afternoon until the alert was over or they were gone.

He was lucky; that evening instead of sleeping in the cot, he laid claim to Cain's bed. It was not as comfortable as the bed at home, but it was a lot better than a canvas cot. He woke up several times reaching for Natalie but finding a small bed with no warm wife beside him. It was hard for him to get back to sleep since Ford snored. It sounded like someone was constantly walking around outside in the hallway.

When reveille came the next morning Dean was already exhausted and the day had not really begun. They had P.T. The battery was called to formation where they learned that the Israeli army was holding its own and that the unit was still on high alert. They were released for breakfast, then the routine started all over again,

On the third day of the alert, Top switched things around. He broke up the Special Weapons section and had them train on the guns. It was a nice break from the routine of putting the weapon together. Dean was lucky; he got put on Sergeant Marks' gun.

Marks started him off as the powder monkey. The eight-inch had seven different bags of gun powder they used during any given fire mission. The job of the powder monkey was to make sure that they got the right number of bags in the tube. If he gave too many bags, the round would go over the target and if he gave to few, the projectile would fall short of its destination.

It was a fairly easy job, so Marks quickly made him one of the loaders. It took four men to lug the round over to the hydraulic lift on the back of the self-propelled gun. It was hard work and Dean had a new respect for the gun bunnies, as they were called. He was taught to cut the fuses again. He had been taught all the basics in AIT but it had been on the 155 self-propelled gun. There were some differences from the weapons and yet some similarities. Marks had him practice being the gunner and the assistant gunner. It was a real break from his regular job.

For the rest of the week, they got stuck assembling the nuclear projectile. Walker would break up the routine with maintenance on the two and half ton van, drills, and P.T. At the end of a week, the Eight Infantry Division was taken off full alert. The Israeli army had made a counter attack, throwing the enemy armies back; the danger had passed. At five p.m. Natalie came to pick him up as usual, this time he had his duffle bag in hand. She gave him a big smile as he got behind the steering wheel of the car.

"Is it over?" she asked hopefully.

"We are still on alert but I guess the Israeli army has gone on the offensive and they are pushing their enemies back. We have to stay close to the phone and I need to keep my gear packed. You need to keep your suitcases close at hand. Tonight I get to sleep in my own bed and have a relaxing dinner."

"I was so concerned, we're about to have a baby and he needs a father. Besides I want you holding my hand when I'm in the delivery room. That would have been hard for you to do in the Middle East," she said smiling.

"Just how do you know it's going to be a boy?"

"I felt like the Lord told me it was going to be a son," she said with deep conviction.

"Well, you have a fifty, fifty chance," he responded as he started the car and pulled out onto the cobblestone road.

Cain and Flander showed up at the battery area the next day. They were happy to be back in Baumholder and sleeping in their own beds. Training was the main focus each day until October 25th when a cease fire was established, ending the Yon Kippur war. The battery went back to training and maintenance mode with fairly regular hours.

Chapter 10

THANKSGIVING

Natalie and Dean had discussed having the section over for Thanksgiving at the beginning of November. Dean could tell Natalie was concerned about fixing the dinner with all the trimmings for a bunch of lonely G.I.s that she hardly knew.

She knew Jack Reed best; Dean had brought him home several times. They learned that he came from upper state New York and that his father worked for the government dealing with hydrology. Walker had visited with her on several occasions and was proud of the fact that he came from Fox Chapel, Pennsylvania. She liked both of these men but had never met Donald Jackson, Dan Cain, George Flander, or Jim Ford.

What's more, she had helped her mother cook the Thanksgiving dinner on several occasions but never prepared the meal by herself. Dean encouraged her since he had not eaten a lousy dinner since they were married.

She cooked his hamburger's a little raw when she first came to Germany, but that was because she made her patties much smaller than his. She took the hamburgers off the stove at the same time. He finally made a comment that he thought his burger was mooing, and he would appreciate it if she kept his meat in the pan a little longer. He could tell that it embarrassed her, but the hamburgers were well cooked after that.

Two weeks before the holiday, Dean invited the men over for the meal. All of them agreed to come and eat except Jackson, who had made other plans. The battery would put on their own Thanksgiving dinner so it was not like Jackson would go hungry. The rest of them were excited about getting two turkey meals. Natalie and Dean went to the PX and bought a couple of folding chairs so everyone could relax in the kitchen for the meal. It was going to be crowded but they all seemed to be looking forward to it.

The day before Thanksgiving, Natalie baked two pumpkin pies, smothered them in whipped cream, and stored them in the fridge. She got as much of the meal together on that day, knowing that the turkey would take a long time to cook. Dean came home early. The smells lingered through their small apartment. He helped as much as he could, but preparing food was not something that he had been taught back on the farm; he was usually out helping his father do the chores. On the other hand, he admired his father who could throw a good meal together without a problem. Bud Larson had become the main cook after his wife had passed away.

Dean got into the Opal station wagon and drove slowly to the barracks to pick up the guys for the meal. It was cold and drizzling rain, which caused him to slow down on the cobble-streets; they were very slick when they had any type of moisture on them. He picked them up and ferried them back to the apartment. Natalie met each one of them at the door, taking coats, and piling them on the bed. It was crowded but they all found a place to sit and Natalie kept working on the meal and visiting at the same time.

Natalie was the center of attention since she was the first American woman some of them had seen in a while. They asked her where she came from and what her parents were like.

"I come from a little town in southern Idaho called Burley. My parents own an acre on the south side of town, where they raised a few chickens, a beef cow, a garden, and my two sisters. My father made a living at one of the potato processing plants."

"How did you meet Dean?" asked Walker.

"We actually ran into one another at a basketball game," she said laughing.

"What's so funny?" remarked Cain.

"Dean lived in Rupert and went to school at Minico. We were arch rivals. He had gone to get a coke and a hotdog at the concession stand. We rounded the corner of the bleachers at the same time going in opposite directions. I knocked his hot dog and drink into him. I was so embarrassed but he was so nice about it. I tried to clean him up, he did not try to stop me. We got to talking and he kind of blackmailed me in going to a movie with him. He sat with me during the rest of the game and I got to liking him. The rest is history."

"How about you Cain, do you have a girl back home?" inquired Natalie.

"No just my mom and two sisters. I sure do miss them. When I get back to the world, I'm going to find a good job and help take care of my mom. She worked hard to provide for me and the two girls."

"I don't want to hit a nerve but what happened to your father?" asked Dean.

"He was killed in a boating accident while fishing on a river. I guess it wasn't much of a boat and he wasn't much of a swimmer. At least that's what my mama told me. I don't really know since I was only four years old when it happened. We were never rich but holidays were always special, she made sure of that. Right about now we would be sitting down to some fried chicken, stuffing, and later pumpkin pie."

Walker had a far-off look in his eyes. "Yeah, only we had goose on the menu, my older brother, or I would have shot the day before. My mother would cook it up with all the fixings and we would gorge ourselves and sit down later to watch some football. My grandparents would come over that evening and we would work on the leftovers."

"What about your father, where is he Alan?" asked Cain.

"My parents got a divorce when I was in fifth grade and he never had much to do with us. In fact, he moved to Alaska and stopped communicating with us after a couple of years. What about you Flander, you go out and shoot a steer and barbecue it for Thanksgiving?"

They all chuckled at Flander's expense.

"Naw, but we once went wild boar hunting a couple of weekends before Thanksgiving and killed two. Brought them home and dressed them out. Let me tell ya, that ham was some of the best stuff I ever ate. The hunt was real special, my father took me and my brother on the hunt and you have to keep on your toes to avoid getting wounded while hunting those things. We had some mighty fine meals off those hogs," he said with a big smile.

"How about you Reed, what would you be doing if you were back home?" queried Walker.

"My parents, I and my two sisters would be going to my grandparent's farm to spend the day. They would kill one of their own turkeys, cook it up and all the goodies that would go with dinner. We would be spending the weekend with them. They would have us grandkids help them around the farm. It was always a great time as a family gathering."

Everyone turned their attention to Ford with questioning looks. "Well Ford, tell us what you would be doing?"

Natalie informed them that dinner was ready and asked them to quiet themselves so she could ask the Lord to bless the food. After all, it was going to be her first solo Thanksgiving. They bowed their heads and she gave thanks to the one that provided them with everything. The guests grabbed their plates and the two hosts dished up the meals.

It was like Natalie had cooked this specific holiday meal all her life. The food was great and afterwards they listened to music and played card games. On the whole, the evening was pleasant and the soldiers that were far from their love ones were a lot less homesick. This is why Natalie and Dean had invited them over in the first place, it was like they were already spending time with family.

While they were playing games; they asked Jim Ford about what he would be doing back home in Oklahoma. He thought for a few minutes, looking like he was far away.

"Well, we would all go to the store and pick the biggest and fattest turkey we could find since I had four brothers and six sisters to share with. Mom and the girls would be in the kitchen most of the day cooking and baking.

"We had a big yard, so my father would take us boys outside and we would play a game of tag football. The captain of the winning team would get one of the drumsticks and of course my old man would get the other one. I remember many a bruise after some of those games. In fact, we had to take Chet, my younger brother, to the hospital for a broken arm one year. We all knew why Dad had us playing the games, it was to keep us out of the kitchen and to get us real hungry. Thanksgiving seemed even more special because of those games. I loved it and I sure miss it. I have to thank you two for the invite. You have made me a little less homesick today."

The rest of them chimed in their appreciation. The party ended late afternoon so they could get back in time for another turkey dinner at the mess hall. After he took everyone back to the barracks, he helped Natalie clean up the mess. They had a quiet evening at home.

When he saw Jackson on Monday, he asked him why he had declined the invitation. Don was polite and thanked him but had instead spent the holiday with a young lady that he met in Germany. He pulled a picture of Greda, a beautiful blond. She was well built with light blue eyes.

"Well, I can see why you declined my invitation."

"It's more than that, I've fallen in love with her and I've asked her to marry me. We made it official at the Thanksgiving meal when I asked her father for her hand in marriage. He looked me over for a while to make me sweat it out. He finally agreed and that's good because I wanted his blessing. He is very well off and after I get out of this man's army, I'm taking her home to meet my parents. We are coming back to Germany and getting married."

"Good for you, man. It sounds like you have a plan. I hope things go well for you, Don. I didn't even know that you knew a girl. Now I have to admit that you definitely know a girl," Dean laughed, patting him on the back.

"I like it here, and her father is going to have me work in his business. Greda is teaching me German and the wedding is set in July. If you want to, you and your wife are invited to come. In fact, I would be really honored if you would, since I'm not going to have many people on my side of the church show up. My father and sister have pledged to come. I'm going to invite the whole section."

"I can't say for sure; I'll have to talk to Natalie. We will also see what the army is doing at the time but if we can, we will be there."

"Great man, I really appreciate it. Afterwards, you guys are invited to come and see us any time."

The wedding did take place in July and most of the men of SW section attended, except for Cain. It was a beautiful affair with the bride picking lavender and white as her colors. One of the old gothic cathedrals was the setting and Dean had no idea what was being said during the ceremony. He enjoyed everything, especially the food afterward.

The bride was better looking than what her picture had indicated and she spoke excellent English. The soldiers were welcome by family and most of Greda's friends. They saw the groom and his wife off for their honeymoon. Dean and Natalie did visit them one time before the winter set in and they seemed very happy.

Chapter 11

V CORP

Dean shivered and gathered the parka closer around his body. They had convoyed out to the firing range near Baumholder. The snow covered the hills around them and the sky was gray, acting like it could drop more of the white flakes on them.

They had just gotten in position and put camouflage netting over the top of the van. He stomped his feet and flagged his arms to get warm. Reed set the last pole to break the pattern of the truck and wandered over to stand next to him. They looked over at the five ton.

Flander and Cain were having a hard time getting their netting up because the wind was whipping it back and forth. They had parked out in a more open area and the breeze would suddenly shift directions this time of year. Reed and Dean went over and helped wrestle the netting into submission, making sure that it would stay in place. Cain looked over at the gun emplacements and shook his head.

"Man, I'm glad I'm not on the gun crews. It's going to be a cold night and they are going to have to sleep in those shelter halves."

"Hey, you guys, get in the van. We need to practice on the round. V Corp is going to inspect us tomorrow, bright and early. At least that's what Lt Danner told me," Walker said waving for them to come over to the van.

"Danner! That butter bar doesn't know how to tie his shoe laces. How would he know when V Corp is going to inspect us?" retorted Flander.

"Just got done talking to him and the BC told him that's when we're scheduled for the inspection. They are inspecting A battery right now, so we can get some practice in before they come our way," Walker commanded.

They entered the van, which was nice and warm. Jackson was sitting on the counter, his gloves and parka sitting next to him. Cain laughed and made a remark about how nice it must be to be a short timer. Jackson just smiled and held his fingers up with a small space between them indicating that he was short.

Walker had Cain and Flander practice first while Dean and Jackson acted as inspectors. Walker did the reading, Reed and Ford got stuck out in the cold guarding the van. Everyone switched positions except for Jackson and Walker.

At three in the afternoon, the guns got their first fire mission and the rounds left the tubes exploding somewhere down range. From then on, they had a mission about every half hour so they could practice different deflections and azimuths. It started snowing about five that evening, a light storm with very little wind. Walker announced that he was going to use the number one team. Cain and Flander on the inspection but that Dean and Reed were doing a very good job. That meant Jackson, Reed, Ford and Dean would be the guards while the inspection would be taking place.

At around six in the evening, the section was playing cards, drinking coffee, and eating rations. They all bedded down for the night in the van, keeping nice and warm while the poor gun crews had to suffer out in the cold. The section was awakened by the first fire mission of the day. They all donned their parkas and packs [boots] to get a cup of coffee and their breakfast.

The snow had stopped, but the wind had picked up a little, making it nasty cold. Reed and Dean stored their coffee and food in the van and found an enclosed area to relieve themselves. As they made yellow snow, they heard some cussing below them on a little knoll. They looked over the edge, catching Huff pissing into the wind. He had made the mistake of not finding an enclosure. As he let lose the wind would blow it back on his pant leg. He would turn and the wind would shift against him, making his pant leg even wetter.

The two men started laughing, they couldn't help it. Huff heard them and started yelling obscene remarks at them as he continued turning to piss on the ground. This seemed to encourage Reed all the more to giggle and make fun of Huff. Dean put a hand on Reed's arm and suggested maybe they should leave Huff alone. Someone might give him live ammo for that M-16 he carried around. Reed sneered and suggested that if anyone gave him live ammunition, they would have to be a fool. Huff would most likely shoot himself in the foot before he killed someone else.

Dean pulled him away from the scene where Huff just could not get a break from the wind which continued to blow the urine back on his pants and boots.

They went back to the van heated up their rations with steno tabs and drank their coffee. They were interrupted by Huff who came stomping up the hill to threaten Dean and Reed. He made several complaints to Walker who was standing by the van.

"What did you two do to Huff?" accused Walker.

"Look at his boots," Reed said pointing at them.

Walker looked down and saw the wet pants and boots. He looked back at Reed and Dean with a question in his stare.

"He pissed into the wind. We didn't do nothing to him except laugh at him," Dean commented.

Walker turned back, looked down at Huff's pants, and started laughing which brought the rest of the section out of the van. The story was retold and everyone else started giggling and pointed at Huff. He became furious and started moving toward Walker in a threatening manner. Walker held up a hand and turned real serious.

"You don't want to come too close with that attitude, Huff. If the guys had peed on you, I would do something about it but my hands are tied, you did it to yourself. If you want to complain about it, take it further up the chain of command but I don't think you're going to get much satisfaction. One good thing about it, you don't have to polish your boots," he said with a chuckle.

Huff turned and stomped off toward the communication section where his section chief was working. Reed shook his head and made a comment that Huff should be back home learning to be a man, and the recruiting officer that talked Huff in coming into the army should be fired.

At ten am, the V Corp inspector showed up and the four guards took their positions around the truck. Cain, Flander, and Walker went into the van with the inspector and proceeded to put the round together according to the book. After they went through that part of the inspection, the captain questioned Reed, and Jackson on their duties as sentries.

He took Walker off to the side and gave him a sheet with the results. Walker came back with a big smile and lead everyone into the van. He announced that the team had gotten only four gigs on the inspection and the captain had suggested that the team had been one of the better SW sections he had seen in the V Corp that year.

Walker got some of the section involved in a card game to kill time until the last fire mission took place, which was supposed to be that day. Dean and Reed went over to visit Mark's gun, where he was the gunner.

Often, Marks would take the time to train them on the 8-inch, but because of the inspection he was all business. He did take time to ask them how they had done on their part of the inspection. He was impressed with the fact that they had only four gigs. They watched the gun fire twice, catching sight of a two-hundred-pound projectile leaving the tube of the gun.

They decided to visit Sergeant Cassidy and his ammo carrier sitting about a hundred yards from the weapons. He would know if the maneuvers were about over. If he delivered the last of the rounds to the guns, it meant that they were about to go back to the barracks.

Cassidy was in the cab of one of the ammo carriers drinking coffee and relaxing. He waved them to come into the cab. Cassidy was always friendly and willing to share the latest rumors he heard from his various sources.

"Well, I heard your section did really well on the inspection."

"Yep, only four gigs," Dean remarked, nodding his head in the positive.

"Wow, that is good. So, who put the round together?"

"Flander was the A man, Cain was the B man and Walker was the reader," replied Reed.

"Flander had been here for a while, so he should know his stuff, but why Cain? Jackson has been in SW a lot longer and should be in the van putting the round together," asked Cassidy.

"He's too short he doesn't want to mess with it. He told Walker he didn't want to be in any more inspections and Walker took him at his word. He has that short timer attitude and Walker was concerned that he would mess up," commented Dean.

Cassidy nodded knowingly. Stared off toward the guns as if he was deep in though. "So, I heard you two caused some trouble today."

Dean and Reed looked at each other, trying to remember what they had done wrong. Reed looked at him innocently and shook his head. "What are talking about? We haven't caused any trouble today."

"Huff," Cassidy laughed at the man's misfortune.

All three of them started chuckling. Reed held up a hand and caught his breath. "It was almost the best part of the trip. The only thing that beat it was the result of the inspection. How did you hear about it?"

"He complained about you two to Top in front of me. I don't know how England didn't laugh in his face. He told Huff that he would look into it. Once Huff walked, away Top burst out laughing and commented on Huff's wet pants. He then looked at me and became really serious and told me that he was going to get rid of Huff one way or another."

Dean whistled and shook his head.

"Good, I'm tired of hearing that shrill voice of his whenever he gets upset. I can't believe he would go to Top and whine about us laughing at him," remarked Reed.

They visited for a couple more minutes and decided to get back to the SW section. They planned to take a short cut through a wooded area, even though they would have to buck some deep snow. As they were passing a group of trees, they heard some harsh words. It was England's voice and though he was not screaming, the voice was stern and anger mingled with each sentence.

Reed pushed Dean in that direction, whispering that Top might be dressing down Huff. They quietly pressed through the foliage and snow to a place where they could see what was happening. It was Top, but to their surprise it was Lt. Danner and he was staring down at the ground.

"Well, I, huh, it was a, I mean."

"Shut the h- -l up and don't make any kind of excuse. You almost killed one of my men, you whimpering little pansy. You don't belong in a combat unit. I have heard enough of your whining about how the men treat you, the lack of respect they give you and all the gross gestures they make toward you. Start acting like a man, an officer of the United States Army, and make wise decisions in the field where lives are on the line. It's too late for that. No one will respect you after what you have done in the field this time."

"Hey Top, I am an officer," Danner said standing a little taller.

"Not in this outfit. I'm getting you out of here, somewhere you won't kill someone." England grabbed him by the front of his parka, lifting him off the ground stared into his eyes. "Don't you understand, sir?" he said sarcastically.

He threw Danner in the snow and turned away from him. "I don't want to see you until I call you into my office to discuss your transfer, so make yourself real scarce. Do you understand? Legally, you can't do anything about this little incident because you have no witnesses. I will deny any accusations that you might make against me. I will also describe in great detail the order you gave that new private that almost got him killed. I might get busted but you will be kicked out of the army."

Danner picked himself off the ground and slinked off toward the battery area.

Top turned to leave the woods and spotted Reed and Dean staring at him. "You two get over here. Well, how much did you see?"

Both of them stammered and kicked the snow at their feet. Finally, Dean looked Top in the eyes and told him how much of the conversation they had witnessed.

"My butt is in your hands. Are you going to help Danner, or are you going to keep your mouths shut?"

"Top, everything you said to Danner was true so, I think what we really want to say is that we only heard you threaten to transfer him to another unit, if anyone asks. Really, I don't think we are going to advertise that we heard any of your discussion with

Danner. Right Larson," commented Reed.

"That's exactly how I feel about it, Top," chimed in Dean.

"Thanks, now you two better get back to your unit. The last fire mission should be coming down soon."

"By the way, Top, how did Danner almost kill someone?" queried Reed.

"He ordered a newbie up in an unstable trailer to wrestle with a round. Several rounds fell over. The man was almost crushed or hurt, it was a good thing he was quick. Danner is an idiot."

Dean and Reed marched back to the SW section looking forward to warming up in the van. Dean looked back to England as they walked. "Remind me never to have a serious discussion with Top without a witness."

They had just gotten into the warm van when they heard the last four rounds go down range. They were soon out in the cold, taking down the camouflage nets and loading up for the wash rack where they would clean the half acre of mud off the vehicles. Dean parked his truck in the motor pool after he got it washed up.

He walked to the barracks with Reed at his side. He made a call to Natalie. She picked him up and took him home. He quickly shed his clothes and took a hot shower. It was the first time he felt really warm in the last three days. Even though they had a heater in the back of the van, they had to keep one of the windows slightly open for safety reasons.

Natalie had dinner ready after the shower. They ate, discussing what had happened on the trip. She was very quiet throughout the meal. At the end she asked him if he thought Huff would become violent and shoot someone? Dean laughed and comforted her with the thought that their weapons were all stored in the armory once again. They went to bed early; he was weary from trudging through the snow and mud.

Natalie was big with child, and feeling ugly, while struggling with her hormones being out of whack. Dean tried to make her feel loved in every way he could, hugged her often, told her she was still beautiful, and that he loved her. He had rejected her weird eating desires on several occasions. The last one was that she had sent him off with a peanut butter and pickle sandwich, which he had tossed out of the window of the van on the way to the field.

In bed he cuddled with her for a long period of time and she snuggled close to him. Even though he was exhausted, sleep was elusive. He thought about the child that they were about to have. Being a father was exciting to him and yet scary. Fatherhood was a new adventure, one with a lot of responsibility. He wanted to raise the child up right. He hoped that Natalie was right, a little boy to wrestle, go hunting and fishing with. He finally drifted off to sleep with excitement and hope for the future.

Top was as good as his word; Danner and Huff disappeared into another part of the army before Christmas. Danner was re-placed by another second lieutenant by the name of Thomas. He was short but stocky with a light complexion and blue eyes. He was quiet and very observant, treating the men well. He pulled his own weight and gained the men's respect quickly.

Chapter 12

CHRISTMAS

A few days before Christmas, Dean and Natalie went to the telephone exchange and placed two calls to the states. Dean got to talk to his brother Jack, who had just come up from the barn. Bud, his father, was on the other side of the canal in the fields feeding the cows.

Back in Idaho they had a little snow on the ground but it was a calm day with the sun peeking through some white clouds. They were doing well and the farm was in good shape, but Dean never got to talk to his father.

Natalie called her folks, Lawrance, and Laura Baker, she asked about her sisters who were out shopping. They asked her about the upcoming baby and what it was like living in Germany. The conversations ended way before they wanted them to. There was a time restriction on how long they could talk. The Bakers informed Natalie that they had invited the two Larson men over for Christmas and they had accepted. When Natalie hung up, Dean noticed a couple of tears were rolling down her check.

They walked out into the cold rain that marked another Baumholder day. Dean could see that this just added to Natalie's mood. She was very close to her family. Dean discussed the

Baker family Christmas traditions with Natalie as the holiday got closer. They got a very small tree for the hallway and decorated it while drinking eggnog. They bought several Christmas albums which were being played constantly. One of the records was put off to the side; it was the one that had "White Christmas" on it. Dean would play it, but Natalie tended to stay away from that music as the song seemed to depress her.

They had gotten a little snow in November and the first part of December, but since then it had been cold rain and grey skies. Usually, Natalie was upbeat with a slight smile on her face. She was shy by nature and it took a while to get her to say much, she had always been cheerful.

Dean tried several things to get her out of her bout with depression, but nothing seemed to help. He brought flowers home but this seemed to be a very temporary fix. They went to the movies several times and he took her to the local guesthouses for dinner to get her mind off home. He knew that she was missing family, friends, and all the things they did at this time of the year.

Christmas was not all that important to Dean. Ever since they had lost his mother to cancer, the holiday had just about become another day in the year. His father tried to make it special, but the farm took up a lot of time, so the boys were on their own when it came to getting the homestead ready for the big day.

Jack and Dean had never gotten along with each other until the last year Dean had been home. They constantly fought over how the house should be decorated. So much for peace on earth, Dean had thought, but that last year at home they almost became friends.

It was obvious that Dean wanted something more than the farm; he wanted an education. Jack was a farmer at heart; he loved growing things and helping his father in the fields. One of the reasons Dean had no desire for farming was because of Christmas.

Even on holidays, you had to get up early, go out feed the animals, gather the eggs, and milk the cows again. Maybe that is why religion seemed to always be secondary; the farm always came first.

It did not help that Dean was putting a lot of time in for the army. During the V Corp inspection, Charlie battery had done well but Bravo battery had done poorly almost to the point of flunking it. If they flunked, the battalion would have gotten a new commander.

Dealing with nuclear weapons was taken very seriously. Walker was putting both teams through the paces, making sure that everyone knew what they were supposed to do. So, while the rest of the battery was dismissed for the day, the SW team was still practicing on the round or dealing with NROSS procedures. Word had come down that USAREUR [U.S. Army Europe] was going to inspect the battalion sometime after Christmas.

It had taken some persuading, but he had talked Natalie into inviting the section over for Christmas lunch. He was hoping this would cheer her up in some way. Walker and Reed were the only ones that accepted the invite.

Jackson was going to spend time with his fiancée and Flander with Ford were invited to a party and didn't think they would be over their hangovers by lunch. Cain was standoffish toward him since Thanksgiving. He acted cool toward Dean and said very little to him outside of business.

The night before Christmas, Dean decided that he was going to talk to Natalie about her depression. He was very concerned about her. She seemed more withdrawn from him every day. It was a cold foggy day when he got home. It was a little after six in the evening and she already had dinner done. He gave her a kiss and told her how good she looked.

She seemed to almost ignore the compliment as she poured him a cup of coffee and set it in front of him. She then dished him up a plate of food as he removed his boots from his sore feet. She poured herself a cup of coffee and sat down in the chair across from him.

"Nat, I know it's Christmas, you're away from home, we have no family here, and the weather stinks. Where is a little of that joy, and peace on earth?" he said with a mischievous grin. Calling her "Nat" fired her up. She hated that nickname; her sisters called her that when they fought. It did the trick; he saw a flash in her eyes and she kicked him under the table.

"Don't call me that, you know it irritates me. I feel like an insect."

"Yes, but at least you don't look so depressed."

"I know, but it is our first Christmas, no family, no mother to help with the baby when he comes. I'm concerned that I'll make a mistake. No snow, just ugly rain or fog. It wears on me. What's more, I have no real friends to share my feelings with." Since Dee left, the new couple upstairs had not been very friendly.

"What about me, we are family now. We may be in this situation for a couple more years. I'm here if you want to talk about your feelings, I will try to be a good listener."

"It's not the same as sharing my problems with another woman, Dean."

"Well, I hope not since I'm a man and that is what I plan on being for the rest of my life. But I think I know what you're saying. I'm sorry. Since Dee left, there have not been any men coming into the unit that are married. I've been watching for one so we could invite them over and you could hang out with the wife."

She got up and smoothed his hair with her hand. She gave him a long kiss and smiled down at him. "I know I've been kind of a 'Scrooge' lately, Dean. You've been working long hours and this up-coming inspection has kept you very occupied. I'm happy that you are my husband and we are about to have a baby. It is a Merry Christmas, I always wanted to be a wife and mother. I should be thankful. I forgot how blessed I am," she said with the gentle smile that had been missing for the last couple of weeks.

Christmas morning brought a rain snow mix which cheered Natalie up. She was back to her old self. They opened gifts early, drinking eggnog, and listening to Christmas albums. They had breakfast, Dean treated his wife to pancakes and eggs with coffee. They got the Christmas meal together and at the proper time he picked up Walker and Reed to share it with.

With less people in the place, the visit was more open and there was a lot more laughter. The two men had found a bouquet of flowers, which they gave to Natalie. Dean could tell that they made Natalie's day. They talked about first Christmases they could remember and the last ones that they had before being deployed to Germany.

They topped it off with eating Natalies world famous walnut cake, drinking coffee, and playing spades. Natalie was not very good at playing card games, which meant that the Larsons lost a lot but they all had a great time. Dean felt very close to these two men by the time the evening was over and he was looking forward to seeing how well Reed and he would do as the A team in one of the next inspections after Flander left.

He took an extra day off with Natalie, so they took a long walk and talked a lot to reconnect. Both of them started reading books that the other one had given for gifts. Natalie also gave him a new 35mm camera so they went exploring the surrounding area; taking photos of the interesting people and landscape. He was glad to have a break from the army. His father had always indicated that you learned by putting your hand to the work. He was getting better all the time with the round.

Later in January they took a quick trip to Idar Oberstein and took all kinds of pictures of the village, which laid in a ravine. The buildings were uniquely German with the smell of animals, a bakery, a butcher shop, and of course the guesthouses.

Two old run-down castles looked down from one of the steep hills, and a church was located at the bottom between the two castles. They went inside, it was a beautiful little chapel with a small stream running down the middle of it out of a rock face in the hill. Natalie felt a real peace in the sanctuary

It was a great weekend for the Larson family. They both felt reenergized and ready to face what came next. The weather had not changed, they were still in Germany without family but they had gained that closeness again.

At this time the couple upstairs had gotten base housing so they had moved out. A week later a small family moved into the apartment above them. He was assigned to Charlie Battery third of the sixteen and was married with a baby girl. He was also a part of Special Weapons so he would take Jackson's place. His name was Eddie Perez and his wife was Maria with Juanita in the crib at six months old.

Chapter 13

PERFECTION

It was cold; it had rained and snowed a little. The day had been a long one; pulling maintenance on both vehicles and they were finishing the day by practicing everything that would be a part of the USAREUR inspection.

Walker was dismissing everyone and Flander was not only hungry but looking forward to his first beer. Walker was warning everyone to be careful going down the steps when Flander's left foot slipped out from under him. He went flying off the end of the van and landed hard on his left arm.

The rest of the section gingerly went down the steps to check Flander out. Perez was the first to reach him, he helped Flander to sit up. Flander was groaning in pain and cradling his left arm. He informed them that he thought he had broken it. Walker ran into the maintenance office and called Top to inform him of the incident. Top called the dispensary and they sent an ambulance with a medic to the motor pool right away.

Perez and Dean helped get Flander's jacket off and they cut the sleeve off his shirt. The arm looked broken. With each movement Flander would let out a painful cry, and his face contorted into an anguished look. He was glad when he was sitting up against a five-ton wheel quietly with a blanket and jacket over him.

The ambulance arrived in a very short time. The medic immobilized the arm in a very professional manner. They lifted him up into the ambulance and he was soon on his way to being treated. They all watched as the vehicle disappeared down the cobblestone streets to the dispensary.

The group moved toward the battery area. No one said a word as they walked together, they were all tired, hungry, and very concerned about Flander. Cain, Ford, and Reed went directly to the mess hall. Walker went into the barracks to talk to Top about the accident while Perez got into Dean's car to go home. There was no conversation on the way home, mostly because the roads were treacherous with snow and ice.

As they moved up the final street to their apartments, Perez reminded Dean that he would most likely be on the A team for the upcoming inspection. Dean was taken aback; he was looking forward to just pulling guard duty on this inspection. He realized that Perez was right and that Reed or he would have to step up.

The next day, Walker had them bypass all the usual battery training and maintenance on the vehicles to start getting ready for the inspection. They had roll call and breakfast. The men retrieved the round from its secure location.

Jackson was doing his paperwork and getting his personal items ready to get out of the army. He was of no help at all. Dean, Perez, Ford, and Cain got the area ready for the training exercises for the day while Reed drove the round over. Walker changed up the teams all day, he would even be a member performing either job allowing one of the others to be the reader.

Flander rejoined the section on Thursday with his arm in a cast. Walker put him to work dealing with guards, informing them of their duties. Because of his injury, they had to use a man from FDC. Perez was not yet cleared to work on the round. Flander would also watch the training and give advice as to how the teams could do things better.

On Friday, Walker announced that he wanted Dean and Reed to be the A team and that they would be carrying out those duties during the inspection. Everyone gave a sideways glance at Cain. You could see a surprised expression course through the emotions that were welling up inside him. Finally, anger took over.

"Whatever man, I earned the right to be on that team."

"Yes, but I think Reed and Larson are doing a better job together," Walker said, standing his ground.

"I see how you are," remarked Cain.

He started walking away from the formation. Walker ordered him back, reminding him that he had not dismissed anyone. He called the section to attention and then put everyone at ease. He got into Cain's face.

"What do you mean by that comment Cain? When you answer me, I want to hear 'Sergeant Walker' do you understand?"

"Mox Nix, Sergeant Walker."   The word "Mox Nix" was a German abbreviation of "it doesn't matter."

"Oh, but it does matter, Spec Four Cain. You're suggesting that maybe some of us are bigots and I don't like the implication. I don't care if you are green, blue, or purple, we will get along with one another as long as you do your job. I have no problem with you, Cain. You have been doing your duties well, but Reed and Larson are a better team. Flander and I have agreed on that evaluation, you seem out of tune with both of them. They had a lot of practice together during the alert. I hope to put you and Ford or Perez together and get the same result. Don't ever pull the bigot card on me again. My great-great-granddaddy fought in the Civil War for the union and lost an arm. He almost paid the ultimate price to see that the nation stayed whole and help make your great-great-granddaddy free. I owe you nothing except what I owe the rest of these men. I hope we understand one another, because if I ever hear you suggest that again, we might have another civil war and it will be between the two of us."

"I agree with him, Cain. Larson and Reed are doing an excellent job," added Flander who was trying to ease the tension.

Walker released them to go to the battery area for roll call so they could go home or to the mess hall.

Dean suddenly felt a lot of pressure fall on his shoulders. He liked Walker and didn't want to let him down. He wanted badly to justify Walker's confidence in him.

The following Thursday, the inspection took place. They designated a part of the airfield the area where the exercise would take place. It was a large field that helicopters used. They chose this location for the inspection because they wouldn't be in anyone's way.

Dean took the van out to the area at the appropriate time and they established a perimeter with the guards. Dean could tell that they were all nervous. He had butterflies hovering in his inners. Before they started, they unloaded the round and started the inspection.

Walker leaned toward the men with a confident smile and quietly declared, "We've got this, just remember everything we have gone over the past few months." The jitters left Dean and he felt at ease. The section went through the procedure of unloading the units from the five-ton and loading them into the van.

The inspector was a captain and watched everything very carefully. It had been raining so there was no snow to deal with. The guards took their post and the captain grilled them on their orders. He then entered the van and watched Larson and Reed go through the procedure of getting an NROSS order to put the round together.

The A team started putting the weapon together while he threw in some problems that they had to deal with. He questioned the men on several regulations. At the end he made them transfer the round as if they were taking it to one of the guns to be fired. He gave no further instructions or made no comments but just left in his jeep.

"What do you think Walker, do you think we missed any-thing?" asked Perez.

"I think it went smoothly; I can't think of anything going wrong in the van. If there was a problem, it was with guards or transporting the round to the gun. We hadn't practiced that too often. I guess we will have to wait for the debriefing," suggested Walker.

The debriefing came a couple of days later at battalion HQ [Headquarters] where the colonel gave the battery commanders and section chiefs the result of the inspection.

When Walker came walking back to the battery from the meeting, the whole section was waiting anxiously for his return outside the barracks. When he saw them, he put his head down and had a very serious expression. This only added to the fears that they had missed something during the procedure.

He called everyone in and they all crowded around him to hear the news. He looked up with a big grin on his face. "I guess the whole battalion did really well on the inspection. All the batteries passed with about eight gigs between us. We, on the other hand, did not get a gig, we were perfect. I can't tell you how proud I am of you all. I am willing to buy a round of beers for you at the local guesthouse. Maybe we can talk Larson into ferrying all of us over to the bar."

"Are you kidding? I would do that just to see you dish out the money for the beer," retorted Dean.

All of them laughed because Walker was known to be tight with his money. You could also sense the stress of waiting for the results had evaporated from them. The guard form FDC had even felt the pressure. Though they tried to coax Cain to come with them, but he would not join in the festivities. Walker bought two rounds with Flander buying another. It would be his last inspection;

he would start getting ready to go back home the first of February. Dean sipped his beers very slowly, since he would have to drive them back to the barracks. He only had the three drinks while the rest of them had more than they should have.

Bravo battery, the section that had almost flunked V Corp was also celebrating, passing with only three gigs. Sergeant Sanders, the section chief went on a binge cleaning beer out of the dispensers in the barracks and having friends bring beer to his living quarters. When that ran out, he called the post commander about the dispensers being empty on a Sunday. The general listened to him and order the machines to be refilled. Sanders continued to drink that day passing out on his bed in the afternoon.

On Monday morning they dragged him down to formation. His acting sergeant stripes were taken away and he was put back on the guns. He was also ordered to drug addiction meetings. It was a good lesson for everyone. It just showed everyone how you could be on the top in the army one minute and busted the next.

The members of Charlie battery were given a certificate of achievement for what they had done during the inspection. Captain Law told the battery that the inspector had been all over Europe doing inspections and it was the first time he had not given at least one gig to a unit. Law was proud of the efforts of the Special Weapons section and wanted the rest of the battery to work as hard.

Chapter 14

A SON

It was a cold Thursday in late February and Dean stood in formation waiting to be dismissed. He wanted to make arrangements to take Natalie to her doctor's appointment later in the morning. Chester dismissed everyone to the motor pool to begin maintenance on the vehicles.

There was nothing exciting scheduled for the day so Dean figured he would have no problems getting permission to take her to Landstuhl to see her doctor. He went to Walker and requested the time off. Walker assured him that it was fine with him, but that he would have to clear it with Chester and England. He told Dean to go to the motor pool and start work on the van, which Dean did.

It was about a half an hour later that Walker showed up at the van. He told Dean that Top had denied him the time off. This took Dean by surprise and he was irritated, his request had never been rejected before. Natalie was due this month and it was too late to make other arrangements. He asked Walker if he could see Chief of Smoke Chester; he was the next man in the chain of command. He wanted to ask him for permission. Walker agreed and told him that he was in Top's office and he could make his arguments with both of them.

Larson marched down to the office and found Lt. Thomas, and Chester in Top's office, talking about the training schedule. Top agreed to see Dean and suggested that the other two leave but Dean insisted that they stay since he came to see Chester and Top at the same time. There was another reason he wanted both of them to stay; he wanted witnesses. Dean turned to Chester first. "Smoke, I requested some time off to take my wife to her doctor's appointment, but Walker told me that I had been denied so I'm here to ask why."

"Because I said no," Top blurted out. He arose in his seat with a stern look on his face." Dean could feel anger arising up but he knew he had to stay cool. He turned and gave Top a slight smile. "Sorry Top but that's not a good enough answer for me. I guess I will take my request up the chain of command. So, who should I see Top, The XO is here so I guess I should talk to the BC?"

The blood vessels in Top's neck bulged, his eyes got big, and he clenched his fist. He started moving around the desk toward Dean.

Larson knew that he had to stop things before they got out of hand. "What do you think Lt. Thomas, my wife is about to pop. I have never been turned down taking her before and she needs to see her doctor. It's too late to make other arrangements so I need to get things changed quickly."

Top suddenly stopped remembering that they were not alone. "Listen, the army never got your wife pregnant. We owe her nothing!" Top blurted out.

"No, but they screw with me enough. I busted my butt on the nuclear inspection and this is the thanks I get, I think...."

Thomas saw what was coming, he interrupted Dean before he could make the threat of not doing so well next time. "Top, that whole section put in a lot of extra time. It seems only right that they get a little extra time off," suggested Thomas.

"I'm willing to go up the chain of command to the post commander if I have to." Dean said in a very determined way.

"Oh, get the h- -l out of here and take your wife to the doctor," Top said with all the tension draining from his face. He sat back down behind his desk and gave Dean a wave to get him out the door.

Chester followed Dean out of the building, stopping him at his car. "I'll inform Sergeant Walker as to what you are doing. Larson, don't think too badly of Top. That order came from Captain Law. I don't think Top was especially pleased in trying to enforce it."

"Thanks for telling me, Smoke. Law is a jerk, a cold-hearted creep. I can't warm up to the guy at all. I'll be back in the afternoon, so I'll see you then."

"Watch what you say Larson, he is your commanding officer so I don't want to hear you repeat those comments in front of me again."

"Yes Smoke." He knew a lot of the people felt the same way.

Dean went home, picked Natalie up, and took the autobahn to the hospital. It was a pleasant journey. He told her about his altercation with Top, but that Law was the one that gave the order. They discussed names again and wondered if they had bought everything they needed to care for their new baby.

It took them about a half hour to get there and they had to wait another thirty minutes before they saw the doctor. As often as she had gone to the hospital, she had only seen her doctor two other times. He checked her closely and came back with the good news that both Natalie and the baby were doing well.

When Dean got back to the base, he reported to Walker at the motor pool. He did some work on the van, then they had close order drill to finish off the day. When he got home, Natalie was feeling uncomfortable and she was having some pain. Dean suggested going back to Landstuhl but she talked him out of it. She eventually started feeling better and they both had a good night's sleep.

Friday, they went out to the firing range where everyone had to qualify with their M-16. Dean, unfortunately got stuck in the last group of shooters. His twenty-five-yard silhouette was mostly shot away. The fifty- and seventy-five-yard targets were shot up pretty badly also. The hundred-yard target was missing its head. Marks was grading him and told him to do the best he could. Dean got into his firing position, took aim, held his breath, and squeezed the trigger. He split the stake on the twenty-five-yard target and with the next shot, sheared the wood off just above the ground.

Marks whistled and smiled at him, stating that he was glad that he was on his side. Dean popped the head off the fifty-yard silhouette. And hit the seventy-five-yard target about seven times. He asked Marks where he wanted him to hit the hundred-yard target, Marks picked the groin area. Dean put eight below the belly button, Marks laughed and gave him a thumbs up.

They also did night firing and Dean again found himself at the end of the line. It would be late before he got home. At about seven that evening, Dean found himself looking down range at his targets. It had grown very cold and a modest wind was blowing. The group was informed they were the last ones and they had a lot of ammo left. Supply did not want to bring any of it back to the battery area. This time Sergeant Cassidy was grading Dean, and Reed was in the lane next to him

Before they started sending rounds down range, Reed came over to Dean and talked to him quietly. "You look worried Larson. What's the problem, don't you think you can hit the target?"

"I'm concerned about Natalie. The doctor said that the baby should come soon and I don't want miss being with her. We made arrangements with Maria to take her if I'm not around. I'm just frustrated I have to be stuck at the end of this exercise. I won't get home until late. Natalie had some pain last night."

"Take a look to your left. See that dead tree? A few tracer rounds should start a little fire. I'm willing to invest a couple of

Uncle Sam's bullets into that particular target if you're willing to add a fair share to the tree. If nothing else, we'll get a little heat and maybe, just maybe, they will close down the range if they know that we're serious about going home."

"That tree has my undivided attention, along with a couple of rounds for my target," Dean said smiling broadly to his friend.

"Give me five," Reed said holding out his hand.

Dean slapped it and looked back at Cassidy. He was talking to Lt. Thomas so Dean didn't think he had caught any of the conversation. Cassidy brought Dean two magazines and informed him that every third to fourth round was a tracer and that he needed to adjust his aim on the target using the tracers.

Dean nodded and stepped up to the firing line. The first magazines, he concentrated on the silhouette and hitting it. The first rounds went a little wide, hitting the target in the shoulder area, so Dean adjusted his aim. After the first magazines he looked over at Reed, who nodded at him. Several of the next rounds went into the dead tree. Nothing happened, but every once in awhile they sent more bullets into the wood. Soon Dean noticed smoke drifting out of the trunk. Dean fired several more rounds into the area. Suddenly, a flame of fire shot up out of the trunk.

Cassidy called for a cease fire but some-one on the other side of the range had the same plan because another dead tree was smoldering. They shut the range down and took fire extinguishers to the flames. It took them about twenty minutes to extinguish the fires. They opened up the range again, but soon the tree near Dean flared up again.

Cassidy looked at Dean for a long moment. "I'm pretty sure I saw rounds from you and Reed hitting that tree."

"What can I say Sarg, I'm a bad shot," retorted Dean with a smile.

"Thats a bunch of bull. Cassidy, you should have seen him take care of business this afternoon," remarked Marks who overheard the conversation.

Nothing more was said and they closed the range down. They trucked the troops back to the battery area. Dean got home about nine that evening. Natalie was napping on the couch waiting for him. He covered her with a blanket and made himself a sandwich, then crawled into bed.

He slept until nine am when he was awakened by Natalie kissing him on the neck. He rolled over and planted a big smack on her lips. She asked him when he got in and he told her what had happened at the firing range. She informed him that she had the coffee on and breakfast was waiting for him at the table. He slowly crawled out of bed and put some clothes on. Natalie had made him an omelet with toast. The coffee especially tasted good, and he needed it after last night.

They lounged around the apartment until about four in the afternoon when he finally talked Natalie into going out in the back yard and having a few pictures taken. They wanted to send some photos back home to show the immediate family how big she had gotten. It was cold and the wind was blowing, so Dean took only three shots of her. They hurried back in and drank another cup of coffee to warm up.

About an hour after that Natalie started feeling sick. It started off like indigestion, but she realized she was having contractions and asked Dean to rush her to the hospital. He packed her bag in the car and hurried upstairs to Eddie Perez's apartment where he informed him what was going on. He ran down to Natalie and helped her to the car.

He made it to the Landstuhl hospital in record time. Neither one of them allowed themselves to panic. Dean focused on his driving using every trick he knew to get down the road as fast as he could. He continued to ask her how she was feeling and she assured him that the contractions were light and that she didn't think there was concern that the baby was going to come real soon.

During their drive Natalie was uncomfortable and had several sharp pains, but he didn't stop the car. He had no desire to deliver the baby himself. He was happy to get her to the hospital before the child came.

When they got to the emergency room, the pains subsided some and Natalie thought maybe she had suffered from false labor. The doctor examined her and informed her that her water had broken, and that the child wanted to become a part of the world. They got her into a hospital gown and provided a room for her. Dean put a chair next to her bed and held her hand.

Time seemed to crawl by as the pains became more intense and her grip on his hand grew more powerful. She often called out for the nurse who would come in and check her out. The child was making progress, but was in no hurry to come out of his comfortable surroundings. After eleven hours the doctor came in to check Natalie. It was not Natalie's regular doctor, which frustrated her, but he seemed like he knew what he was doing.

"I'm afraid you're too small down there and that is prolonging your labor," he told both of them looking over the sheets of the bed.

"What needs to happen?" asked Dean.

"I'm going to have to cut her near the opening, or I'm afraid when the child does come, it will tear the opening."

"Cut her? Do you really have to cut her? I mean ..." stuttered Dean.

"Do it! I am tired of this pain. Dean, you're never going to touch me again," she said through clinched lips. She squeezed his hand even tighter to keep him quiet.

Dean couldn't look as they cut her in the vaginal area, the thought bothered him so deeply, that she was in even more pain. They gave her a local anesthetic to ease her suffering, but Dean couldn't get past his imagination and what was taking place a couple of feet away.

After just over twelve hours, John Larson was born. He was nine pounds, five ounces. Natalie had pushed so hard that little red spots had pushed to the surface of her skin all over her arms and face. The doctor assured her that they would disappear; that she had strained so hard that she had broken small blood vessels during her travail. The pain seemed to disappear from her face as she held her son for the first time.

Finally, Dean got to hold his little boy. So many emotions flooded over him. The first was love, not only for his new son, but a deeper emotional attachment for Natalie. She had suffered so much to bring forth the new life that he held in his arms.

The next emotion was great concern, what kind of father would he be? He was afraid that he might fail at this job and he could not contemplate that being an option. He felt pride; he was a father and he had always wanted to be a father, to have a son to wrestle with and read to. A great sense of happiness caused his weariness to vanish for about an hour.

They took the baby, cleaned him up, and made a place for him in the nursery. They also cleaned up Natalie and make her comfortable for some well-earned rest and sleep. They found an empty bed for Dean and allowed him to sleep a little before he went back to Baumholder.

He slept a couple hours and feeling rested enough, he went to give Natalie a kiss. She was still sleeping. He checked on John before leaving for home. He took a shower, laid down for a couple of hours before he was awakened by Eddie. He informed him that Maria wanted to see the new baby and Natalie. Dean got dressed and loaded them all up in the car.

Natalie was breast feeding John when they arrived. John almost looked bald but at close observation he had a lot of really light blonde hair. Maria held him for a little while, but John had not gotten all he had wanted when it came to food. He let everyone know it, so Natalie had to finish feeding him before Dean could hold him. The emotions had not gone away; all of them washed back over Dean as he held his new little boy.

They left about six that evening. Dean and Eddie had to be in formation early the next morning. Dean slept well, he was exhausted but he had this alarm clock inside his head and was up at five a.m. He drove Eddie over to the barracks. He had cigars in his pockets and went to the second floor of the barracks to announce John's birth to the section.

He was about to knock on the door when Top England interrupted him. "Larson, I hear you are the proud father of a son."

"Yes, I am," stammered Dean.

"Congratulations, Larson. I bet you're going to be a good father." He held out his hand to Dean and they shook.

Dean offered him a cigar, which he accepted. Walker had heard the announcement through the door and patted Dean on the back. The rest of the section came out congratulating him and grabbing cigars.

A couple of days later, Dean asked Walker if he could go get Natalie and John from Landstuhl to bring them home. He had no problems getting permission.

Chapter 15

A HAND AWAY

It was April and the battery of guns was set up at the direct fire range. It was muddy, and everyone was wading through the puddles that the rain had left the night before. It was overcast and a little cool, but Spring had chased the winter away. Everyone was complaining about the lack of sun, they had only twelve to fifteen days of sunshine last summer. The men had not seen one ray during the winter and the spring had no indication of changing the trend.

Reed and Dean were standing behind Sgt. Mark's gun, watching the crew work the eight-inch guns. They were firing at moving targets that were being manipulated mechanically by soldiers behind the guns. Everyone was warned to stay at the rear of the weapons for safety reasons. A berm was set up in front of the guns to help shield the crews from any stray shrapnel.

The crews could not depress the tubes below the berm which would have caused major problems. Some of the targets were stationary; old tanks, trucks, or jeeps. Every once in a while, Dean heard the zing of a piece of metal flying overhead. The sections were told not to watch the rounds go down range, but to duck behind something solid before firing the round.

It could not be helped; crew members would watch the rounds hit the targets every so often. Dean and Reed poked their heads over the vehicles to observe the rounds making big round holes in the moving targets. They were using big blue dummy rounds. It was an awe-inspiring show. Sgt Marks crew was doing a pretty good job; they had only missed once and that had been one of the first projectiles they sent through the tube. They had led the silhouette too much and it had blown into pieces in front of the target. The moving targets did not last long; they were quickly destroying them with the two-hundred-pound rounds.

Sgt. Cassidy came running up to them, hunched over to make himself small for any flying objects. He leaned against the massive spade that held the eight-inch guns in place. They dug the large scoop into the ground to keep the recoil of the gun from getting the weapons out of position. "You two be careful; I saw a guy lose an eye from this kind of fire one time."

"We just look every once in a while, Sarg," replied Dean.

"It only takes one time, Larson. By the way, how is that kid of yours?"

"He's growing like a weed. He has blonde hair, blue eyes, and has little rolls of fat on his legs and arms. He loves to eat and I'm glad Natalie decided to breast feed the little squirt. She is the one that usually has to get up in the middle of the night to take care of him," beamed Dean.

"Well, if you need some help, my old lady would be glad to come over and give Natalie some tips. After all we have three kids so Sandi has some experience in the matter."

"Thanks, but the Perez family lives above us and she has been giving Natalie pointers on how to take care of John. He is flourishing. Every time I hold him at night, I repeat 'Daddy' about ten times in his face. I'm betting he says it before 'Mommy.' He just smiles at me but I think he understands. It irritates Natalie who does the same thing when I'm not around, during the day," laughed Dean.

Cassidy smiled and both of them looked over the spade and watched number four gun send a round down range, hitting a tank dead center. The guns fired at different intervals but once in a while, they would discharge at about the same time which caused the booms to sound like echoes.

"Dean, I hear you're going to rotate back to the states soon?" asked Cassidy.

"Yes, the bum is going to be leaving us this summer after Grafenwöhr," piped in Reed.

"You're just jealous, man. I'll be back in the world while you'll be stuck here in beautiful Baumholder, with all the rain, snow, fog, and boars," laughed Dean.

"You know how to hurt a guy's feelings," retorted Reed.

"So what duty stations are you going to put in for?" asked Cassidy.

"I want to be close to home so I'm going to be requesting Ord in California, Lewis in Washington, or Fort Carson Colorado."

The three of them noticed a jeep pulling up behind the battery. Cassidy waved Marks down and requested a cease fire. It was Captain Clark, the new battalion S-2 officer.

He was tall with dark hair and seemed to wear the perfect uniform. His dark combat boots always had a high shine. Dean had never talked with him but he seemed friendly and had good knowledge of the NROSS program and the nuclear weapon protocols, at least that is what Walker had told him.

Walker had several conversations with him over the last three months since he came to the battalion. He parked his jeep just left of the number four gun and went to the FDC tent where Captain Law was. Once he had disappeared into the tent, the guns returned to their direct fire missions.

Cassidy had been to Fort Carson so he started telling Dean about the place, the town nearby, and the firing range. He described several areas where he could get affordable housing and the best places for shopping. They were into the conversation for about fifteen minutes, and no one noticed Clark walking out to his jeep. Each crew had loaded a round into their guns and had one more projectile to go before they could call it a day.

Number four gun was ordered to fire. Reed watched Jeff Carter twist his body, pulling the lanyard. The tube belched it's projectile out of its maw sending it through the center of the target. Reed saw the back portion of the round shear off, flying backward ratcheting off the back of the berm. Its rotation sent it downward instead of up. At that moment Clark was climbing into his jeep. He had his right hand behind the seat, pulling his body into position to get behind the steering wheel. The shrapnel sheered his right hand off slightly above the wrist.

"My God!" yelled Reed.

"What's up?" asked Cassidy.

"Captain Clark has been hit!" shouted Reed with panic in his voice.

Cassidy looked at the jeep and observed that Clark was on the ground and a large blood stain was on the back of the driver's seat with a chunk of it missing. He ordered Reed to get the guns to cease fire, looked at Dean and told him to see if he could help Clark. He ran to the FDC tent to get the medics and a helicopter out for a medivac.

No one else had noticed what had happened. Dean sprinted to Clark's side where he found the man groaning in pain and the arm gushing blood with each pulse. He pulled his belt off and grabbed the bloody stump but it was slippery from the blood and mud. Clark added to the problem by trying to pull it back to his chest and hold it. Dean could tell that he was in shock and didn't know what he was doing.

Dean finally put his knee on the shoulder and pulled the arm to him. Clark seemed to submit and allowed Dean to tie the belt around the wound making a tourniquet with it. Reed cornered Clark's arm and held it up, letting gravity help slow down the blood flow. Dean held the cleanest cloth he could find on the wound to stop the bleeding.

Marks had Carter hunt up a blanket and covered Clark up and propped Clark's legs up in case he was in shock. Clark kept looking around and started insisting that someone find his hand. Marks had the crew look for the severed limb.

At this time, Captain Law, Cassidy, and part of FDC was out at the jeep surrounding the wounded man. Marks produced another blanket trying to keep Clark warm. He continued to order those around him to find his hand. Law ordered others to help in the search of the area and the hand was retrieved.

They found a bucket, filled it with ice from a cooler with a plastic bag and stored it. This seemed to satisfy Clark and he settled down to wait for the chopper to come get him. He was very pale and continued to moan with pain.

To Dean, the medivac seemed to take forever. In reality, it only took the chopper ten to fifteen minutes to get to the accident. The medic came to Dean first, and asked if he was all right. Dean was surprised at first and then looked at the front of his fatigues, seeing all the blood on it. He pointed to Clark.

Thats when the adrenaline subsided and he slumped to the ground near the jeep. He had been focused on what needed to be done, using his training to help Clark as much as he could. The terror and stress were gone and exhaustion took over. He felt anxious, starting to rethink about what he had done. Did he help save him or did he add to Clark's problems.

He watched the medic put on a proper tourniquet and hooked him up to an IV. He turned to Dean and asked him if he had applied the first tourniquet? Dean just nodded. The medic complimented him on it.

They took the hand and the patient to Ramstein Air Force Base where he was treated. The shrapnel had severed his hand at an angle with ragged edges not allowing them to sew the hand back on. Clark was honorably discharged from the Army and Dean saw him at a battalion formation just before he left for the states. He came over and personally thanked Dean, Reed, and Cassidy for what they had done to help him. The Army, in its wisdom, presented him with a very expensive wrist watch for his service.

When Dean went home that night. Natalie looked at him, grew pale, and almost fainted; seeing all the blood on his utility uniform. It took Dean a few minutes to calm her down and explain what had occurred. He threw the fatigues away. What he could not get rid of were the memories of Clark wallowing on the ground spraying blood all over the mud and grass, the paleness of his tan face, and him insisting on them finding his hand.

Chapter 16

VISITORS FROM HOME

The international airport in Frankfort was busy. Several flights had arrived and people were coming and going everywhere. Dean held John tightly in his arms while Natalie scanned the faces of passengers coming in on a flight from America. Dean did not know his in-laws very well. He had focused on getting to know Natalie, but he liked his father-in-law.

Lawrance Baker was five foot, ten inches tall with a mustache, glasses dirty blond hair, and was slightly bent from years of hard work. Laura, his wife, was a little shorter with dark curly hair framing a round face.

Natalie started waving and pushing through the crowd toward her parents. She helped them wade through the people to Dean's side where Lawrance shook his hand and Laura Baker gave him a stiff hug. Grandma tried to whisk John out of Dean's arms, but the baby would not allow it. He started crying and clutched at Dean's neck, holding on even tighter. Grandma gave up for the moment.

They all made their way to the baggage claim and retrieved the large suitcases the Bakers brought. Dean had taken a twenty day leave and the Larson family planned some special trips with the Bakers. Dean was really excited about their visit; he was hoping to cement a relationship with the two. He gave John to Natalie as he helped Lawrance pack the baggage to the Opel station wagon. They were soon on the autobahn, traveling back to Baumholder. It was late May and spring had come to Europe with flowers blooming and deep green grass everywhere.

Lawrance sat in the front, taking in the scenery and talking to Dean about what he was seeing Laura sat in the back with Natalie and John. She was trying everything she could think of to win her grandson over. She finally caught his attention with her blue sparkling necklace. She would let him play with the jewelry and he would allow her to touch him without crying. Eventually he let her hold him while he chewed on the pretty thing that hung around her neck.

"Guess what?" Lawrance said eyeing Dean.

"I don't know. Huh, this is your first trip to Europe." Dean responded.

"Well, yes, it is. But your brother Jack is dating Natalie's sister Helen. They seem pretty serious, don't they Laura?"

"Oh Lawrance, I don't know if we can say that, but they have been spending a lot of time together."

"About three or four nights a week. That seems pretty serious to me. Don't you think so, son?" he said, looking at Dean.

"I guess so," Dean choked out. He did not know what surprised him most; Lawrance calling him son, or the fact that his brother was dating Helen.

Helen was a handsome young lady. She was a blonde, blue eyed gal with long legs built for track meets. If she wanted to catch Jack, he didn't have a chance. She was apt to run him down and was bold enough to propose marriage herself.

"It would be great if those two tied the knot for everyone."

"How so, Dad?" asked Natalie.

"Well, I would have two of my three daughters married and out of the house. Jack and Dean would be able to help each other remember birthdays and anniversaries. When one of you boys want to buy a gift for your wife you can run and ask your sister-in-law what your wife would like," he said laughing.

They all had a chuckle. Dean turned to Natalie, smiled and declared that he had gotten the pick of the litter. She beamed back at him and the conversation returned to what they were seeing out-side the windows of the car.

Rolling green hills sped by with villages or cities breaking up beautiful green plants and the flowers that doted the fields. Eventually they got off the autobahn on to a secondary road climbing steady up the mountain to Baumholder. The road was lined with trees and ravines. The first houses that made up Baumholder were a welcome sight, the long trip for the Bakers had made them very weary.

That evening the Bakers got the bed, while Dean and Natalie slept on the uncomfortable couch. The next day the Larsons took Lawrance and Laura to Idar Oberstein and told them about the history of the little hamlet and the beautiful church with the stream flowing through it. They took them to a guesthouse and bought them a schnitzel with mushrooms, and French fries. The dinner was comprised of deep fat fried veal smothered with mushrooms. It was Dean and Natalie's favorite German dish.

After a good night sleep, it was off to England by bus on a USO tour. They passed through the country side of Belgium. It was beautiful farm country with pastures and crops everywhere they looked. They boarded a ferry at Zeebrugge and crossed the English Channel to Ramsgate.

The seas were a little choppy, causing Natalie and her mother to get a little queasy. They held down their lunch and eventually, everyone saw the white cliffs of Dover come into view. It was just the way Dean had pictured them; the chalky cliffs suddenly jutting up out of the sea.

They soon disembarked from the ferry and found themselves in London. They crossed the Thames River, moving toward the hotel that they were going to stay at. Off in the distance, they saw London Bridge and Big Ben. They would get a closer look at them as the tour progressed.

They stopped at their hotel where they ate dinner and got settled in for the evening. The night clerk gave them a list of plays that were playing in the theater district. They picked one starring Hayley Mills. Grandma and Grandpa were only too happy to watch John for the evening. Dean called to make reservations and to get the best seats in the house.

"Do you have a tux?" asked the ticket agent.

"Da, well no. What does that have to do with the price of the ticket?" asked Dean a little surprised.

"Your seats will be in the balcony. I have two seats reserved for you and you can pay for them at the theater. Please be on time so that you do not interrupt the performance," the man said in his English snooty accent. He hung up the phone.

Dean looked around the room at everyone with a very surprised look on his face. Natalie questioned him about the conversation and he told her what had been said. She questioned him again about the tux but he could give her no explanation about the clerk's question and attitude.

Natalie and Dean dressed in their nicest clothes to see if that would help with where they were seated and ticket prices. It didn't faze the people that were selling the tickets. They were escorted to the balcony where they were assigned to sit. They could see from their vantage point the first two rows of seats. Every man was dressed in a tuxedo and the women wore formals.

The play was excellent and Dean got to see Hayley in person. When he had been younger, he had a crush on her. It was a real treat for him, but who knows if he had worn a tux, he may have gotten to go back stage. The seating arrangement was fairly good but once in a while because of the positions of the actor or actress, they could only see them from the neck down.

In the morning they had the usual continental breakfast, roll, a variety of meats, cheese, and coffee. They had this same meal in Holand, Luxemburg, and Switzerland when they had toured those nations. Fritz, the bus driver had taken them to all those destinations. He was an excellent driver, getting everyone quickly to the places of interest in a safe manner.

Laura seemed to go along for the ride. She was much more interested in her new grandson. She doted on him, holding him whenever she could. The sights and sounds of London were just a by-product of her visit with the Larson family. She was fascinated by the Old Curiosity Shop. She spent money on her daughters and John in this store which had been around since the 1400's. Lawrance, Dean, and Natalie were enthralled with everything from the history, architecture, and the people. In Madame Tussaud's Wax Museum, the figures looked so real and life like. Natalie was checking out a guard that was wearing garb from what Dean thought came from the 16th century. The man suddenly moved and Natalie almost fell over a prop. It was funny and Natalie caught her father and Dean snickering at her. She warned them to never tell her sisters.

They were all awed by the sights and sounds of London, England and Dean wanted to come back some day to see more of the country.

After a few days in England, they crossed the Channel once again and traveled to Brussels, Belgium. Before they went into the city, Fritz stopped at a beautiful manicured park. All the parks in Europe seemed to be manicured, the flowers set in rows trees lining the walks for shade and the green grass cut to a certain height. It was just nice to sit, eat a lunch, and walk among the foliage.

Dean quizzed Lawrance on how his father was doing. Lawrance told him that his father had started looking pretty wore down so he had made Jack his partner. This seemed to have taken some of the pressure off his father. They had bought another farm next to them at a good price, enlarging the land to about five hundred and twenty-five acres. Since Dean's father had made these changes, he seemed to be doing better health wise and acted more content emotionally.

"How do you feel about the business going on between your father and Jack?" asked Lawrance with an inquiring expression on his face.

"It's fine, Dad. I have no interest in the farm. Once I get out of the army, I'm going to college. I want to be a teacher. I'm thinking about teaching history and English. Jack was more like Dad; he loves the land and growing things," Dean said with a smile. It seemed to be a little strange calling his father-in-law 'Dad' while talking about his real father. Lawrance had insisted on it and Dean was finally getting used to it.

"Where are you going to go to school?"

"I plan on going to Twin Falls for my first two years and finishing at Boise State College. I want to work part time to take care of the family and go to classes part time. I know it will take longer that way, but I'm not the sharpest tack in the world."

"It sounds like a good plan to me. You'll have access to the GI bill, and they'll pay for a lot of your college. Twin and Boise are growing at a steady rate, so you should be able to find a job easily. Idaho always needs good teachers. You do plan on staying in the state?"

"Yes, I've already discussed all this with Natalie. We want to raise our kids near our families. We both agree that family is very important to us."

"Good, we want to be a part of your lives and to watch our grandkids grow up." He patted Dean on the arm and suggested that they get back to the bus.

Fritz, the driver loaded everyone on the bus and drove them into the heart of Brussels to look at the Atomism which looked like a big atom. It was left over from the World Expo in 1958. It was magnified 165 billion times the size of a molecule. It had nine corridors running to nine chambers. Two of the giant spheres displayed art and science while three of the others had permanent records of Expo 58.

A short walk down the street brought you to Min-Europe. The place had beautiful miniature replicas of many of the architectural achievements of Europe. They had miniatures of the Eiffel tower, London's Big Ben, and the Tower of Pisa to name a few.

Dean thought the contrast in the Atomism and the Min Europe was funny. Min Europe was like seeing all the important places in Europe at one time. The details of the buildings were exact and Lawrance was especially fascinated by London Bridge. He had been a part of a construction group when he was in the Army during the Korean war and had built several bridges.

Fritz took them to their hotel and they all got checked in. They settled into their rooms and had a nice dinner before turning in. They were all tired and even John didn't fuss but was soon asleep.

After breakfast Fritz drove them to a central place and allowed them to wander through the shopping areas that made up Brussel. It was a beautiful city. They observed Manneken Pis which was a statue of a little boy pissing in a fountain. For some reason Europeans rarely took their babies out in public so John usually drew attention from people. This time he drew more than the Larsons wanted. The crowd kept pointing at the statue and then at John. Soon a crowd surrounded them comparing John and the statue. When Dean looked closer, he had to admit that the little boy pissing in the fountain looked very similar to John. The people would touch John's fat little checks, and arms. They finally backed off when John made it quite clear that he had enough touching.

The drive home the next day, it was obvious that everyone had enough traveling for the time being. It was good to be back in their cramped little apartment. That Sunday, they lounged around at home. Monday Dean took everyone to Baumholder and they explored the town and the base.

Chapter 17

OFF TO BAVARIA

Monday, Dean took Lawrance into the base to pick up his paycheck. He had worked his leave time out in such a manner so they could afford the next adventure. Dean had arranged for them to go to Innsbruck, Austria and to tour around the Garmisch area in Germany starting Tuesday.

He introduced Lawrance to Top England. The two hit it off right away, both of them had served in Korea and had passed each other several times. England had been involved in a couple of retreats that took him over bridges that Lawrance had help blow up after they crossed. On the other hand, he drove over some bridges Lawrance had helped construct. Dean found Walker and they visited for a while and he introduced him to his father-in-law.

The next morning, they were on the road again. The landscapes were beautiful as they traveled through Germany toward the Austrian Alps. It turned into thick forest and they were told that it was the Black Forest. The interesting thing about Germany is that it is all privately owned land and they take good care of what they owned.

They passed through Germany into Innsbruck Austria and the scenery looked the same. The Olympic games had taken place a year or two before. They checked into their hotel and went out exploring the city. The guide suggested going to the Golden Roof in the Innsbruck, Tounge Goldenes Dachl. It was set in a large square where Emperor Maximillan addressed his subjects or observed his troops when they were on parade. The roof looked gold but the shingles were fire gilded copper.

Laura insisted on taking a picture of Dean, Natalie, and John in the square. She was trying to get just the right photo. She moved several times because of the sun and she fiddled with the setting on more than one occasion. All the time John was wiggling, but they continued to pose. She put the camera to her eye, suddenly Dean and Natalie felt strong arms encircle their shoulders.

They didn't turn to see who it was, thinking it was Lawrance. She snapped the shot and someone started laughing. They turned to see a big Austrian smiling from ear to ear. Lawrance was looking in the window of a bakery nearby. The smiling Austrian waved and ran off down the street never to be seen by them again except in the photo. They walked to a guesthouse where they ordered dinner.

They took a walking tour of the city. It still had a Medieval feel about the place. Emperor Ferdinand built the Court Church in honor of his father Maximillan. It was a Gothic Church, and the architecture was awe inspiring. They traveled to Stadtturm to visit a watch tower that had been built in the 1400s. It had a copper clad onion dome like the Tounge Goldenes Dachl.

They crossed the border back into Germany. They stopped at the Chapel of Tears. It was a simple church from the outside. Inside, one of the walls was lined with prayer requests written on paper neatly pinned to cork boards. The ceiling had a door painted on it, no matter where you were in the sanctuary, the door faced you.

At the front, near the alter, stood the crying Christ. He was carrying His cross with wounds and a sad face. It was a wood carving and the story that surrounded him was that it used to be located outside in one of the little prayer booths that lined the roads of Bavaria. One day, his owner was praying before the statue when he noticed tears running down its wooden checks. They told their neighbors and they also witnessed the event. Soon, the chapel was built for the Crying Christ and many of the prayer requests had been answered over the years.

The next item on the agenda was to visit Garmisch which was not an average German village. It had cobblestone streets and the houses were like most of the architecture in Bavaria, Germany. There was one big difference, many of the homes had murals on them that told fairy tales such as Red Riding Hood, or The Three Little Pigs.

They walked through some of the neighborhoods looking at the stories being displayed on the Tudor homes. The group continued down town to visit some of the stores that sold wood carvings. The pieces were very detailed and carved from the wood that came out of the Black Forest. Natalie decided to buy a figurine of an old man guiding a horse driven cart of logs.

They passed by what they thought was a pet shop. Dean suddenly stopped and walked back to the store. Everyone just watched him, then he called them over. They were all tired and ready to go back to the hotel but he insisted. They wandered back and looked into the window where there were two dogs. A Saint Bernard and a Cocker Spaniel but neither dog moved and that was because they were full sized wood carvings. The details were amazing, you could even see individual hairs within the carvings.

The next day our guide drove us to the Neuschwanstein Castle that sat up on a hill overlooking a village. It was nice walking up the hill to view the insides of the structure. It looked like the castle at Disneyland. It took a little while to get to the castle, it was a steady incline and half way up an old Bavarian man was sitting on a log watching them climb.

He wore traditional garb; short paints held up by suspenders, a Bavarian shirt, and a hat with a feather in it. His face had a big smile and a well-trimmed beard that framed it. The group stopped and talked to him for a few minutes. He gave them a small history lesson and allowed them to take some pictures.

He told them that the castle had been built by King Ludwig. He had built three of the structures in the area. He was considered crazy which led to his assassination.

They continued to the top of the hill into Neuschwanstein castle. It was very impressive, this one had wood carvings everywhere, some of the most beautiful detailed work Dean had ever seen. The ballroom was magnificent and took up most of one of the upper floors.

They ended the day by touring Linderhof Palace which was also built by Ludwig. There were intricate gardens off every room and windows that you could peer out to look at them. The building had running water and in the dining room they had a table that lowered to the kitchen. The servants would put the food on it and raise it back up to the dining room.

On the way back to the hotel their guide offered to take the group over the border to a small village in Italy but everyone except Dean declined the offer. Dean realized at that point that he had scheduled too much traveling in too short of a time.

Natalie grabbed a hold of his arm and suggested that they all go home. Her smile and pleading eyes told him the story, so he agreed. They did not stay in the hotel for the night but talked Johanna into taking them back to Baumholder. It was late when they got into town, they all collapsed into their beds and didn't wake up until noon.

Dean took his in-laws to the airport on a Monday a week later. Dean and Natalie got them checked in and sat visiting with them while waiting for their departure. They gave them some messages to take home to brothers and sisters. Dean apologized to his father-in-law.

"Don't think anything of it, Dean. I enjoyed all the trips. If I had been a few years younger I would have argued for the trip to Italy. We are getting a little older so we don't travel as well. I know Laura loved the parks, flowers, and shopping. She came over to see her new grandson most of all."

"Still, I should have been more in tuned to your needs," Dean replied." He suddenly noticed that he had lost Lawrance's attention. His father-in-law was staring off to the right and his head was bobbing up and down.

Dean looked in the direction that Lawrance was staring. It was a young German lady that was well endowed and she was wearing a white see-through blouse with no bra. Laura, who was sitting behind Lawrance, turned to say something and caught the infraction. She slapped him softly in the back of the head and reminded him to keep his eyes on Dean. Everyone laughed, even Lawrance. They saw them to the gate and said goodbye as they entered the gate to their plane.

Dean and Natalie were glad they had come but it was nice to get back to the routine. Dean had to get back to work. In two weeks, he would be going to Grafenwöhr for thirty days.

Chapter 18

ON THE ROAD AGAIN

Dean shifted the truck into gear and pulled in behind Reed who was driving the five-ton. They were headed for Grafenwöhr and Dean was excited about this trip. It would be his last battery test and maneuvers in the toilet bowl of Germany.

He liked driving on the autobahn, the van did have a govern on it which meant that he couldn't go over a certain speed. Still, they were traveling and seeing different country. His assistant driver was Eddie and they had grown close; being neighbors and in the same section.

They would visit with one another about their wives and children. Eddie was curious about their destination since this was his first trip to Grafenwöhr. They were soon on the German highway, traveling about fifty-five miles an hour.

"So, what's Grafenwöhr like?" Questioned Eddie.

"It is the armpit of Germany. It was located near the Cech Border, in fact if you take one road, you end up in the Cech Republic and If you take the other one, you end up where you're supposed to be."

Eddie patted his M-16 and smiled.

"Don't worry Dean, I'll hold them off with the five-rounds they gave us if you take the wrong road."

They both laughed, Dean shook his head and thought about

how much trouble they would get into if they took the wrong road. It was true Reed was transporting the nuclear round and packages in his truck, so Cain, who was his assistant driver, was also packing his rifle with five rounds.

Dean and Eddie had the NROSS in the back of the van, which contained the secret messages that pertained to the nuclear round. It would be bad news if either truck got captured by the Cech military. He was also carrying Walker, Ford, and a new man by the name of Donald Henry in the back.

"Tell me about the village of Grafenwöhr" Eddie said.

"I don't know what it looks like, I've never been there. Some of the NCOs might have gotten passes to go into town but I doubt that any of us EMs [enlisted men] have ever been on the other side of the fence that surrounds the base."

"You're kidding me, you mean we're stuck on base for thirty days with no reprieve. What about beer and snacks, man?"

"There is a commissary you can get those items at. This is where we will be doing our battery test. We'll also be putting the round together in front of USAFER inspectors. You can't get any higher than that when it comes to inspections. This place is all business, so they keep us locked up, that way we keep focused."

"Shoot, this place is not going to be any fun at all," Perez whined.

"It's true, but I have to tell you, the time flies by. You're so busy all the time that you're traveling back to Baumholder before you know it. You are humping all day long."

"Well, that's a plus. What kind of weather and ground are we talking about?"

"Last year, the weather was nice, we only had one day of rain. The ground is rolling hills with a white dust that covers everything. The one day it did rain, that white dust became oozing mud that stuck to everything. You'll become a white boy like me. We'll have to call you Eddie England, making you Top's son," Dean said laughing.

"You're cold, man, and that is not funny," Eddie said with a smile.

"Back to Grafenwöhr, it has beautiful forest, be careful of the wild boars, I've seen a lot of them roaming around. I did spot one deer, I guess that is what you call it, she was no bigger than a large dog back home. They are not worth the shooting, if you ask me."

"Hmm, I'm not much of a hunter anyway."

"I used to hunt with my father and brother back home. It was great being out with those two. I never had any pleasure in killing a deer, they are beautiful animals. But it was good being out in the high country and getting closer to those two. There's nothing like it."

"Maybe you should take Cain hunting. I don't think he likes you and I don't know why," Eddie said thoughtfully.

"I really don't give a crap; I've never done anything to the guy. I invited him over to Thanksgiving, treated him like everyone else. He hasn't associated with me since. He suggested to Walker that he was playing favorites when he made Reed and me the A-team. Walker jumped him hard and then Reed and I came away from the inspection with no gigs, it shut him up somewhat."

"You know when Maria and I invited you all over to our house for dinner and drinks, he wouldn't come. He asked me if you were coming and when I said yes, he told me he couldn't make it."

"I figured that if we were in a real war, I wouldn't jump in the same fox hole that Cain was in. I don't trust him."

Dean peeked out the open side window toward the front. Their convoy was starting to pass another unit. He didn't like the idea that they could get tangled up with this new outfit and get lost in the shuffle. He took a deep breath and decided he was going to stick to Reed's tail no matter what. The radio crackled and it was Cain informing him that Captain Law had decided to pass this other convoy.

"Do you know what the most dangerous thing is in Germany?" Dean asked Eddie with a smile. "It can kill quicker than lightning."

"No what is it?"

"One German in a BMW. We'll see if we can survive Law's brainless scheme," Dean said grinning.

The radio crackled again. This time it was Cassidy and Dean could tell that he was enjoying himself. He rarely showed much emotion but Dean noticed the excitement in what he was saying.

"Dean, I got me one. It's a comrade, believe it or not, a BMW car. He must have the pedal to the floor board. I guess I'll just have to slow him down a bit."

Cassidy's driver pulled out in the fast lane. Dean could see the change of lanes in his side mirror. He did not see the results, but he knew that the German driver was furious for having to slow down. He was probably weaving back and forth trying to find any opening.

The five-ton slowly inched forward and then Cassidy came on the radio suggesting that Dean should pass the vehicle in front of him. Just as Cassidy started to pull in, Dean pulled out in the fast lane. Sure enough, there was a beautiful white BMW that zoomed past Cassidy, only to slow down because Dean's van was blocking his way.

The German was shaking his fist and honking his horn, trying to get Dean to pull over. Larson and Eddie were laughing at the sight in the mirrors. Dean slowly inched ahead of the vehicle they were passing. Before they got back into the right, they informed Cain of the BMW, as they inched in front of the other vehicle, the German quickly passed them.

Reed pulled his truck out into the fast lane in front of the German. As the BMW passed Dean, the German gave them an obscene gesture. Dean and Eddie smiled and waved at him as he passed by. He didn't get very far, Reed pulled his truck out in the fast lane, blocking the German from speeding around the rest of the convoy. Reed also took his time getting back to the right. The BMW driver continued his frantic shifting back and forth but it got him down the road no faster.

"You guys are mean," Eddie laughed.

"You have to do things like this to keep yourself entertained."

"You're leaving soon, have you put in your dream request as to where you want to go when you get back to the states?"

"Yep, I put in for Fort Carson, Colorado, Fort Lewis, Washington, and Fort Ord, California, those are the three choices I made," Dean responded.

"All out west so you can get home once in a while. You're hoping to get in another Special Weapons section?"

"That would be really nice, the duty is good compared to being a gun bunny on an eight-inch howitzer."

"No kidding, I'm glad my scores were high enough to get me into Mike Five school, it's nice being in a heated van when it's cold outside," Eddie said with a big grin.

Charlie battery had finally passed the other convoy and was making up some lost time. Dean paid close attention to the road for a while. Eddie sat back and watched the countryside pass by almost in a trance like state. Suddenly he blurted out a question that caused Dean to jump in his seat.

"We're going to have to sleep in our pup tents?"

"No, man. The advance party that went up with the guns on the train have erected large tents for us. They put them up over concrete slabs which are our floors. You will be issued a cot, it's not as comfortable as your bed at home but it's a lot better than the ground."

"That's good news. You know Maria and I were discussing the other day how lucky we were to get stationed with you two nearby. You guys arranged for us to get the apartment above yours. You drove me to work until Maria and I bought our own car, and we share the rides, which cuts down on our expenses. Maria and

Natalie have become good friends, and well, I kind of like you," he said with a laugh.

"Well, I like you too Eddie."

"Maria tells me that Natalie suspects that she is pregnant. Are you hoping for a girl this time?"

"Yes, all the signs are there that she is going to have a baby. If so, it will be due in October, and I'm hoping it's going to be a sweet thing like Natalie. Another boy would be fine, whatever comes is good with me. We've told the folks back home about our suspicions, and Reed and Walker know, but no one else."

"Your wife has been a good influence on Maria. We fight a lot less now that those two have a Bible study every Monday. Maria always tells me about it that evening. Natalie knows some good stuff. We were both raised Catholic but we haven't gone to mass for a lot of years. Most of the verses she discusses are new to me, things that are in the Bible that I had never seen."

"Yes, Natalie is a sweetheart, we tried a few churches in Baumholder but she didn't like any of them. My mother told me not to date girl's that drink, or smoke and Natalie fits the bill. I tried to talk her into having a glass of wine with me when we celebrated our first wedding anniversary but she would not partake."

"Natalie also talks to me about the Bible. It's good stuff but I consider myself a decent guy and God is loving so I figure I got a foot in the door. If nothing else, I can point to Natalie and say I know her. I know that I have a few rough edges, but I don't beat her or John. I figure I've met God's grade so far," he said, smiling at Eddie.

"I agree and that's how I feel about the situation, but still it's nice to learn more about God. It's not going to hurt me."

Dean nodded in agreement and thought about what Eddie had said. His own mother had insisted that they go to church once in a while when she was alive. Dean had been polite and respectful at the meetings but had not gotten much out of them. It was quiet for a long time, each man wrestling with his own thoughts.

They exited the autobahn and drove down a secondary road. There it was before them, part of the vast military complex near Grafenwöhr. They passed several tent cities until they were guided by one of the advance party members down to a tent. Private Tom Adams pointed out a large tent indicating that it was their home for the next thirty days.

Dean stopped the van behind Reed's truck and got out from behind the steering wheel. He stretched his legs, arms, and back; he was stiff all over and it was good not to be in the truck. He was also hungry and was looking forward to some mess hall cooking and coffee.

Walker stepped out of the back of the van with Ford and the new man, Henry who joined the section two weeks before Grafenwöhr.

Private Donald Henry stood five foot, nine inches. He was built like a football player; very little neck, broad through the chest. He had a handsome chiseled face that the ladies would like. Light hair crowned his head and he had blue eyes. Everyone made fun of him for having two first names. They didn't tease him too much because it looked like he could take care of himself but he took the jokes with a smile.

Walker ordered everyone to get their gear stowed away in the tent. He told Ford to stand guard over the round and the NROSS. After everyone got their bunks and gear stowed away, Walker ordered Perez to watch the two trucks while Ford took care of business.

Ford had to play guard while the rest of the section ate dinner. After dinner Reed took the round and components over to the armory, where it would be guarded twenty-four hours a day.

Dean took the NROSS over to the headquarters' tent where it was offloaded and put into a secure place. The SW section had to share their tent with part of the FDC crew.

Chapter 19

DIRT, MUD, AND
BOARS

The unit stayed in base camp for two days, getting gear ready for the rest of their time in Grafenwöhr. Walker checked out the team members practicing on the round one more time before they went to the field. He chose Dean and Reed to stay as the A-team; they would do the inspection when they went through the battery test. Things went by slowly during those two days. In the evening, most of them would drink some beer and play cards. Dean would read a good book for a while, then gather around a cot, play spades, and drink a couple of beers to keep his mind of his wife and son.

On the third day, Walker called Dean and Donald Henry out of the tent early. He told them to get over to the mess tent and have breakfast before everyone else. He wanted those two to go out on advance party with Captain Law and Top. Dean was supposed to show Henry how to direct the SW Section into their first positions out on maneuvers. They were to gear up, toss the rest of the things they needed in the van, and meet the rest of the advance party at HQ [Headquarters] at 0700 hours.

Walker had not given them much notice so they hurried over to the mess and ate their breakfast. They went to the tent, gathered what they needed, tossed it in their duffle bags and loaded them in the back of the van. The two men checked their weapons out of the armory and donned web gear, canteen, and helmets. They made the advance party team with a few minutes to spare. Sergeant Marks got them loaded in a Gamma Goat. It was an ugly little vehicle that they used to carry a lot of different cargos in. Most of the goats for Charlie battery carried communications equipment in them.

It was a beautiful sunny day with a few clouds roaming around in a bright blue sky. Unfortunately, Dean and Henry were in the last vehicle of the small convoy. The white dust of Grafenwöhr rolled up off the dirt roads as if one of the white clouds had drifted down from the sky and was covering everything on the road.

Dean prepared himself by covering his nose and mouth with a red handkerchief. Henry put his shirt over his face as much as possible but because of his broad chest, the shirt was not doing a very good job. He was soon coughing and using the sleeve on his left arm to keep the dust out of his mouth. His right hand was covering his eyes from the swirling powder. It was an hour before they pulled off the road into their first firing position.

Henry cussed as he crawled out of the Gamma Goat. His hair was no longer brown but a pepper gray like everyone else. The dust had caused him to tear up, so he had a couple of muddy tears running down his face. He started beating the powder off of himself. Everyone else was doing the same thing and it took a few minutes before the clouds settled to the ground around the soldiers.

"Why didn't you warn me man?" Henry asked, irritated.

"Didn't have time," Dean retorted with a laugh.

"That is not funny," Henry said stepping toward Dean. Dean stepped back, and got into a fighting stance.

All of a sudden, laughter broke out behind Henry. Henry turned around with a snarl on his chiseled face. He was about to say something but stopped in midsentence.

"What are you going to do soldier? You look pretty tough, but if I hear you threaten anyone again, we'll see how tough you are between two MPs as they cart your butt off to the brig. If Larson has any problems with you; I will take great pleasure in seeing you end up in Mannheim. I suggest you smile and get a sense of humor. Understand?" Sergeant Mark said quietly.

"Sorry, I guess it is funny," Henry replied holding a hand out to Dean.

"No problem," Dean said, shaking it.

"What's he doing?" asked Henry pointing at Captain Law.

"He's laying out the positions of the battery. Top will be coming over here in a little while to tell us where SW will be located. Once the rest of the battery comes in, we will be directing Perez and Reed as to where they put the trucks. Then we'll help them put up the camouflage netting to hide our positions from the air. That's the drill Rookie."

"Law looks like he knows what he's doing out there."

"Yeah, he can get the guns in firing position in quick order. Technically, he is a really good BC but he is a jerk as a person in my opinion. He has been aloft, ever since he took over the battery. I think he has said about twenty words to me since he arrived. It's not like I want to be friends. I don't think we would get along outside the Army. In fact, from what I hear, he has very few friends."

They watched as Law's long gangly frame moved from position to position with Top at his side. They looked like Mutt and Jeff; while the BC took his long strides, Top, with his shorter frame, had to double-time to keep up.

A sudden crashing sound directed their attention to their left. Apparently, the advance party had disturbed one of the wild boars in the area. He came out of the thick brush to see who was bothering his morning routine. He snorted at the men in front of him about thirty yards away.

"What the h--l is that thing," asked Henry?

"It's a wild boar. Where do you come from, man?" Retorted Dean with an incredulous look on his face.

"New York, but I didn't know there was anything like that in Germany."

"Well, that critter is the meanest thing in this neck of the woods. Stay clear of them, they will tear you up in a minute, so just leave him alone."

"A boar is just a big pig, isn't it?"

The boar continued to stare at them, he was broad through the shoulders, weighing over 200 pounds Dean guessed. Small tusk protruded from his mouth. He turned to leave a different way than he had come. Thats when Henry picked up a rock ran forward, and heaved it at the retreating beast.

The boar turned and charged the group of soldiers. His speed belied his thick body. Everyone was climbing trees, and jumping up on vehicles, to get away from the charging animal. He closed in on his antagonist in a matter of seconds. Henry just made it upon the hood of a jeep before the boar would have raked him with his tusk. Dean almost laughed at Henry; his face was a mask of fear and terror. The boar kept trying to get at Henry, but his short legs could not propel him high enough to get to the soldier. He circled the rest of the advance party in the area. No one else was ignorant enough to take on the angry pig. It grew weary and raced off into the woods. Dean started laughing as it disappeared into the forest.

"What are you laughing at?" asked Top.

"Here we all are, about a dozen soldiers, and one little boar had us retreating and peeing in our pants."

Everyone laughed as they considered how it must have looked.

"Didn't anyone warn you about wild boars?" asked Top, looking at Henry.

"Well, yes Larson told me to stay away from them."

"Oh, so you're a block head? You have to learn everything the hard way. Well, I suggest that you listen to Larson the next time. If you don't, I'll throw you to the wild boars myself, get the picture?"

Henry bowed his head and nodded in agreement.

Top dealt with the gun crews first, indicating where they needed to put the four eight-inch howitzers. He took each section to their designated positions. After he told Henry and Larson where Special Weapons were to place the two trucks, they were left alone.

"I think he would throw me to the boars, Henry remarked.

"You haven't listened to me too often rookie, but you mess with Top and you will be sorry. I've seen him deal with some people before. You don't want to get in his sights, he is very good at squeezing the trigger at the right time."

Henry didn't say much as they waited for the rest of the battery. Henry and Dean guided the trucks into their positions. Perez was driving the van and he was still missing a gear once in a while but he was starting to get the hang of the stick shift. They set up the camouflage nets in pretty good time. Henry was ordered to go out on the perimeter as a guard. Walker went and talked to Top about how long he thought they would be in this position. Top advised him not to practice on the round, so Walker went through the manual with the section.

The exercise they were going through was to get them ready for the battery test that would take place at the end of their tour in Grafenwöhr. It was a matter of speed and accuracy in everything they did. The night moves getting from one position to another, getting the rounds down range quickly and accurately.

The guns had to get in place with camouflage with the rest of the battery. FDC had to have their tent up and calculate deflection, and azimuth before the guns were ready. Ammo with powder bags had to be off loaded behind the eight-inch guns. Communication had to be established between everyone that was involved with the fire mission.

As long as Dean had been with the unit, it had never flunked a battery test. They did not want to find out what would happen if a unit did not pass. The word was that they would spend most of the rest of their time in Baumholder out in the field practicing until they got it right. Once the first rounds were out, most of the sections could relax somewhat. They just maintained what had been established. FDC and the guns were always on alert, waiting for a fire mission.

Henry was relieved after two hours on the perimeter by someone from the Commo unit. Several of them settled down to read a book or play spades. Dean went out, and watched the batteries do a night fire. To him, it was better than the fourth of July. He would stand behind Mark's gun and watch the round leave the tube. A bright flash of light would engulf it and the smell of burnt powder would fill the air. He stood there for about half an hour, observing them send two rounds to a target about seven miles away. Reed showed up and they talked for a while.

"What did you do to Henry? He's not the arrogant little creep he has been?"

"He almost got his tail feathers singed by a boar I told him to leave it alone. I think the icing on the cake was when Top threatened to throw him to the animals if he didn't start paying attention to what we have been telling him."

"He might be worth hanging out with after all. I think we should throw him into Top's office if he gives us too much trouble," Reed said smiling.

"Good plan. Well, I think I'll hit the sack. It's been a long day, being bounced all over Grafenwöhr in a goat and then being chased by a wild boar."

Everyone was getting the same idea. Dean rolled out his sleeping bag on the counter, since he was the driver, he got first choice even over Walker. Walker picked a place on the floor while

Reed got the next place. Reed chose the front of the five-ton, which was long enough with a door slightly ajar. Henry was the new man so he had to sleep in the back of the five-ton. Instead, he decided to sleep outside.

"Make sure you sleep under the five-ton so we can find you easy," Walker told him.

"But I was thinking about sleeping under the stars."

"No, you want to sleep under the five-ton so we can find you. That way, no one will trip over you and hurt themselves like the BC or Top. If we get marching orders in the night, I don't want someone running over you with a truck. Understand! Reed remember the 'cruit' is asleep under the truck. I don't want to have to do all that paper work if you kill Henry so be careful."

"I know. I heard about that idiot in that 155 unit that fell asleep in front of the treads without telling anyone. They got marching orders and they ran over him with the tracks. He was only a wet spot in the grass when they went back looking for him," remarked Reed.

"I get the message," Henry said nodding.

They found him crawling out from the truck when everyone went to chow the next morning. The cooks fixed a decent breakfast with a good cup of hot coffee. After the meal it was all business. They packed up and moved to another position where the battery fired three rounds each. SW had barely gotten their camouflage up when they were pulling it down to move to another place.

Walker and Cain went on advance party this time and guided them into another firing position. They set up and practiced on the round. The battery stayed there all night. The next day, at about noon, they went back to base camp where they got a hot meal and a warm shower.

They stayed at base camp for two days, then they were back out in the field for four days, setting up firing rounds and moving to new locations. One day the battery left base camp, but they left

Walker and Dean behind. It was raining and the roads had turned to mud with little streams of water running everywhere. Dean was not upset about being left behind, but he couldn't understand why the rest of the section had to go. It made no sense to him. He understood if they were all left in base camp, they could work on the round together. He asked Walker about it, but he had no definite answers just some guesses.

At noon, Captain Pickett the new battalion S-2 showed up at the mess tent and told all the special weapon units to fall in outside right away. Dean noticed that there were two men from the SW sections of each battery left behind in camp. The six men left the tent and formed a line in front of Pickett. None of them had finished eating lunch.

Pickett was tall clean shaven, good looking and his uniform was immaculate. He usually had a slight smile and was single. The smile was gone, he was all business-like. He informed them they were going to convoy the vans to the battery and that he would be leading them to their destination. He ordered them to go in, clean off their trays, and have their trucks lined up for the trip in twenty minutes at the motor pool with gear inside.

Once they were dismissed, Dean and Walker rushed into the mess tent. Dean took one big bite of mashed potatoes and gravy, threw the ham into the middle of a biscuit and scraped the tray clean into the garbage can. They ran to their tent, threw the gear they needed into the duffle bags, and were stowing the items in the back of the van with ten minutes to spare. The battery vans were lined up and ready to go within fifteen minutes. Dean's van was the last one in the convoy because they were Charlie Battery.

Pickett led them over to headquarters to pick up the NROSS and then they went to the armory to check out the rounds and the packages that went with it. Pickett had them on one of the dirt roads and on the way to join the batteries in thirty minutes. Pickett told each of the section chiefs how to get to their battery if they got separated, giving them maps of the routes they should take. It was still raining but Pickett was wasting no time getting from point A to point B. Walker urged Dean to keep up. He did not want to have to find the battery by the map coordinates that Pickett had given him. The captain passed a convoy which was scary at times because of the hills they had to climb, not knowing what was coming at them.

"What's this guy doing? Is he going to a fire?" asked Dean.

"I don't know, but don't lose him Larson." Walker said with some stress in his voice. Halfway down the hill, Dean watched Bravo Battery van hit the bottom of a hill where a large pool of water had collected. The truck splashed mud and water halfway up its sides. Dean started to slow down but noticed that Pickett was way ahead, almost to the top of the next hill. He stepped on the gas to catch up.

"Shoot a bear, I wish Bravo would get their tails in gear."

"Slow down!" yelled Walker.

It was too late. Dean had been concentrating so much on Pickett's jeep that he didn't see another convoy nose up to the road at the bottom of the basin. It was an infantry unit and they had just exited a wooded area nearby. Dean slammed on the brakes, but the van started fish tailing so he let off the brake, hitting the puddle about the time the first jeep had pulled up to it. The van splashed the mud everywhere. Dean started slowing down.

"No! Go, man don't even stop. That Lieutenant or Captain is madder than a hornet. We do not want to deal with these guys!" shouted Walker.

"Why? What happened, man?"

"Well, that officer was a white guy, but you just made him a black man. The only thing white on him is his eyeballs. Do you get the drift? Move it."

Dean floored the gas, the truck grabbed mud but they were making good time. Once again, their plan did not go well for them

Bravo Batteries van topped the hill, they hit a large bump and the step ladder that was supposed to be secured on the back popped out of its brackets, landing in front of Dean. He skidded to a halt just a few inches in front of the ladder. He would have gone around the ladder on the left, but Spec Four Harold Mueller had seen the ladder pop off and stopped the Bravo battery's van at the top of the hill. He was backing up to retrieve their wayward property impeding any attempt of escaping. Walker cursed under his breath.

"We are in big squat man."

"Yeah. You're telling me," Dean said as he watched the jeep advance up the hill toward their position.

"You let me do all the talking Larson and whatever you do, don't laugh."

The jeep pulled alongside them and it was all Dean could do to stifle a belly laugh. The driver was a black man, at least Dean thought he was. As the lieutenant started chewing Dean and Walker out, the driver gave them a big toothy grin. The man that sat in the back was a first sergeant and he was a tall white man covered in mud, but after bathing the vehicle in black murky water, the only white on him were his teeth and eye balls. Mud and water slushed around in the bottom of the jeep. It was easy to see why the lieutenant would be a little upset. He walked over to the back of the van and wiped the mud away from the area where the unit designation was painted on the truck.

"They are part of Charlie Battery, third of the sixteenth. Please make a note of that, First Sergeant. Indicate that the vehicle is a deuce-and-a-half van."

He was a skinny first lieutenant, his face was contorted from rage. He had not cleaned all the clumps of mud away from his face. The man had gotten all the mud off of his eye lids, the blue orbs showed nothing but anger. He berated Dean's driving skills and Walker's ability to lead. What irritated Dean most was that

Mueller saw what was happening and retreated over the hill without a murmur.

"What's your names?" demanded the lieutenant.

"My name is Henry Larson," Dean said without thinking.

"Write that down, First Sergeant. And yours Sergeant?"

"Reed Walker," stammered Walker.

"I'll be talking to someone about you two, and real soon."

"We're a part of a convoy, sir. Can we catch up to them? It is important, Lieutenant."

"Yes, get out of my sight, and if you ever pull another stunt like this, your heads will roll. Do you understand me?"

"Yes sir," they both said as they pulled away from him.

"Why did you give him a false name, Larson? We could be in a lot more trouble if he finds out that we lied to him."

"I would have given him a false last name if it wasn't sewn on our jackets. Don't worry Walker, he's a grunt officer and I doubt that he will be able to find us considering that there are so many units in Grafenwöhr this time of year. Relax Walker, and try to find out where we are going and how to get there."

Walker took out the map and compass and tried to figure how they were supposed to get to the battery position. He looked for landmarks and the map several times.

"We should be coming to a fork in the road go to the left. Take that turn and it should take us to Charlie battery."

Pickett was parked at the fork. He waved them over and asked them where they had been. Walker recounted their encounter with the infantry officer. Pickett shook his head and started laughing, remarking that he would cover their butts if they found themselves in trouble. Dean described what the three men in the jeep looked like and all three of them started roaring with side-splitting giggles. Pickett turned his jeep around and escorted them to the battery area.

They set up the camouflage netting, then Walker checked with the rest of the section. They didn't talk to anyone about their little encounter with the other convoy. Top came by at seven that evening. He informed them that they were going to do a night move.

"We will be taking up a position in a small valley with a stream running through the middle of it. You make sure you stay on our side of the stream. The Czech Republic owns the other side and the State Department would not appreciate the time it will take to retrieve you from a communist country. Do you understand, Private Henry?"

"Yes Top. Has anyone ever done something that stupid?" asked Henry.

"I heard of one genius some years back being lured over to the other side by some blond beauty. You all make sure that you think with your head and not your third leg. By the way, I don't know if we ever got that dumb private back."

He smiled and ordered them to get ready for the move. They tore down their camouflage netting and packed up the rest of their gear. They lined up in the convoy and were on the move to their next position. A night move was always difficult. They did not use headlights, only black-out lights.

The lights appeared like red cat eyes on the back of the vehicle in front of the next driver. The trouble with getting too close was a sudden stop could cause an accident but if a driver got too far behind, the night lights would suddenly disappear.

It took the battery about two hours to get into position. The meadow on the German side had a flat open space for the guns, but there was thick forest everywhere else. Walker guided Reed and the five-ton in through the trees to their place for the night. He turned his attention to Dean, guiding him to his spot. It was great to be able to park in the woods. They didn't have to throw up the camouflage when that occurred. The moon was out and Dean considered some of the old horror films and thought about vampires coming out from behind a tree.

They were about to turn in for the night when their battery area was engulfed in brilliant lights. It came from across the stream and it was a Czech tank unit. They had turned on their high-powered spot lights to check the unit out. Everyone scrambled to their weapons.

Law and Top went through the battery, calming everyone down. They didn't want to start World War III by accident. The tank unit finally shut their lights off and Dean settled down and got some sleep but he was restless most of the night.

After firing several rounds the next day, the battery moved to another location to perform more fire missions. They finally went back to base camp in the evening. On the way back, they witnessed a Cobra gun ship coming in on target. It rained down a steady stream of rounds on the position. It looked like red hot fire coming down from the chopper to the ground.

When they finally got to camp Dean and Walker checked in the NROSS and the round. Everyone else was asleep, one of the guys from the FDC section was snoring louder than a chain saw going full bore on a tree. Dean grabbed up his cot and moved it outside. His head hit the pillow and he was fast too sleep. When he woke up at ten am the next morning, he was wet from a rain storm that moved through the area that night. It was sunny now, so he opened the bag up to dry. He went and had a shower, breakfast, and relaxed for an hour reading his novel.

They went out several times on fire missions and the time flew by. They stayed two days in base camp, made sure their equipment was ready for the battery test. In the evening they played some cards and drank some beer. Everyone was ready for it to be over.

Dean was especially looking forward to the end. He missed his family and he would be getting his orders for the states soon. He would know where he was going to be stationed. Dean would have to arrange for the airline tickets for Natalie and John to go home. They would stay with her folks until Dean caught up with them. He would stay in the barracks for a couple of weeks. Dean was really hoping to get stationed at Fort Carson, Colorado so they could go home often. It would be his last inspection on the round here. Walker would have to figure out who would be the next A-team.

Chapter 20

BATTERY TEST

The white dust was like a shroud over everything as Dean drove the van down the road with the rest of the convoy. The canvas top was off and Walker stood on the seat with his M-16 in hand, watching for aggressors and enemy aircraft.

Dean laughed to himself, with all the dust, they could hardly see the vehicle in front of them. It was doubtful they would see an enemy soldier since they could barely make out the trees along the road. Still, they had to play the game in case war became a reality. The convoy snaked around the hills that made up Grafenwöhr. It was a warm beautiful day with the sun shining brightly and a blue sky dotted by the occasional white cloud drifting by.

They finally pulled off the road and set up a firing position. Dean threw the camouflage netting up with Henry's help. The four guns fired about twelve rounds down range at a fairly rapid rate. The average rate of fire was supposed to be a projectile out of the tube every one and a half minutes.

The eight-inch gun was declared one of the most accurate weapons in the US Army arsenal. They bragged that they could put the two-hundred-pound round on a dime twenty miles away. The section ate rations around noon and waited for their inspection. At eight in the evening, they were ordered on a road march. It took them most of the night to get to their next position.

They had to wrestle the camouflage up over the trucks. The guns fired a couple rounds, then all became quiet. The gunners and assistant gunners fell asleep at their instruments while the rest of the crew members threw their sleeping bags behind the guns and laid down for a quick nap. They were up often throughout the night sending rounds down range. The cooks had the coffee on by six am and they provided a hot breakfast.

At ten am the battery was hit by a group of aggressors. They were soldiers from another unit that pretended to be enemy combatants. Half the battery fought with the aggressors while the rest of the crew completed two fire missions.

The battery had several 'casualties' but they had driven the enemy from the field. Walker placed the section at strategic positions to make sure the aggressors did not get near the nuclear round or the NROSS. Cain was left in the van with the five live rounds, guarding all the packages. When the battle was over, they returned to the van, finding Cain sitting on the floor with his rifle between his legs and his head leaning against the weapon.

"What's up with you, man?" asked Walker.

"I'm sorry, Sarge. I made a big mistake."

"Get it over with. Tell me what you did and we'll see if we can fix it."

"Well, when the aggressors attacked, I got excited and forgot that I had live rounds. I took a shot and then I realized what I had done and put it back on safe. Man, I'm sorry Walker. I didn't mean to pop off a live round," Cain said with wide eyes.

"Crap. Cain, I signed for those rounds and I have to account for all of them," Walker said, his face turning a white ash color.

"Well, did you hit anyone?" inquired Reed with a smile.

"Yeah, I don't want to have to sneak out later tonight and bury a dead body," piped in Dean with a grin.

"I don't know, I didn't even think about that," Cain said with his eyes as big as saucers

"You smart alecks. Larson, you go check and see if there is a body. Cain, show him the general direction you were aiming when you fired," ordered Walker.

Cain pointed out the area that he had been aiming when he discharged the weapon. There were a lot of trees with brush covering uneven ground. Dean started down the steps to accomplish his assignment. He stopped at the bottom and looked up at Cain.

"By the way, what kind of marksman badge did you earn in basic?"

"Expert."

Dean beat the bush around the area Cain pointed out but he didn't find a dead body, nor did he find a bullet hole in any of the trees in the area. He reported the good news to Walker. He looked relieved, but paced back and forth in the van. That was hard to do with all the bodies that were in there.

"I guess I'll tell them in the armory that Cain dropped the magazine in the dark and that the round must have popped out. That is the story that I'm going to give them. You all have my back, right?"

"For five bucks," Dean said with a smile.

"Bull, or I kick your butt between your shoulders," Walker retorted with a big grin.

"Thanks for covering my tailpipes, man. I'm the one that shot the round. It's my neck in the noose. I know it was a mistake and I don't know how much trouble I could get in, but I appreciate you guys taking care of my six."

"No problem. We're a team and we need to stick together." Walker affirmed.

After that, the guns had five more fire missions, then they were on the road again to another position. Two hours after setting up the section was given a message to put the round together. It was confirmed through NROSS and soon the inspector was on the door step of the van.

Walker rounded up another perimeter guard from FDC. Once the guards were set, Walker took the reader's position. Dean was the A man and Reed was the B man. The procedure went well. The inspector threw a few problems into the mix but the team handled them all. He asked several pointed questions at the end, but one of the team members had the answer every time.

The inspector, a captain, shook his head in approval. "You soldiers are good. I don't even have a gig against you. I've done a lot of inspections with teams all over Europe and you three are the first ones I've inspected that didn't get a gig. Congratulations Sergeant." He shook Walker's hand and left the van.

The team tore the round down and Walker invited the rest of the section into the van, plus the FDC man. He promised them some beers on him when they got back to base camp. The guards had been just as impressive when they had been questioned. They pulled out their sleeping bags to get a little shut-eye, but before they could get situated, they were told to pack up, they were moving to another firing position.

It was another long road march and Walker had to continually talk to Dean to keep him awake. They fired about ten rounds and then they were on the march again. The battery got to the next place about the time the sun came up. Dean got to lay down for about an hour, then had to relieve Henry on guard duty.

Aggressors attacked them about noon but they were better prepared for them and drove them off with only a few soldiers declared wounded this time. Dean was guarding the van when the attack occurred.

He kept the four rounds in the magazine and watched from one of the side windows as the enemy was being repelled. The battery stayed in this position throughout the day with sporadic fire missions. The members of the sections took turns getting some shut eye. The battery test lasted seventy-two hours and, in that time, Dean figured that he got about two hours of sleep.

Late that night, they got a knock on the door. It was Top England and he was looking for a place where he could get some shut-eye and not be disturbed. The whole section was in the van, but they made room for Top. He informed them they were almost done and that they would be going back to base camp soon. They were going to do a battalion time on target and that it should be quite the show.

Henry left the van and went to the back of the five-ton to catch a little sleep. Top got up on the counter and was soon in deep slumber. Dean went out and sat in the driver's seat to watch the fireworks.

The battalion was made up of twelve 8-inch guns and a bunch of 155 weapons that had six guns a piece. Dean figured that he might see a large flash in the distance because all the rounds would explode above the ground. They would fit all the rounds with timers, figure the time to target and cut the detonator so that it would explode the round at a certain distance above the ground.

They were slow in getting all the battery's coordinated for the [TOT], Dean fell asleep leaning his head against the steering wheel. Suddenly there were loud explosions in front of him. He woke up seeing fire and smoke belching out the gun tubes. A few seconds later the horizon lit up and the rumble of thunder rolled across the landscape ending the battery test.

He exited the cab of the truck and went to the back of the van. Everyone was asleep except Ford who was sitting up on the floor looking dazed. Reed was standing in the corner dozing standing up. Dean roused them out of their slumber. They pulled down the netting and made sure the round and NROSS was all secured.

He saw men on the move, pulling camouflage nets down, loading up equipment, and making sure everyone was accounted for. They did not want to run over anyone in the dark. Dean pulled the van up behind Cassidy who was driving one of his big ammo carriers. It was just a square box on treads with a big bed for rounds and Reed was behind Dean in the five-ton.

Dean had an extra passenger, Top England had decided to ride up front, sitting between him and Walker. They pulled up to the powder pit just as Chester was torching off the unused powder bags. The flame caught and the bags produced a white-hot fire consuming the old powder. It messed up Dean's night vision and he didn't realize Cassidy had taken off. Top prompted him to move, telling him next time not to look directly at the flame. Dean quickly caught up with Cassidy but it took all his concentration to make out the cat eyes on the ammo carrier.

At some point in the midst of the trip, Top suddenly grabbed Dean's arm and yelled at him to stop. Dean had been so focused on Cassidy's vehicle in front of him that he did not realize that it had left the road and was traveling over some rough terrain.

The ammo carrier stopped about thirty yards down the hill. Top and Walker left the van and ran down the hill to see if Cassidy was alright. He had fallen asleep at the controls and by some miraculous act of God, the ammo carrier had gone off the road between two giant boulders without hitting them. They got him turned around on the rough ground and guided him back on the road.

Top acted as his assistant driver and led the rest of the convoy back to base camp. The vehicles pulled in about twenty minutes after the rest of the unit. Law was getting back in his jeep to find the rest of the battery just as they pulled in. Reed soon had his truck locked up and was sleeping in his cot with the rest of the section. Walker and Dean had to take the NROSS safe over to headquarters and the round to the armory to secure them.

Walker also turned in the rifle rounds minus one. The armory sergeant questioned him for a few minutes about the missing round, but when Dean affirmed the story, the sergeant let the subject drop.

They dragged themselves to the tent, even though Dean was exhausted, the same man's snoring kept him awake. He was wondering if he could get away with murdering the guy by stuffing his pillow down his throat suggesting that his intake of air acted like a vacuum and he had inhaled the pillow.

He grabbed up his cot and sleeping bag and set them up outside. He couldn't remember laying his head down, but he must have. Dean didn't wake up until eleven am the next day. He put his things inside the tent, got some breakfast, a hot shower, and clean fatigues. He joined the rest of the section at the motor pool. Reed had taken Henry with him to the wash rack where they were cleaning some of the dirt off the truck. Walker suggested that Dean take Perez with him and wash the van.

The wash rack was about a mile down the road, so Dean had Perez drive the van to the rack to get practice on the stick shift. He missed a gear or two, but was getting a lot better with the clutch each time he drove. They cleaned most of the dirt off the duce and a half. Dean took it to the fuel dump and they got her fueled up for the trip home. They checked out the fluids; the water was good but they had to add a half quart of oil to the motor. They cleaned up the inside and called it a day.

That afternoon they played cards and drank some beer. Dean was involved in a game of spades and had a really good hand when he was interrupted by Top. England was at the tent flaps and he summoned Walker and Dean outside. He walked them a ways from the tent and turned to them with a serious, and stern look.

"I Just got done talking to an infantry lieutenant that had a complaint against two men who were supposed to be a part of this unit. Thank goodness the battery commander asked me to look into the matter. He told me that a Spec Four and a Sergeant were driving recklessly on a dirt road and splashed mud all over him and two others. I asked him what their names were but I didn't recognize the two names he gave me. Do you two know anything about what this grunt is talking about?"

Dean and Walker shuffled their feet and looked down. "Well Top, suppose that van was in a SW convoy and the captain that was in charge was hauling tail like he was going to a fire? The driver was just trying to keep up, if you know what I mean. By some strange fate, that driver hit the bottom of a hill on a rainy day just as this infantry unit started to pull out. Now at the bottom of that hill was a rather large mud puddle and the sergeant yelled to slow down but it was too late if you know what I mean?" said Dean.

"If those two were going that fast, why did they get caught?"

"Well, suppose the van in front of theirs lost their stinking steps and they fell off right in front of them? Before they could take care of the problem, the lieutenant caught up to said driver and sergeant. The two were very apologetic but the three muddy men did not see the humor in the situation," explained Walker.

"A certain Captain Pickett said that he would cover for those two men," added Dean.

"Well, I know you two are not the men I'm looking for, but if you had been there, can you describe what these men might look like after the incident?"

"Was the lieutenant clean shaven and white, Top?" questioned Dean.

"Yes, he was."

"I guess if you can see him with mud covering him from head to toe and his passengers the same way, that is a start. The jeep would have about an inch of muddy water sloshing around on the floor boards," described Dean with a big smile on his face.

Top started laughing and Dean and Walker joined in. Top had to wipe tears from his eyes.

"I would have paid money to see that cocky little twerp with mud in his eyes. He came into my tent acting like he was someone special. Now that I've heard the story, I will take care of this little problem. Of course, I will have to talk to Pickett. Next time come and tell me little things like this so I can prepare for them. You two behave yourselves and if you see that lieutenant poking around, hide yourselves. He's a grunt. You would think by now that he'd be use to eating a little dirt. It should be a part of his diet."

Dean and Walker heard no more about the incident with the mud and the infantry lieutenant. They went back to playing cards and drinking beer. They all turned in early in anticipation of getting ready for the road trip home.

They had regular formation the next morning where Captain Law praised them for their efforts in the field. They were dismissed to various areas to get their gear ready for the convoy back to Baumholder. Dean had Perez check the truck over one more time while Ford took care of their personal gear. Dean pulled rank, had Perez drive the van home while he got some extra sleep.

Reed got stuck tearing down the battery's tent city so he would be riding with the gun crews back on the train. Cain would be driving the five-ton home with Henry as his assistant driver. Walker and Ford would be riding in the back of the van, probably sleeping. They loaded up as much gear as they could that evening. The only thing Dean had left out was his sleeping bag, the cot, and the clothes that he would be wearing home.

They were up by six am, ate breakfast, and were lined up in the convoy by seven-thirty. The vehicles moved off the secondary roads and onto the autobahn in a hurry. Once they hit the German highway, Dean leaned into the corner of the seat and laid his head against the door window. He mumbled to Eddie that he better not get into an accident or he would kill him.

Two hours later, he woke with a start, not knowing where he was. He looked over and saw Perez driving the van and realized what was happening. They talked about wives and the Army. Eddie was thinking about making it a career. Dean was determined to get out at his earliest convenience. He wanted to raise his son in Idaho and get started on perusing his dream of becoming a teacher.

They found themselves in Baumholder in late afternoon. Dean informed him that they needed to go to the headquarters building first where they could off load the NROSS. After that, they preceded to the barracks where they started unloading the personal gear. Dean went into the office and called Natalie so she could come and pick him up. He told her to go upstairs and inform Maria that Eddie was home and he needed a ride.

It took the ladies about ten minutes to get to the barracks. By that time, the trucks were off loaded and Eddie and Dean were sitting on the back curb waiting. It seemed like a long time, but it was worth it.

Both women were dressed up and Natalie rushed into Dean's arms and kissed him several times. John was in her arms looking a little concerned. After Natalie released her husband, Dean grabbed up John and lifted him over his head.

The little boy started crying and reaching for his mother. Dean brought his son down and looked into his face but the little boy cried even louder. He grabbed Natalies's arm and tugged on her. Dean tried to soothe him but he would have none of it. He would not stop crying or wiggling until he was in his mother's arms.

Dean had never felt so bad. His son had forgotten who his father was during the thirty-day absence. Dean wiped a tear away as he felt his heart breaking over John's behavior. He knew it wasn't John's fault, but it still hurt. It would take a couple of days to win his son's heart back. It would be nice to pick him up again and wrestle with him.

On the way home, Natalie had some exciting news. Jack, Dean's brother, had proposed marriage to Helen, Natalies's sister.

They wanted Dean to be the best man, Natalie to be a bride's maid. They were planning to have the wedding when Dean was on his two-week leave between duty stations. They were going to have it at the church that Natalie and Helen had grown up in.

Pastor Gordan Baker had shepherded the church since he had been a young man of thirty-five years old. He was now sixty-four and just as spry as a forty-year-old and was Natilie's uncle. He wore glasses, and hearing aids, he had white hair and was slight of build.

He had married Dean and Natalie. The ceremony was beautiful and Baker made Dean think about what marriage was all about before he allowed Dean to make his vows. Baker had emphasized purity to both of them several times and afterwards had confronted Dean about not knowing the Lord.

Dean had been polite toward him and had insisted that he knew that there was a God. Barker persisted by declaring that he may have known that there was a God but that he did not know God. Every once in a while, his words would come back to haunt Dean, but he just pushed them aside.

After dinner and John was asleep in his crib, Natalie poured one last cup of coffee for Dean, but he put it aside. Dean pulled her down so that she was sitting on his lap. He gave her a big kiss which she was embarrassed by, but after it was done, she pushed up and looked him square in the eye.

"I have some more news," she said with a bright gleam in her eyes.

"Well, is it good news?"

"I think it is Dean. I hope you will too. Any guesses?"

Dean shook his head no.

"Our suspicions have now been confirmed, we are going to have another baby. I saw the doctor a couple of days ago."

Dean smiled, knowing it was not exactly a surprise. "That is not good news, that is great news," he proclaimed.

"I thought you would be happy. We not only suspected it but we have discussed how we do want four children."

"Oh, I am happy. I hope it's a little girl and that she looks like you," he said with a laugh.

"Then you're happy about this? After all, it's too late to send the little one back. Besides I don't want John to get too old before he has a playmate."

"Well, I hope I don't have to leave her for thirty days and she or he forgets me again," Dean said wistfully. "It hurts."

Natalie touched him on the check and assured him that John would be back to normal in no time. She suggested that they go to bed, it was late.

Two weeks later, Law came out to the formation and announced the results of the battery test. The unit had passed with a few suggestions as to where it could improve. He also informed them that the whole battalion had been given a very good rating. He then called the battery to attention and called Reed, Walker, and Larson out in front of the formation where they were given certificates of achievement. He thanked them for their diligent work in the nuclear program.

He dismissed the battery and Dean started to follow Perez to his car. Top stopped him and told him that he wanted to see him in his office. Dean thought for sure that he was in trouble about something but he couldn't think of anything he had done wrong.

"Your orders have come in Larson. You will get your leave time but you are to report to the 101st Airborne Division, Fort Campbell Kentucky on the specified date. You are assigned to Alpha Battery third of the three nineteenth."

"You're kidding, right Top? I'm not Airbourne qualified."

"The 101st is an air assault unit now, they fly into an area in choppers, set up fire rounds, and move on."

"But I'm Mike five, I deal with nuclear weapons. The Army made a mistake, don't you think?"

"The Army never makes a mistake. The orders stand and you will report to Fort Campbell as ordered on the date specified. Understand Spec Four Larson. Good luck to you."

"Yes Top. Thank you."

Dean didn't know what to think. It would be different, an adventure to say the least. He had always been interested in Daniel Boone and the Civil War battles that had taken place in Kentucky and Tennessee, maybe he would find some time to visit some of them. He would have to see how things turned out.

Natalie was waiting for him at the door with a hug and kiss. After sitting down, he said, "Well do you want the good news first or the bad news?"

She sat down beside him and waited for him to unload on her. "The good news first I guess."

He pulled out the certificate and held it up to her. She read it and gave him a big hug. "I've been praying that you would do really good on your inspections and the Lord has answered my prayers. Did Reed and Walker get one too?"

"Yeah, we were all called up in front of the formation and Law praised us for our efforts." Dean felt a little deflated with the pray comment and the thought that the Lord had something to do with all his hard work.

"Well, what is the bad news, Dean?"

"The Army in all its wisdom is sending us to Fort Campbell Kentucky for the rest of our time in the service. No way will we be able to go home until our time is up. I will get my leave time so I will be a part of the wedding party."

Natalie looked troubled but made an off-hand comment about the wedding. She got up and went into the kitchen to fix his supper. She seemed distracted for the rest of the evening.

Chapter 21

BARRACKS RAT

Dean pressed the gas pedal down a little harder. They were running a little behind, but they were making good time on the autobahn to Frankfurt. He was going to put Natalie and John on the plane to go home. It was going to be a long flight, but John was a very good traveler. He usually fell asleep and rarely woke up until they stopped moving.

Dean wished he was going with them, but he was scheduled to travel to Kentucky next week on a military flight, which cost him nothing. From there, he would catch a commercial flight home. He had some final business to take care of in Baumholder. Dean would spend his last night in the apartment that they had rented and move into the barracks for about a week.

They sold the car to one of the new soldiers that came in from the states. The man was going to get paid in two days and he was going to pay the rest of the money to Dean for the Opel station wagon. Dean was not going to take any chances with the guy. He didn't know him. He was going to take him to the bank when he got his check and grab the money right after he left the teller.

"You ready for this, Babe? I wish I was going with you, but we can't afford to pay for a ticket for me."

"John and I will be fine Dean; you just make sure you get home on time. You're going to be standing tall beside Jack. You need to be there to steady him so he can answer that all-important question."

They exchanged a knowing smile between them. Jack was shy around girls and they found out that Helen had asked Jack to marry her. Jack could face down cows and bullies at school but had a yellow streak down his back when it came to women and alters.

"Yes. Brother like, brother, huh Dean?"

"What do you mean? I asked you to marry me, didn't I?"

"Yes, but we would have never dated if I had not run into you at the basketball game. I don't know how we ever got together, you're shy and I'm not exactly forward when it comes to men."

"It must have been fate or something, because you're the only one I ever dated except Mary Hastings. She was the one that asked me to the Fall Dance and then she tried to run my life after a couple of weeks. Had it all planned out when we were going to get married and where we were going to live. Boy, I did not like the control that came with her."

The traffic was getting heavy as they got closer to Frankfurt, so Dean concentrated on the cars that surrounded him. He had to watch closely for the sign that would direct them to the airport. Dean did not want to miss the exit otherwise they would end up where he had never been before. He spotted the sign after a few more miles and got off the autobahn.

The airport was well organized and easy to get around in. He parked the car and lugged their baggage over to the airline counter and got both of them checked in. He soon had Natalie and John at the gate they were going to fly out of.

They had a few minutes before they had to board the flight, so Dean sat with them. He held John close to him reminding him that he was not to forget his father this time. Natalie assured him that she would take a large picture of him out every day and show it to John. It was hard for Dean to say good-bye, he lingered with them, finally giving John a big hug and kiss on the check. He gave Natalie a long kiss and escorted them as far as he could to the gate.

Dean got into the little Opel and maneuvered it toward the autobahn. As he was going down the ramp. He hit a large pothole. It caused the exhaust system on the car to break. Instead of sounding like a quiet, small four-cylinder vehicle, it made the racket of a large truck that was out of tune.

The law in Germany was that you had to keep your vehicles in good running order and the police gave large fines to drivers that did not obey that law. One of Dean's friends had been fined seven hundred Marks for bald tires. That was roughly two hundred and fifty dollars and something Dean could not afford. He had to get it back to Arnold's mechanic shop, Arnold had fixed Dean's car on a couple of other occasions.

It was a good thing that there was a lot of traffic. Many drivers looked around for the noise maker but they could not pick out which car was making the racket. Dean suddenly spotted a German policeman pulled off on the side of the highway. They heard Dean's car and pulled out into the traffic. There were so many vehicles that it took them awhile to get into the flow of cars. Dean watched them as they darted in and out between the vehicles. When they started getting close to him, he pressed in the clutch which brought quiet to the exhaust system. The police passed by him. One of the officers had his window down and was listening to each car as they drove by.

Dean sighed in relief. He didn't get caught. He drove the car on the outskirts of Baumholder to Arnold's where he parked it. Arnold was working on a truck when he drove up. He came out shaking his head with a big smile.

Dean explained what happened to him and they looked under the vehicle. They found the exhaust pipe had broken in half near the middle of the system. Arnold went in and ordered the parts they needed and told Dean that he would have the Opel ready on Monday. Arnold told him to call before he tried picking it up.

Dean hiked over to the apartment where he would stay one more night in their first home as a family. It was too quiet, but Eddie showed up on his door step and invited him up for dinner. It was good not being alone thinking about Natalie.

The next morning Eddie gave him a ride over to the barracks where he would spend the next eight nights. The rooms where the section was located was filled up. He would have to stay in one of the rooms where FDC was located. They had an empty bunk and locker for him. He had already transferred most of his gear from the apartment to his new living quarters.

He had dinner with Reed and Ford. He was hungry and the mess hall food was good. As they ate, Dean explained what happened to the car and Reed asked him about Natalie and John. They had a couple of cups of coffee.

Ford invited him over to play a game of spades, drink some beer, and listen to music. Dean gladly accepted the invitation. As they approached the room, Dean could hear Cain responding to someone in an angry tone, not shouting but speaking back with a stern voice. "What do you mean we don't need farmers, man. My granddaddy was a small farmer and he worked his tail off to grow crops."

"I'm not saying that he didn't work hard, I'm just saying that we don't need farmers," Henry spouted off.

Cain was getting more irritated by the minute. He rose, but Reed got in front of him to calm him down. Dean couldn't believe what he was hearing. "Where do you come from Henry?"

"Well, from New York. You know that Larson, why do you ask?"

"Not everyone in New York is as ignorant as you, right?"

"What do you mean by that remark?" Henry asked, rising out of his chair.

"Where do you think we get food?" asked Cain.

"From the store of course," snarled Henry.

"You better settle down," Ford said, pointing at him with his big index finger.

"I'll take on all you SOBs at one time, or one at a time!"

"Sounds good to me!" shouted Cain.

He charged in on Henry, hitting him like a linebacker, shoulder to ribs knocked him over his chair. Reed shut the door. Ford grabbed a blanket threw it over Henry's face while Dean stomped on Henry's right hand, busting several fingers.

Henry tried to rise up using his left hand but Dean threw his full weight on his chest and got his head in a half-nelson. Henry was still resisting until Ford kicked him between the legs. Henry tried to double over but Dean still had the half-nelson on him and had turned him over on his stomach. He was able to grab himself with his left hand and cry out in pain.

Dean asked him if he wanted to continue the fight. Henry just continued moaning and shook his head no. Dean released his half-nelson little by little until they were sure Henry was calmer. About halfway through the fracas, Walker had opened the door, saw what was happening, and closed it.

Walker came in looking from Henry to Dean to Reed, Ford, and then to Cain. He made the rounds twice more but no one said anything.

"What is this all about?" he asked staring at Dean.

"Just a little misunderstanding, right Henry?"

"Yeah, man." Nodded Henry, still holding his midsection with his hands.

"Listen Henry, ever since you came into the unit, you have been nothing but a problem. You talk way too much and don't know nothing. My old man gave me some advice and I'm going to give it to you. He told me that I was born with one mouth and two ears and that I should listen twice as much as I talk. I suggest you make that a rule of thumb around here from now on, or I'm going to ask Top to put you on one of the gun sections. How would you like to be a powder monkey for one of the guns?"

"I don't think I would like that," Henry said looking at the floor.

"So What started this fight?"

"He said that there was no need to have farmers anymore!" Cain blurted out.

"We tried to correct him, kinda called him ignorant. He suggested that he would take us all on, so we obliged him," explained Dean.

"What, you got pissed because they suggested that you were ignorant Henry?" Walker asked wide eyed. Henry looked down and nodded.

"You are ignorant man; farmers grow crops and raise animals to feed us. Where do you think food comes from?"

"The store."

"It comes from the farm first, city boy. You better go get that hand taken care of. Are there any more issues that need to be dealt with before I leave?"

No one spoke a word.

"You all remember this, if I catch any of you fighting, especially amongst the section I will recommend an Article 15, loss of rank, and some pay. You, Henry will be gone; humping two-hundred-pound projectiles on one of the gun crews, do you understand?"

"I get the drift Sarge, I will try to behave myself," he said nodding.

"You get things right for a while after your corrected but you fall into the same rut. This is your last warning, understand?' Walker turned and left, the group broke up, but Larson, Reed, Ford, and Cain watched each other's backs for a couple of days, making sure Henry didn't try to get revenge on any of them.

They were quite sure that two of them could take him, Reed may have been able to hold his own, but Dean and Cain alone could not have handled Henry. Henry seemed to forget the incident and acted like one of the team again.

On Monday, Dean had some final paper work to deal with at headquarters. He caught a ride to Arnold's where he retrieved the Opel. Dean drove it over to the motor pool where he picked up the young soldier that wanted to buy it. They went and cashed their checks at the bank.

Dean was given the final payment for the Opel station wagon. He signed the paperwork for the change of title and gave the man the keys to it. Since he was in transition all he had to do was to show up at formation in the evening and the morning

At evening formation, Dean reported in and when they were all released, he went with Reed to have dinner. They were sitting by themselves when Cain asked if he could join them. Dean and Reed looked at each other and then waved Cain to the next seat over.

He usually sat with some brothers at another table, so they were surprised. It was a good visit, Cain seemed to have a different attitude, he was less guarded and more open to both of them. They came to find out that Cain had two sisters and they had no idea until that evening. He even showed them pictures of them and his mother.

They were pretty young ladies and he seemed to be proud of them. One was in college and the other one was a senior in high school. At the end of dinner, Cain invited them to come to the EM club [Enlisted Men's] and have a few drinks.

Reed declined; he rarely went out drinking on week nights. Dean accepted the invitation, and they walked the few blocks to the club. Neither one of them said much. The evening was warm and very few people were out, since it was a Monday. Their boots made a hollow tone on the cobblestone road as they trudged by the motor pool with its smell of engine oil. They passed a couple more buildings and found themselves in the EM club.

Both of them ordered beers and they took a seat at a table in the corner. They surveyed the crowd and counted eight other enlisted men sitting in the joint sipping on beers also. Even though it had been a payday, few people were out, but the place would be crowded the coming weekend.

Cain cleared his throat and looked earnestly at Dean. He drummed a finger on the table and looked down for a few seconds. "Man, I have to apologize to you. I figured you all wrong. I thought for sure you were a bigot. When you helped me with Henry and backed me up on the missing rifle round, I figured you're alright. Then come to find out your Daddy is a farmer, well I'm sorry for being such a jerk all this time." he said looking down at the table.

"You're forgiven Cain. After all, I took you all wrong, I thought for sure you were a Russian spy."

They both broke out laughing and any problems that were between them melted away. Cain was roaring so hard that he almost fell out of his chair. He had to wipe tears from his face before they gained self-control. Everyone in the club was staring at them. "I didn't know they had black Russians." He commented as he started gaining self-control. This brought on some more giggles.

They took a few sips of their beers and started discussing what they were going to do after the Army, when they got back to the world. It was a pleasant visit, they each had four beers and slowly walked back to the barracks. It was nine in the evening, so Dean took a quick shower, got his uniform ready for the next day and was asleep by ten-thirty.

After morning formation, Top called him into the office. England talked to him about the 101st Airbourne division. He had served with some of them in Vietnam and informed Dean that they were a tough bunch of soldiers. He told him several stories about some tough battles they had participated in during the war. Larson was impressed, he loved history and knew that the 101st had been involved in the invasion of France on D-Day and the Battle of the Bulge.

He wandered to the PX and the Commissary as kind of a good-bye to Baumholder. He also walked through town. He could never get use to the smell of cow dung coming from some of the houses in the village. It did remind him of home. He expected it on the farm, but Germany was different, they kept their livestock at home. The farmers didn't live on the land but in the villages nearby.

He went to his favorite guesthouse and had lunch, a beer, and schnitzel with mushrooms and fries. He would miss Germany and the friends that he had made. Still, he was ready to go back to the states.

He went back to the barracks to make the evening formation. Perez invited him home for dinner. Maria was fixing enchiladas when they arrived at the apartment. Dean left for a few minutes to say a final farewell to his landlords. They gave him a soft drink and had him sit down. They talked a few minutes and then he went upstairs.

Dean spent the rest of the evening visiting with Eddie and his family. They were very grateful to Dean and Natalie for all the help they had given them to get started in Baumholder. Eddie was now paying part of his rent in cigarettes, which helped with the bills. They didn't go many places because of their expenses, they didn't have the opportunity to travel like the Larsons.

Dean and Natalie had taken the Perez family on several excursions. They had taken them to Trier, one of the oldest cities in Germany. It still had Roman ruins you could visit. They had also help finance a USO tour to Holland. They talked about those trips and the Bible studies Natalie had shared with Maria. Eddie took Dean back to the barracks at about nine that evening.

He continued to make morning formations and participating in the battalion run. They would get a two or three mile run in after physical training. He wanted to stay in shape for his next duty station. He would disappear in his room after breakfast, take a shower to wash off the sweat and get into the book that he was reading. He wanted to finish it before he went home.

It was a book written by James Michener with about a thousand pages. He only had a couple more chapters and he was enjoying the novel. That evening he played cards with Henry, Cain, and Reed.

Henry seemed to have a different attitude; the cockiness was gone. He seemed to have taken Walker's advice and was listening a lot more than he was mouthing off. Walker brought in a couple of six packs later in the evening. They drank beer and played more card games, dealing Walker in.

Friday evening, they all went out to a guesthouse and enjoyed each other's company. Eddie also joined the festivities. They wouldn't let Dean pay for anything; they bought him beer and dinner. About eight that evening, Eddie informed them that he had to get home. They talked him into taking them to the EM club where he left them.

Dean usually limited his beer intake on such occasions, but they kept setting another round in front of him. He finally talked them into taking him back to the barracks. They rolled him into his bunk, took off his shoes and hat. Reed covered him with a blanket and that was all he could recall until morning.

He slept until ten am and woke up with Reed hovering over him. He smiled and helped Dean sit up in bed.

"You okay man?"

"I think I'll live," replied Dean holding his head in his hands.

"You missed breakfast, you feel like eating?"

"I guess I could eat a couple of eggs and some ham. Let's go to the EM club and I'll buy the meal this time Reed," invited Dean.

"Naw, you can buy me some coffee and I'll watch you eat. I made it to chow before they closed things down. I didn't drink nearly as much as the rest of you," he said with a big grin.

Dean pulled himself out of his bed, changed shirts, washed his face, and combed his hair. They wandered up to the club and put in their order. They sat in one of the corners and talked about the night before. Reed changed the subject once Dean got his order of food. "Hey man, I want to keep in touch with you. Give me your father's address and his phone number. I plan on seeing you someday."

"Are you kidding me? From upper state New York?"

"Yeah, man. You're one of the best friends I've ever had. We made a great team. Besides that, your wife is a great cook. For all those reasons I would gladly come out and see you."

"Do you even know where Idaho is, Reed?"

"All I have to do is drive out of my parent's driveway, turn west, and press the gas pedal. If nothing else, I learned how to read a map while I've been here. I was also taught how to put a bullet hole in a man's chest at a couple hundred yards, and assemble a nuclear round in no time at all. I wonder if I could get a job off any those skills?" He said laughing.

"I don't know, but I would hire you in a second. Oops, I better get a job first before I make any more promises. I give you my word that if you show up on my doorstep, you will have a place to stay and some of Natalie's fine cooking," Dean said with a broad smile.

"Sounds like a deal, man. Oh, now that you have become a barracks rat, how do you like it?"

"You can have it. I would rather go home at night to Natalie."

"Yeah, I don't blame you. I hope I find someone like her someday."

Dean finished up his food and they wandered back to the barracks. Larson went back to his room and took a shower. He cleaned up his area after dressing in some fresh civilian clothes. Walker invited him, Cain, and Reed to go to an afternoon matinee. They got back in time for dinner at the mess hall. They played cards and had a couple of beers. Dean turned in early, he was tired from the night before.

Sunday, he finished his book, got his gear packed in the duffel bag. He got his class A uniform ready, arranging the ribbons and the marksman badge in the proper place for Monday. He would go to Ramstein Airforce base and catch a military flight to Kentucky. He was feeling the excitement and the anticipation of seeing Natalie, John, and the family.

He was happy for his brother's upcoming wedding and being the best man. Dean was fairly sure that he would still be suffering from jet lag, he was hoping that he wouldn't do anything stupid to embarrass himself or his brother during the ceremony. Eddie Perez was going to take him to the air field. He tossed and turned for a couple hours Sunday night going over every detail for Monday, until he fell asleep.

He woke up an hour early, snuck out of the room and took an early shower. He made his bunk and made sure his area was squared away. He went downstairs and visited with Sergeant Marks who was on duty at the time. They talked for about a half hour before they had morning formation. Captain Law and Top shook his hand before they allowed him to go to breakfast. Reed and Walker gave him a hug and several of his other friends shook his hand.

Eddie loaded him and his gear up in the car drove him to Ramstein where he loaded on the plane and left Germany. It would take him about eight hours to get to Kentucky where he disembarked, and from there he would catch a commercial flight to Denver and then to Salt Lake. The final leg of his trip would be to Boise where his father and Natalie would be waiting with a car. It would be about another three hours by car before he got home.

Chapter 22

IN TRANSITION

He woke up with a start. Someone was running their hand through his hair. He focused on the face that was hovering over him. It was Natalie smiling down at him trying to gently wake him. He grabbed her and pulled her down to him. Their lips locked and he kissed her long, hugging her tightly.

He remembered meeting her with his father at the airport and giving her a small kiss. What surprised him was that his father gave him a hug; his father rarely showed affection. Once they were in the car, he fell asleep and didn't wake up until they hit the driveway at the farm.

He stumbled into the house, retreating to his old bedroom and collapsing on the bed. Natalie must have undressed him and got him under the sheets. He had not slept much on his trip from Germany, the seats were too close together for his long legs.

"Well, are you awake?"

"Yes, I guess so," he said stretching and yawning. "Where's that son of mine? I want a hug and kiss from him."

"He's downstairs, playing with his Aunt Helen. I didn't know if you would be ready to wake up or not. You acted exhausted yesterday. Do you even remember hugging your brother?"

"No. You mean Jack hugged me?"

"Yes, what is strange about that?"

"Just everything. I can't believe my father embraced me at the airport."

"A lot of changes have taken place since we left Dean. Your father and brother have become Christians. They attend church with my folks and I have never seen your father so at peace or your brother with so much joy. It would be good if you took some notes from their pages Dean."

"Hey love, we have a good life and I treat you good, don't I? I don't beat you or make you plow the back forty. I love you like crazy. Isn't that enough?"

"That is enough for me Dean, but I don't think it is enough for you. I know that you have some deep hurts surrounding the death of your mother and what happened afterwards. I know that you have a hole in your heart that only God can fill. I love you Dean, and I want you to make it to Heaven," she said in a pleading voice.

"Can we skip this conversation for now? What is on the agenda for the day?"

"You need to get up and have some lunch. And then it's off to the tailor and getting fitted for a tux. You will be in the practice run tonight and then after that they are going to have a dinner. You are going to have a busy day, so hop to it Spec Four Larson. Duty calls."

"How about a little breakfast instead of lunch before I start the day?"

"You shower and I will fix a breakfast of eggs, ham, and taters. When you get downstairs, John will be waiting for you with a cup of coffee and cream right from the cow."

He slapped her on the behind as she turned to leave the room.

"You behave yourself, Mr. Larson. Let's get the day started," she said with a broad smile.

He found an old robe and stared for the bathroom, but was ambushed by John who ran into his father's arms. They kissed and hugged for a few minutes before his Aunt Helen grabbed him up and whisked him back down to the living room. The shower felt good and Dean started feeling alive again. Natalie had ironed some of the wrinkled clothes and had them laying on the bed for him after he showered and shave.

Dean just sat down for his breakfast, when his father and brother came in from the barnyard to have lunch. Bud Larson was a tall man, standing about six foot two, with broad shoulders, a square face, and arms that rippled with muscles. Dean had rarely seen him smile after his mother died. There was also a lack of spark in his eyes. Now as Bud picked him up out of the chair and gave him a bear hug, not only was the spark back, but a smile creased the wrinkles of his sun-tanned face.

He admitted to himself that he did not know his father well. Jack gave Helen a kiss first, then gave Dean the same kind of hug. It took Dean's breath away. Helen placed lunch before the two hungry farmers and as they ate, Dean gave his brother a hard time about marrying his wife's sister.

There was laughter and storytelling until Helen put her foot down. She reminded all of them about the agenda. Jack and Dean quickly finished their food. Helen herded Dean and Jack to the pick-up where Jack drove his brother to get fitted for the tux.

On the way to town, Jack told Dean how he started courting Helen, the time frame of falling in love with her, and their plans for the future. They went to Burley to get fitted for the tux and it took them a little while to get to the store.

The seamstress quickly got the measurements from Dean. Dean offered to buy Jack a couple of beers at the local bar, since he couldn't give his brother a bachelor party, but Jack declined. Dean continued to pressure him to have a least one beer. Dean blamed Helen, suggesting that she had gotten him to stop drinking completely. He informed Dean that he felt like the Lord had asked him to stop boozing it up. Dean finally talked his brother into going to a nearby restaurant and getting a cup of coffee.

Dean asked him about his conversion. Jack told him that the Baker's had invited them to go to church several times. Finally, Bud and Jack had accepted the invitation and found the congregation to be loving and caring people. They started asking questions about Natalie and Dean all the time. They asked Bud and Jack if they needed prayer.

Bud confessed to the pastor that they needed to expand the farm because they couldn't make enough money off their current acreage. Members of the congregation gathered around them and they prayed that the Lord would intercede in their behalf. Within a month, they had purchased more farmland at a very good price. Jack declared that it was miraculous as to how it came about. "We saw God's hand in it," declared Jack.

Bud and Jack had talked it over and decided that there must be a God and that He must care for them because He worked out the purchase of the land. A couple weeks later, both of them asked Jesus Christ into their hearts.

Dean remained silent for a little while, thinking about what he had just heard. He figured it was a coincidence, but he would not play down what had happened. He did like the changes he saw in his father and brother. He suggested that Jack keep pursuing God. That he would have a better relationship with Helen and their father.

Jack came back and invited him to become part of the church and to accept Christ as his savior. Dean told him that he would think about it, but he had already decided that he was basically a good guy. Natalie and he were doing well right now and he really had no need for God.

They finished their coffee and went back to the farm. Bud Larson and Lawrance Baker were finishing up the arbor where the wedding was going to take place. It was a beautiful setting with an apple orchard in the back ground and a large grassy lawn for the audience.

Bud and Jack had cleared a large part of the barn of any items that would hinder the reception and the dance to take place after the nuptials were taken care of. The next day they would set up about sixty chairs for the guest and the barn would have tables, chairs, and a stage with a live band. The tuxedos were black with dark red shirts and bolo ties. The groom would be the only one to wear a black Stetson. The bride was decked out in white of course, but she would wear a dark red flower on her wrist. The bride's maids all wore dark red dresses, the same colors as the men's shirts.

Dean grabbed John who was in the way of the women getting the wedding dinner ready and took him outside to play. He wrestled with him and chased him around the yard, getting him tired so that he might sleep through most of the night. He tried to teach him to play catch by rolling his old ball to him.

Baseball had been Dean's sport; he was third baseman and had a decent batting average. John was catching on, running quickly to the ball and retrieving it up until dinner was ready. The food was set up out in the barn. It was a picturesque structure, red with a hay loft and two doors that slid side to side. The stalls still had hay in them, but no animals. The hay was fresh letting off that sweet grass smell that Dean always loved.

He entertained Pastor Gordan Baker and his wife Sandra who were Natalie's aunt and uncle while everyone put the finishing touches for the evening festivities. Gordan would be officiating the wedding and Sandra was to play the wedding march on her guitar.

Sandra was a petite woman and she always smiled, but Dean detected a sadness in her. He later learned that she lost a daughter just a couple years before. Gordan was a very nice guy of medium build with expressive blue eyes. Whenever Dean was around him, he felt like Gordan was looking right through him. It made him uncomfortable so he avoided him as much as possible.

Dean was best man and Randy Alder would be a groom's man. Randy, a tall lanky young man, had been Jack's best friend since grade school. Troy, the Baker family's youngest daughter, would be a bride's maid along with Susan Smith, who was Helen's best friend through high school.

Troy was still in high school, a junior with fair skin, brown hair and thick glasses. She had a sweet nature about her and a pretty face. Susan was chunky, cute in the face, and had an outgoing personality. She always had a smart remark about any comment that was make and a contagious laugh.

Gordan started things off with prayer and then everyone dug into the food. They had a variety of meats, potatoes cooked different ways, and vegetables taken right out of the garden that morning. Natalie made her famous walnut cake with various other deserts.

After the meal, Gordan got everyone situated and they did a practice run of the wedding. Natalie and Dean were given the responsibility of the rings. The little flower girl was not at the rehearsal which was scary, but they were hoping she would do a good job. It was a long day for Dean, he snuck out as soon as he could and went to bed. He was suffering from his trip, succumbing to the nods at the practice. He quickly fell asleep.

He woke up too early, donned a T-shirt and a pair of exercise shorts. He went downstairs and warmed up a cup of coffee. He started out the door to sit on one of the chairs on the porch, when Jack showed up on the staircase.

Dean poured him a cup of coffee and they went out on the step to sit. The sun was just starting to peek over the mountains to the northeast of them. The rays were chasing the shadows away and the coolness of the morning made the coffee all the more refreshing to both of them. For about a half-hour, they said nothing to one another, just taking in the view and the sounds of the morning. A frog was croaking from the canal bank, a cricket would chirp once in a while. The birds were the main entertainment, as the various species called for their mates, or warned others to stay away. It was the crow of the rooster that brought them back to reality.

"Well, are you ready Jack?"

"It's kind of scary, taking a wife, all that responsibility, loving her the right way and providing for her. I do love Helen and I want to face whatever the future holds for me with her. I not only love her but I like her and consider her to be a friend."

"That sounds like the right attitude if you ask me. That is how I feel about Natalie. Don't worry, you'll get the hang of marriage. It's tough at times. You will butt heads with her but just remember this rule: don't go to bed angry, and enjoy making up with her. Apologize and try to work things out at some other point in time," Dean said with a broad smile.

"That coming from a man that has only been married a couple of years."

"What can I say? I have to try to get you started off right."

"I guess you must be right, I already talked to Dad about it, and he said the same thing."

"Where do you think I got my advice. By the way, where are you taking her on your honeymoon?"

"We're going to Yellowstone National Park, but Dad paid for a night at one of the better hotels in Pocatello to stay at," Jack said, looking down at the porch floor with a red face.

"Don't worry my brother, things will come naturally. There is the joy of exploring and finding out how to give each other pleasure. You have had plenty of lessons here on the farm, the sheep, cats, and other critters," Dean said laughing at his brother's embarrassment.

"I hope so," Jack replied wistfully.

"Where are you guys going to live when you come back?"

"The other farm we bought has a four-bedroom house a couple of miles down the road. Dad and the Bakers have been giving us some odds and ends. Helen and I went out and bought some of the things we need. The house needs a little fixing up so the furniture goes along with the inside of our new home. Nothing fancy, but we look forward to repairing it and making the place ours."

"Good, it sounds like you have a plan. I wish you the best Jack, all the good things in life plus a dozen kids," Dean said laughing again.

"Hey, not that many. We would like a few but not a dozen," he said with a big grin. Jack turned and looked out at the barn for a long moment. Dean wondered what he was thinking, he looked so serious. Dean figured that he was thinking about the wedding, so he remained silent.

"Hey bro, I want to apologize for treating you so mean when we were in high school. I was concerned that you would want the farm for yourself and I figured since you were the oldest, Dad would give it to you. I love farming and well, I wanted the old homestead. We have so many good memories here, memories of Mom. Anyway, I wanted to say that I'm sorry and if you want to be a partner, I would gladly share the farm with you."

"No man, I want to be a teacher. I figure that we both gave our teachers all kinds of problems and I should be punished for all the stuff we got away with by becoming one myself."

They both gave a big belly laugh.

"Well, your right about that, and I'm glad you're being punished for the both of us. You will probably be a teacher for a long time to make up for all we did," Jack said grinning.

Dean nodded and then he was attacked from behind by John. The little boy had awakened his mother, wanting some breakfast. Natalie appeared at the door and asked if they wanted some pancakes. They both nodded and the day officially started.

After breakfast, the morning was spent getting the tables, grounds and stage ready. The women became the bosses and directed the men on how to put the finishing touches on the barn, the house, and where the ceremony itself would take place. Of course, things had to be changed around several times to make it look perfect. After lunch, it was time to get themselves ready. Randy had picked up Dean's tux in Burley for him. Dean dressed himself first and helped Jack with getting everything just right. The Stetson was a nice touch. Once Jack was ready, all he could do was pace the floor in his room.

Helen showed up ten minutes before the ceremony. When she stepped out of the car, Dean was taken back by her beauty. She was stunning and Dean had only seen one other bride more beautiful; Natalie. Dean went in and reported to Jack that Helen had showed up and he was in for a treat when he saw his wife-to-be. He then went and found Pastor Gordan to see when he wanted Jack and his attendants at the arbor.

Gordan checked with the rest of the parties involved in the ceremony and then waved Dean to bring the groom and his party to the arbor. As Dean was walking with Jack to stand before the pastor, he remembered the ring and checked his jacket pocket to make sure it was there. It was and he breathed a sigh of relief.

Once the groom and party were in their proper places, Gordan gave his wife a nod. She got her guitar and started strumming the bridal march. A few seconds later, Helen appeared at the back door and Dean heard Jack take a deep breath. He heard him say "gorgeous" in a low tone.

He looked at his own wife in her red dress and thought the same thing, how beautiful and different looking the two sisters appeared. John was sitting in his grandfather's arms and being very good. The audience was standing to the side of Helen who slowly circled them and marched down the center, toward her future husband. The flower girl in front took four steps down the center aisle, threw her basket of flowers, and went crying to her mother. When that happened Dean could see the stress come over his brother.

"That's a good sign."

Jack looked back at him with a question in his eyes.

"Remember when I got married and you drove us into the ditch during that snow storm and we were forty minutes late?"

Jack smiled and the stress lifted from him.

"It was good, a wedding that is perfect indicates the marriage will be riddled with mistakes. Yes, Natalie was flustered because I was late, but I did show up," Dean said smiling.

The rest of the ceremony went without any problems and they became Mr. and Mrs. Jack Larson. When Jack kissed her, it was long followed by a loud applause. Everyone went to the barn where the music started. Jack danced with Laura Baker and Helen cut the rug with her new father-in-law. The festivities continued and everyone seemed to have a good time. The bride and groom snuck off for their honeymoon around six p.m., but the party continued until about nine that evening.

Dean was sitting down feeding John but his son was nodding off. It had been a busy day for little John also. All the ladies would pick him up and dance with him in their arms. He had gotten more dances than all the other men at the party. Dean was worn out, but he was going to help Natalie clean up after John was completely under the spell of the sandman.

Gordan came and sat next to him with a slight smile on his face. "So, how do you like the army?"

"It's alright, I guess. I'm not interested in making a career out of it."

"That's what Natalie was telling me. How is your relationship with the Lord, Dean?"

"Just fine," Dean said hesitantly.

"Well, hold on to your boots. I know you don't know Him but you will and He has a special plan for you. You have a special calling on your life and you are to learn as much as you can at your next duty station. Do you mind if I pray for you?"

"I guess not," Dean said, confused.

Gordan grabbed a hold of Dean's hand and started praying. "Lord, I would ask you to move in a mighty way in Dean's life, leading him to the river of life and into your kingdom. We ask you to make yourself very real to John that hc might come to know you at a very early age. May you bless their marriage and make it strong so they can weather every storm that comes their way. Now the ministry you are going to place on Dean, may you led and guide him that he might fulfill all the purposes you have for him and give him the heart of King David. Amen. We love you Dean and if you need anything just give me a call." He patted Dean on the back and left for home.

Dean sat there pondering what Gordan had said. He rejected the idea of ever becoming a pastor to a church. That was not him. Some of the prayer he didn't understand and he kept trying to figure out all Gordan had spoken over him and the electric currents that went up and down his back. What was all that about? He was questioning everything the pastor had told him. Still, the words stayed with him and the things he remembered rolled around in his head until Natalie sat down next to him. She questioned him about what Gordan talked to him about, but Dean did not want to discuss it with her at that moment.

They put John to bed and came back to the barn where he danced with Natalie to several tunes until his father cut in. He went to the bar and had several beers with Randy. Randy questioned him about army life until Dean called it a night.

For the next week he helped his father on the farm and did some of the repairs that needed to be done on Jack and Helen's house, getting it ready for them to live in. They had already done a lot of work on the place but his father and Lawrance with the help of John made the place even nicer.

He had long visits with his father who apologized several times about being an absent father after his wife had died. It was strange to see Bud Larson so open about his feelings. Dean had never seen him that way before and he wasn't sure he liked it. The newlyweds came back after a week of camping. Dean asked his brother if everything came naturally. Jack didn't catch on until Dean winked at him. Jack turned a little red and told Dean that he was right concerning his advice on nature.

He continued his visit with family and friends in the area. The important thing was to make as many memories with John and Natalie as possible before he left for Fort Campbell. He decided he would leave a day early; he did not want to be late for any reason for his new duty station.

Jack and Helen volunteered to take him to Boise and put him on his plane. He gave Helen and his brother hugs, teasing his brother about if he should consider him a brother or a brother-in-law. He gave John a big hug, kissed him, tickled him on his belly, then gave him another big hug. It was tough saying good-bye to them. He held Natalie's hand, hugged her several times, and gave her a long good-bye kiss. He promised her that he would start looking for a place to rent right away.

He boarded the plane that started his trip to Clarksville, Tennessee. Part of the base was in Tennessee and part of it was in Kentucky. He was hoping things would go smoothly and they would find a place to live in and some transportation; he wanted to be able to see some of the country. He was especially interested in civil war battlefields. The traveling would have to wait until after their baby was born. He got in late that afternoon and it was raining. It was pouring rain like he had never seen before. It was more like someone turning on a water spigot. The rain drenched everything and little streams ran down the sides of the road.

A taxi took him to the guard station at the gate, where the MP checked his papers, allowing him to step out of the vehicle. He was then directed to the building where he was to report.

"We don't want you to wait in the guard station. I'm sure someone would be glad to give you a ride to your destination," suggested one of the MP's."

"Thanks, Sarg, does it always rain like this in Tennessee or is this unusual?"

"When it rains, this is what it does. Now you know what Noah had to contend with." He said with a big smile.

Several cars went through the gate before the MP waved Dean out to a car going his way. He was an E-5 Sergeant and he was traveling past the building that Dean needed to check-in at.

"So where are you coming from?" asked the Sergeant.

"I'm coming off leave. I was with family in Idaho from my last duty station."

"Idaho, beautiful country. I grew up in Washington and we had family in northern Idaho that we would visit often. Where were you stationed before you came here?"

"I did about two years in Germany."

"What was it like, the terrain and weather? Are the people friendly?"

"A lot of it is rolling hills. Where I was stationed, we had a lot of cloudy days with rain and snow. Most of the people are friendly. Why do you ask, are you being transferred to Germany?"

"No, haven't you heard most of the 101st is going over there on Reforger 76. It should be an interesting time to say the least."

At that point they pulled up in front of Dean's destination and Dean got out of the car but he had a lot of questions that he wanted to throw the Sergeants way.

He quickly ran to the appropriate office and hurried inside out of the rain. He placed his paperwork in front of the Specialist Four that was sitting behind the desk. There were other desks but they were empty. He was busy with some other work and asked Dean to take a seat, that he would get to him in a few seconds.

Dean gathered up his folder and sat on one of the chairs. Finally, the soldier looked up and wave him over with a smile. Dean placed the folder on the desk and the specialist rummaged through it. He shook his head a few times and then looked up at Dean.

"So, you came from Germany?"

Dean nodded a reply.

"You are assigned to Battery A, third of the three-nineteenth. What is this Mike five on your job description?"

"It indicates that I can put nuclear rounds together for the eight-inch gun," Dean replied.

"Well, we are not nuclear capable. Just like the army to send you here. I guess you're going to be a gun bunny again. Captain Knight will be your battery commander I hear he is a good BC. First Sergeant Barrett is your top NCO. He is gung-ho and I hear he is an ornery SOB." He said quietly leaning forward so no one else would hear him even though no one else was in the office.

I hate to tell you this, but this unit is going on Reforger 76. You will be going back to Germany this fall. In fact, you came here at the right time. In about three weeks, your battery and several other units will be going to Fort Bragg to participate in war games against the 82nd Airbourne Division," announced the Spec Four.

"Damn, I'm married and I need to find some housing for my family. Got any suggestions as to where to look?"

"I've got several suggestions. First, don't report to Barrett without the proper uniform. Get rid of the saucer cap; you will be wearing a blue beret on your head with a rope on your left shoulder. You will not need the dress shoes but will blouse your dress green pants and wear jump boots.

Second don't give Barrett any problems, or you might find a boot up you-know what. Third, don't give the local police any problems; none of them are very fond of us soldiers. Fourth, there's an office in this building that can help you find housing. I suggest you make friends with a married man quickly so he can take you around to look at rentals. Most of the guys I know rent mobile homes." He pointed down the hall toward more offices indicating that someone could help him with his housing problem.

"Fifth, you don't have to check in until tomorrow, so I suggest you go to the PX and get the items for your uniform plus the unit crest and come back here. We will provide you with a cot for the night." He pointed out the PX on a map of the base. "Sixth, I would get to humping, if I were you. You have a lot of things to do before mess. You can eat with me tonight. Stow your gear behind me, I'll make sure it stays secure."

"You got a jeep up your sleeve I could use by any chance?" asked Dean.

"No, I guess a little rain must fall on all of us. You better hurry."

Dean went to the PX and got the items for his uniform. He was soaked to the skin by the time he had make it to the housing office. They pointed out several mobile home parks that had rentals up for grabs. They would help him with the landlords and the paperwork that needed to be done so that he could live off-base. He made it back just in time for chow.

After eating the Spec Four showed him a pay phone and he called Natalie. He informed her about the day's events and went back to his room. He got his dress uniform ready for the next day, took a shower, and went to bed early.

Book II

101ˢᵗ AIRBOURNE DIVISION

105-gun under a Chinook

FORT CAMPBELL KENTUCKY

Chapter 1

FIRST IMPRESSIONS

Private Brian Clark waved Dean toward a chair. It was Monday morning 10:00 am. He was the battery clerk, seemed to be friendly, but was busy at the moment. He had a slight smile as he spoke to Dean, informing him that Top Barrett was busy with the Battery Commander at the time. Brian was about five-feet ten-inches and a little chubby. He wore round wire rim glasses that seemed to emphasize his round face.

Dean took a seat and looked past the main door to a man that was sitting on another chair waiting to see either Top or the BC. He was thin for his six-foot stature. He had sharp blue eyes that took in all the details around you and about you. He was agile, but Dean could see the strength in his shoulders, legs, and arms. He held out his hand in an act of friendship and introduce himself as Private First-Class Kevin Morton. Dean took the hand and told him his rank and name.

"Where were you stationed before this?" asked Morton.

"Baumholder, Germany with the Eight Infantry Division."

"Man, why did they send you to us? We could have picked you up when we go over there this fall on Reforger 76," Morton said laughing.

"They probably thought you guys would need a guide before you landed in country," Dean responded, smiling broadly.

"So, what's your MOS, man?"

"I'm thirteen bravo mike five."

"What is mike five, I figure you would be a regular gun bunny."

"That means I used to put nuclear weapons together for the eight-inch guns."

"What the h-- I are you doing here man? We're not nuclear capable," Morton responded with his eyebrows disappearing into his hairline.

"I have no idea. So, what do you do in this man' outfit?"

"I'm the forward observer, I hump all day and night with some grunt outfit, calling in the rounds when the troopers get in trouble. It's a lousy job, but someone has to do it," he said, chuckling.

Top Barrett appeared in the doorway; he had a handsome face marred by a scar over his left eye. It was large, coming close to his hairline starting near the bridge of his nose ending near the end of his brow. He was all of six-feet one with strong arms that tried to break out of his shirt sleeves every time he bent his elbows. He looked at Morton and told him that the BC was ready to see him. He turned his attention to Dean and grunted that he should come into his office. Dean went into the office and Top motioned him to take a chair.

"So, you're Spec Four Dean Larson. I've been going over your record, you have some excellent marks. A certificate of achievement on some inspections concerning nuclear rounds. I guess you know we do not have nuclear rounds. Unfortunately, you are stuck with us and we are stuck with you. I do have to say you made a good first impression, you have the right uniform on. To be in the Mike Five program, you have to have some brains, so we are going to throw you in the FDC section to see if you can call out coordinates fast enough.

I want to get you straight right away. I don't put up with any stinkin' thinkin'. I don't care how well you did in Germany. You will have to prove your worth to me and this unit. Do you have any questions?"

"No questions, but a suggestion. I don't do well with numbers. I think FDC would be a bad marriage for me."

"Now you could be getting off on the wrong foot. I didn't ask you for a suggestion Larson, I asked if you had a question for me. You keep your suggestions to yourself, understand?"

"Yes Top, I'll keep that in mind."

"Sergeant Ellis will be your section chief, you will report to him after you see the BC. He will get you squared away with your quarters and your duties. The captain should be coming for you shortly. Welcome to the 101st Airborne Division soldier." With that Barrett turned to some paperwork on his desk and Dean went to the outer office.

Captain Harold Knight appeared at the doorway a few minutes later. He was thin with sharp features. He had kind brown eyes and was built like a runner. He stood about five-foot eleven-inches and Dean could tell after he talked with him for a few minutes that he was very intelligent. Knight took him into his office and explained what he expected of Dean. He was impressed with his record and asked him pointed questions about the nuclear program.

At the end of his questions Dean responded as he had to others. "Do you really want me to answer those questions about eight-inch nukes sir?"

"Well yes, if you can," responded Knight. I can tell you all those things, but then I would have to kill you sir," Dean said with a smile.

"I see, then I won't bother you about those weapons again. I have not been in a unit that deals with such systems so I was curious about them. I should have known that they were classified and not just anyone can know about them."

"Yes sir, that is the story concerning them."

"When you were in Germany, did they have a run in the mornings?"

"Yes sir, we ran between two and three miles a day after doing PT."

"You're going to have to crank up the output Larson. We will be running between three and five miles a day. We will give you two weeks to get into shape. If you fall out of rank after that, you will have extra PT at the end of the day, so get ready. I see that you are married so I imagine you're going to need housing off base. Sergeant Ellis, your section chief is also married and living off base. I imagine that he can help with that little problem. Ellis is a good man and is very good directing things in FDC. It looks like you have one child."

"Yes, a little boy and one on the way, so I would like to find a place to live as soon as possible, sir."

"You know that we will be going to Germany on Reforger 76 this fall and that in about twenty days we will be in the midst of war games with the 82nd Airbourne Division. I'll ask Ellis to give you as much time off as possible to take care of your responsibilities. The problem is that you don't know any jobs around here. You have most likely forgotten what a section does on the guns and you have not been trained for the FDC."

"This is true sir, but my wife is due this fall and I can't have her living with her folks all the time."

"Yes, this is true we will see what we can work out. Now, do you plan on making the army a career? You have some very good marks on your evaluations and this certificate of achievement would help at the promotion board."

"No, sir I plan on using my GI bill, going back to school, and becoming a teacher."

"That is too bad I think you could go far. May I suggest that you sign up for college classes here on base. The period starts in September and they will work around the times you are out in the field. They will cut you slack to make up the time lost in the classroom. I would highly recommend you getting signed up. If you decide to stay in the service, college classes will go a long way toward promotion. Do you have any questions for me Larson?"

"No sir, and thank you for the heads up concerning the classes. I'm going to take full advantage of that program."

Knight dismissed Dean, and asked Clark to escort him to where the FDC was located. They found Ellis in a room where a lot of the FDC equipment was located. Clark introduced Dean to Sergeant Ellis. He was twenty-five years old, a buck sergeant; a very stout man built like a triangle that wore black framed glasses with a crew cut hair style. After a few minutes of talking with him, Dean could tell that he was also very intelligent. There was another man in the midst of the equipment, he stood quietly watching the exchange of words being played out between Dean and Ellis. Dean had to explain about his mike five status. Ellis asked him several pointed questions on nuclear weapons at which point Dean informed him that he could tell him nothing.

Ellis nodded that he understood. He pointed at the other man in the room introduced him to Private William Clinton and then gave him his nickname. "But you can call Clinton "Wild Willie" because that fits him to a "T".

Willie held out his right hand and Dean clinched it hard. Willie had a strong hand shake and a twinkle in his eye that said he was full of mischief. He had brown curly hair and an infectious smile. He had boyish good looks a thin physique in a six-foot frame. Dean instantly liked him and he had hardly said a word.

"So why do they call you Wild Willie?" Dean asked.

"I've been in the service for over two years and I'm still a private. Trouble tends to follow me wherever I go," he responded with a broad grin.

"Bull. You cause most of the trouble you get in. I have to say he is good at plotting out fire missions, otherwise I would have gotten rid of him for all the headaches he gives me," remarked Ellis.

He instructed Willie to take Dean to the room that the section was assigned and give him the bunk next to his. Willie showed Dean the room, as well as where the supply room was located. Dean got his bedding, pillow, and bathroom items from the supply sergeant and got his area situated. He got out of his dress greens and pulled on a utility uniform. Willie showed up at noon and walked him to the mess hall where he ate a fairly decent meal.

Dean found out that Willie came from Ohio and that he had several girlfriends waiting for him back home. The girls were the ones that usually got him in hot water with the army,

Every time he took leave and went home, they hung onto him and got him drunk. He would be late getting back to the post, thus he would be considered AWOL. He was reduced in rank and money was held out of his pay.

It was the same way every time he went home. Willie couldn't break the habit. He had also been in several fights which had not endeared him to the higher ranks. He had gotten in trouble with the law before the service and they had given him the option of either jail time or three years in the army. He had chosen the army but trouble still plagued him.

They were joined by PFC Richard McDonald, a tall skinny young man that stood about six-feet two-inches. He was another member of the FDC section. He had brown eyes and dark hair with a crooked smile that quickly emerged every time someone told a joke. Even a bad joke would bring on the crooked grin. He sat quietly as Dean and Willie talked about their military careers. The only thing Dean found out about Richard before they had to go to the noon formation was that he came from Flagstaff, Arizona.

Ellis got his men formed up with the rest of the battery. He had four other men besides Willie and McDonald. Smoke James Ashton called the formation to attention and received the report from the individual section chiefs that everyone was present and accounted for. Ashton reported to Captain Knight and he gave the battery into Ashton's hands, leaving the area.

Ashton put everyone at parade rest and looked over the battery for a few minutes. "Listen up, I want you to grab your ears and pull real hard. Pull until you get your head out of your tail pipes and take a deep breath. We need to start thinking about the things that are coming up."

Dean couldn't help it, he smiled at the ear joke because Ashton made sure that everyone had grabbed their ears. Smoke stopped and pointed at Dean with a scowl on his face. "You think that is funny soldier? I suggest that you wipe that smile off your face before I put you digging a fifty-foot trench behind the barracks. Do you understand?"

Dean instantly wiped the grin off his face and affirmed that he had understood. Ashton looked around at the others and walked back to the middle of the formation.

"We are about to go down to Bragg and play war games against the 82nd Airbourne Division. I don't plan on losing to those pukes, do you all understand? I want everyone to do their jobs and know them in, out, and sideways. Have all your gear ready and in good working order. All the goats better be in perfect running order. If one goes down, I'm going to clean a toilet with someone's face. The guns need to be bore sited and all the components in readiness. I know that I'm speaking English, but if someone doesn't understand, your section chiefs better sort things out or I'm going to be all over you like flies on a dead carcass. Any questions?"

He gave everyone just a few seconds to respond and then he dismissed the battery to get to work. He pointed to Ellis and Dean and called them over to him.

"Who's this new soldier Sergeant Ellis?"

"This is Spec Four Dean Larson, Smoke."

"So do you know your business when it comes to FDC mister?"

"Actually, I dealt with nuclear rounds at my last duty station."

What the h-- I you doing in this outfit? Listen, we don't need to coddle anyone, so you better learn to be useful in short order or I'll make your live miserable. Ellis, get him squared away and productive, do you understand? Soldier, never smile in my formation again. We are warriors in this outfit. Our job is to kill the enemy, I doubt if you are a good soldier, yet."

With that, Ashton turned toward the motor pool. Ellis shook his head and turned toward the barracks and the FDC room which was located on the first floor.

"Sorry Larson, but you just saw his good side. Some days he is nastier than today. I'll try to get you trained before we go to Bragg, but both of us have a lot to do and not enough time to get it all done. I'll tell you what, why don't you go down to the housing office and see if you can get some leads on rentals and I'll take you out to look at some tomorrow night.

"Thanks, man. I have to warn you. I am not good with numbers. I told Top that, but he figured if I was good with nukes, then I'd be good with deflections and azimuths."

Ellis shook his head again and turned back to the barracks. Dean continued to the sidewalk and down the road to the housing office. He noticed the weather was a lot different from Germany and Idaho. The sun was out but it was humid and hot. He was sweating up a storm. He hoped it would not be like this all the time.

He got several leads on rentals and returned to the barracks to help Willie with some of his work on the gear. He gave Ellis the addresses and he went into the office and to the local phone book which had a map of the local area. Ellis figured out the route he would use to taxi Larson around and check out the rentals.

After evening formation, Dean went to have dinner at the mess hall. The food was not as good as it had been in Germany. He played with it more than he ate. He was thinking about the day's events. He was fairly certain that Ashton and Barrett didn't like him for whatever reason. He didn't like them much either. He thought of several plans that might get them to have a more favorable attitude towards him, but all of them would be considered kissing up by the others and he was not into doing that.

He was interrupted by Wild Willie who flopped his tray down next to him. He looked at Dean long and hard.

"What's up, man? You look like someone shot your dog."

"It feels like I'm already on the wrong side of Top and Smoke and I've only been here one day."

"Don't worry about those two. They'll leave you alone as soon as you show them that you know what you're doing."

"That's just it, I don't know much of anything about FDC."

"I'll try to help you out. Lighten up, man. I'm always in trouble, but when the calls come down to work out fire missions, I do my business and they cut me a lot of slack." He nudged Dean and smiled at him making Larson feel better.

Before he bedded down for the night, he called Natalie and told her about his first day on the job. She told him that she loved him and that she would pray for him.

Chapter 2

FRUSTRATIONS

Dean stayed away from Ashton and Barrett as much as possible. He soon lost his smile and he took to heart everything Ashton said in formation. The unit seemed to be more disciplined than the eighth, but it was also a more elite group of soldiers. They did the run the next morning and Dean made it all the way. They only did a three-mile run and Dean was glad that he had continued to run while he was home on leave.

Ellis sat up an area that he could practice finding the deflections and azimuth on imagined fire missions to help Dean get ready for his new job. Dean started getting the hang of working out coordinates, but he was very slow at it. Ellis suggested that he would speed up after a while but Dean knew his own limitations and when it came to working on the nuke, speed was not required but being precise was a necessity. His father had nagged him over fixing machinery at home when he was younger but Dean had ignored him and did it his way. His father had to admit that when Dean got done, the piece of equipment worked well and ran longer. When he was in school, Dean had two math teachers and had not gotten along with either one of them. This could be one of the reasons he had such a hard time comprehending the subject.

That evening, Ellis took him around to the possible rentals that housing had given him to check on. They only had time to check on four of them. They were all in mobile home parks and were on the Kentucky side near Hopkinsville. As Dean checked on the rentals, he soon learned that you had to be quick looking into them. Two of them were already rented out and Ellis suggested that they bypass the third one because it sat in a hollow and that when the wind blew through them, it could destroy a home. They didn't get to the fourth one until after dark. The trailer was still available and the rent was a little lower than the rest of them. As Dean looked at the place, he realized that it was older and more run down. It had enough rooms and everything worked in it. He was talking to the landlord about rent and the down payment when Ellis shut the lights off on them. Ellis told them to be quiet. Dean suddenly heard the scurrying of little feet. Ellis turned on the lights and Dean saw large bugs running back into the shadows.

"Larson, can your wife live with cockroaches?"

"No, I don't think she can," Dean said with a little awe in his voice.

"Sir, you don't spray for bugs. Do ya?"

"No, that is why the rent is a little cheaper."

"I don't think this is the right place for my family," stammered Dean. With that, he turned and exited the rental with Ellis right behind him.

They both got into Ellis's car and started back to Campbell.

"Those things were cockroaches?" asked Larson in an incredulous voice.

"You don't have cockroaches in Idaho?"

"No. Those things were fast and I think two of them could have carried my little boy out of the mobile home. Natalie would have been screaming all the time. I couldn't have gotten her to live there."

"Well, you better keep looking, then. I suggest that you ask the next one if they spray for bugs."

The next day, Top called Dean into his office and asked him if he had an international driver's license. Dean affirmed that he did, so Top asked him to give the rest of the drivers lessons on the signs and ins and outs of operating a vehicle in Europe. He sent him to Ashton to work out a schedule for the classes. Smoke also made him the assistant driver for FDC's Gamma Goat. This was fine with Dean, he didn't mind driving, in fact he enjoyed it.

Ellis had Dean working with McDonald since he was the driver and suggested he get to know him a lot better. When McDonald had enlisted he had gotten a large bonus. Richard used part of that money to buy himself a fairly new Dodge Charger. Ellis suggested that Dean could maybe strike up a deal with him to take him around to the rentals. Ellis had a lot of things going on and didn't have a lot of time taking Dean places.

Richard was a little taller than Dean and he wore dark rimmed glasses with almost a walrus type mustache under a broad nose. He was stout and very good at the jobs in FDC. He agreed to take Dean to look at rental as long as he bought the gas and a couple of beers afterwards. McDonald was not very friendly at first but he started warming up to Dean after a day or two. Dean found out that he planned on making the army a career and he had at least one more year in Campbell. About a month after Reforger 76, he would be going on leave for thirty days. He loved hunting so they both enjoyed talking about their adventures.

Dean did not get to the housing office until Thursday and was too busy Friday to go hunt for a home. Saturday, McDonald took him to three different places to check out the mobile homes, but the first two had just been rented. The last one Richard drove him to, they stopped outside the park. He looked at the name of the park for a few minutes, turned to Dean and shook his head. He informed Dean that he would not want to live there. One of his friends had lived there about a year ago and a bad wind storm blew in and it had picked up about six of the mobile homes moving them off their foundations. His friend never found some of his household items. After that Larson agreed that he did not want to put his family in danger, so they did not check on the last possible rental.

Dean took Richard to a pub. He bought him lunch and they had a couple of beers. McDonald asked him about Idaho and his family. Dean bragged on his wife and John. As he was talking about them, he became very homesick and realized how much he missed them. It brought on depression and he hardly said anything to Richard as they drove back to the barracks.

He went to a pay phone and called Natalie, and told her the bad news. Hearing her voice only make things worse. He felt frustrated because things were not going his way. After the conversation he went to his room and laid down on his bed. His mind went in all kinds of directions as he tried to think of a way to change his circumstances

Another problem arose on Friday; the battalion ran five miles. Dean fell out with several others. When they got near the battery area, one of the gun sergeants wrote down their names.

They were required to do extra PT. Dean told the NCO that he was exempt for another week but the sergeant shook his head, saying that no one had told him. He took his complaint to Barrett who looked at him, then informed him that a little extra physical training would do him good. He tried to argue the point but Barrett gave him a look and told him to take it like a man and to do what he was told. He suggested that he would like to talk to Knight about it but was informed that the Captain was at a meeting at headquarters.

That's when Barrett came around the desk toward Dean. "You moron, don't you ever question one of my orders." Dean quickly stood and opened the outer door and called for Clark, the clerk, to come in. Barrett stopped and Dean smiled, apologizing for irritating him in front of Clark. He did the extra PT, but it made it too late for Dean to check on rentals. He also realized that he had made Barrett a real enemy now.

All of the next week, Dean went out looking for a place but all of them had been rented or they had insect problems. Training was not going well; he was slowly gaining in speed but it was not good enough for the standards of the battery. Ellis tried several things to help him get faster and slowly helped him speed up. He also fell out of another run, so he had to do more PT. He was getting the hang of driving the goat and maintaining it. It had been two lousy weeks and he was wondering when he would get a break.

To add to his stress, Ashton was harassing him whenever he got a chance. The only good thing was that he was getting along with Ellis and the section. He had got to know McDonald and the rest of the section a lot better. McDonald loved to listen to heavy metal and wore some wild clothes when off duty. Willie had invited him to go drinking with him but Dean was using every spare minute to look for a place.

Morton had been in and out of the unit since Dean met him in the offices, but they had not connected except to say "hi" occasionally. While Dean was having dinner in the mess hall, Morton came over and sat next to him.

Morton had been on several field exercises, not only calling artillery in, but also working with air strikes. It was a Thursday and Morton smelled like a goat. He had not taken a shower yet, but he was more hungry for real food than hot water. He told Dean that he was going on leave and that he was going to get married this weekend. They were going on their honeymoon for a week in Nashville, to take in the sites.

Dean congratulated and listened to him as he talked about his bride-to-be and everything else he was going to see on his time off. A thought suddenly came to Dean. "Hey man where are you going to live?"

"I've got a rental all ready for us after my leave."

"I've been looking all over the place and I haven't been able to find a place for my family. Do they have any other rentals in that park?"

"I don't know Dean, but the landlord and I are friends. I'll tell you what, I'll call him tomorrow before I leave to go back home and get hitched."

"Thanks, man. How's the rent and does he spray for bugs?"

"Yes, there are no cockroaches and the rent is reasonable for me. You will have to talk to him about the prices. It depends on how many bedrooms there are and what the place looks like, I guess. If he has something coming open, I'll arrange for you to meet with him."

"Sounds good, Morton. I can't tell you how much I appreciate it, Kevin."

Dean asked him about his field exercises and how he did. Morton thought they had gone well and that he was not only ready for the 82nd, but he was ready for Reforger 76. He asked Dean how well he was doing with FDC.

Dean admitted that he was too slow and that no matter how he tried he was not getting much faster at the job. Morton tried to encourage him, but Dean had this feeling of impending doom though he was hopeful to get a place to live soon. A nagging doubt ate at his heart as to if he would ever get his family to Kentucky. He was suddenly wishing that he had never left Germany.

Friday, Morton came into the FDC room at about eleven in the morning. He was dressed in civilian clothes and had a large suitcase in hand. He asked to see Dean and informed him that the landlord had a vacancy coming up at the end of the week and he was willing to talk to Dean about it.

Morton told him that Dean would be over to see him Saturday at around ten in the morning. He gave Dean the address and told him that the man he wanted to see was Jon Kelly. After he left, Dean talked Ellis into giving him a ride to see Mr. Kelly

Jon Kelly was ex-military and Dean guessed that he was in his late twenties or early thirties. He was on disability. The chopper that he had been in, had lost power and came down hard, messing up his back.

He stood about six one, had a handsome face with a barrel chest. He told Dean that the couple was moving out so the mobile home was a mess and that he would have to look past that. The couple had given him permission to look the place over as they were out having breakfast.

Dean was impressed with the park; many of the mobile homes had tie downs. They were thick straps that went over the roof and hooked into anchors in the ground. The home that Jon took Dean to had this feature. They went inside and Dean liked what he saw, it was fairly clean and the furniture was in good shape. Lights all turned on and the faucets gave good clean water. It had three bedrooms and one-and-half baths. The fridge and stove seemed to be working well.

Dean asked about bugs and Jon assured him that they sprayed for the little critters once a month. Dean took a deep breath and inquired about rent and utilities. Jon gave him the prices and the down payment but added since he was a friend of Kevin that he would lower it by twenty dollars.

Dean did the math in his head and realized that it would be close but they could do it. He shook Jon's hand, took out his check book, and paid him the down payment. Finally, he could give Natalie some good news. Ellis took him back to the barracks and he called Natalie right away.

She would make arrangements for a flight to Campbell the next day and leave that week, so she could come right way before he left on maneuvers. It was a Saturday and hopefully Dean could help her get things arranged and a way to the store so they could buy food. He told her to send out his 30-30 rifle; he might find some time to do some hunting.

He went to his room where Willie was talking to McDonald. They wanted to go out to one of the bar and grills that evening. They invited Dean to go along with them since he had something to celebrate. Willie also invited his buddy Arthur Garcia who was a gun bunny. He owned an old Chevy that was as big as a WWII tank and they decide to take it.

At six that evening, the four of them piled into the Chevy and headed off to the bar and grill. They all paid for their own meals but Dean bought the first round of drinks. They only had two beers a piece and left for a bar down Ft. Campbell Blvd., a couple of blocks.

It was dark, crowded and smoke filled. Dean quickly saw why they came; it had women. One of the ladies hit on him, but he told her that he was married. She informed him that she didn't care, but he made it obvious that he was not interested and nursed his beer while the other three men hit on some ladies.

He held himself to four beers total for the night because he realized that he was going to have to drive everyone else back to the barracks, The rest of them were downing the beer fast and the women helping them enlarge the amount on the drinking tab. Three men appeared in the door of the bar and they seemed to be looking for someone. It was so dark, they had to get fairly close to individuals to make out faces.

One of them got close to Garcia and yelled at one of his friends over the music. The man was big and stout standing at six-one or so. He came over and pulled Arthur away from the woman and pushed him up against a wall. He made some comment that Arthur was dancing with his girl and raised a fist to punch him. Dean had no idea where Willie came from but before the guy could throw the fist, Willie had slapped him upside the head, knocking him off balance. The guy shook it off and looked Willie over.

"I have nothing against you. Why don't you go stand over in the corner before I hurt you?" The man spat out in anger.

"He's my friend, redneck, and when you hit him, it's like you're hitting me. Now the girl seems to prefer Art's company and I can see why. You're as ugly as the backside of a pig."

All three men went for Willie at once. Dean had positioned himself close to the man on Willie's right side so when the man moved, Dean hit the man in his right ear, causing him to stumble into his friend. Dean kicked the man between the legs, causing the man to go down to his knees groaning.

Willie moved like lightning, he hit the man in front of him twice, knocking him over the man that Dean had knocked down. Art was going to take the other man on, but before he could get involved Willie kicked the man in the chest, knocking him down. As he tried to get up, Willie hit him with his forearm in the temple, knocking him unconscious. The boyfriend was starting to stand, but he should have stayed down. Willie kicked him in the back of the head and everyone thought it was all over.

Willie yelled out a challenge to anyone that came from Kentucky. Several men stood up, but more soldiers stood and the fight moved from Willie to other parts of the bar. Willie stared in that direction, but McDonald intercepted him.

"We need to get out of here, the barkeep called the police."

"H-- l, I'll take them on," declared Willie.

"No, you're not. We're getting out of here. I'm the only one that will go to jail if they catch us," shouted Dean. He had thrown the first blow. He could not afford to lose rank and money if they gave him an Article 15.

Dean grabbed Willie and forced him toward the exit while McDonald had Garcia in tow. Garcia gave Dean the keys to his old red Chevy Impala, telling him that he was too drunk to drive it.

Dean got behind the steering wheel and started the big V-8 up. His first inclination was to stomp the gas, but that would bring attention to their getaway. He got out on the boulevard and slowly sped up. People were pouring out of the bar. Some of them were escaping the fight, others were running away before the police got there. A couple of them were looking for the four trouble makers. Dean was sure that he had put enough distance between them that they could not tell what the license plate number was. He could hear the sirens closing the distance between their position.

"You two in the back, get your heads down. Someone may have told them that there was four of us," Dean suggested.

"Man, I'm going to hang around with you Dean. You had my back when things went crazy?" Willie suggested with a laugh.

"Are you kidding me, I don't have enough time in the day to take care of you and still get my job done. You are trouble, man, and if you don't cause problems, Art finds it for you. You two should get married. It is clear you both could go through life causing revolutions wherever you go."

Garcia laughed, his cheesy mustache making a half circle around his upper lip. His medium frame bounced in the seat at Dean's comment. McDonald and Willie gave big belly laughs, but kept their heads down.

The police passed them, they didn't even slow nor did they look in Dean's direction. Dean stopped at the gate. They could smell the beer and asked Dean to step out of the car. They made him walk a straight line and touch his nose. He passed so they sent them on their way. Willie suggested that they go out the next day, but Dean and McDonald declined. Dean liked Willie and wanted to stay close but, there was no way he could afford hanging around with him. He was glad to hit the sack, and was soon asleep.

Dean awoke and went to the mess for breakfast. He was drinking his second cup of coffee when McDonald joined him. "A real exciting night, wasn't it?"

"Yea, I don't know if I could handle that too often," Dean responded.

"I'm with you. I think I'll pass on a lot of their invitations for now on."

"They're going to ask you if you want to go out tonight again Dean. They were looking for you a few minutes ago."

Willie and Garcia appeared in the doorway. They looked around, spotted Dean and came over to the table. "Been looking for you Larson. You want to go out on the town tonight?" Willie asked.

"No thanks, man. One night a month with that much excitement is enough for me. Besides I'm an old married man and my wife will be here in about a week, so you need to find yourself another wing man."

"Man, that's too bad, we could have some good times together. If you need any help, man, just tell me and I'll be there for you."

"Thanks Willie, I'll keep that in mind."

Garcia and Willie went to get their food. They came and sat with McDonald, but Dean finished his coffee and went back to the barracks. He could not rely on Morton to give him a ride to base because of his schedule with the infantry. It was out of Ellis' way to come and get him for the morning formation and he could not afford to have McDonald coming out to get him every morning. Richard was nice, but he did not think he would want to get up that early. Dean started asking around and found out Sergeant Ross Porter was living in the same court.

He was told that Porter was a very nice guy and he was waiting for housing on base to come open but nothing was available. He also had a pickup and Dean was hoping to talk him into picking up some house hold items that Natalie had sent by freight. They were supposed to arrive the day before Natalie flew in.

Monday morning, he introduced himself to Sergeant Porter after PT and the three-mile run. They were right, Porter was a very nice guy. He was a short buck sergeant with a wife and two daughters. He stood about five one with dirty blonde hair; blue eyes, and a dry sense of humor.

Dean told him his situation and Porter immediately consented to help him. He was glad to give Dean rides until he got his own vehicle. This took a lot of pressure off Dean, and things were beginning to look up.

PT and runs were miserable for Dean, he never liked running in the first place. It was worse in Kentucky since the heat and humidity sapped all his strength. He would walk out on the PT field and before they started calisthenics, he started sweating around his neck line and in his arm pits.

By the time the run was over, he could take his T-shirt off and wring it out. He started getting a rash in a very awkward place at the top of his legs. Willie told him not to wear underwear during the run. This seemed to help but felt weird to him so he started wearing lose fitting boxers. They also gave him ointment to help heal things up.

On Friday, they had another five-mile run and Dean didn't make it. Ashton was at the finish line and he belittled Dean in front of everyone as he had on several occasions. He ordered him to do extra PT after the work day. Dean asked him if he could skip it, but Smoke gave him no mercy and told him to be there at five in the afternoon.

He told Porter what happened and he agreed to take Dean to the freight office and pick up the house hold items after he was done. After they off loaded pots, pans, towels and the rest of the goods, Porter took Dean right back to the barracks. Dean packed up his gear that evening after dinner so he could move it over to the rental when they picked Natalie and John up at the airport.

Richard had Dean at the airfield just a little before two in the afternoon on Saturday, the jet was few minutes late. It made Dean all the more anxious, but that vanished as soon as he saw Natalie and John at the gate. This time John came running into Dean's arms which made his day.

Natalie looked worn out and was starting to show with the new baby. She had that look that said that she felt ugly and don't touch her. It also said Dean better hug her and tell her that he loved her like crazy. He waded in cautiously, telling her how much he missed her and that he was so glad that she was finally here. He gave her a hug and kissed her with the longing that he felt in his heart. She responded and kissed him back. He introduced her to McDonald who shook her hand gently. He tried to win over John, but the little boy would not respond, he just hugged Dean's leg.

Richard got them home and the two of them started putting things away. John was wide awake because he slept most of the way on the flight. He helped and was also getting in the way. They finally found some of his toys and got him playing in his room. Dean had bought some of the things that he knew they would need for a couple of days.

Natalie fixed some spaghetti and meat balls. They ate in silence until Natalie complained about the humidity. Dean told her that she better get used to it, the weather was either hot and humid or raining and humid. She gave him a small laugh and returned to her dinner.

After they got John settled down, they sat on the couch discussing their problems. In two days, Dean would be going to Fort Bragg for a week to play war games against the 82nd Airbourne leaving Natalie on her own. He hated it, but that was how it was going down.

Ashton and Bennett were not giving Dean any slack, it was like they decided they didn't like him and they were going to get rid of him. The more pressure they applied to him, the more mistakes he was making. Then there was Reforger 76. Dean could be in

Germany when Natalie was having the baby and he didn't want to be absent when the little one came.

Natalie listened intently and finally told Dean that she would pray about it and hopefully the Lord would move in their behalf. She finally admitted that she was ready for bed. They called it an evening. At first Dean slept well, but woke up about two in the morning and thought about his problems some more.

Chapter 3

FRIENDSHIPS

It was late morning when they got a knock on their mobile home door. It was Ross Porter with Suzan, his wife, and their two daughters. Darlene was the oldest while Angela was two years younger. Both of them were brunette with bright blue eyes, and were slightly taller than their parents. They were well developed with beautiful round faces.

Suzan was about as tall as Ross, but thinner with short brown hair. She had sad green eyes, setting it off with a thin smile. She brought over a casserole dish and welcomed Natalie to the neighborhood.

Natalie invited them in and offered them drinks. They accepted the invitation. Natalie apologized for the mess and Suzan readily forgave, suggesting that they had moved several times and expected things out of order. They wanted her to know that the Porter family were only eight homes down and were willing to give the Larson family any kind of help they needed.

The girls were instantly attracted to John and quickly made friends with the little boy. He was shy at first, but was soon sitting in their laps showing them his toys. Darlene was about sixteen and Dean saw a babysitter in the future.

Ross asked Dean about the places they had been to while in Europe. Dean described the eight countries that had visited while on the continent. Ross would interrupt every so often to ask a question. He was hoping that his next duty station would be Germany. About the time they were going to leave Natalie asked Suzan if she knew where there was a good church. Suzan's smile grew large as she said yes.

They offered to pick up the Larson family the next day, but Natalie declined because of the chaos they were living in. She did ask the Porters to pick them up the next Sunday. She didn't ask Dean if he wanted to go, she decided the Larson family would be attending church the next Sunday.

After the Porters left, Dean and Natalie argued over the church decision, but Natalie had made up her mind that it was not going to be like Baumholder. They were going to find a good church and attend. Dean tried to give some excuses, but even as he spurted them out, they seemed lame. Natalie spoke out the right reasons and Dean could not argue with them. She told him they had nothing but trouble since they left Germany and maybe they needed God on their side, maybe He was making it tough on them so they would start to seek Him. With that kind of reasoning, Dean put all other arguments aside. They continued to put the house in order.

At about five pm that evening Morton showed up with his new wife Carrie. She had fried chicken, potatoes, and salad. They brought them over to welcome the Larsons as neighbors. Carrie had been married before and had a daughter Joan that was four years old. John and Joan became fast friends as long as Joan didn't play with his favorite toys.

It took Natalie and Carrie a little while to become close because both of them were shy. Once that barrier was broken, they could spend hours talking. The Morton's stayed an hour that evening with Morton and Dean doing most of the visiting.

Most of the weekend was spent getting settled into the new home. Suzan Porter came over Sunday after church and drove Natalie to the Commissary to pick up food for the week. It was just the two ladies and they seemed to forge a close bond quickly. Dean was glad because he would soon be gone for a week to Fort Bragg. He was looking forward to it in a way. He had never been to North Carolina and he was excited to see how his new unit did things in mock combat.

The rest of the week, the battery continued to get ready to deploy to Bragg. In the midst of that, Ellis tried to make Dean useful to the section by having Willie and McDonald work with him on fake fire missions. Dean did gain some speed, but he was still considered to be too slow.

He also improved on the runs, and finished all of them. It was not so humid that Friday and the five-mile run drained him, but he was able to come into the barracks area with the rest of the battery. He noticed that Smoke Aston seemed disappointed when he came in with the rest of the men.

It was like he was hoping that Dean would mess up so he could discipline him. By Friday night, the battery was ready to load up on C-130 transport planes to fly down to Fort Bragg on Monday morning. Dean had never flown on the C-130s, so he was excited about the new experience.

He was worn out by Friday when he walked into Natalies's warm embrace after work. She was ready to talk, so Dean sat down in one of the overstuffed chairs in the living room to listen after grabbing a cup of coffee from the kitchen.

"Did you know that Ross spent two tours in Vietnam?"

"I heard that he had seen some serious action in 'Nam,' but he never talks about it," replied Dean.

"Well, he's a hero Dean. He has a Silver Star, and two Purple Hearts to name a few decorations. I guess that last medal, the Purple Heart kept him in the hospital for about a month."

"Who told you that, Babe?"

"Sue, she was over for about two hours today, responded Natalie. Yeah, they got married right out of high school. He had a good job at his father's business. I guess they were doing really well when he got his draft notice from Uncle Sam. They had the two girls and he was older than the average draftee. He was really different when he came back from his first tour. She thought that he would go back to working for his father, but he signed up for another two years in the army. She said that every once in a while, she will see the old Ross, the one she fell in love with."

"Very interesting. I guess war would change you a bunch. He seems to be adjusting and he is a very nice guy. He is becoming a good friend and will watch my back. He told me that he overheard Top and Smoke talking about me the other day. They were not happy with my progress with FDC, they consider me dead weight and were discussing different options about getting rid of me, one way or another."

"Those two are still messing with you Dean. Don't worry about it. I've been praying and I had a dream the other night. I believe it was about God helping you. I saw this man standing at the top of a tree. He was looking down on everyone else and commanding these little trees to go here or to go there. A finger appeared out from a cloud and flicked him off the tree.

Dean took a long sip of his coffee. Natalie had told him about other dreams she had and they often came true. He could not see it happening, both men were at the top of the heap and he was at the bottom. He couldn't see them making a big mistake in their careers at this late stage of the game. Of course, they could get sick or maybe a helicopter would land on one of them, not that he was wishing for it.

He took another sip of coffee and looked at Natalie. "I guess we'll see what happens, Natalie. They are at the top of the food chain and both of them look healthy. It would have to be a God thing, but I am fed up with them riding me all the time."

"You watch, Dean. I am betting on God. He is going to do something on your behalf. I told Sue and she felt the Spirit. She thinks something is going to happen also."

Dean said nothing, but he was doubtful. Why would God do anything in his behalf? He was not a believer like Natalie. He looked over at her and she was giving him the look that said she knew what he was thinking. They smiled at each other and Natalie went to the kitchen to fix dinner.

Natalie had decided to go to church. The Porter family showed up at their home at 10:30 am, Dean hauled his family out to the big station wagon and they were off to the services.

It was a beautiful sunny humid day in Tennessee and they got to the church about fifteen minutes before service. Dean wanted to sit in the back pews of the church, but Ross led his family to the second row and Natalie followed, sitting next to Sue. Dean was the last one, squeezing into the pew next to the aisle. He was thinking about a quick escape if things got too weird.

Pastor Jethro Jackson came over and introduced himself to the Larsons. He held out a thick hand to Dean which had a solid strong grip when he shook Dean's hand. Jethro gave them a warm welcome and pointed out his wife who was up on the stage getting ready to lead worship. Sally Jackson was big chested with dark hair. She dressed well and wore a fair amount of jewelry. She had a handsome face, a nice figure and a wonderful voice for singing.

The service started with her leading the congregation in several worship songs that touched Dean. He enjoyed that portion and was awed by her voice as she sang a special song with the piano accompanying her. Jethro gave a sermon on the third person of the Godhead, the Holy Spirit.

Dean had never heard anything about the Spirit before, he had only heard about the Father and the Son. The message caught his attention and Jackson was an exciting speaker. He was walking back and forth in front of the first pew.

He suddenly stopped in front of Dean, leaned over the first seats and laid a hand on Dean's chest. At the same time he said, "And you can sense the Holy Spirit when He touches you."

Dean felt the jolt of electricity go from Jethro's hand, through his chest, and down to his toe nails. It scared him; he had never felt anything like that in his life. The sensation immediately left him, but he knew that his eyes had gotten as big as saucers. He moved a little closer to the aisle and he lost all presence of mind concerning the message. He noticed Natalie watching him closely and she leaned over and asked him if he was alright. He just nodded back at her and looked away.

Pastor Jethro was at the door shaking hands and saying goodbye with Sally. Jehtro introduced his wife to the Larsons and they spoke for a few minutes. Ross invited the pastor and his family over for a barbecue in the evening. The Porters had also previously invited the Larsons and the Morton family over as a goodbye bash before they went to Bragg.

Dean was hoping the Jacksons would decline, but they agreed to come. He'd had enough weird for one day, but it looked like he was going to have to put up with some more.

When they were at home, Natalie talked to him about the sermon. It stirred up a discussion, allowing Dean to understand what he had heard better.

"So, what happened to you, Dean, when the pastor touched you on the chest?"

"I felt this jolt of power go through me. It didn't hurt. It was good, but so strange. It scared me. I have never felt anything like it before."

"That was the Holy Spirit moving on you Dean. God is trying to get your attention. You need to take heed. God loves you and has a plan for you." She caressed his cheek with her soft hand

and leaned over him, kissing him on the forehead.

"What could He possibly want with me? I have no outstanding talents, nor am I very smart."

"Maybe that is exactly why He wants you, or maybe He sees something in you that you don't see. Don't fight against it to long Dean. I don't want you broken over this. I know you can be stubborn. Don't be, I love you."

He had a lot more questions, but he didn't want to get into a deeper discussion than the one he had just climbed out of. He didn't say much for the rest of the day. He concentrated on packing and getting ready for the trip to Ft. Bragg.

As he packed, he mulled over what had happened that morning. He tried to explain the jolt away in his mind, he'd had a few minor encounters when Natalies's old pastor had talked to him. This one was more powerful and it was still causing him to question the very things he had always believed.

Kevin and Carrie joined them as they walked over to the Porter's rental for the barbeque. Carrie and Natalie fell behind as Natalie told Carrie about life in Idaho. Kevin drilled Dean on what he was taking with him to Bragg. Dean was an old hand at deploying to other places, so he had all his equipment ready.

The Jacksons were already at the barbecue, they had a daughter by the name of Sarah. She was built and looked a lot like her mother but her hair was loose and long coming past her waist. Tom was their son and he looked a lot like Sally also, just a smaller version with less hair. He was three years younger than his sister who was seventeen.

Ross introduced the Morton's to the Jacksons and a friendly conversation ensued. When the food was done, Jethro blessed it. Ross Porter was a great cook; the hamburgers were grilled to perfection. After everyone ate, they played some games and the Jacksons had to excuse themselves for evening church.

Jethro invited the Morton's to attend a service and he asked if he could pray for the men for their safety and the women since they would be alone. They also offered help for the women while the men were gone. After they ended the prayer, the Jacksons started walking away, but Jethro suddenly stopped and turned around. He walked up to Dean.

"I feel like I'm supposed to confirm something to you. You were made for such a time as this and the Lord has a special plan for you. Be warned, there are some real obstacles ahead. Just in case there are any doubts in your mind, He touched you today." With that, he turned and walked away.

"Wow, that was a real interesting word, has someone else told you that Dean?" asked Suzan.

"Well, kind of. Natalie's pastor spoke a similar word over me back home."

"So, that is what he said to you at the wedding? Why didn't you tell me when I asked you about it, Dean?"

"Well, it's out now. I'm interested to see how it all comes about," Ross spoke up.

"Yes. Let's just drop the subject for tonight. The men are leaving tomorrow. Let's enjoy the last few hours before they take off," Sue interjected.

The two older girls kept John and Joan busy while the adults talked among themselves. Kevin and Carrie seemed to be glad to get off the subject of God. Both of them believed in a God but saw no real need for Him in their lives. The ladies talked about getting together several times to keep each other company. While the men talked about the upcoming maneuvers. The party ended early, since the men had to get up early.

Chapter 4

82ⁿᵈ AIRBORNE DIVISION

Dean almost lost his balance as he ran out of the back of the C-130 cargo plane. The prop wash from the big engines created a wind that almost knocked him off his feet. The rest of the men had the same problem. Sergeant Ellis was in front of him and had to retrieve his helmet. Wild Willie had to grab Dean by an arm to steady himself as they came down the ramp.

McDonald drove the goat out of the back of the plane and joined the rest of the section in a wooded area that Ellis led them too. They heard the engines grow loader in pitch, the ramp went up, and the plane taxied down the runway. It gained speed and took off, slowly gaining altitude to clear the area.

Another plane landed and it disgorged the number one gun and crew. The planes continued to land and take off until the whole battery was on the ground. Captain Knight and Barrett got the convoy arranged and they started down the road at a nice pace.

Dean was sitting with Willie and the rest of the crew in the back of the Gamma Goat with the FDC equipment. Dust poured in from every crack in the canopy that covered the back end. They traveled for about an hour and pulled off the road to set up base camp.

They parked the guns and set up their tents for the night.

A truck came out that evening and they had hot chow with a nice cup of coffee. Dean and Willie set up their shelter that they would share together. It was a soft night. A breeze kept the heat down but it was humid, even more so than in Kentucky. Moss hung off the trees and a fungus smell would drift in with the light wind every now and then.

Willie had been to Bragg a couple of times, so he gave Dean instructions on what to watch for. Snakes were common, so they never picked up any object with their hand. They rolled it over with their foot and stepped back. They talked about going to the clubs after maneuvers, but they needed to be on their toes in case someone from Ft. Bragg was in a nasty mood. Ellis came by around nine pm and ordered lights out.

The next morning started off with a hot breakfast, but that was it for the hot meals for the rest of the exercises. The rest of the time, the unit lived off rations.

The first exercise was deployment. The 82nd airborne soldiers jumped out of C-130s at a low altitude while the 101st troopers air assaulted with Chinook helicopters. The advance party of the 101st repelled out of the Hueys, beating the airborne soldiers to the ground.

The low-level jump allowed the paratroopers to hit the LZ [landing zone] before the 101st soldiers could air assault into position, but it cost the 82nd. They had one of their troopers draft below another, taking his wind from his chute. The man in the higher position did not have enough altitude to fix the problem and plunged to his death. Dean never heard about the incident until they were back in Kentucky. He felt real sorrow for the man's family and it happened during a test and not combat.

Both units were attacked by aggressors from each unit. The 82nd inflicted more casualties, on the 101st but the 101st units were able to evacuate the wounded back to the medical facilities faster.

The 7th Cavalry that flew the 101st around not only did a great job with the wounded, but gave excellent air to ground support.

At one point, one of the Chinooks lifted off with a gun crew, got about a hundred feet off the ground and the engines died. It came down hard. The rotors did slow the descent, but not good enough for Dean, who observed the men getting off the chopper. One of them was complaining about his back, while some of the others were shaking cobwebs out of their heads. Those that felt alright were put on another chopper with their gun and flown to the next position. The back injury was medevacked to the base hospital.

Both units participated in a fire mission concerning direct fire. The 101st had more direct hits, so they won that part of the test. Dean felt like the third wheel, he was put near the door as a guard by orders of Top.

The battery set up in a position where they caught a large number of enemy troops in the open about two hundred yards out. They simulated using the bee hive rounds on them. The bee hive round is like a shot gun round for the 105s. The enemy units were ravaged according to the referees. The battery was not the only unit to get a jump on the 82nd, several other units of the 101st pulled off similar feats during the simulated combat test.

The next mission was indirect fire on targets several miles away. Morton called the shot and was laying the rounds in the pickle barrel. Dean was allowed to participate in calculating one of the fire missions. He was accurate, but slow, and McDonald relieved him of his duties after a few minutes. He found himself watching as the rest of the section worked the table, giving the guns deflection and azimuth. The rounds went out quickly and hit the targets with great accuracy. The batteries put the rounds where they were supposed to go, beating the 82nd in the war games.

The battery hooked up the six guns to the Gamma Goats and road marched back to Ft. Bragg. They got the final decision from the referees when they got back to base camp. There was a lot of yelling and cheering when they got the news that they had won the contest. They cleaned up the equipment with zeal and quickly. Most of the battery was released to celebrate their victory. Captain Knight advised the troopers to stay out of trouble and to limit their intake on the alcoholic beverages.

Willie grabbed Dean and Arthur Garcia by the arms and directed them down a street where everyone else seemed to be walking. Clark, the battery clerk, fell in behind them, keeping a distance from them.

"Well, what do you think of Bragg, Larson?"

"It's hot humid, with a lot thicker vegetation, but the nice thing is that we're about to go home and we kicked the 82nd's butt in a big way, Willie."

"Now you're talking, Larson! Let me buy you the first beer. Not only as a celebration, but because this is your first time at Bragg."

"Well, I don't know. I'm getting a lot more pay. You finally have your PFC strips back, but you can't be making much."

"Another reason I should be buying; celebrating my promotion. Right, Clark? Join us. Don't hang back like you're my ugly little brother."

"Right, Willie. Thanks for inviting me. You should buy the first round, but I get to buy the second round. That's only right, Larson since you have been officially baptized under fire with the 101st."

"Okay, but I get to buy the third round."

Everyone started funneling into a large building. Men from both divisions were crowding into the facility. Dean suddenly got a very uneasy feeling about this little venture. He became even more concerned when Willie looked at him, and asked Clark and Garcia if they had his back because he had theirs.

They entered the smoke-filled bar and moved to their right, looking for a table. At the first table they passed, Larson spied Barrett sitting with two section chiefs downing his first beer. This sight put him at ease, Top would make sure things would stay peaceful. They grabbed up a booth and ordered their first beers. Clark asked Dean about the beer in Germany, which started a long discussion. They were in no hurry so Dean sipped his brew slowly. Clark ordered the next four beers and the conversation focused on Dean.

"Larson, watch yourself around Smoke, I take it from some of the conversations I've overheard that he doesn't like you much. In fact, you have two strikes against you. Barrett isn't really fond of you either.

"What the h-- I have I ever done to those two?"

"They expected you to do well in FDC and they are disappointed with your performance. You made them look bad in front of the others. You do have a plus, Captain Knight and Lieutenant Mark Patton both like you and think you are a good soldier."

"Don't worry about Aston, he's a big jerk. I have your back when it comes to him. I know the kind of crap he pulls. He didn't like me either, but we both came to a mutual understanding. I'll take care of you when it comes to Aston, but Barrett is another matter. That's the one you need to be concerned with," Willie spoke up.

"I'll keep my ears open for you, Larson. If I hear any of them talking about you or Willie, I will inform you," Clark remarked.

An 82nd soldier bumped into Willie, causing him to spill some of his drink. Willie stood up and got into his fighting stance. Dean tapped him on his arm and reminded him that he had just got his PFC stripes back. Another trooper grabbed the man that had bumped Willie and calmed him down. Both backed off from one another. Willie sat down and smiled at Dean.

"I don't know, Larson. A good fight might be worth a stripe."

"Man, you don't need to get into a fight here, we whipped them on the battlefield. You can go back to Campbell, thump someone, and keep your rank."

"That's true," Willie said laughing.

There was sudden movement toward the front door and some swearing. Several people stood up in front of Dean. This caused the four soldiers to stand up to see what was happening. All of a sudden, Dean saw fists and chairs being thrown. Dean heard Willie yell "fight' and saw Clark dive under the table.

Dean observed Willie kick an Airbourne soldier in the chest. He started putting his arms up in a defensive posture, when he saw movement to his left. He started to turn when he felt a fist connect with the left side of his head. It was so violent he thought his teeth rattled. His glasses went flying toward the big wooden bar. Dean thought he reached out toward a chair or table but it mattered little, he slumped to the floor in a heap.

When he awoke, the fight was over and he looked into the face of an MP who was slapping him lightly in the face to wake him up. Dean shook his head, trying to clear the cobwebs. The MP asked him if he was alright. Dean tried to comprehend what was being said and finally was able to answer him that he was fine.

The MP looked at his hands, smiled, and proclaimed that Dean had not started the brawl. He touched several of Dean's fingers, which made him wince and curse quietly. His two middle fingers on his right hand were broken. Someone had stepped on them during the fight. He realized that he hurt in a number of places on his body. A couple of places on his legs and several areas on his side, near his ribs. Dean also realized that everything was out of focus and started searching for his glasses.

The MP called a medic over to check him out. Dean was sat up against a wall. From what he could see, furniture was turned over and soldiers were leaning against the bar or being helped by other MPs. The medic checked over his body and concluded that he was bruised and had broken fingers but was otherwise fit for duty. The MP brought Dean a pair of glasses. They kind of looked like his frames but they were useless, bent in various directions. He helped Dean to his feet, that's when Dean saw the full extent of the damage to the bar. Tables and chairs were turned over and broken, only a few bottles and shot glasses were intact. Men were laying on the floor bleeding or leaning against a wall so they could stand. He looked toward the doorway and saw what looked like Barrett and Willie talking to MPs.

Dean looked at the MP. "Will I get in trouble since I didn't even throw a punch?"

"No, in fact it looks like your 1st Sergeant is in a lot of trouble. The man with the highest rank is held accountable on both units. It looks like he also was the first to punch out an 82nd Airbourne soldier. It's that staff sergeant that the medics are working on over in the corner. He sure laid him out, both of them will lose rank and pay, I would guess."

Dean felt a lot of relief come over him. He didn't need no trouble and was just getting by financially as it was. He was also hoping it was true about Barrett. He didn't want to see him in trouble but it would release him of some stress that was in his life.

Not too far from him, a medic was helping Clark stand and was directing him toward the door. Clark looked at Dean and asked him if he was alright. Dean shook his head, held up his glasses, and informed him that he wasn't sure. Clark agreed, he wasn't sure that all his body parts were attached either. Both of them were led to one side of the bar where some of the 101st soldiers were gathering.

"So, what started the fight?" Dean asked Clark.

"Don't know man, I saw you go down. That guy took a cheap shot at you, Larson, but I saw Willie go after him. Willie kicked him in the stomach, he doubled over and Willie kneed him in the forehead. That was all she wrote. I didn't see the guy move after that. I got in trouble and Willie came over and rescued me."

"I hope Willie doesn't get in trouble over all this. I hate to see him lose a stripe for taking care of the guy that hit me," Dean responded shaking his head.

"I saw him take two more out before someone punched my lights out."

Dean spotted one of the section chiefs that had been sitting with Barrett. He went up to him and asked him if he had seen who started the fight. The sergeant had a black eye and a bloody lip. He was pressing something against his lip and Dean leaned close to him and questioned him if he had seen who started the fight. He looked around and whispered that a sergeant from the 82nd had bumped Barrett's drink.

Barrett looked up, waiting for an apology but the man spouted off some ugly slurs and blamed Barrett for bumping him. Top got up, grabbed the man by his collar and punched him so hard that he hit the wall about five feet away. He didn't think the man touched the floor while he was in the air. He wasn't sure about military law, but he thought Barrett could be in a lot of trouble.

A few people were taken out on stretchers, but everyone else walked out on their own accord. All of the 82nd Airbourne personnel were taken to a large facility where they were questioned. The soldiers from the 101st were put in a bus and taken to a gym. Concertina wire was strung around the building and guards were put on duty.

The trip back to Kentucky was delayed for two days until everyone was interrogated. The men that stayed with the equipment were ordered to load up on the C-130s the next day and go home. Willie sought out Dean, who was sitting outside enjoying a cool breeze out of the east.

"You okay, Larson? Man, you fell like a sack of crap."

"Yeah. How about you, Willie?"

"Man, I barely got touched. I'm going to lose a stripe and some pay."

"Why, what did you do this time Willie"?

"Well, when the MPs showed up, one of them tried to restrain me and I got carried away and tapped him on the chin a little. Those guys have no sense of humor."

"Willie, Willie. When are you going to learn to behave yourself? At least you still have your private stripe. You going to keep it?"

"Maybe, maybe not. Look what I have." He pulled out three berets from his shirt that he had taken off unconscious soldiers from the 82nd Airbourne Division.

"What do you plan on doing with them?"

"Let's do a foray on base and get even for the ugly southern hospitality these guys have shown us. No telling what kind of little things we can get away with. I'm giving you the opportunity to exact a little revenge on these guys for the cheap shot in the head they gave you."

"No thanks man, you don't want me along. I have no glasses and I can't hardly see. I would just slow you down."

"I figured that Larson, but I felt like I should invite you. Clark is coming and I guess I'll invite Garcia. He is always up for a little excitement."

"What about those patches on your shoulders?"

"We're going to wear T-shirts and dirty ourselves up. If they stop us, we're going to tell them that we were on a late work detail. I also found that the concertina wire is not real tight in the back of the gym, easy to escape. I have it all planned. Don't worry, man."

Dean shook his head and was glad that he had his glasses as an excuse not to go. He wasn't feeling up to running and dodging MPs. In fact, he was looking forward to getting a good night's sleep in the gym.

Late in the evening, Dean helped with concertina wire, allowing the three to escape. He crawled back into his sleeping bag soon afterwards and fell back to sleep quickly. He woke the next morning and instantly looked Willie's way. He squinted and made out Willie's head peeking from the sleeping bag. He couldn't tell if Garcia or Clark had made it back safely. Larson crawled out of his bag and snuck over to Willie. He shook him awake and asked him about the raid. It took a while before Willie could wake up enough to respond. He wagged his head and frowned.

"Wish you had been able to come along, Larson. Clark got himself caught; he didn't make it back."

"Where is he now, Willie?"

"Don't know, the last I saw of him was when a MP was pulling him up off the ground in front of HQ [headquarters]. He froze and fell to the ground when one of those guys fired their .45 in the air."

"What were you doing at HQ?"

"We stole their unit crest off the top of the building. Boy was it heavy, Garcia and I had the top of it while Clark was packing the bottom. We had started across the parade ground when a jeep turned this corner. Wouldn't ya know it, they were MPs. They stopped and asked us what we were doing. We informed them that the crest needed some repairs and we were taking it to the shop. They told us to stay right where we were, no one would have us doing that type of work at that time of the morning. We thought they would buy the explanation since they were MPs and part of the 82nd."

"Did you really think they would buy that story?"

"Well, no. But they had to stop and think about it, which gave us some time to start running for it. We picked a bad route; too much open area. They started chasing us and they yelled 'halt' and fired a round in the air. That's when we lost Clark. He dropped his end and raised his hands. They ordered him to his knees.

The other MP wouldn't give up and the crest was really heavy. Garcia suggested that we drop it, but no way. I had worked too hard for the damn thing. The cop was a little overweight and I figured we could outlast him. Besides, as we continued to run, the crest seemed to get lighter. I thought our adrenaline had kicked in-to high gear. That wasn't the case when I looked down the thing was falling apart. We must have left over half of it all over Bragg," he said snickering.

"Where is it now?"

"That's the beauty of it, we took it back to where all the equipment was parked. We put it in the FDC's Gamma Goat under the tent. Our buddy McDonald was on guard duty and he knows about it. He is going to sneak it into the barracks and hide it for me. They must be loading up now on the 130s. It was great, Larson. You missed out."

"You know, Clark could finger you."

"I don't think so. He knows I'll smack him upside the head and besides that, we are in the same unit and we wouldn't tell on each other. Would you?"

"No, especially on you Willie. You're too good of a friend."

The sergeants started rousing everyone out of the sleeping bags for roll call and breakfast. The 82nd sent out a truck with rations and they served the troopers from Kentucky some hot nasty tasting coffee. Willie wouldn't drink it because he believed the cooks had pissed in it before serving it to the unit. Once Willie made that statement several soldiers threw their coffee out, including Dean.

Roll call was made and Clark came up missing. They searched the gym and the surrounding area and he was not found. He was declared AWOL [absent without leave]. During this time, ten MPs showed up and started taking statements from everyone that had been at the bar. Dean's interview lasted only a few minutes. They checked his knuckles which weren't banged up again and released him.

Halfway through the interviews, a jeep pulled up in front of the gym. Clark stepped out with two MPs in tow. Captain Knight quickly intercepted the three soldiers. He listened intently to the report from one of the MPs. Dean had never seen Knight lose his cool, but he was sure that Captain Knight swore as he pointed to a chair, indicating that Clark should sit. He talked to the police for a while longer, signed some paperwork and the MPs left. Knight stayed away from Clark and walked with his head down through the soldiers not saying a word.

He finally went up to three of the NCOs and ordered them to check inside the gym through all the gear and any possible hiding spots looking for the stolen unit crest. He went over to Clark and questioned him for about a half hour. Dean could see the frustration on his face as Clark continued to give him the same answer.

After the MPs finished interviewing everyone, Knight held a formation and told all the men what Clark had done. There were a lot of laughs and comments made about the crest until Knight called everyone to attention. It didn't matter Clark had become a hero in the eyes of most of the battery.

"This is no laughing matter, so keep your comments and snickering to yourself. Now, Clark swears that he thought he was helping two men from the 82nd take the crest to the wood shop to be repaired at about 0200 hours in the morning, but I don't buy it. I think someone from this unit helped steal the crest. Is there anyone that would like to confess?"

Barrett walked up and down the lines of men. He would stop and look at a man, asking him if he knew anything. Of course, no one knew anything. He stopped in front of Dean, but looked to his right where Willie was standing in formation.

"You know, Willie, as I consider everyone in this unit, you're the one that I would pick to pull this off."

"Thanks for the complement, Top but I was fast asleep," he said looking up at him with an innocent expression. Willie had a childlike face and even when he got caught doing something wrong, he looked innocent.

"Bull, I would bet you were in on this little foray. I also think you were with him, Larson."

"No way, Top. I'm as blind as a bat," Dean said holding up his broken glasses.

"Then it had to be Garcia. That little jerk and you can create more havoc than Patton could with fifty tanks under his command during World War II. Is there anything left of the crest?"

"Well Top, if I was smart enough to pull that little raid off, do you think I would keep any evidence around to get me in trouble?"

"No, you wouldn't, but if I ever find any, your can is mine. Do you understand, Willie?"

"Yes, I do, Top."

Barrett went back to the BC and shook his head. He called the unit to attention and dismissed everyone. About an hour later, buses pulled up and A Battery was taken to the airfield where they were loaded on a plane. They were flown to Fort Campbell, where Porter picked Dean up and took him home.

Chapter 5

CAUSE AND EFFECT

Dean was so worn out that he gave Natalie a quick kiss and a short explanation about the bruises and the broken glasses. He crawled into bed without supper and faded off into a deep sleep. He was up early the next morning and told Natalie a more in-depth story about what had happened during their visit to Fort Bragg.

It was great having a good breakfast and some excellent coffee. He found an old pair of glasses so he could see again. John had been asleep when he came in that night and Dean would not see him until that evening. He was still hurting from the fight, stiff in some of his leg joints and a few of the bruises were very tender.

Porter picked him up and questioned him about what had occurred at the bar. Porter had been with the equipment so he missed all the excitement. Dean rehashed the tale one more time. When he talked to him about Clark's adventures, Porter laughed and told him that he would have liked being in on that raid. Dean did not tell him who were Clark's partners in crime.

As usual, they fell out in T-shirts and pants with combat boots. Smoke was smiling as he told the battery "At Ease" and then walked in front of the first section, then to the middle of the formation.

"You will be happy to hear that we are going, to run five-miles today. It is to remind you that you are in the Army and that you are to be disciplined soldiers, even in a bar. Anyone, and I mean anyone, falls out of the run, he will have to do extra PT tonight."

He called two of the section chiefs out and told them they were to run at the back of the formation and take down the names of those individuals that didn't complete the run. The BC and the XO came out of the building and fell in beside the battery. Smoke yelled out "right face" and marched the men out to the road where he called out "double time" and they all started the five-mile jog.

Dean hated running and this day was no exception but this time he started with pain almost immediately in his right leg. It hurt from his knee to his hip. He had hurt his knee sliding into home playing baseball when he was in high school. It must have sustained some kind of blow during the fight, aggravating the old injury. He was going to tough it out, he didn't want to do extra PT. After two-miles, he fell behind a little but kept close enough to make up the distance. He could see one of the sergeant's write his name down.

He caught a second wind and closed the gap. The sergeant wrote something in his note pad, but Dean fell behind again after about a half a mile. He picked up the pace, catching the formation again. He stayed with them for a large distance but the pain in his leg and constant pounding on the pavement was too much for him and he fell out. He was limping down the road when a duce and half truck stopped next to him on the road.

The passenger door flew open and he heard a feminine voice ask him if he wanted a ride. He grabbed the door and swung up into the passenger seat. The woman was petite, blonde, with bright blue eyes. Dean swung the door shut and she got the truck rolling down the street. She smiled at him. She had very bright white teeth.

"You a part of this formation up ahead?"

"Yes, I hurt my leg the other day and I just can't keep up with them."

"What would you like me to do?" she said looking deeply into his eyes.

It's the way she said it that bothered Dean. He wasn't sure but he thought that she might be flirting with him. He coughed and cleared his throat, feeling uneasy.

"Well, if you would drop me off at the corner of that building. I would appreciate it. I think I can sneak out and become a part of the formation without getting caught."

"Sure thing, is there anything else you need?"

The way she looked at him made Larson blush. He had never had a woman come on to him before and though he was flattered by it, he was also embarrassed. More than that, he was reminded of Natalie and the child they were about to have.

He was not interested, but then he thought, it didn't matter, the base was big and she most likely flirted with a lot of men. It was unlikely that they would run into one another again. She checked her mirrors and pulled to the left, near some cars which were parked alongside the road. He started out the passenger door, but she suggested that they would see him going out that door. She moved on to the running board, and he slid under the steering wheel. As he stepped on to the running board, she grabbed him and kissed him on the check. He almost fell off but caught the door, easing down on to the road.

"I have to tell you that I'm married."

"I don't care. You can find me at one of the bars outside the main gate every Friday night. I'll let you buy me a beer for rescuing you. By the way, my name is Ann," she said with a big smile.

"Thanks" he yelled, waving back at her.

He waited near the corner of the building. The first part of the formation passed by and toward the middle of it he jumped out near Willie and McDonald, who quickly made room for him. Dean looked around. Several men had seen him jump in but he did not think any of the sergeants had noticed him sneaking into the battery. Smoke called the formation to a halt and lined everyone up. He asked the two sergeants at the end who had not made the run. They named off the men and they put them to the side as they came straggling in. When they called Larson's name, he raised his hand, quipping that he was with his section.

The sergeant shrugged and admitted that Dean had fallen back, but had closed the gap several times. No one in the formation told on Dean, so Smoke let it go and Dean was off the hook. The unit was dismissed but before Willie and Dean could get too far, Clark caught them by the arm.

"Willie, they are going to search all the equipment and rooms for any part of the 82nd Airbourne crest. I overheard Knight talking to Smoke and Top this morning. You need to hide that thing real good or you're going to be in hot water like me."

Willie thought for a long moment and suddenly smiled. "I guess I will never be able to keep my trophy. If they catch me with
that, they'll fry me. I guess I'm going to give you an early Christmas gift, Larson."

"No, you don't, Willie. If I get caught with that thing, it's my hide, and they will hang me out to dry."

"Now listen, they don't suspect you because of the broken glasses. I'll bring the Gamma Goat in after breakfast since McDonald didn't have the opportunity to get it unloaded yesterday. I'll bring it to the battery area after breakfast to unload the gear. I'll put the crest in a laundry bag with some of my dirty clothes near the tailgate and create a diversion. You grab it up and put it in Porter's car to take home. It is yours, after all you did help us get past the wire."

Dean thought for a while and decided the odds were in their favor. The BC didn't know that they knew his plan. He would get to keep the prize and it would be a conversation piece for visitors. Porter's car would never be searched. He would have to get his sleeping bag to take home, so they would probably pay little attention to him if Willie kept them looking the other way.

"Sounds like a plan, I'm in, but what is your diversion going to be?"

"You'll know it when you hear and see it. Make sure you're in FDC room and be watching for me."

Dean stationed himself near the window, putting away equipment that had already been brought in from the C-130. McDonald had tried to sneak the crest into the barracks but Porter had kept him so busy that he didn't have a chance.

It was a good thing he didn't accomplish the mission, Willie thought it would be easier to transfer it from the goat to a car. They were interrupted by the XO, Lieutenant Patton. He questioned Ellis if he had checked all the gear yet. Ellis informed him they were just going through it now. Patton started helping them dig into the equipment. He asked Ellis if all the items had been brought in. Ellis told him that Willie was driving the Gamma Goat in from the motor pool but a lot of those items would be going into the connex. The large things such as the tent, poles, and generator would be put in that building.

Dean observed Willie drive the goat to the connex which was a metal shed located near the barracks. He opened the tailgate and then the two doors to the connex. Just then, the Gamma Goat from B battery drove up to unload their equipment into their connex which was located on the other side of A battery's building. At the point of the driveway that B battery's driver needed to get around Willie, it narrowed so badly, he could not squeeze the vehicle pass. On one side, a tree blocked the way and Willie's vehicle on the other side was impeding his progress.

Dean watched with fascination as the driver stuck his head out the window and said something to Willie. Willie shook his head and more conversation ensued until Willie held up a fist with one finger sticking in the air. The driver became very animated and jumped out of the cab.

Ellis interrupted Dean's train of thought by asking him what he was looking at. Dean kept his eyes focused on the scene out-side and described what he was observing. Ellis and Patton immediately ran to the window with the rest of the section following close behind.

"What the h-- l is Willie doing? I told him a half dozen times to let B battery in first so they could unload their equipment. Those two do not get along at all."

"We better get out there and break up things before they get started," Patton ordered.

Willie was getting up on the wheel well, as if he was going to drive the vehicle out of the way. He was taking his time and said something to the other driver with a big smirk on his face. That did it. The other soldier started running toward Willie. He covered the distance in a couple of steps. He was a lot bigger, weighing around 220 pounds.

He reached for the smaller man, but before he could pull Willie off the goat, Willie kicked him in the face, knocking him back about five paces. Dean followed the rest of the section out the building. When they got outside, Willie was pummeling the other soldier at will. While Patton and Ellis were separating the two, Dean moved to the back of the goat and retrieved the laundry bag with the crest. He slowly walked to Porter's car where he stowed it on the back floor board. When he got back to the fight area, everyone was starting to disperse.

Ellis had Willie by the arm, dragging him toward the building. Patton and a sergeant from battery B were helping the other man off the ground. He looked dazed and was bleeding from the nose and lip. McDonald moved the Gamma Goat out of the way so battery B could pull their vehicle in and off load. Dean started to follow them in, but Ellis pointed to the connex and told him to store the equipment.

Dean would have liked to hear what was said, but he would get the lowdown from Willie later. Patton came back and helped him unload. Dean asked him why he was helping and he told him that he was looking for the crest. He inspected all the equipment but didn't find the it. Later they assumed the two perpetrators had thrown it away.

It was a Saturday so they called a halt to the day at two pm. Porter took him home, as Dean retrieved the laundry bag from Porter's car. He told him it was dirty laundry he had forgotten. Porter leaned out the window, smiling at Dean.

"When I come over tomorrow to get you for church, I want to see that crest."

Dean stopped dead in his tracks. He turned to Porter and observed the smile.

"You got it Sarge, but I want you to know that I had no hand in stealing this little item."

"Sorry to hear that. I would have thought more highly of you if you had been in on that incursion," Porter said grinning.

"How did you know I had it?"

"None of us had that much laundry and I saw you go to the back of the goat. You did a nice job of walking slowly to my car while everyone else was watching the fight. I try to look for the unusual and you should have been rooting Willie on but you were dealing with laundry instead."

With that, he drove off and Dean entered his home. Natalie was sitting on the couch in front of a fan trying to cool down from another hot humid day. He went over and kissed her, but she did not stir much. John was playing on the floor with some toys. He immediately jumped up, ran to his father, and wrapped around one of Dean's legs.

Dean grabbed him up and started kissing and nibbling on his neck. The little boy squealed with delight and laughter. Dean questioned him about what he was doing and if he was having a good day. John showed him the toys he was playing with and how he drove his toy truck.

"Why don't I make us some breakfast for dinner?" Dean suggested looking at his wife.

"That sounds good," she mumbled

"What's up, babe. You look exhausted. John wearing you out?"

"No, he's been good. I'm tired of the Army, Dean. I would like you to get out as soon as you can. You go to Fort Bragg for about a week and soon you'll be running off to Germany. You have been away more than you have been around, lately."

"I know Natalie, but I just can't get up and quit the service. I have to finish out my enlistment or I get in big trouble. We need to stick to the plan; the army and then college."

She looked at him for a long moment closed her eyes again. He turned to the kitchen, mixed up some batter, and cooked up pancakes and eggs. He served the food to her on the couch with a fresh brewed cup of coffee. She took the food and coffee with little enthusiasm.

"You need to stay out of the bars and away from Willie. You have gotten in more fights since we got here than in your whole life."

"Not true. When I was in grade school, I think I fought more often. I do have to say that trouble seems to follow Willie around. Look at what he gave me today."

He retrieved the top of the 82nd Airbourne crest from Bragg.

"Big deal, Dean. It doesn't look like something to lose your life over."

He became silent. She had deflated him in quick order. The top of the crest was like a scalp, an enemy flag, a Roman Eagle. She did not see the significance of the prize. They ate the rest of the meal with only John interrupting the peace. That evening, they went to bed and Natalie rolled over and went to sleep without kissing him.

Sunday morning, Natalie was having some pain so they skipped church and Dean wasn't sure if she was miserable or had real pain. She did talk more. They had gotten a phone call from home and they discussed the news from the family. That evening, she was more loving towards him again and he got some very nice hugs.

Dean was about to start college classes. Porter took him to several car dealerships looking for a good running vehicle they could afford. They struck out that evening, but the second night Dean found an older red Dodge Cornet that he bought outright. The V-8 was in good condition, the inside was a little faded, but there were no rips in the carpet or seats.

The body was another story, there were several dents in various places and some of the body had rust spots. Dean tuned up on the engine with the help of Morton. Kevin had the tools and equipment to get the motor running better than before. Dean took the family for a drive after dinner, it was good to be independent again.

About two weeks later, Dean found himself in class with about twenty other people. It was a college history course. He had enjoyed the subject in high school and after looking at the outline he saw no reason for not excelling in this class. On Wednesday, he was taking an English class.

As he surveyed the rest of the students, he picked out a familiar face. It was the little blonde woman from the truck, Ann. She smiled at him and waved. He nodded and smiled back. He was glad the rest of the seats were taken around him, at least she could not sit next to him.

As they left the class, she intercepted him and suggested that they study together once in a while. He informed her he would see how the class went, but he told her that just to get rid of her.

On an overcast Monday, as Willie escorted Dean to the mess hall, Clark caught up to them. He looked around to see if anyone was in ear shot.

"Guess what guys?"

"No. You just tell us, Clark," stated Willie.

"Well, Top got busted to an E-6 and is being transferred out of here in a week."

"That was quick even for the Army. I've noticed that he had been real quiet ever since we got back from Bragg," observed Dean.

"Well, I hope we get a good Top soon, one that will be a buffer between Smoke and us. He had been riding us pretty hard since Bragg. It's like we didn't win the war games."

"Yes, but the one person that started the whole thing was Barrett and he's out of here," Dean chimed in. Then he remembered Natalies' dream. She had seen it before it had occurred.

"We're going to get a new First Sergeant right away. Knight wants one before we go to Germany. I don't know who it will be, but I will keep you two posted. They decided to keep you with FDC at least until after Germany, Larson. You'll be driving the lead goat, since you know all the traffic signs and laws. Otherwise, you will be on the radio or on guard," reported Clark.

"That is great, Larson. We'll be hanging out. You can show me around all the bars and keep me out of trouble."

"Willie, no one can keep you out of trouble and they're guesthouses. I'll show you around but I'm warning you that you don't want to have a run in with the German police," Dean said smiling.

That evening, Dean told Natalie the news about Barrett and she reminded him of the dream she had about the finger coming out of the cloud and flicking a man off the top of the tree. Dean told her that he had thought of that the minute he heard the news from Clark.

Chapter 6

TOP JASON CHILDS

He showed up without any fanfare and stood in front of the battery while Smoke gave a short introduction. Top Jason Childs was average in every way with brown hair and eyes. He stood about five-feet eleven inches with broad shoulders and muscular arms. He had a mustache that hugged a wide nose.

He inspected the ranks of men that stood at attention and stopped to talk to one of the men that stood before him every so often. He spoke to Sergeant Ellis about the FDC section and asked him where he was from.` Ellis answered him with quick concise sentences.

He stopped and looked Willie over for a few minutes, but said nothing to him. Dean sighed a breath of relief as Childs passed him, but Childs halted and turned around, pausing in front of Larson. He said nothing for a couple of minutes. Dean felt uncomfortable. Top seemed to look right through him, probing the very deep places in his soul.

"What's your full name Spec Four Larson?"

"Spec Four Dean Julias Larson, Top"

"Where do you come from, son?"

"A little town in southern Idaho called Rupert. And it is Idaho, Top."

"I know where Idaho is, Larson. It's a nice state. Are you married, young man?"

"Yes, Top. With a little boy and another one on the way."

Top said nothing else, looked him over for another few minutes, and then continued his inspection of the rest of the battery. Dean wanted to stay off his radar and already the man had stopped, inspected him like a rancher inspects a cow, and had asked him some personal questions. Dean didn't think that was a good sign. Besides, Willie had heard his middle name and instantly teased him about it. Dean explained that Julias was the name of his grandfather on his mother's side. The explanation did not stop Willie from giving him a hard time. Of course, others heard the remarks and joined in the bantering.

After lunch, Dean was called into Top's office. As he reported to the outer office, he gave Clark a questioning look.   Clark shrugged his shoulders, suggesting that he knew nothing. Childs indicated a chair with a gesture while he read a file. Dean took a seat in the chair and waited patiently until Top spoke. "Larson, I'm going over your file. You have some very high marks on your evaluations. I see you were in the nuclear program in Germany and you have a couple of letters of achievement. How did you get stuck in the FDC here in Campbell?"

"They thought that since I did so well in SW, I would really do good at figuring where a round would land but I'm not very good with numbers. I have to think about that stuff when we're getting fire missions."

"Yes, I've talked to Ellis about your problems. I've decided to put you back on the guns when we get back from Germany. I agree with the BC on you driving the goat on Reforger 76, since you know the rules of the road. I see you're also taking college classes, English and History. Do you plan on making the Army a career?"

"No, I'm doing my time and getting out."

"You would be a great candidate for Sergeant stripes. In fact, I'm going to recommend you for the board sometime this winter."

"That would be kind of a waste of time, since I'm planning on leaving."

"We'll see what happens, you might get to liking the Army. I would also suggest that you go to Air Assault school and get your wings."

"I will consider that Top."

"Good. On that note, you are dismissed, Larson."

Larson shook his head as he left. He didn't know what to think. He was excited about getting back on the guns, where he could be productive again. It concerned him that this guy was paying so much attention to him, but maybe he was doing it with everyone in the battery. Still, it bothered Dean and it troubled him the rest of the day. He went home and told Natalie about Childs, she agreed with him that it was strange. He hurried, ate dinner, and got into some civilian clothes to go to class.

After his history class, he went to the library to do some research for a paper that needed to be done. As he roamed through the books, he was surprised to come face to face with Ann Hunter. She said "Hi" in a coy tone. She acted shy, but he knew different and it took him back. He stumbled, but recovered and had to think about what he should say. She took advantage of his surprise and moved in grabbing him by the arm. He finally blurted out a hello and asked her what she was doing there. She informed him that she was in the other history class and that she was doing some research. He pulled away from her slowly withdrawing his arm from her grasp.

"So, I haven't seen you along the road lately. Have you been making your runs?"

"Not always, but I haven't needed a ride lately."

"Well, I'm always willing to give you a ride, Dean. All you have to do is call," she said moving closer to him.

He caught a whiff of her perfume. It was a beautiful scent and her smile and eyes were intoxicating. He shook off the thought even though she had him trapped up against one of the book cases. Suddenly fear rose up in his very being as he thought about the fact that she knew his first name. They had used their last names in class. He pushed past her to the end of the book cases.

"How do you know my first name?"

"I went over to Battery A one day and hung out. I saw you with your section and asked a man about you and all your buddies. He gave me all your names, I also know that you are a member of the FDC," she said with a large smile.

"Well, I think I better go right now. It was nice seeing you again, Ann."

"No, the pleasure was all mine Spec Four Larson. Hope to see you again real soon. Oh, did you get the book that you were looking for? I don't see you with any extras."

"No, I will get it some other time. I need to get home to my wife," he said over his right shoulder as he left.

He got in the Cornet, inserted the key, the car roared to life, and he started for home. He had never been chased by a woman like this. He didn't consider himself very handsome or charming, so why was Ann pursuing him so hard? To come over to the battery area and find out about him was scary. He was in love with Natalie and he had never spoken about Ann because he didn't think he would ever run into her again.

Natalie was very pregnant and very touchy about everything. She might demand he stop going to the college classes if he told her what was going on. She wasn't normally jealous he didn't think, but she had been acting so strange lately. Sometimes she was the old Natalie, loving, shy, and reserved. Other times she was angry, depressed, and distant. He blamed it on the weather and her condition.

Carrie, Morton's wife, had advised him things might get better after the baby came. Suzan Porter also gave him the same message. Some days, Dean would stay outside, working on the car or visiting Kevin or Porter because Natalie was in such a foul mood. He also took John with him to give everyone a break in the hope that Natalie would feel some relief from her surroundings. Dean knew who Natalie was and felt lucky to have her as his wife. He was determined to wait this out for the real Natalie on the other side.

As he pulled into the driveway, he thought it would be best not to tell Natalie about Ann. He did not want to upset her in any fashion. He just had no way of measuring her reaction to the idea that another woman was hitting on him.

It wasn't very late, but he found Natalie asleep on the couch. He covered her with a blanket quietly went into the bathroom, and took a shower. He checked on John and went to bed. He read a chapter in his history book until he nodded off.

Friday, early in the morning, the battery fell out for the run, it was five miles again. Childs had been running with the battery most mornings. Barrett used to run a few of the shorter distances but, Top Childs had only missed one. He was in formation for the five-mile run and this caused Dean to respect him even more.

At about four-miles, Dean started lagging behind with a couple of other men. He had gotten use to the idea of staying behind Friday evening and doing extra PT. There was just something about five-miles. Childs fell behind with them, which caused Dean to smile. He wasn't as fit as he acted. Top came alongside them and looked them over.

"I'm an old man, so I should fall out. What are your excuses?" He spoke in a low controlled voice. He wasn't even panting very hard.

"You a football player in high school, Robinson?"

"Yes, Top. I was a defensive linebacker."

"See that last man in formation? I want you to picture him as the other team quarterback and you better tackle him before we get back to the battery area, or I'm going to make you low crawl for a half hour when we get back. I want you to picture him about to throw a touchdown pass. Now go!"

Robinson had been running right next to Dean. He suddenly got a second wind and took off, closing the space between him and the last man. Top looked at Dean with a questioning look.

"What sport?"

"Baseball."

"You just hit a hard ball between center and left field, which will give you a stand-up triple.   If you run like crazy, you can make home but if you don't, I'm going to make you do a dying cockroach for thirty minutes."

A dying cockroach, laid on your back, putting up legs and arms straight up in the air. It was a painful exercise, and one Dean did not want to do. The idea that he had hit a stand-up triple was motivating, but the dying cockroach was terrifying. He started gaining, not as quickly as Robinson, but he did catch the unit before they reached the battery area. Top motivated several others in the same way, so the battery only had a few stragglers when everyone was called to attention.

Everyone was dismissed except the stragglers and the ones that Childs had motivated. He told them that as long as he was Top, everyone would finish the five-mile run as a unit. He was not interested in having anyone falling out of formation. He pointed to the three that did not make the run and told them to go to the armory to check out three rifles. They would run a mile with their weapons over their heads and he would run with them.

He informed the rest of them they needed to get past their thinking and the pain to accomplish the runs. They may not like running, but they better embrace it, pain was a part of life.

Dean spent most of Saturday studying and doing assignments for his college classes. He was doing work ahead of time so he would not be so far behind when he got back from Germany. He worked until it was time to go to bed. Natalie gave him a hard time about spending very little time with her or John. He was too worn out to even argue with her, and he fell into bed and was sound asleep in minutes.

The next morning, he tried talking her out of going to church, but she insisted on it. She dragged him to the third row as usual. The pastor came by and talked to them for a few seconds and then walked up to the podium and started going over his notes. The Porter family came and sat down beside them.

Dean and his family sat in the middle of the row. Someone sat down to Dean's left. He looked over, and it was Top Childs with a beautiful blonde lady sitting next to him and a teenage boy and girl.

"Surprise," Childs spoke in a low voice.

"It certainly is, Top. In fact, I can't tell you how surprised I am!"

"Your worst nightmare. You're stuck with me on base and now you find me in your church."

They were interrupted by Pastor Jethro, who came over and introduced himself to the visitors. Dean pointed to Top and gave Jethro his name. Childs took Jethro's hand and shook it vigorously and then introduced his wife Eve, Esther, his daughter, and Isiah, his son.

Eve had dark hair with sea green eyes. She was about as tall as her husband with a nice figure and a pleasant smile. Esther looked like her mother, the same color of hair and stature. Isaiah was taller than his parents, he was clean cut with brown hair and green eyes. The music started so the introductions ended and Jethro ran up to the podium.

Dean didn't hear the message at all. He was uncomfortable with Childs sitting next to him. Dean was aware that he was sweating up a storm and he could not concentrate on the worship music. He did notice that Childs seemed to enjoy every aspect of the service, which made Dean wonder if he was a Christian or that he was being forced by his wife to come to the services. Dean considered how he did things and decided that he must be a Christian.

Dean could not remember him cussing or verbally abusing any of the soldiers. Still, the only person Dean could remember professing to be a Christian in the Army, besides Porter, was a sergeant in Baumholder.

After the service, Dean introduced his family to Childs. Porter also got in on the action, throwing out the names of his daughters and wife. Both of the girls gave Isaiah the once over. He seemed to be embarrassed by all the attention. Childs tried to make Dean feel more comfortable about him being a part of the congregation. He teased him, promising that he would not make him do any laps around the sanctuary or push-ups in front of the pews.

Dean felt better, but still had some misgivings about being in the same church as Childs. He talked to Natalie about checking out other churches, but she stood her ground, they were going to stay where they were. She liked Eve and Jason and thought that Jason might be a good influence on Dean.

Chapter 7

NEXT STOP
GIEBELSTADT GERMANY

Dean moved his body into a different position, so the blood would circulate to some other extremity. He looked toward the back of the C-140 that was taking them to Germany. The Gamma Goat that he would be driving was in front of him.

He felt lucky because it was newer, so there would be a lot less maintenance on it. A lot of the men were sleeping, but he could not stop thinking about the last few days he had been home. Natalie and him had been fighting off and on most of the time. He had gotten ahead on his homework from his two classes, but it had taken a lot of family time.

He asked Childs if he would send him home as soon as possible because of the baby coming due. It was September, and the child was due to appear on the scene in October. Top assured him that he would send him back to Kentucky as soon as possible. Dean felt bad, he was so irritated at Natalie, he had not given her a kiss when they embarked on the plane. He wished he could take that moment back, but it was too late for that.

School had been going well for him. He had gotten decent grades in spite of the army and Natalie. Still, he was bothered by Ann. He had dodged her most of the time, but she ambushed him several times in the library. She was aggressive, hugging him from behind once, and touching his hand several times. He broke the hug quickly and rebuked her for doing such a thing. He was completely beside himself on the mysteries of women and what he should do about her. On the one hand, he couldn't seem to get rid of her no matter what he did, but Natalie, the one he loved seemed to be drifting away from him.

He unfastened his seatbelt and went to the restroom. He passed Childs, who was sitting next to Aston. Both of them were sleeping. Aston's six-feet, three-inch frame seemed jammed into the row. Childs' smaller body looked more at ease in his position.

Dean had to admit that Top was a Godsend because he had made Aston ease off riding him so much. One of the other reasons was Reforger 76. Dean was helpful by getting the drivers ready for the roads in Europe. He was also driving the goat for FDC. Still, Dean would sometimes catch Aston watching him with a creepy look in his eyes.

Clark had overheard several conversations between the two high ranking NCOs discussing Dean, and Childs was always sticking up for him. Dean had been able to finally conquer the five-mile run with Childs' motivation. He only failed a couple times, often because of a hangover.

After the bathroom, Dean wandered around the goat to see how they secured it in the C-140. They also had a Mule in the big cargo plane. It was a small four-wheel all-terrain vehicle that they used to transport small amounts of supplies or the TOW missile, which was an anti-tank weapon. It had side rails above the bed and a motor in front with steering wheel behind it. Dean went back to his seat as he was starting to feel drowsy. He buckled up and feel asleep.

He woke up when he heard the tires touch down on the airfield in Germany. Willie was sitting next to him. He stretched and hit Dean playfully on the head, announcing to him that he was back in Germany. Smoke appeared in front of them and declared it was time to haul their tail ends off the plane. They grabbed their gear and headed out the back.

Once the goat was off loaded, Dean checked it over. He got into the driver's seat with Ellis as his assistant driver and waited for the other equipment to be off loaded. Smoke got them lined up and they convoyed to Giebelstadt, a small village surrounded by forest. They did not pass through the town, but went directly to the old-World War II fighter airfield on a secondary road.

A tent city had already been erected by an advance party. After securing their gear, they had a late dinner and found the tent that they were assigned to. They pulled out their sleeping bags, laid them on cots, and were soon asleep.

Reveille was late and another hot meal was provided with a good hot cup of coffee. The meals were provided by the mess crews at various stations within the compound. Dean and Willie stood behind three pilots from the 1st Cavalry. The men discussed how they hated flying the big choppers and how unreliable they were.

They flew Chinooks that taxied the 101st Airbourne wherever they needed to go as well as the Cobras that flew cover while they were on the ground. The air fleet was parked along the broken pavement of the airfield. A fixed wing plane could not land on the runway, but the place was well suited for the choppers.

While in line, Willie talked Dean into asking Childs for a pass into town. Dean resisted for a while. He didn't think they would let anyone off base, and he didn't want to put Top in the position where others might think he favored him.

After the meal, he went in to ask for the pass. Childs told him no, that he had guard duty that evening. He would be posted at 11pm for a two-hour shift. In the mean time they were to get their area and gear ready for the upcoming maneuvers.

He indicated that he was willing to give him a pass for the next day. Clark stepped in and asked for a pass and Dean inquired for Willie. Top wanted to know if Dean could keep Willie out of trouble. Dean assured him that he would keep a tight leash on Willie, so Childs approved the passes for the next day.

At 10:15 pm Dean was awakened, driven to the motor pool, and relieved the man that had stood watch before him. He was given a radio and an unloaded M-16 as a weapon and a flashlight. Dean walked the perimeter four times when he spotted a dark shadow moving toward one of the vehicles. He intercepted a soldier that was unlocking a jeep. He shined the flashlight in his face, which caused the man to stop what he was doing and raise his hands to his shoulders. "I'm here to pick up the commander's jeep, he stammered.

"Who are you?" Dean asked harshly.

He had seen this trooper before but he couldn't place him

"I'm PFC Stone, the colonel's driver. He's been ordered to the General's tent right away."

"Stone. Where have I heard that name before?"

"I've been at Campbell for about a year, now."

Suddenly, it came to Dean like a light turning on in a dark room.

"No. You're the SOB that stole a jeep in Grafenwöhr when I was standing guard at that motor pool. Turn toward the other jeep now, before I club you to death with this M-16," Dean shouted sternly.

Stone turned toward the other jeep, dropping his log book on the ground. He put his hands on the hood. He turned to say something, but Dean told him to shut his mouth and pressed the barrel of his rifle into his back to show that he meant business. He got on the radio and called in to see if Stone was really authorized to take the jeep. The sergeant of the guard verified Stone's story. The jeep was needed by the colonel. Dean was really hoping Stone was stealing the vehicle so he could get a little revenge.

"Hey, man. You were the guard on duty with 3/16th. Did you get in trouble when I took that jeep?"

"No. they tried to give me an article 15, but Top Eagle stood up for me and they dropped it. Why are you still in the Army? I thought they court marshaled you and were going to send you to Mannheim?"

"They were, but I went AWOL instead. Two days before they declared me a deserter, I turned myself in. By that time, they had prosecuted the other cases and had no witnesses. To save on money, they gave me an article 15 and busted me to a private. I finally got my PFC stripes back and have been behaving."

"Well, good for you. The way things are going, you're going to be a lifer in this man's Army," Dean said sarcastically.

"Hey man, I like the Army, I have reupped and I'm thinking of making it a career. I'm sorry if I caused you any trouble before."

He held his hand out toward Dean and they shook. He mentioned that he should get the jeep and pick up the colonel. He was gone in a flash and Dean was left alone again. The rest of night went without incident. Dean was glad to crawl back into his sleeping bag.

The next evening, Dean lead Willie and Clark to a guest-house where they served excellent food and beer. It was a two-story structure that was not too far from the base. The bar maid was quick and efficient, bringing the three large mugs of beer they ordered. Dean suggested they order a bratwurst or deep-fried breaded veal for dinner. They all ordered the veal. Dean noticed the other two were eyeing the young lady. She was brunette, had a great figure, was well endowed, and stood about five-feet eleven inches.

"Don't even think about it," Larson remarked knowingly.

"What? She is a fine-looking woman. It would be nice to get to know some of the natives. She might want me to come back and get to know her a lot better," remarked Willie.

"Yes, she is a beauty. Maybe she could handle two boyfriends," suggested Clark.

"She is too young. I bet you she's fourteen, maybe sixteen at the most."

"You're crazy. The way she looks? She has to be at least eighteen. Look how big busted she is," Willie commented.

"She is jail bait and her old man is behind the bar, watching us like a buzzard eyes road kill. I would imagine he owns this establishment and she helps the family out by taking orders."

Clark and Willie glanced at the big bar keeper, who was staring long and hard their way. Willie looked away and smiled. "I could take him. I bet he's slow. What is he doing, having his minor daughter wait tables?"

"I don't know what the laws are concerning minors, but I bet you that she is too young to accept a date with either one of you. If I'm right, you two pick up the check for everything, if I'm wrong, I pay for both of your meals."

They both agreed to the bet and when the young lady brought them their meals Dean questioned her after complimenting her on her English. "How long have you lived in Giebelstadt?"

"I was born here; my father owns this guesthouse."

"My friends and I were wondering how old you are."

"I'm fourteen and my father won't allow me to date yet." With that she turned tossing her hair in the air and adding a little more swing to her hip. Clark and Willie's jaws dropped. They shook their heads and took another sip of their beers. The food was good and Dean complemented their host on the meal and the brews as Willie and Clark paid the bill.

They walked through a portion of the town, stopping at several stores to purchase gifts for family and friends. It was late afternoon before they got back to the base in a taxi. Dean gave them the lowdown on what to do in a taxi. He emphasized the fact that they better never rob one.

It was nice to get a full night's sleep. He would have written Natalie a letter, but there was no way of getting it to her. He slept soundly for the night and felt rested the next day. He pulled maintenance on the goat and cleaned gear so everything would be ready for the war games they would be involved in soon. He noticed the absence of any women as he went about the base. He observed that there were a lot of men locked up in one area and they weren't letting very many of them go into Giebelstadt.

The Army in all of its wisdom set up a beer tent and invited a band to entertain the troops. After duty the next day, Dean, Willie, Clark, and Arthur Garcia wandered over to the tent to have a couple of beers and listen to the music.

It was a beautiful September day, so they had the sides of the tent up with a mesh hanging down to keep the insects out. The place was crowded, so they had to grab seats near Smoke Aston. He glared at them from dark eyes, his large frame leaned over the beer that he rolled back and forth on the table in his large hands. His red hair was cropped close to his face.

Willie greeted him, but he just continued to stare at his beer and the group. They were all given beers and Dean took his first sip. He didn't like the taste. It was the first time he had a German brew and didn't like it. It was green like it had not been aged long enough. He made a comment on that very subject, but Willie reminded him it was free, and Dean should shut up and enjoy the stuff.

After they had their second beer, the band came marching in. It was a band of seven women, dressed in gold hot pants with skimpy blouses and boots. It was hard not to notice them, but Dean already had two beers under his belt and was very happy. He looked over at Aston, who was not happy. His facial expressions indicated that he was a very mean drunk and he continued to glare at them.

Dean decided to ignore him and ordered another drink. All four of them were having a good time. Clark looked a little white around the gills, but was laughing and joking. They were about five tables away from the band and men were standing in front of them cheering the ladies on.

The band just started their fourth song when the fight broke out. It started with some pushing and shoving from men trying to get closer to the ladies so they could touch them. Soon there were flying fist and kicks swinging through the air. Willie jumped up on the table then jumped down to the bench on the other side of the next table.

Dean watched as he hit a helicopter pilot with a hard right. The man crumbled to the floor like a sack of potatoes. Garcia was right behind, plowing into the melee, but Dean wanted no part of it. He sat back and watched Aston go flying by, and slide under the insect mesh. He was running for his tent, not wanting to have the same problems as Barrett.

Dean turned his attention to Clark, who was taking on a shade of light green. Suddenly he heaved into Willie's litter mug of beer and rolled off the bench into the grass, where he threw up again. Everything seemed funny to Dean, he just kept laughing.

Eight MPs showed up, surrounding the band and escorting them out of the tent with some difficulty to a waiting van. They waded through the fighting men and rescued the instruments. The ladies were driven away, never to be see again. The MPs entered the fight one more time, breaking up the conflict. It had settled down a lot since the band left the tent.

Willie came back to the table with bruised knuckles and a sweaty face. Garcia was right behind him. Willie made some comment about Clark not being able to hold his liquor. Dean was still laughing, he held out a hand trying to stop Willie from drinking from his mug.

Willie ignored the gesture, hauling the large mug up to his lips with a quick swoop of his hands. He spit the mouthful of beer on the ground and swore, using some words Dean had not heard before. Willie turned to Dean with an angry look on his face. He started moving toward Dean. Dean held up a hand and pointed toward Clark. He was getting up on his hands and knees after getting rid of everything in his stomach. Willie could see where he had vomited. He kicked him in the mid-section, knocking him over into his own puke. Clark cursed and got up, wiped away his face, turned to take on the person that kicked him.

Clark suddenly realized it was Willie and bowed his head and apologized for getting sick in Willie's mug. Dean was still chuckling when Willie came around the table and slapped him in the back of the head. That stopped the laughter and Willie in-formed him that the smack was for giggling and for not warning him. Dean told him that he tried to stop him but that he was too fast with the drinking.

They decided they'd had enough fun, so they went back to the tent. As they walked, Dean told the others how Smoke had slipped out under the tent netting in such a hurry. Willie loved the story and started spreading it around the battery that Aston was a coward and he had run from the fight with his tail between his legs. Word eventually got back to Aston, and Dean could tell that he hated the four of them even more. They had one more day to relax in base camp before they went out to the field.

Chapter 8

AGAINST THE HORDE

The war games started off with the premise that the Soviet Union had launched a massive attack over the border. The 101st was to hold them off the best they could so that reinforcements could come stop them and counter attack. The 1st and 2nd Armored Division were the aggressors, stationed in Nuremberg. The operation was called Gordian Shield and started off on a crisp cool day in September.

The battery convoyed out to their first firing position early in the morning arriving just as the sun was peeking over the horizon. Ellis was Dean's assistant driver and they were pulling the generator that the FDC needed to do their job.

The games soon began. The battery had completed several fake fire missions but were being pressed by the armor units. The battery had to pick up and withdraw to a safer position. The battery had several more fake missions but had to move back again.

The battery went through all the motions of firing the weapons and the referees estimated where the rounds would have landed. If an enemy unit was in the area, a judgement call was made on how many casualties the unit suffered and those soldiers sat out the rest of the battle at base camp.

Alpha battery got into their final position about an hour before dark the first day. They set up and were given hot coffee and rations for the evening meal. It had been a long day with a lot of physical activity. Dean was worn out, but the Sergeant of the Guard woke him up at midnight to pull perimeter guard for two hours.

He caught a group of infantry trying to sneak through the camp. He challenged them and they gave the right password. It was a squad of grunts doing some recon late in the evening. They asked Dean what kind of unit he was guarding. Dean would not tell them but called the Sergeant of the Guard over to talk to them. After a brief discussion, the unit skirted around the rest of the battery. Dean could not help but wonder why they were scouting in the wrong direction.

When he was relieved, he fell into his sleeping bag and fell quickly to sleep. He was rudely awakened the next morning. Willie gave him a cup of coffee as he dragged him out of the mummy bag. He told Dean to keep low and motioned for him to follow. They were located in a tree line with a large open meadow in front of them. A crossroad was on the other side of the meadow. The road that ran alongside the field was clear, but the other road that intersected it was filled with tanks and they were coming directly toward the battery.

"The enemy," Willie said pointing at the tanks.

"Where are the grunts that are supposed to be in front of us?"

"Most likely high tailed it to a safe spot behind us."

"Well, that's a fine howdy-do. What are we going to do?" asked Dean.

"We've called in an air strike."

Dean took a drink of the strong black coffee and watched the long line of tanks. He could make out a least ten of the M-60 tanks. Suddenly, a jet appeared above the monsters and the battery went to work on the line of tanks adding to the make-believe destruction of the unit in front of them. After about twenty minutes, the tank unit was considered destroyed with a small fraction of the unit getting away. The battery was ordered to pack up, and retreat to a place where the infantry was in front of the guns.

As Dean was about to go help pack up the equipment, he noticed movement in one of the bushes in front of them. It was two mechanical mules with mounted TOW missile launchers on them. The TOW was built for the sole purpose of destroying tanks. The two little mules that had been hiding in the bushes quickly vacated the area.

Dean didn't even get breakfast; they were in such a hurry to get out of the area. They were soon driving at a high speed down a dirt road. Ellis was able to eat his cold rations while Dean drove the goat. They came to a fork in the road, Knight took the road to the left. Half of the battery had gotten through the intersection when Knight halted the convoy.

In his hurry to get out of the area, he had read the map wrong and the unit was supposed to go right at the crossroads. The road was narrow so they had a difficult time getting the battery turned around and moving down the correct road. Dean found himself at the end of the convoy with the XO as his assistant driver. Lieutenant Patton had to be at the end of the convoy in case a part of the battery got separated from the rest of the unit. He knew the map coordinates and how to get any stragglers to the next firing position.

The battery continued traveling on the dirt road, but Patton warned Dean they should be coming to a secondary road. Secondary roads were paved but they had only two lanes which would allow them to move much faster. They came to a lazy corner that went right. Dean saw the BC's jeep disappear around it, then gun one and so forth.

There were a lot of shrubs and trees on the corner so Dean slowed. Patton warned him not to lose the rest of convoy. Still

Dean felt a little uneasy about the road. He started around it and then he saw the barrel of a 105-howitzer sitting in the middle of the lane. They had come to the secondary road and a stop sign was posted at the corner of the dirt road. It would have been all right if the command jeep had been able to take off immediately, but there had been traffic causing the convoy to wait until the road was clear. Dean jumped on the brakes and shifted down, causing the Gamma Goat to slide a little, but Dean brought it out of the skid, bringing the goat back to the middle of the road.

The generator with trailer behind him added to the momentum and Dean knew instantly that he was not going to be able to stop in time. Patton had been leaning toward Dean talking to him. He looked forward to see the barrel of the 105 coming right at him. Patton quickly moved back toward the passenger door, but he had help.

Dean with his right hand, pushed him by the shoulder with all his might thrusting him away from the barrel. At the same time he had to push the brake as hard as he could. Larson pulled his hand back just as the tube came crashing through the center of the windshield. They both turned their heads so that Dean only got a small scratch on his cheek. The goat came to a sudden halt with the barrel ripping through the cab to the canvas that covered the cargo area.

Clark, who had been driving the command jeep, heard the skidding of tires and the impact of vehicles. He pointed the accident out to Top and the BC. They scampered out of the jeep and came running back to the end of the convoy. Dean and Patton looked at the tube in the cab and then over it at each other.

"I think I wet my pants a little," commented Dean with a small smile.

"You're lucky. I think I did something worse and I hope it doesn't stink too much."

"You two okay?" asked Childs.

"We just need to change our drawers," Patton breathed out.

The crew came staggering out of the back. They were cussing and making vivid threats on Dean's life. Some of them had been banged up pretty good, a couple of them came out with cuts that had to be bandaged, but nothing serious. The trailer with the generator had jackknifed but not turned over. The goat in front pulled up as far as they could, extracting the barrel from Dean's cab. They swept the glass up, getting it out of the cab. They unhooked the trailer and strong armed it into the proper position.

"Well, this is a combat situation, what are we going to do?" asked Top.

Patton started to speak up, but Childs cut him off by raising a hand. He looked at Dean with expectation.

"Well, Larson? Have you lost your voice, or do you have an answer for me?"

Dean stammered, wondering why he was picking on him. He looked over the goat and suggested dealing with the unsecure glass and frame of the vehicle and they would need goggles."

"Good answer, Larson. That is called adapting and overcoming the situation. You'll need to know that in the future. I'm glad you thought about the problem and worked out a solution."

The mechanics removed the frame.

"Mount up, we need to get out of here," Knight commanded.

The convoy proceeded down the secondary road coming to a village about twenty minutes later. That is where they finally caught up with their infantry. They proceeded through the village and took up their next firing position about a half hour down the road. Dean finally ate his first meal of the day. Even the cold rations tasted good. Coffee and another set of rations were given to everyone.

After talking to Patton, the BC decided that Larson was not at fault concerning the accident. They fired some more fake missions from this area and moved back once again, setting up camp in the dark. Dean threw his shelter half over a log, pulled out his mummy bag, and tucked it underneath. He crawled in and fell instantly into a deep sleep.

"Hey, wake up Larson," Willie was declaring as he shook Dean.

"Damn, man. It's still midnight, Willie. Why are you bothering me?"

It was still dark and Dean was exhausted from yesterday. It was cool and he did not want to get out of the sack.

"It's 0500 am and Ellis wants you in the FDC tent. From what I heard, you are going on advance party, so up and at it. They are going to put you on a chopper. Thank God. Maybe the rest of us will live through the rest of the day without you driving the goat."

Willie rubbed his shoulder and back which he had hurt in the accident.

"Quit your whining, Willie. It could have been much worse. After all, you could have been driving."

"That's true. You know I don't believe in going slow," he said laughing.

Dean grabbed up a cup of coffee on the way to the tent. He wanted some bacon and eggs really bad. At least he wouldn't have to wait until the middle of the day before he got his first meal. Knight, Aston, Ellis, and a couple of men from each gun were in the tent.

Knight informed them they were going to do an air assault behind enemy lines. They would set up, fire the rounds and return back to their own lines. An infantry unit would fly in before them and establish security.

They were taken by Gamma Goat to a meadow not far from camp. Two Chinook helicopters were standing by. It was always the same story, both units stood nearby waiting for the pilots to show up. The pilots appeared twenty-five minutes later. During that time, Dean gulped down his food and drank his coffee.

The pilots started the engines. Dean sat near Ellis, close to the back where the large door was. He would be one of the first ones off when the chopper landed. The helicopter took off at a steep angle. They wasted no time getting down range. They were flying combat mode, following as close to the terrain as possible. Up and down hills, around and through the valleys. A couple times he was sure he felt the chopper scrape the top of trees. He never lost his breakfast, but he had to concentrate with all that was in him to keep it down. A couple of the soldiers lost it, and Dean being at the back of the aircraft caught whiff of the odor once in a while. He was glad that the wind was blowing through the cargo bay.

The chopper with infantry landed first. The soldiers ran out in every direction, making a perimeter for the artillery. The second helicopter landed and Dean ran out of the backend taking a position behind some bushes near the center of the meadow. Ellis came and crouched down near him. After the Chinook had taken off, the BC and Top surveyed the area and laid out where the units were to take up their positions.

Suddenly, to the north of them they heard screaming and several blank rounds being fired off. Childs ordered Dean and several other advance party people to the area to make sure that it stayed secured. Before they could get into position to repel any aggressors, wild boars came shooting out of the shrub. They were hauling tail, running as fast as they could, crossing the meadow for the forest on the other side.

A grunt came out of the woods where the pigs had just exited. He called for help and waved them toward the area. Dean rushed toward the man and followed him into the tree line. One of the soldiers was down on the ground, holding his leg. He had surprised the boars and one of them had turned on him lacerating the right calve of his leg.

Dean helped the other soldier put a bandage on the wound while an infantry sergeant supervised the operation. They pulled out his poncho and laid him on it. Dean and three others hauled him to an area near the LZ [landing zone]. There were no medics in the advance party, so they found some painkillers someone had brought for headaches and gave him several, which helped some. The large bandage that had been applied to the wound seem to slow down the bleeding.

The next chopper brought more grunts in, they came rushing out to strengthen the perimeter. Some of them slowed with startled looks as their buddy was carried onto the chopper. One of them fell back to take care of him as the aircraft whisked him to a medical unit.

The next six choppers brought the six guns and crews of Alpha battery in. The guns were strapped to the underbelly of the choppers. A man would have to carefully unhook the strap from the hook without touching the metal itself. If he touched the hook, he would get a nasty shock because the whirling rotor blades of the helicopter produced powerful static electricity.

Next came the FDC's Gamma Goat, it was Dean's turn to unhook it. Once it hit the ground, he climbed up on it and pulled the straps off the hook. He forgot to take his helmet off, so it went flying off into the grass because of the swirling winds. Ellis retrieved it for him. The chopper landed and the rest of the crew pulled out the generator. After all was clear, Dean hooked up the generator and towed it to the position that the BC had mapped out for them.

They set up, shot about fifteen rounds, and flew out without getting caught by the armor divisions. Dean wondered if it made any difference in the war games. The Chinooks came flying in with Cobra attack helicopters as their escorts. The guns and crews were taken out first and then Dean had to hook up the goat to the chopper.

He had done it only one other time, but this time he got a lesson in pain when the hook swung and touched his arm. The shock knocked him to the ground and dazed him for a few minutes. Ellis and Childs were at his side in a few seconds. Ellis pulled him up on his feet and offered to hook it up himself but Childs insisted that Dean finish the job. Dean gingerly climbed up in the cab of the vehicle and moved with the swinging hook attaching the straps to it without another shocking experience. The next chopper took the advance party out and flew them to their own lines. They flew combat mode and Dean had to hold down his lunch as the Chinook lurched this way and that following the terrain.

The 101st gave ground, but they never broke and they inflicted more casualties than they received. Alpha battery was constantly on the move, but put out a lot of rounds. The first few days the enemy never zeroed in on the unit but at the end of the maneuvers it lost several men to the fighting. Dean was one of them, he was marked as "wounded" and they evacuated him back to base, where he caught up on drinking beer and reading a book for a couple of days.

When the rest of the unit came back to base, they looked worn out, dirty, and hungry. Willie complained about the food out in the field, never cooking them one hot meal. Back in Kentucky when it was all over with, the cooks would get citations for their outstanding work during Reforger 76. The only thing they fixed for the soldiers was hot coffee and it was not good coffee. The next day, after showers and hot food, they started cleaning the equipment and relaxing a little.

Chapter 9

DOWN TIME

After a couple of days cleaning up equipment and repairing things, they started the runs and PT again. They were getting hot food and time at the beer tent. Aston called A Battery out after breakfast one morning and they were loaded up on a bus. As they were traveling down a secondary road, one of the men up front yelled that there was a woman going to the bathroom on the side of the road. The car that she was trying to hide behind was a white BMW, turned out on the left side of the curve. She would have stayed hidden but the bus was high, allowing the soldiers to look down and over the vehicle.

All the men on the right side of the bus ran to the left side to gawk at the poor woman. The only one that stayed seated was Dean, who had run into such sights on his trips all over Europe. The nations of Europe did not provide rest stops, so people stopped at a convenient place to take care of business.

The bus was taking a tight corner and with all the weight on the left side and the vehicle being top heavy, it leaned hard to the left. The bus driver's eyes were as big as saucers. Top yelled at everyone to get back into their seats and the bus came back down, bringing all four wheels back down on the ground again.

The bus took them to the east border and the soldiers of the 101st were given a practical lesson in what it was to lock up a whole people, the East Germans behind the iron curtain. They were taken up on a hill and shown one of the border crossings.

The check point was placed in between two small hills and had two large metal slabs of metal on each side of the road. If the communist wanted to block the road completely, all they had to do was throw a switch and the metal slabs came rolling across the road on rails.

Next, they took the unit to a town that had a stream running through it. On the east side was East Germany and the iron curtain while on the west side was freedom. The East German government had established a fence about fifteen-feet high with strands of barb wire on strong poles. It ran along their side of the stream.

In some areas, large dogs roamed freely between another fence of barbed wire, but it was not as high. The only thing that stopped the fence was a building. They were always built with brick and they never had windows.

Guard towers sprang up every once in a while. They always had two guards. The guide told them there was always a Russian soldier with an East German trooper. Otherwise, the Germans would try to escape to the West. The guards would scope out the 101st soldiers and take notes on units and names. It was unsettling to Dean to have two soldiers with AK-47s watching him through binoculars.

The guide stopped everyone at one section of the fence to tell the group about an escape that had occurred in the last six months. He pointed out the road that went into the town. It ran up a hill and at the top on the right-hand side was a guesthouse. The road was used to feed the two soldiers in the guard tower which stood about forty yards to the right of the gates. The road ran through two fences and if a vehicle entered, they would have to maneuver it through one gate and then a man would have to go through a small gate with the food on foot.

A large brick wall was erected in front of the gates, it had not been there before the escape. A beer truck driver stopped at the guesthouse to off load his order of beer. He got into his truck, got back out and drank some beer which was unusual. He got back into his truck, backed up, and started down the access road. He was traveling at a fairly high rate of speed when he busted through the first gate, surprising the guards. They shouldered their rifles by the time he hit the second gate making it a lot larger with his truck. He had to cover about seventy-five yards before he made the creek. The guards had started firing.

The rounds came zinging through the window splashing glass all over him. He was laying on the seat, head down, but his foot was pressing the gas pedal all the way to the floor. Once he came to the stream, the truck turned over on the right side. It protected him from the searching AK-47 rounds, which were sprouting up everywhere. The windshield had been shot out, so he kicked out any glass left in place and crawled out to the front of the truck. Some West German police came to his rescue and helped him escape to the west.

They continued to walk along the border discussing more points of interest. A few more stories were told of other escapes to freedom. Dean noticed that one of the dogs was just a little smaller than a bear. Yet with every story told of people risking their lives to ditch the enslavement of the east, he wondered how often he had taken his own freedom for granted.

He lived in Baumholder for almost two years and had never seen the iron curtain. It was a real education, and the message of the tour guides would stick with him for a long time.

A few days later, Dean was ordered to be an usher for some of the big brass in NATO. He had to spit shine his boots and iron his utility uniform. It was hard finding an iron, but he did get a crease down his pants and shirt sleeve. He showed generals and colonels from various countries where to sit during a demonstration of the fire power the 101st could bring to the battlefield. They started with soldiers repelling out of helicopters near the seating stands. It was fun watching the brass trying to keep their hats on their heads from the rotary wash of the choppers.

Next, some of the mechanical mules and crews fired their TOW missiles from camouflage positions on several vehicles that were in the area. The next demonstration was the Cobra Attack Helicopters. One suddenly appeared from below a grove of trees and unleashed its Gatlin guns on the targets, the rounds ripping great gaping holes in the vehicles and a great explosion consumed one of the targets in the middle of a cluster of machines. The instructor pointed at a puff of smoke about a thousand yards out. It was a Cobra hovering off the ground that had sent the missile into the targets.

Dean could tell the audience was impressed with the demonstrations. They asked a lot of questions of the instructor and he answered most of them. They asked how many rounds the Gatlin guns could put out and how far could the TOW missile be fired and still hit its target. Once all the questions were asked and answered, a final demonstration took place.

A Chinook helicopter flew a 105-howitzer in underneath the chopper. It lowered it to the ground and a man came running out of the bush to unhook the gun. The Chinook went forward a little distance, landed, and the gun crew disembarked from the back of it.

They were carrying their rounds with them. Within a few minutes they were ready to fire. They fired three rounds each and the demonstration came to an end. The audience asked a few more questions and they left talking among themselves about what they had just seen.

Dean was given the privilege of going with a group of soldiers from Alpha Battery to celebrate Octoberfest in Munich. They had beer tents everywhere and the city was alive with party goers. Willie and Clark stuck close to Dean. He found the beer that he thought was the best tasting and about five men from the 101st settled in for the afternoon to eat great German food and drink the beer. Willie almost got into it with several Germans over a big busted blonde woman. Dean stepped in, reminding Willie of German police and being thrown into prison. They relocated to a new beer tent and the afternoon wore on toward the evening. Dean got Clark and Willie to go with him to see some of the sights in the city before they had to go back to Giebelstadt. It was a pleasant day, but he was ready to get back to his tent and his cot.

He was in Germany for about forty days when Top called him into the command tent. He was told they were sending him back home on the advance party. He could hardly contain himself; he was so happy. He was more than ready to get back to his wife and John. Besides that, Natalie would be fairly close to giving birth to their next child. Two days later, he was in a C-140 with a bunch of other soldiers flying back to the states.

Chapter 10

A WARM WELCOME

It was a cool evening as he stepped off the plane onto the Kentucky landscape. There was no fanfare and Dean had decided to surprise Natalie by not telling her that he was coming home early. The rest of the unit would have to pack up gear and do a couple more demonstrations and visit more sites before they got back to Fort Campbell.

A truck picked them up at the airfield and about a dozen men climbed aboard. The duce and half carried them back to the various barracks to drop them off so they could report in. Dean made known that he was back at A battery, then he called a taxi so he could get home. It was about eight o'clock Friday night. He would have the weekend to get rested up and spend some time with John and Natalie.

He caught a ride to the gate and waited patiently for the taxi, which seemed forever before it picked him up. He had the taxi drop him off a couple mobile homes down from his place. He paid the driver and shouldered the duffle bag and slowly walked the short distance to their home.

He could hear music seeping through the two large windows that framed their kitchen. He crept up the steps and knocked on the door. The music stopped and he heard a rustling inside. Natalie's gentle voice asked who it was at the door. Dean kept quiet and knocked again. Natalie was a little louder, with a touch of fear, as she asked the question again. Dean remained silent but knocked again. He heard a flurry of activity and then heard Natalie ask the question again. Dean smiled to himself and was about to knock again when he heard the metallic click of the lever on a 30-30 charge a round into the magazine. Dean remembered the rifle and realized that Natalie was about to protect herself and John.

"Who is out there? I'm going to shoot!"

"Hold fire, Natalie! It's your loving husband Dean!"

There was a moment of silence and then the door flew open and Natalie came flying into his arms. She hugged him so tight he couldn't catch his breath. She planted a kiss on him and told him the fight they had before he left was forgotten. She was just glad to have him back. He felt a tug at his leg and his son was clamped around his left one. When Natalie let go of him, he picked John up and clutched him to his chest. He had missed his son so very much he kissed him and tickled him until his laughter filled the area.

Natalie hit him playfully on the arm, "You almost got yourself shot Dean. What were you thinking? I didn't expect you for another two weeks."

"Top let me come back early because of you. He wanted me to be around in case the little one came early. He sure has been nice to me. It almost scares me at times."

She dragged him inside. He looked to the left of the door and the 30-30 was leaning against the wall. The hammer was still cocked open, he picked it up and emptied the round out of the chamber. He put the weapon up in the closet, then pulled off his field jacket, boots, and hat. He took a seat on the couch.

Natalie brought him a cup of coffee and he relaxed. The trip from Europe had sapped him. She questioned him about Reforger 76 and he answered a couple of her questions before falling asleep. She took the coffee out of his hand, leaned him full length on the couch, and covered him with a blanket.

Dean woke with a start, not knowing where he was. It was still dark and everything seemed so unfamiliar until he made out the items in his living room and remembered the warm welcome he got from Natalie. He smiled to himself and was comforted by the fact that she would have protected John and herself from any intruders. He sat up, took off his shirt, and wandered over to the stove where he turned it on to warm up the coffee.

He knew his inner clock was messed up and sleep was going to come at some very inopportune times. He sat and savored his coffee for a while. Natalie knew how to make a good cup. He rummaged through the drawers on the desk and found some letters from Natalie's sister and parents.

It looked like everyone was doing well. Jack said the farm had been very productive this year but his father was slowing down even more. Jack was going to be a father which was exciting to Dean. Natalie's other sister was dating a guy she had been going to school with. Dean found a newspaper that was two days old and consumed it and a magazine before Natalie started rousing up out of bed.

When she emerged from the bedroom her hair was in tangles and the robe hung over her stomach like a tent. He loved her and thought she looked beautiful. Her first comment was on how bad she looked, but their first kiss was long and intent. The hug told him she had missed him and was glad that he was home. She fixed him a breakfast of pancakes, eggs, and bacon with fresh coffee and they talked while they sat at the dining table.

"So, what are your plans for today?"

"I'm going to relax and spend time with you and John. Nothing exciting, if you don't mind today."

"No, that sounds good to me, but if you don't mind, I would like to go to church tomorrow and we need to go to the store tomorrow for groceries."

"Sounds like a plan to me. How did the car run for you while I was gone?"

"She ran good. I had no problems. I did go with Carrie a lot of times."

"So, I read the letters. I guess we are going to be an aunt and uncle."

"I called Helen when I got the news. She is so excited and my parents are about to burst. A grandchild close enough to spoil."

Suddenly, they were interrupted by John, who came running out of his bedroom and jumped into his father's lap. Dean threw his son up in the air with squeals of delight coming from the little boy. He wrestled him to the ground, tickling him and kissing him on the neck. The little boy laughed all the more until Natalie broke it up to get her son to eat breakfast. Dean talked to John about his days of playing around the house and what Mommy had been doing.

It was late morning Natalie was about to fix him lunch. It had been a special time with all of them getting connected. His peace was interrupted by a ruckus outside. He could make out Carrie Morton's voice but couldn't understand what she was saying. She sounded agitated and he could make out a man's voice, but did not recognize who it was. Natalie turned from the kitchen and announced that Jon Kelly, the landlord, had been trying to seduce Carrie almost to the point of harassing her.

Dean got up and looked out the window, Jon had grabbed ahold of Carries arm and was gently but firmly pulling on her. It seemed he was trying to entice her to come along with him. Dean started for the door, but Natalie grabbed him before he could exit.

She asked him if he thought he should get involved. He told her he thought Morton would get involved if Jon was bothering her. She nodded and let go of him.

As he walked down the step, he thought about how he should handle it. He wanted to go over and punch him in the face. As he turned the corner of the mobile home and came in on the scene, he decided that he would give him a warning and hopefully Jon would go away.

"Hey. Let her go right now, Jon, or I'll kick your butt up between your ears."

Jon and Carrie were taken by surprise.

"Ah when did you get back?" Jon asked, releasing Carrie's arm.

"Last night. What do you think you're doing, bothering Morton's wife while he's gone? If he ever found out, he would break your face and I would help him."

"Just because you're in the army, doesn't make you so tough. I was just trying to be friendly, no harm in that."

"It started about a week after you guys left. He started coming around the place suggesting that he could fix things that didn't need fixing. He has become more aggressive lately, grabbing me and making nasty remarks," Carrie complained.

"Jon, you're a real low life. I thought you were Kevin's friend and I think you should trot on home before I lose my cool."

"You don't scare, me," Jon yelled, rushing forward and raising a right fist at the same time.

Dean ducked under the punch, charging forward and catching Jon with his shoulder in the belly. Dean then forced him back with a charge of his own. Jon lost his balance, but gained it when Dean drove him up against the wall of Morton's home. Jon put his hands on Dean's shoulders, trying to push him back, but Dean flung his arms up, driving Jon's arms away and at the same time stepped back, arched his elbow using his hip, and he drove the forearm into Jon's face. Jon slumped to the ground and Dean kicked him between the legs.

Dean could see that he had broken Jon's nose, it was spirting blood at a good rate. He was doubled over and groaning. "If you ever come on to Carrie or any of my friend's wives again, you're going to get some more of the same," Dean hissed.

"Come, Dean. Let me get Joan and we'll go see Natalie," Carrie said as she pulled Dean to her front door.

"You all right, Carrie?"

"Yes, thanks to you. How is that husband of mine?"

"He is fine. I just saw him a couple of days ago. He misses you and Joan, told me to tell you that he loves you both. He sent me back with a letter for you."

They went to her door, grabbed Joan and went to Dean's place. Jon was still on the ground as the three of them went to see Natalie. They sat down and Natalie served them with coffee. John and Joan went into his bedroom to play. Dean retrieved the letter from Morton and gave it to Carrie.

She read it over a couple of times while they sipped their coffee. Dean got up and looked out the window and didn't see Jon. He had crawled or walked to his home hopefully. Carrie wiped a few tears from her eyes and commented that things would be different if Kevin were home. Dean assured her that he would take care of her until Morton was back. If she had any trouble with Jon, she should come running and he would step up to the plate.

Carrie changed the subject to what had happened in Germany. She wanted to know when Morton was coming home, how did he look, and was he doing well. She questioned Dean why he got to come home early. Dean pointed at Natalie and Carrie laughed. She had forgotten how close Natalie was due with the new baby. After about an hour and half of visiting, she scooped Joan up and they went home.

Dean dug a letter out for Suzan Porter and walked it over to their place. She made him sit down and tell her about Germany and how Ross was doing. He made it quick as he could, he just wanted to get back home and relax. He visited with her and the two girls for about a half hour. Suzan had also been bothered by the landlord, but had threatened him with a shotgun. He never came back.

Dean sat down in his easy chair and was taking a nap when someone started pounding on the door. He was concerned that it might be Jon wanting a little revenge, so he peeked out the window. To his surprise it was two police officers. One of them spotted him and told the other who pounded on the door again. He opened it and asked the officers if he could help them. They asked him his name and he informed them that he was Dean Larson. They pulled him out of the house and shoved him against the wall. They frisked him and put handcuffs on him.

Natalie was crying and asking why Dean was being arrested. They wouldn't even speak to her until she started down the steps. They warned her that she should stay in the house unless she wanted to be arrested. John was wrapped around her leg crying. It was a horrifying sight to Dean and he was angered by what was happening.

They threw him into the back of the police car. They never told him what he was arrested for or any of his rights. They took him to the Hopkinsville's police station and reported in at the desk. He finally found out what he was charged with. It was assault and battery on Jon Kelly. He tried to tell his side of the story, but they dldn't want to hear it. They just threw him into a jail cell.

He tried to think of a way of getting out, but nothing came to mind. He had never been a guest in a jail before and he did not like the circumstances that he found himself in now. The thought of the one phone call came to mind but he didn't know any lawyers. What's more, the friends he did have that might know a good attorney were all in Germany. He got up and paced, but that didn't help at all. He still didn't have a clue as to what he should do.

He relived the fight, how it became so natural to him. When he saw Jon come at him, he ducked under, moving in, pushing him to the wall of the mobile home and rotating his hip back and then forward to get the maximum power as he swung his forearm into Jon's face. The blood oozing from his nose while Dean knew for sure that Jon would have at least one black eye from the deal. The defining touch was the kick in his groin. Now he wished he'd given him a few more kicks to make it worth his while.

It had paid off doing hand to hand combat with Willie during their off time in Germany. One time when they were playing around, Dean was behind him while Arthur was to his right, and Clark was on his left. He was smiling and warned them not to attack him. Arthur yelled "go" and the three of them ran in on him at the same time. He slapped Clark and Arthur in the face and kicked back, hitting Dean in the chest stopping him in his tracks. The slaps were playful and the kick had no power in it. They all laughed and the three of them jumped on him, playfully roughing him up. Willie was so quick with his hands and legs.

It made Dean smile and he wondered if he should not have stayed in Germany. He took inventory of what had happened so far since his return. He was almost shot by his wife. His friend's wife was being sexually harassed by the landlord so he took care of business. For doing a good deed, he was arrested and thrown into jail. Would Jon try to raise the rent on him for what he had done? So many thoughts were flying through his head that he was getting a headache.

He was interrupted by a ruckus in the outer room. The noise started rolling toward him and he could make out Natalies's voice. He had never heard Natalie yell at him even when they fought, which wasn't often. She always spoke at an even keel, but her eyes would flash and her words were always biting. The door flew open and a police sergeant stepped through with Natalie close behind and Carrie behind her.

"Well, did you ask him, his side of the story sergeant?" asked Natalie. Dean could tell she was livid. He had never seen her so angry.

"No Mrs. Larson we did not," the policeman stuttered.

"Is that how you investigate everything around here? Just because Jon was a hometown boy, you took his word as gospel and didn't even talk to my husband."

"Well Mrs. Larson we have a lot of trouble with soldiers from Fort Campbell. We eventually find out their side of the story."

"My husband just got back from Germany last night. You sure know how to throw a welcome home party, sergeant. Here I am, pregnant, and those two gorillas come in our home, they don't say a word, they threaten me with jail time if I come down off the steps. They cuff him and bring him here, and you still don't investigate the charges that were brought against him. I'm thinking about suing everyone involved. What kind of lousy police force is this anyway?"

"I'm sorry, ma'am. I will have a talk with the officers that were involved."

He opened up the cell door, releasing Dean from his confinement. Natalie grabbed his hand and dragged him toward the front door.

"Do I need to come back?" Dean asked stunned.

"No!" The word exploded out of Natalie.

The policeman waved him toward the door.

One of the policemen that had arrested Dean was walking up the steps while the three were descending. The policeman looked surprised and Natalie glared at him. "Sir, it is only because I'm a lady that I don't tell you what I think of you. I warn you, if we ever have another incident like we had this morning with you or your partner, I will be speaking with an attorney, the press, the mayor, the general at Campbell, and anyone else that will listen to me. You, you policeman," Natalie had wanted to call him a name, but held it in.

She rushed Dean and Carrie to the car. Dean could do nothing but smile at the policeman as Natalie led them to the Cornet. She was going to drive, but Dean guided her to the passenger seat, where he opened the door and helped her in. He drove them back home, but Natalie was not done. She went over the incident several times, fuming all the way.

Dean did get the rest of the story. After the police had carted him off, she had gone to Carrie and both women had called the desk sergeant. Carrie told the man what had occurred and that she was going to charge Jon with attempted rape and that Dean had defended her. They were going to file a law suit against the city for false arrest and they would be talking to the press and the mayor's office if something wasn't done immediately.

She suggested that they tell Jon that if he tried to raise the rent or evict them that they would take legal action against him. As they drove up to the driveway, Dean made the comment that he would have bet they had never seen Tornado Natalie coming until it was too late.

Dean went into the house while Natalie retrieved John from the Porter home. Dean remembered sitting in the big chair and leaning back. He started thinking about the events of the day and realized how weary he was. Before Natalie got back home, he was asleep and didn't wake up until ten am the next morning. That Sunday they lounged around, talking, laughing, and watching television. They did not make it to church after all.

Chapter 11

A LITTLE GIRL

Dean was waiting by the airfield, watching the sky for the next C-140 to land. It was a very cool day in late October. A couple of weeks had passed since the problem with Jon Kelly had occurred. He was going to pick up Knight, Childs, and Aston and ferry them back to the battery area. After that he was supposed to come back and help the rest of the unit unload the equipment and get it stored away. It was late afternoon and he was considering all the events that had occurred.

They had not seen Jon since the fight, which was fine with everyone involved. They were going to watch very closely to see what happened with their rents. Dean would wake up randomly and walk around Morton's place, which Carrie appreciated to the extent of baking the Larsons a cake.

Natalie was feeling miserable lately. It looked like the baby had dropped and she was visiting the bathroom a lot more. Dean started taking classes again and had run into Ann a couple of times. They were cordial to one another, but she didn't seem to be pursuing him like she had been. This took a lot of pressure of Dean, and he felt more relaxed during lessons.

He heard the rumble of the big plane engines and looked up to see the sun glinting off the silver wings of the aircraft. It was arching and turning to make its approach on the runway. The landing was clean and the pilot taxied off the main landing strip toward the tower. Dean drove the jeep near the plane.

The BC, XO, Top, and Smoke were the first ones off. They packed into the vehicle with their duffle bags. It was crowded and Dean had to take it easy driving them to the barracks. He let them off and was about to drive back to the airfield when the duty officer came running out and stopped him. He informed Dean that Natalie had just called to say Carrie was taking her to the hospital. She was having contractions. Childs told him to get his tail end over to the hospital, that she needed him more than the army did.

He parked the jeep, dashed to his Dodge and took off for the hospital. It took him about ten minutes. They were admitting her as he came running into the waiting room. She smiled at him, but he could see her grimace in pain from a contraction.

John came running into Dean's arms and asked him what was wrong with Mommy. Dean told him that she had a tummy ache and that she would be well soon. Carrie retrieved John from his arms. Dean suggested they go home because Morton would be home soon.

The nurses came out and gowned him up and took him to Natalie's room. About ten minutes after that, the doctor came in and checked her out. He confirmed what they suspected the baby was coming and he ordered the nurse to come in and check her every fifteen minutes or so.

Dean held Natalie's hand and wiped her forehead as she struggled with the contractions. He saw the same inner strength and determination in her that he had seen when John was born. After two and a half hours and much pain, the doctor held up a baby daughter. Natalie instantly asked why her little girl wasn't crying. She had entered the world without saying a word.

The doctor took her to a table and spanked her on the bottom a couple of times. She let out a loud cry and the parents felt a lot better. The doctor brought the baby over to them and Natalie started breast feeding her which stopped the crying. Dean ran his hand over her face, stroking her check. She was so soft and seemed to smile at his touch. After she had eaten, Dean took her in his arms and checked her over. She seemed to have all of her body parts.

All through the examination, she had this expression of peace on her face and didn't even whimper while she was being handled. She was a lot smaller than her older brother when he had been born. She either had dark blonde hair or real light brown hair. They had already decided to call her Melody. As he held her, she seemed to relax in his arms and suck on nothing.

Dean stayed with them for about an hour in the hospital. They were going to keep both of them for a couple of days. He found a pay phone and called the Morton family to let them know about Melody and Natalie. They were going to pass it on to the Porter family. Dean put a call into the company clerk's office but it was late and Clark was no longer on duty. Childs was just leaving and picked up the phone on his way out the door. Dean gave him the news about his little girl and Childs congratulated him.

He had to go get a box of cigars on the way home, get his uniform ready for tomorrow and pick up John from the Morton's. He picked up the cigars and some beer, the beer would help him relax after a tense day. Kevin met him at the door when he knocked. He had just started thanking him the instant he walked over the threshold. Carrie interrupted him to find out about the baby.

Dean told her about Melody and Natalie and informed Kevin that he didn't have to thank him, Kevin would have done the same for him. Dean told them about the labor and that Natalie was doing well. They had already fed John and he was already sleeping in Joan's room. They suggested John stay overnight.

Dean accepted the invitation, gave Kevin a cigar. He took one out for himself and they lit up smoking them out on the porch. It was an old tradition smoking cigars when a new child was brought into the family. Dean didn't know where it came from but it was a matter of pride and declaring that the baby was special and already loved.

He went home fixed his uniform for the next day and got some dinner. Dean called his father and gave him the news that he was a new grandfather. His father sounded very excited about having a little granddaughter. He hung up and immediately called the Bakers and gave them the news about Melody and Natalie. They asked all sorts of questions and he didn't have all the answers but promised to get them and call them again the next day. He admitted that he was wore out and needed to get some rest. At that he ended the conversation, sat down, had a couple of beers and fell asleep in his overstuffed chair watching television.

Kevin woke him up the next morning by banging on the door. Dean quickly got dressed, drank a cup of coffee, and ate a piece of toast as Morton drove them to the battery. He was able to give Knight and Childs a cigar before he had to go to formation. After the roll call, he gave everyone in the FDC section a cigar. He made sure Porter got one, but when he offered it to Aston, Smoke turned it down and gave some nasty remark about rug rats that Dean didn't quite hear. It irritated him and he thought about making some smart remark about his ancestry, but let it slide.

Clark came out from the office and informed him to report to Childs when he was done handing out his cigars. He was informed by Top that he needed to report to Sergeant Porter on Monday.

Porter was E-6 sergeant and had earned the right to run gun six, so Dean was going to become a gun bunny. He had forgotten almost everything he had learned in AIT about the guns. The 105 mm howitzer was nothing like the 8-inch gun. Childs informed him that he needed to learn everything about the gun because he planned on recommending him before the NCO board to get his sergeant's stripes.

Dean was happy with the assignment. He was excited about being a part of Porter's gun crew. Arthur was also assigned to that crew, so he knew the eight-man crew already. Dean didn't understand why Childs wanted him to try out for sergeant; he didn't plan on staying in the army, it seemed like a waste of time.

The day dragged. He helped FDC clean up their gear and store it away. They all seemed to go through the motions, with everyone moving at a slower pace. Willie admitted smuggling some hashish back from Germany. He offered to share it with Dean but Larson rejected the invitation. He had hidden it in the breach of gun number six, the one that Dean was going to be assigned to. Garcia had helped him ship the stuff back home in the hopes that he would share it with him.

That evening, Dean took John to meet his new sister. They imparted to him that she was very small and that he had to be careful with her and that it was his job to protect her. He seemed to get the message and he treated her with loving care. He continued to be that way when they brought Melody home Friday afternoon. Saturday morning, Natalie sat straight up in bed. It woke Dean up.

"What's wrong, Natalie? Did the baby cry?"

"No, that is what worries me. I haven't heard a whimper out of her."

Natalie jumped out of bed and rushed to the crib. She felt the new child, her chest was heaving up and down. She was still breathing.

"Is she alright?" asked Dean with great concern.

"Yes, she is fine. Sleeping like she doesn't have a care in the world. By this time of night John was always waking me up to eat." she said with a sigh of relief.

It took them two weeks to get used to Melody sleeping through the night most of the time. They would often wake in the midnight hour wondering what was wrong with her. She rarely cried, only complaining when she was hungry or needed her diaper changed. She seemed to smile often and cooed when someone talked to her.

Chapter 12

PORTER

Porter picked Dean up on Monday morning. They had decided to share rides since they were going to be working together. Dean noticed on the ride to base that Porter was different somehow. He couldn't put his finger on it, but he was keeping Dean at a distance emotionally. He didn't say much on the ride except that Childs had told him to give Dean a crash course on the M101, which was the army's nomenclature for the 105-mm howitzer. Usually, the crew was made up of nine men, but one of Porter's crew had just gotten out of the army.

After formation, Porter threw the manual on the gun to Dean and told him to study it. The crew would have to do some maintenance on the goat and the gun. There were six guns that made up the battery and the 105 was a pop gun compared to the 8-inch. It was a towed weapon, meaning they had to use the goat or a helicopter to get it where they wanted it. The gun could send the thirty-three-pound round down range about seven miles. Still, it was a very accurate weapon for close infantry support.

The ammunition was semi-fixed, in other words it looked like a regular bullet, but the brass, casing could be pulled off the round where the bags of powder were stored. The bags that were not needed were pulled out of the casing and burned. The powder could never be used again because the potency changed with age.

Dean studied the manual while the rest of the crew worked on the equipment. Dean did notice that Porter was very good at his job. He was not a dictator, but would jump in leading the way on any task that he assigned the crew. He didn't mind getting dirty, in fact he seemed to enjoy that part of the job. In between tasks, he would come over and ask Dean about what he had just read. He was also very good at answering any questions Dean had on the weapon. Porter was always patient with him, taking time to show any part of the gun that he had a question on. Dean knew that he was busy because he had to get everything ready for the battery test which was going to take place in January, just a couple of months in the future.

At lunch, they sat together and Porter asked him about his life before he joined the army. Porter had a general idea about Dean's history on the farm in Idaho from earlier conversations. He seemed more attentive to details and asked a lot of questions.

"What about you Porter? Let's start with the army. Where did you do basic?"

"Fort Bliss in Texas. It was as hot as Hell, that's when I decided I didn't want to go to Hell. It was in the middle of summer. Then I went to Fort Sill Oklahoma for AIT. They taught us about artillery on the self-propelled 155s."

"Same here, except I took basic at Fort Ord in California. Where was your first duty station?"

"Nam," Porter said quietly. He gave Dean a distant look, then turned away and his shoulders sagged a little.

"If you don't want to talk about it, don't. It can't be good memories. We can talk about your family, or how it was growing up and family."

"No, that's fine," he said with a smile. He seemed to be a little uncomfortable with the subject, but it had come up, so he decided to share his experiences with a fellow soldier.

"It was hot muggy, and ugly. I hated it right off. They assigned me to a 155 unit, took me to the supply depot and gave me all the gear I needed to survive out in the field except for a good rifle. They gave me a M-16 with a broken extractor. Once I fired the weapon, I had to pull back the charging handle to get rid of the brass casing, chamber another round, then I was ready to fire another round. The second day in country, they took me by chopper to a fire base where I was assigned to gun three. I met the BC and he gave me a little pep talk and told me about the crew I would be working with. I told him about my problem with my rifle and he told me to inform the sergeant in charge so he could take care of the situation."

"They gave you a rifle that didn't work properly?"

"Yep, a h-- l of a way to go to war, but no one seemed to be concerned about it except me. I was escorted to a bunker where some of the crew was staying. I found me an empty cot and stowed my gear away. A couple of guys offered me a beer and we talked for a little while. Most of them had already crashed.

They had several fire missions the night before and were exhausted. My sergeant came in and introduced himself to me. His name was Kaleb, he was a nice guy who seemed to care about his men. He took me over to the supply man where we ordered a new extractor or a new M-16, Porter took a bite of his food and drank some water. He looked away to some noise that was taking place somewhere in the mess.

He took a deep breath and continued his story. "I got a working rifle that evening. We were hit by a large body of enemy soldiers. I was separated from the rest of the crew in the midst of the confusion and fighting. I shot at several enemy soldiers, but I don't know if I hit anyone. I decided to hide in a bunker. When I ran in, I found 'Charlie' hovering over a dead GI he had just killed. He tried to swing around to shoot me, but I was faster. I shot him in the chest. He went down like a sack of wheat. I must have hit him in the heart. I've never seen so much blood. I went over to get the dead GI's rifle. I looked down into the face of the man that I shot. He looked like he was about fifteen years old. That face still haunts me to this day. We lost two members of the crew that day. I couldn't even remember who they were. All I could think of when Sergeant Kaleb told me, was that I was glad it wasn't me."

About that time lunch was over, Porter picked up what food he had not ate and consumed it on the way to the motor pool. He had the crew practice going through fire missions. He had Dean work with fake powder bags. Dean would practice putting the right number of bags in when told. If you got the order for charge three, he would cut the extra bags off and brought the round to the gun. He announced 'charge three' to the gun crew and then went for another round. They practiced the rest of the day. All the crews were getting ready for the battery test coming up in January.

The rest of the week went about like Monday. Dean would study the manual in the morning while the rest of the crew did what had to be done on gear. Porter would have them practice fake fire missions in the afternoon with Dean doing a different job each time. He tried to get Porter to open up more about his time in Nam, but he would side step the subject. Willie invited Dean and Arthur to one of the local bars for a few drinks. They found a table and Willie asked Dean how he liked working with the gun.

"It's alright. You know, it's a lot warmer in that tent during the winter," Dean said, smiling.

"Well, we miss you man. I don't have enough people watching my back now," Willie said laughing.

"As much trouble as you cause, you need the whole 101st Airbourne watching your back,"

"He's got your number," Arthur chimed in laughing.

"What do you think about Porter?" asked Willie.

"I think he's a great guy, why?"

Willie and Arthur exchanged looks. It made Dean uneasy and he was wondering what they were thinking. "Is there a problem with Porter that I don't know about?"

"Well, you know that hash we smuggled back to the states. Porter helped us hide it in return for some of it. We don't know if he used it or sold it. I know that you go to church with him, but I don't think he is what you think he is Dean. Just watch yourself. I like you man, and I know you don't partake in drugs, but he's doing something with them and he will do all kinds of things to protect the image that he has made."

Dean looked down at his beer. He took a sip. He took his index finger and traced the rim of the glass with it. He didn't know what to say. He knew that Porter had changed when he came back from Germany. He had never seen any indication of a drug problem with Porter. His family seemed like the average American family. No one said anything for a long time.

"What are you thinking Dean?" asked Willie.

"Well, I can't think of one reason why you would lie about it, Wilie. You have nothing to gain by fabricating a story about Porter. Were you there also Arthur?" Dean asked turning to him.

"Yeah. In fact, Willie and I were discussing how to smuggle the stuff in when Porter overheard us. He said that he would help if we gave him some hash and the rest of it is history. I never saw him smoke any of it, but what do you do with hash besides smoke or sell it.

"How many others of the crew know about it besides us?"

"No one, just us three." Arthur said quietly.

"What do you think he did with it?" wondered Dean out loud.

"I don't know for sure man. But I think he smoked it. I saw him a little blurry eyed and very happy a couple of days. He calls himself a Christian and it's against the law if not against God's law. Maybe it was a onetime deal, who knows," declared Arthur.

Everyone became silent again and the mood to discuss things, or even drink beer had ended. Dean couldn't get past what he heard. He admired Porter. Several times in church services, he had seen Porter pray for people and they had been healed. One had been a burn victim and after Porter prayed for the woman, her burnt skin turned pink and the pain disappeared. It was a confusing tale of contradictions. Porter had two daughters. What if they found out, what would his actions say to them? Maybe it would stay hidden.

Dean wasn't going to tell anyone, not even Natalie. But it changed Dean's opinion of Porter and Christians. He had felt like he was getting closer to Porter but now he was wondering what other secrets he was hiding. Willie suggested they call it a night. They finished up their beers, piled into Arthur's car, and he took them back to base.

Arthur and Willie started for the barracks while Dean walked toward his car. He was still deep in thought about Porter when he started reaching for his car door. He saw a dark shadow come out from behind the car next to his. He turned to look that way, when a long arm snaked out caught him in the side of the head. The blow threw him against the side of the car and he slumped to the ground. He tried to turn over and get on his knees, but a blow by a long leg and a large foot knocked him up against the vehicle again.

"Call me a coward, you sniveling little jerk," hissed Aston.

Dean could not make out his face, but he knew the voice. The frame that stood over him was large enough to be Smoke. He saw him raise a leg to kick him again, but Dean put up his arms, catching the leg, and pushing it back causing him to lose his balance.

"I didn't call you a coward Smoke," Dean said getting to his knees.

"I heard it all over camp after the fight at the beer tent," Aston said as he came running at Dean with a raised fist.

At the last minute, Dean rolled to the side and Aston hit the side of the car with his knuckles. Smoke yelped in pain. Dean had very little room to maneuver and knew Aston would get him with the next punch. He tried to crawl out from behind the cars where there was more room to maneuver or at least duck a blow. He was out matched and was considering running from this fray and trying to reason with him when others were around.

Aston grabbed him by the back of the collar and pulled him off the ground. His legs dangled in the air for a few seconds. Dean brought his arms up to protect his face. He could see Smoke bring his fist all the way back.

"You hit him, I'll kick your butt. You know I can," Willie said in an even tone.

"And I will help him," Arthur chimed in.

Aston looked behind him seeing Dean's two friends. He dropped his arm and set Dean on the ground. Dean dropped to the ground, feeling for his glasses which had went flying off his face with Aston's first punch. Arthur asked him what he was doing. He explained to them that he was missing his glasses. Willie told Aston to help him. Smoke hesitated, then complied. Dean came up with them. They were bent, but he was able to get them back in shape enough to wear them.

Willie asked why the altercation had happened. Aston remained silent while Dean told his two friends the reason Smoke had used to attack him. Willie laughed out loud and Dean wanted to know what was so funny.

"Aston, Dean never started that story. I did," Willie said with a big smile on his face.

"Why, you little jerk," Aston said moving toward Willie.

"Come on, you know I want you to. You know why I call you a coward? Not because of what happened in Germany. No, it's because you do crap like you did with Dean this evening. You tried it on me, but you got the worst of it. You know what, Smoke? If Dean or any of my friends come up with even a bruise and I suspect you had anything to do with it, I'm going to catch you in the dark out in front of your house and break your face. Do you get my drift?"

Aston turned white; they could see it even in the dark. He said nothing, got in his car, and drove off. Arthur came over to Dean to see if he needed any help. Dean had a gash over his eye brow, his glasses sat cocked on his nose, and a cut near his lip oozed blood. The real hurt was his ribs, which would be sore for about a week. He thanked both of them profusely and patted them on their backs. He started for his car but stopped and turned to Willie.

"How in the world did you kick his butt?"

"I have to jump extra high and be really fast but he learned the hard way that it is better to have speed than might." Willie said with a big grin.

When he got home, Natalie nursed him, placing bandages on the wounds. She asked what happened but he only told her that he had a disagreement with someone and they settled it. He assured her that everything was fine and he shouldn't have a problem with the guy again.

Chapter 13

BUD LARSON

The phone was ringing as Dean came through the door. He was glad that Natalie answered it. It had been a long cold day working on the gun, then he finished the day off with college classes. He was struggling with math and the light had not come on concerning some of the problems he was dealing with.

He was deep in thought when Natalie ushered him over to the phone. She indicated that it was his father. Alarms went off in his head, his father rarely called. The first thought was that someone had been hurt or was dying.

Bud Larson gave him a cheerful hello and they discussed what was happening in each other's little worlds. Eventually his father got down to business and asked if he could come see them for Thanksgiving. Dean was taken back; he didn't know what to say. He couldn't imagine that his father would leave the farm to come and visit them in Kentucky.

He had thought about inviting the Porters over for dinner, since most of their family was up north. They had also discussed encouraging some of the single men that would be stuck at the barracks over for the celebration. His father heard the hesitation in his voice as he ran through this check list. Bud apologized for inviting himself on such short notice and trying to force an invitation. Dean promised him they had not made plans and he was just surprised that he was going to leave the farm.

Dean looked at Natalie and she nodded her head to affirm that she wanted him to come. Dean turned his attention back to his father and extended the invitation to him to join them for Thanksgiving. He asked him why he was coming out at this time. Bud reminded him that he was a grandfather and had not hugged his granddaughter yet. Dean laughed and made a joke about finally finding a reason for his father to leave the homestead. He asked Bud how he was traveling and was surprised to find out that he was thinking about flying.

Bud had often shaken his head at the mention of flying and made disparaging comments about men not being birds. Dean had loved the thought of flying and was not disappointed when he flew to California for basic training. It had turned out to be a fun adventure. Bud informed him that he would work out all the details and get back to Dean.

Natalie was excited about her father-in-law coming to visit. It was the first time Dean had seen her smile since he had come home from his fight with Aston. She had been withdrawn and cool toward him, he had tried to talk to her about things, but she just clammed up on him. For a kiss, she usually gave him a peck on the lips and that was it. He had too many other things to deal with right now.

Math was consuming his study time. He was trying to become a part of the gun crew and Ann was starting to haunt him in the library again. Another concern was little Melody, she slept throughout the night most of the time, but sometimes she would wake up crying. When she did this, she always had a fever. Dean figured that this was some of Natalie's problem; she was concerned about Melody.

They had taken her to the doctor a couple of times, divulging their concerns but the doctors found nothing. Aston had not bothered him physically lately, but Dean found himself doing a lot of extra details. He asked Porter about it and he indicated that Smoke was ordering Porter to have Dean do them.

The airport was crowded on the Tuesday before Thanksgiving as Dean waited for his father to exit the plane. It had been delayed in Denver because of a snow storm by twenty minutes. His father should be standing about a head above everyone else, he was surprised to find Bud stooped when he came through the gates into the terminal. Dean immediately came to his side and looked him in the eyes. He smiled but his eyes were a little sunken and it was the first time that he considered his father looking a little frail.

"How was your trip Dad?"

"What an exciting feeling I got flying. Too bad I didn't try it years ago. Where are Natalie and the kids?"

"We didn't know how long we would be waiting for you, so Natalie thought it would be best that they stayed home."

"That was probably a good idea. I bet that John has grown a couple of inches since I last saw him. What is Melody like?"

"She is as sweet as she can be. She sleeps through the night most of the time and rarely cries."

"I can hardly wait to hold her," Bud said with longing in his eyes.

They moved to baggage claims, picked up his one suitcase, then proceeded to the car.

"Are you all right, Dad? You look a little under the weather."

"I'm fine, Dean. Your brother just worked me too hard this harvest." he said with a grin.

Dean unlocked the trunk of the car and threw Bud's bag in. Bud stepped back and looked the vehicle over. "This thing actually runs? No wonder Natalie stayed home."

They both laughed. The red Cornet had rust and dents. The color had faded and she was as ugly as a pig in a wallow. Morton and Dean had her running well; the V-8 engine hummed like a well-tuned church choir. The drive was nice as his father took in the scenery. The day was cloudy, but the temperature was in the high 60s and a little muggy.

John ran into Bud's arms, beating his mother by a few steps. Dean grinned. John had not forgotten what his grandfather looked like. Dean had put in for leave on Wednesday, Friday, and Monday, only to find out that Smoke had put him on the rooster for barrack's guard. Porter had gone to bat for him, talking to Smoke about Bud coming to visit. This had not changed Aston's mind, so Porter went up the chain of command, telling Top what was going on and about all the other extra duties Dean had been given. Childs called Smoke into the office and they had a serious discussion. Clark told Dean about it later. He heard several loud phrases and when it was all said, Dean had his days off. Dean had a lot fewer extra duties after that.

On Wednesday, the family went for a ride and they showed Hopkinsville to Bud, they then drove to Clarksville. They showed him the sights and spent some time in one of the parks. He spent a lot of time playing with John and holding Melody.

They bought Thanksgiving dinner at the PX. Natalie had bought the turkey several days earlier so that it would be thawed out. She started the dinner that evening while Dean took his father over to the Porters to visit for an hour. John had to come along, he wanted to hang around with his grandfather.

When they walked into their home, supper was cooking, and the smells saturated their nostrils. It was a quiet evening with John pestering his grandfather. This gave Dean a chance to do some of his homework. He glided through English with ease, but struggled with math. He was pulling Ds and Cs, so he needed to get the concepts down, or he was going to flunk the final test. He was supposed to be finishing up in December, but they were going to extend it until after the battery test in January.

They welcomed Thanksgiving in with cold rain and gray clouds. That was alright; it was warm in the house and Dean found a hot cup of coffee on the stove. His father had woken earlier and put the pot on. He was reading his Bible, but he put it down when Dean took the chair across from him. "So, how are things going with you Dean?"

"Oh, fair to middlin! I'm having a hard time with math, just like when I was in high school but otherwise, things are going well."

"Bull, I have never heard you feed me such a wheelbarrow full of manure before. Natalie was telling me that you got into a fist fight with one of your sergeants not too long ago."

"You don't need to worry about that happening again. Some of the other guys are watching my back. He knows to leave me alone from now on, or he is going to have all kinds of trouble."

"But I heard that you've been in several fights. What is that all about? You use to avoid confrontations like that in school."

"I don't know what it is about this unit, but they are always looking for a good ruckus. I had a couple of fights in Germany but it seems like I'm either dodging them or I'm in the midst of one since I came into the 101st. I think they are constantly trying to live up to their reputations as the 'Battling Bastards of Bastone'. They are still trying to live up to their image of World War II."

"Is all this fighting causing Natalie to be tense and stressed out?"

"I don't know what her problem is, Dad. She has been cool toward me since I came home from that fight with my Chief of Smoke. I'm not the one that started it, in fact he ambushed me. I was trying to run away, but he had me trapped. I just think that she feels like she is under a lot of pressure. Melody wakes up at night every so often crying and with a fever and the doctors can't figure out what's wrong."

They heard Natalie stirring, so they changed the subject to what was going on in Rupert, Idaho. The small town was growing a little. The town square was still the main hang out during the day and the bars were the gathering places at night. Natalie came out in her robe with a smile. She put the turkey in the oven and started breakfast. She got the latest news on her parents and her sisters as she cooked up some pancakes and eggs for the morning meal. John came running out with all the energy of a wild pony, interrupting the conversation. Natalie had most of the breakfast done when Melody started crying. She went in and fed her while Dean finished cooking the morning meal.

In the afternoon, Dean helped Natalie with the rest of the dinner, while Bud kept the kids busy. Dean kept football games off, since his father was more of a baseball fan. It was a quiet peaceful day. The meal was served at about two pm. Natalie had out done herself, everything tasted so good. John went down for his nap afterwards and once Melody ate, she was soon asleep. Bud wanted to see their pictures of Europe. They spent much of the evening talking about their adventures overseas. After that, they played some card games, went to bed, and Thanksgiving became history.

Friday found them exploring some of the Tennessee countryside. They went to several lakes and roamed around the lush farmland in that area. It was a long day and Dean noticed that his father looked worn out by the time they got back home. He had dinner and went to bed. Once Natalie got the children in bed, they had a cup of tea, talked for a little while, and also retired for the evening. The conversation was about Bud; that he was looking frail and didn't seem to have the energy he once had. They both suggested that it was most likely due to his age.

Saturday, they hung around the house and spent some time with the Porters. Bud didn't have much in common with Ross Porter. They finally got on the subject of the Bible and Dean was surprised how knowledgeable his father was about the scriptures. The ice was broken and they spoke about their experiences with the Lord. After leaving, Bud mentioned how much he had enjoyed the visit with Ross. He also suggested that he was broken and he thought he needed some inner healing from his time in Nam.

Sunday morning found them in church where he met Eve and Jason Childs. They hit it off but Eve took Bud aside and talked to him before the service, ministering to him. Whatever she said, it brought tears to Bud's eyes. Dean had never seen his father cry, not even when his mother had passed away. He caught only bits and pieces of the conversation, so he didn't know what she was saying to him. Natalie was closer so he was hoping that she could fill in the blanks later. When they talked after the service, she had picked up the thought that God had heard his prayers and that he would answer them.

The rest of the church service was great, with wonderful worship and a powerful message on God's love for mankind. Pastor Jethro and Sally Jackson talked with Bud for a long time afterwards. Natalie had planned to fix them a great lunch at home, but Bud insisted upon taking them out to dinner, so Dean taxied the family down to Clarksville to one of the better restaurants.

It was good and the conversation was all about Dean and Jack when they were growing up; the trouble they caused and the funny stories and the problems they found themselves in on the farm. The stories made everyone laugh.

The mood changed when they got home. Bud became real serious and he asked, if he could pray for all of them. Natalie gave her consent, so he grabbed Melody up in his arms and lifted his eyes to Heaven. "God, I bring my granddaughter before you and I ask that you heal her of this infirmity that she has. She will be your handmaid all her life and she will love you with all her heart. She was named Melody because you will fill her mouth with praise and lead her all the days of her life."

He picked John up and kissed him on the check. "Lord, you gave John to us as a gift. His name means 'gift,' my first grandchild and my son's first son. He will be a pastor to pastors, physically strong, and a man of integrity, and honor. The Lord will never leave you nor forsake you all the days of your life."

He turned to Natalie and laid his hands on her shoulders, "My beautiful daughter-in-law, you are being troubled in many ways. Some of it is your own doing, but the Lord is going to see you through it. You will come out more refined and become the woman He wants you to be. Remember to forgive and love, for He forgives you and loves you much."

He grabbed Dean and pulled him into a hug and started praying over him. "Dean, I'm going to leave a father's blessing with you. You know not God, but He knows you and loves you the way you are. You will come to know Him in a powerful way. Remember, in some cases failure is an option. In your failures you will find victory and out of that the Lord will show you the Kingdom and the King."

As he prayed for Dean, Dean felt this power shoot through him and if he could have, he would have run away because it scared him. His father held onto him tight and didn't let go until he was done. Bud pushed him to arm's length and looked into his son's eyes. He reaffirmed that he loved him and he was sorry that he had not done this before. Bud looked drained and excused himself for the evening.

After he went in his room, Dean asked Natalie what had happened. She told him that Bud had blessed him as a father and had prophesied over him. This concerned Dean. How was he going to fail? Was it math? He needed it to get into college. Maybe he could get ahead of the game. He decided to make a bargain with God, so he promised the Lord that he would serve Him if He helped him through math. That made him feel a little better about the whole situation.

He questioned Natalie further about what she had heard Eve Childs pray over his father. Natalie told him that Eve had prayed for his strength and peace. She also told him that it was good that he was getting his house in order. There had been some other things but she had not caught that part of the conversation.

Bud Larson stayed Monday and went home on Tuesday. He spent Monday playing with the grandkids and visiting with Natalie. Dean spent half the day studying and the rest of it visiting with his father. He also went to class that evening and found out that his grade average was a D+. He needed a C to pass, so he was determined to study harder to get better grades. It seemed like no matter how hard he worked on the books, he still didn't understand this new math. Dean understood adding, subtracting, and so forth, but this new stuff just didn't make sense to him.

He took a couple of hours off and drove his father to the airport on Tuesday. Dean was concerned about his father. He had seen him grimace with pain a few times during his visit. Dean had asked him if he was alright, but Bud had assured him that he was doing well, that it was just old age. Now as Bud boarded the plane, his father looked more bent and wearier. Bud gave him a final hug and told him that he loved him. Dean noticed a tear come with his final goodbye. The farewell sounded strange and then Bud was gone.

Chapter 14

NO COLD WEATHER GEAR

The cold penetrated everywhere as they bumped along the dirt road toward their first firing position. It was January and they were doing their battery test. It would be one of the coldest winters in that area in many years.

Ft. Campbell was not considered a cold weather base, so they were not issued cold weather gear. They had no packs for their feet, parkas, or mittens. They only had their thermos, inserts for their jackets and gloves. Dean figured it was hovering around the low twenties and it was supposed to drop to around zero in the morning hours.

He felt sorry for Porter, who was sick and sitting up front in the assistant driver's seat with the canvas top removed. Even though his teeth were chattering and he was sitting as close to the man next to him as possible, his thoughts were somewhere else.

Two weeks after his father had left for home, they got a call from Jack telling them that Bud was dying from congestive heart failure. He had grown sicker since his trip to Kentucky. Dean was wondering if he had told his father how much he loved him. Did he tell him how proud he was of him. He wanted to express how he appreciated what he had taught him.

Bud had known that he was dying when he had spent Thanksgiving with them, but he had not wanted his son feeling sorry for him while they were visiting. He didn't want Natalie hovering over him, treating him like he was sick. Dean had called him several times and had tried to express all the feelings he had toward his father. Bud had listened intently to every word and had turned it around on Dean.

He told Dean how much he loved him and his family and this time Dean heard his father choke up and weep. Dean could not hold back the tears. They both knew that they would not see each other alive again in this world. The words they spoke to one another could never convey what their emotions were churning up.

Bud never had a daughter and since Natalie was his first daughter-in-law, he treated her as a daughter. He also adopted Helen as one. They had grown very close to one another in the short time they spent together.

Natalie tried to comfort Dean at first, but he had rejected her attempts in very nice ways. He lost himself in work and school. It paid off in history and English, taking the tests before Christmas. He got As on both of them. He had added math later and at first he was doing well but his grades had gotten worse, his average was a D- now. When he cracked the math book, he could not concentrate. He started thinking of anything else, most often about his father.

Natalie had been withdrawn before the visit, but now she was building a cocoon around herself. She seemed more depressed and only responded to the cries of the children. He could tell she wanted to be home to help take care of his father. She was homesick, missing her parents and sisters.

The ladies came over often to try and cheer her up, but it only seemed to be a temporary fix. Sometimes, Natalie would apologize and suggest that she was not feeling well. A couple of Sundays she would not even go to church. Dean realized that he was no help to her and often made things worse.

A day after he had passed his test and a couple of days before Christmas, Laura Baker, Natalie's mother, called to tell them that Bud had passed away with a massive heart attack. He had died at home with many of his close friends and loved ones surrounding him. It was like a punch to Dean's guts. Nothing could take the cold feeling he felt in his heart by hearing that his father had passed away. Natalie cried her eyes out hugging John and Melody. Dean tried to comfort her, but as he had rejected her arms when he got the news about his father, she turned away from him.

The Gamma Goat jolted to a halt, bringing Dean back to reality. His feet felt like ice and his fingers were numb. He started stomping his feet on the floor and beating his hands together. Porter's face appeared at the back of the goat. He released the tailgate and told them to get to it. They got the gun in place and made sure it was anchored. All the activity helped warm them up. Dean could not help but notice that Porter looked like death warmed over. He was pale, lethargic, with a running nose. He stopped once and vomited. Garcia got his small stove going and brewed up some coffee. They had to drink it fast or it soon became iced coffee. The men took turns warming up their extremities around the small fire.

They soon got several fire missions, which helped keep their minds off the bitter cold. Dean thought of Morton, who was out in front of them directing the fire. He had to be miserable, it was spitting snow as they sent some more rounds down range. It did not warm up at all as the day grew to an end.

Dean found out quickly that he was odd man out; the number of the crew was uneven and he had no one to share his shelter half with. This had not bothered him during the summer, but now he could use the body warmth of another in a tent. He was wishing that he had made the FDC crew; they were sitting in their tent and it had heat.

He shook the snow off of some branches with pine needles, laid them in a dry area, then propped his shelter half over it. He crawled in it for the night stacking more branches at one end and closing off the other with his poncho. He took his boots off, cleaned them off as much as possible, and stuffed them into his sleeping bag. Dean took off his field jacked and snuggled down in his bag, putting the jacket over him and his wool blanket over that. This seemed to stave off some of the cold and he fell into a restless sleep. They had two missions that evening so Dean learned the hard way to keep his boots on his feet while he slept.

He woke up around midnight. There was a breeze swirling around the trees and through the brush he had put at one end of his shelter half. The temperature was hovering just above zero and the wind made it even colder. No matter what Dean did, he could not get warm nor could he get back to sleep. He could hear the hum of the generator that kept the heaters working in the FDC tent. All the high-ranking people were inside keeping warm, the privilege of rank had its perks. There were no missions after two a.m.

As he laid there with his arms wrapped around himself and his teeth chattering, he started thinking about Christmas. It had been the worse celebration he could remember. Even the Christmas that had come after his mother's death had been better. The day was gloomy, with no snow on the ground and the mood inside the house was as gray as it was outside. At least Dean was warm, but Natalie was very cold towards him.

She had wanted to go to the funeral, but when Dean checked their finances, they couldn't go home to say goodbye to Bud. Porter found out about the problem and had brought it before the church, they were willing to take up donations for it, but Dean couldn't swallow his pride to accept the money.

Natalie had pleaded with him, but Dean couldn't accept the money. Dean used the money problems as an excuse, the real reason he did not want to go the funeral, was because he didn't want to see his father dead. He wanted to remember him when he was alive.

He could never get past how cancer had destroyed his mother. She was 86 pounds when they laid her in the grave. Afterwards, he and Natalie had a fight about not going back home. A lot of words had been exchanged and none of them had been nice. He played them over in his head now and knew that she was right on several accounts.

She had called him arrogant, self-centered, and a lousy father and husband. The last two names had deeply wounded him, but he had turned and walked away from the conflict, not revealing his true motive for staying home.

Well, if he had accepted the money, they would be in Idaho now and he wouldn't be freezing his buns off in Kentucky. It was too late to change his mind now. He would go home to Natalie and try to smooth things over.

He digested their conversations again and tried to think of some way to restore peace between him and his wife. Some carnations and a night out without the children might do the trick. He would have to apologize, even though he was right. It's not like his father would care anymore but Natalie did and that's what mattered.

At seven in the morning Smoke appeared over his hovel to wake him up. He told him that there was coffee over at the mess truck and they had cold rations waiting for everyone. Dean wiggled into his field jacket and wrapped the blanket around himself. The cold nipped at every exposed portion of skin. He was sorry he had forgotten his wool scarf. He was one of the first ones in line and got his coffee and rations. He drank the coffee quickly, warming his insides and stopping the chattering teeth. He stayed near the heat as long as he could, but others moved in, displacing him to the bitter cold.

Top appeared near the mess truck and told everyone to gather around. He informed everyone that the range had been shut down because of the weather conditions and they were going to airlift them back to base. They were already sending the pilots out to the flight line to get the choppers off the ground. He also told them that they were going to medivac Porter out; he had a fever and couldn't hold anything down. Dean went to see Porter. They had put him into the FDC tent but they wouldn't let him in. They said that he was out of it and the medic thought he should be left alone.

A Huey chopper showed up about twenty minutes later and Porter was taken to the base hospital. That's when Top called all the men to him at the mess area again. He told them that they couldn't get enough Chinooks in the air to transport the whole unit back to base. We were all going to have to convoy back home.

Dean could hardly feel his feet and beating the arms back and forth wasn't helping his body heat. He was sure that the wind had picked up even more. He was designated assistant driver since Porter was at the hospital. They loaded up their gear after having one last cup of coffee.

The trip home was beyond miserable. They were only traveling ten to fifteen miles an hour adding to the hardship. Dean had his rifle in one hand propped up on the seat near the driver. The driver had the windshield to help protect him, but Dean's head was above that. He held his rifle near his side and had the wool blanket wrapped around himself. He would look out of it every once in a while, making sure they were still on the road and the driver had not succumbed to the frigid cold that was pressing in everywhere.

It seemed like an eternity before they reached the motor pool. Personal gear and sensitive equipment were off loaded and stored away. Dean could not remember ever being that cold before. They opened up the mess hall and provided coffee and a hot meal for everyone. Dean stayed there for a couple of hours thawing out. He was told later that it had dropped to five to ten degrees above zero, but the wind is what had closed the range.

He loaded up his gear in the Cornet. It didn't want to start at first, but the eight cylinders finally turned over and got him home.

The reception at home from Natalie was just about as cold as it had been out in the field. John on the other hand jumped into Daddy's arms and hugged and kissed him. Natalie gave him a peck on the check. She also provided a warm snack for him before he went to bed. Dean was too worn out to try to make amends with her and was quickly asleep.

"Dean wake up." He heard it but he couldn't comprehend what he had to do. "Dean get up, Melody has a high fever." Now it sank in. He crawled out from under the covers.

He swore under his breath, wondering what else could go wrong. Dean quickly dressed and took Melody out of Natalie's arms. He put his check against hers. She was very warm. "How high is the fever?"

"It's a 103 so let's get her to the doctor right away."

Dean rushed her out to the car and strapped her into the car seat. Natalie got John tucked into the car. Little John looked confused. Several yawns broke across his face before Dean got the car started.

Dean had to take it slow, the roads were slick. By the time they got Melody in to see the physician, her fever was starting to recede. It was now 101 and she was crying less. Dean sat with John out in the waiting room while Natalie stayed with her daughter.

After an hour and half Natalie came out with the doctor. Again they had found nothing wrong with their little girl. The physician suspected it had something to do with her kidneys or bladder. He suggested a specialist.

Dean and Natalie suspected that she had about eight episodes with fever but they had brought her into the doctor only three times for various reasons. They took the name of the specialist and went home. It was after three in the morning. Now Dean was wide awake and pacing the living room floor. Melody was sick and that was a major problem. They had not paid off the last doctor bill and that was another issue that needed his attention. So far they were taking payments.

Chapter 15

OUT FLANKED

Dean sipped his beer and retrieved the wadded paper from his pocket. He put his beer down and pressed the paper out on the bar. He read it again, it was his final grade in his math class. Porter had let him get off early so that he could pick it up and go home.

It gave him a sick feeling in his mid-section when he had read it the first time. The queasy feeling did not go away the second time. His final grade was a D+ and he had busted his tail trying to bring it up. He looked at it a couple of times hoping that it would change to a C or a B, but no, he had flunked the class and would have to take it again.

This time he wadded it up, put it in his pocket, not to return to it for a couple of days. He took a chug on his beer but this didn't cheer him up, so he took another big gulp. He stared off down the long bar and realized that the place was fairly empty still. It was early and most of the units had not released their men from duty.

He thought about going home, but the first question Natalie would ask was about the grade. Once he told her, she would give him that look, it would be one of disappointment. He had seen it several times lately. When he had rejected charity or the loans to get back to his father's funeral. She had insisted that he go hear a guest speaker at church, but this one had used the words 'hell' and 'damnation' too often and Dean had tuned him out.

When she had asked him what he thought, Dean had put him down and would not go back the next night. Melody had another bout with fever and even though they had rushed her into the specialist he had found nothing unusual. He was an older doctor and he advised them to call him at home if need be. He would meet them at the hospital, he believed he knew what was causing the infections. Natalie never said anything, but her looks at Dean made him think she blamed him for their daughter's sickness.

All these reasons made home an unfriendly place to be. John was still happy to see him, running into his arms, but Dean was lucky to get a peck on the lips from Natalie. He decided he would stay at the bar and have a few more beers until it didn't matter how Natalie treated him when he got home. He finished off his first two beers and ordered another one.

The third one started doing the trick, he thought about the D+ and it seemed funny to him. He considered how one little letter out of the alphabet had made him so miserable. He chuckled to himself and took another big swig of his beer, but his mood suddenly changed from happy to depressed.

He considered the D and how it was going to put him behind on his goals for college. He would have to take the class again. What if he flunked it the second time? He took a gulp of beer and someone slapped him on his back. It was Willie and Arthur, they asked him if he wanted some company. He was polite, but made is obvious that he was in no mood for visiting.

In most cases, he would have wanted to talk to Willie, who had gotten in trouble and been busted down to E-1 again. Dean heard that he had taken leave during Christmas and failed to return on time. They busted him for being AWOL, but Dean would have liked getting the story from the horse's mouth so to speak.

He finished his third beer, but the depression hung over him like the clouds hung over the Idaho mountains in the fall. The brew did not help, he seemed more depressed. Willie came over and offered to take him home, but Dean rudely rejected the offer and ordered another drink. Everyone seemed to leave him alone after that. He was downing his seventh beer when he felt an arm snake about his shoulders. He looked to his right and there stood Ann, with her blonde hair pulled back and a large smile breaking across her face.

"You look miserable, Dean. What's the problem?"

"I failed my math class," he said moving away from her.

"I can help you with it next semester," she said tightening her grip on him.

"I guess that would work. What was your grade in math?"

"I got a B+ and I know I can help you get a C, if not better, Dean. Don't worry. We will get you through that class yet," she said as she sat down on the bar stool next to him.

She started talking to him about the army, school, and what his plans were for the future. She also bought him a couple more beers and Dean started talking openly about his dreams. She suggested that she take him home. He rejected the idea at first, but she finally talked him into going with her. She supported him as he walked to her car.

She put him in the passenger seat, and strapped him in. Ann got behind the wheel, but before starting the car, she kissed him hard on the lips. He gave some faint resistance and then responded by kissing her back. She didn't even ask him how to get to his house. She took him to a motel nearby and disappeared into the office, coming out with a key to one of the rooms. She drove him to the room and helped him out of the car into the motel room.

He knew what was happening but, in his drunkenness, and numb state his resistance to her advances were gone. He was no longer concerned about sleeping with her. She helped pull his clothes off, then she climbed in beside him and they made love several times. It was wild and intense like a dream and as though he was moving in a fog.

He awoke with a start, not knowing his surroundings. He rolled over to see a blonde head of hair and then the fog started lifting. Dean remembered the beers and then Ann coming in on the scene. He felt a panic as he remembered the sex and what he had done that evening. He fished around on the floor, finding some of his clothes. The guilt churning inside him almost stopped him from breathing. He struggled to pull air into his lungs. She rolled over, smiling at him. She grabbed his arm, trying to pull him down towards her. He shook her off and told her that he needed to get home.

She tried to coax him to come to her and make love one more time, but he refused. She stood naked before him and he had to admit that she was beautiful and enticing. He quickly got dressed and hurried out of the room toward the street.

He was disoriented, and didn't know if he should go left or right back to his car. He tried to remember the trip last night and finally figured out that the shoulder of the road had been on his right. He turned left and, after about twenty minutes of walking, came to the bar he had been drinking at.

His red Cornet was parked where he had left it. He started it up, but sat there wondering what he should do for a long moment. He drove to one of the local parks, and decided that he could not face Natalie at that very moment. He sat at one of the picnic tables and tried to think about what he would tell his wife. The thought was so very ugly and yet, he could not tell her a lie. Maybe he could tell her about getting drunk, but leave out the part about Ann. That was about as bad as a lie, but things were not going well with their marriage. This could cause a divorce and he loved Natalie no matter what.

He could not imagine what life would be without her. He couldn't blame her if she kicked him out of the house. He was so intently thinking about what he could do that he didn't hear a car drive up and park behind his, nor did he hear the footsteps as a man approach behind him until Childs said something to him and put a hand on his shoulder.

Dean was taken back and didn't know what to say. He finally found his voice after a few minutes and asked Childs if Natalie had sent him.

"No, the Lord sent me Larson."

There was a moment of silence as Dean considered what Childs had just told him and Childs let the words sink in.

"He spoke to my heart and told me to go find you, that you have really screwed up. Well, maybe not those words exactly, but that was the jest of the conversation."

"Well, He was right about that. I messed up big time, I bought a one-way ticket to hell" Dean said looking away from Childs.

"You need to ante up today and get things right or you could lose everything even your life Larson. The Lord has been dealing with you on a lot of issues and in all kinds of ways. Don't look at others Dean and how they are living their lives, you just consider what Jesus did for you on the cross. Porter and I are not examples to follow; Jesus is. This is your "Valley of Decision.""

"I'm kind of slow. Maybe you better explain what you mean by all that."

"The guest speaker talked about hell and damnation and that message was for you. The good Lord was trying to get your attention and warn you of the wages of sin, which is eternal death and hell. You were offended, I could tell but you being a good man did something that will get you a one-way trip to fire and brimstone.

You have been going to church for a half year now, and you still have not caught the message of salvation in your heart. The Lord has been trying to woo you to Him for some time, but you are not only slow, you are self-centered thinking the world rotates around you and your world is going to fly out of control if you don't get things right. The scriptures say that all have sinned and come short of the glory of God. Now you have committed adultery."

Dean didn't respond, he just looked down at the ground and thought about all the words Childs had spoken to him. More than that, he remembered what his father and Natalie had said. They had told him the same thing, but in a gentler way. They had been kinder, but Childs had not held back on him. He had declared him a sinner and that he was not a good man, but Dean finally realized that was true and last night was an indication of what a big jerk he was and that he did deserve hell.

"What should I do?"

"You need to confess what you did last night. I don't need to know the details, so tell me the short story."

"Well, I got drunk and had sex with another woman."

"Yes, that is what God told me. What brought all this on? How is home life and your marriage with Natalie?"

"Well, if God told you that I committed adultery, why did I have to confess it?"

"You need to know what you did and get clean of it and God needed you to say it so He can forgive you. So, what brought on this bad behavior?"

"I flunked my math class. That started me drinking, but home life has not been going well, Natalie is always depressed and never very loving. She wants me to get out of the army at any price, she is not willing to wait until August when my enlistment is up. Melody Is still having bouts of high fevers and every time we go to the hospital Natalie looks at me like I'm the one at fault."

"It sounds like it is time for you to give your life over to the Lord, Dean. He has big plans for you, it sounds like you have not been doing a very good job running your own life."

"I'm tired of it all and I see my need for Jesus finally."

"If you plan on saving your marriage and your own life, then you must give it all to the Lord. Are you ready for that?" Childs said with gravity in his voice.

"Yes, I haven't been doing a very good job at anything I've put my hand to. I might as well see if the Lord can make something out of it."

"Okay, repeat after me. Lord, forgive me of my sins, come into my heart. Make me the man you want me to be and the husband Natalie needs me to be. God, I give up my will and desires to do what you want me to do. Jesus, I give you my family and the mess I've made of my life and I ask that you would fix things, not for my benefit, but for your glory. Amen"

Dean said the prayer just as Childs had told him. He sensed a heavy weight lift off his shoulders. He also had a feeling that everything was going to work out between him and Natalie. This brought a smile to his face, which had been missing for a long while.

Childs informed him that Eve, his wife, had gone over and picked Natalie and the children up earlier. Dean was going to have to follow Childs to the base and into the housing area for NCOs. On the way over, Dean repeated the sinner's prayer a couple of times to make sure that he was forgiven and saved. He did not want to go to hell.

The guest speaker's description of the place did not make it an enticing place; constant torment, brimstone, and the smell of sulfur permeating every breath of air taken in. He parked behind Childs, who pulled up to one of the housing units. Childs led the way through the front door. Natalie brightened up when she saw her husband, ran into his arms, and gushed her fears that something terrible had happened to him. John also grabbed a leg and was hugging him. It was the first time in a while that Natalie had shown any kind of strong emotion toward him. He hugged her back hard, knowing that things might change again quickly.

Dean suggested they pack up and go home, but Childs stopped him, suggesting that Natalie and him talk things over at their place, that they might need some counseling. Eve grabbed Melody while Top lead John into the other room. Natalie looked earnestly into her husband's eyes and questioned him about what had happened the night before. He looked away from her and confessed that he had gotten so drunk that he had lost control. He pulled out the wrinkled paper and showed her his math grade.

"It's okay Dean, we will work on it together and figure things out," she moved closer to him to console him.

"That's not the whole story, Natalie," he said quietly, holding up a hand to stop her.

There was a long pause, finally she broke the silence. "Well, what else happened Dean?"

"I slept with another woman Natalie," he said looking into her eyes.

She looked confused at first, then it registered. He saw the deep hurt flood over her and tears welled up in her beautiful eyes. He looked away from her, wishing that she wouldn't cry but would slap the h-- l out of him instead. She just stood there weeping.

"Natalie, I was a big jerk and I have been a jerk for a while, not thinking about you or the kids, but what I wanted. I am sorry for what I did and the kind of man that I have been for about a year. I want to change things around and win you back. I can't see me living my life without you. Please give me another chance."

There was another agonizing long silence before Natalie did anything. She wiped away the tears and came to Dean where she gave him a kiss on the check. "You are forgiven, after all I haven't been much of a wife. We start new. I would like to go out on some dates and really talk about things. I know I have been depressed and not very loving. We take things slow if that is alright with you."

He nodded and gave a big sigh of relief. He was willing to play by her rules, whatever it took to bring healing to the marriage. He knew that he was going to have to win back her trust and was willing to show her that he was worthy of her love.

Childs stuck his head through the doorway and asked how things were going. Dean invited them back into their living room. Childs announced to Natalie that Dean had given his life over to the Lord.

Dean, dreading the confession, had completely forgotten his conversation with God. Natalie looked happy, but he could tell that she was not sure she believed he did it for the right reasons. Childs took Dean off to the side and counseled him that he should slow down on his drinking and spend more time with the family. He also suggested that he take math as his only class and concentrate on that while fixing his relationships. The Childs family offered to watch the children free when they went on their first date.

He then pulled out his wallet and handed Dean a ten-dollar bill, telling him to stop and have some ice cream on the way home. Dean was a little hesitant, but Childs insisted upon it, stating that Dean most likely had no spare money after all that drinking last night. Dean thanked him and leaned closer to him. He told him that Ann, the woman that he slept with, was taking college classes and he didn't want to run into her again. He asked Top if he could find out her schedule so he could get his class on another day. Top agreed to look into it.

Eve took Natalie off to the side and prayed for her. She asked the Lord to set her free from the depression and to heal her emotionally. She also prayed for Melody that he would heal her physical problem.

Dean took his family home after they stopped for ice cream. He slept on the couch for a couple of nights. He had fun dating his wife and having some serious discussions with her. He realized that he had been taking her for granted and he was seeing her in a whole new light.

They worked a lot of problems out and started praying together. At first Dean had trouble finding the words to speak. He eventually started looking forward to talking to God every evening before supper.

Chapter 16

ANSWERS TO PRAYERS

Dean was doing some light maintenance work on the Gamma Goat, concentrating on the task in front of him. He was about finished when he heard footsteps behind him. He turned to see Smoke diverging on his location. Dean jumped down off the wide fender in case he needed to defend himself.

Aston staring at him for a few minutes, it was as always, a hateful look. He finally asked Dean what he was doing, so Dean explained that he had fixed some minor problems with the goat. Aston got a little closer and looked around to see if anyone was near. He informed Dean that he knew he was getting out in a few months and that he was going to give him a big send off before he left for home. He started moving off, but before he got too far, Dean felt a boldness that he had never had before with Smoke.

"What put the bee in your bonnet about me, Smoke? What did I ever do that pissed you off at me?"

"I just never liked you. I think you're a wimp, coming into the army just for the bennies. You're no patriot and I don't believe you're a good soldier," he said with surprise on his face at Dean's directness.

"Well, you're as wrong as you can be. I felt like I owed my country something for the freedom it's given me. I joined because

I love my country and was willing to defend it, but I don't think I owe it my whole life. I will take advantage of the things that it offers me to accomplish my dreams. I believe I have proven my patriotism just by putting up with people like you and not running away."

"You have seen nothing, nor have you faced the enemy on the battlefield. You are still nothing to me and you have proven nothing to me." he said coming closer.

"I can see that nothing I say to you will change your mind," Dean said standing his ground.

"No. I think you would run after the first shot. I also believe you will run when I meet you outside the gates." He turned to leave.

Suddenly Dean felt a power come over him, it was strange, but he remembered the feeling it in a church service once. Again, with boldness that Dean had never felt before, he said. "That fight you're talking about will never take place because you won't be around to participate in it. God is about to shake your world and turn you upside down."

"I don't believe in God," he spoke looking back at Dean.

"It doesn't matter. He lives and knows all things."

The boldness and power left and Dean was wondering what he just did. How could he say such things? Where did all those things come from? Dean was going to get his head handed to him. In fact, Willie was going to leave the service before him and Dean was not going to talk to Willie about it, nor was he going to tell Childs. He was just going to have to defend himself as best as he could. He felt fear trying to climb up into his throat, but doing some of the things he had done in the past cause him to recognize the symptoms and swallowed it.

He turned back to the goat, and he continued working on it for another half hour when he was interrupted by a ruckus toward the motor pool gate. He saw someone laying on the ground. He couldn't make out who it was because several people had formed a circle around the man.

Dean could see that he was tall and as he drew closer, he made out some red locks flowing down over his forehead. When he saw the hair, he knew it was Aston. He picked up the pace and noticed that Porter was one of the sergeants standing nearby. Dean nudged him and asked what had happened to Aston.

"Well, he was talking to us when the right side of his mouth drooped down and his speech became slurred. I asked him if he was alright. He told me something, but I couldn't understand him. He turned, dragging his right foot behind him, and then collapsed out the door."

"Wow. Natalie and I have been praying that the Lord would move him out of my life, but I didn't mean for God to do this."

"Maybe you should be more specific when you pray. There is a verse in the Bible that states that no one should touch God's anointed. I do believe you have a calling on your life. It should be interesting to see what He does with you."

Dean thought these things over as others tried to make Aston more comfortable. Aston was combative, pushing people away with his left arm. The ambulance finally pulled up and hauled him away. Dean didn't want to look too stupid in front of Porter, but he wondered what "calling' meant in this case.

Natalie and him were now reading the Bible every night together, but he had not run into that term in their devotions yet. He decided that he would ask Natalie that evening. He went back to tinkering with the goat until Porter checked his work and they went to lunch.

At the evening formation, the battery was told that Aston had a massive stroke and that anyone that wanted to visit him would have to wait a while until they got him more stable. Dean thought to himself that he had no intentions of seeing Aston ever again, unless he was forced to. He was glad the day was over.

It was off to math class and he was doing much better. Top had suggested which class to take and he had not run into Ann yet. He was always on the lookout for her. He did not want any more contact with her than was necessary. Since he had gotten saved, Childs acted like a guardian angel, helping to keep him on the straight and narrow. The class went well, it was like his mind had finally opened to the concepts they were teaching. He had decided to take Top's advice and had limited himself to taking just one class.

It was great coming home now. Natalie was back to being the woman he had married; the depression was gone. Every once in a while, Dean would see a sad look come over her and they would talk about his father. Through their discussions, he had come to realize that he had not taken time to mourn his father's death. Sometimes, they would cry on each other's shoulders and other times they would discuss a story about him which would bring laughter.

The evening that Aston had his stroke, Dean went home and Natalie met him at the door with a big kiss and hug. After Natalie finished, John attacked him and they wrestled around for a while. He then went over to his daughter, picked her up, and loved on her. She was such a quiet, beautiful child.

Dean showered, sat at the table holding John, and discussed the day's events. He told her what had happened to Aston. She looked concerned and suggested they send flowers. He reminded her that they had prayed that God would take him out of his sphere of influence. She agreed, but she was hoping that he would simply be transferred to another unit.

After dinner and some TV time, Dean studied his math. They put John and Melody to bed and had their Bible devotion. He asked her about "calling" and she showed him where it was used in the Bible. It said that many are called but few are chosen. Calling was the job that God gave you to do for Him. Dean looked over the verse again and determined that he wanted to be chosen.

He was being patient with his wife who was warming up to him. Dean was learning more and more about Natalie. She was shy in most cases but she could insert herself if need be. She was also sharing more of her feelings now. Maybe she had been before all the problems but he had not been paying attention to them.

The next morning in formation, the battery was informed what they had expected. Aston had a stroke, it affected his right side causing paralyzes in his arm, leg, and his face. Childs called Dean over after everyone was released to perform their duties. He suggested that Dean should go see Aston when the hospital allowed visitors.

Dean couldn't believe his ears and asked Childs why he would ever want to do that. After all, he was not exactly fond of Aston. Childs told him that he needed to forgive Aston so that he could be free of him. This didn't exactly make sense to Dean, but it would be a great discussion point with Natalie when they talked about the Bible that night.

About a week later, Childs invited Dean to go with him to see Aston. Dean made a couple of lame excuses as to why he couldn't go, but Childs blew them off. Top finally gave him the option, but suggested that he thought he should go. Dean eventually relented.

He called Natalie at home and told her that he was going to see Aston. She encouraged him to meet with him, reminding him of their study on forgiveness. He remembered that discussion, that in forgiving Aston, it sets him free and allows God to do a work in both their lives.

On the way to the hospital, he asked the good Lord to help him to forgive Smoke, not only with his mouth but in his heart. It was a little easier with the thought that Aston would never abuse him again. They both trudged into the hospital and went to the elevator and Childs gave Dean the low down on Aston's family. Dean had no idea that he was married and had two children, a boy and a girl.

They walked into the hospital room and Aston laid limp on the bed, his large frame covering most of it. His wife Florence, sat at his side holding his left hand. She was tall with a pleasant face that was tear stained with a strained expression. She stood up and greeted Childs, thanking him for coming.

Top immediately introduced Dean and she shook his hand. She introduced her two children to Dean and Childs. Eric, their son had a distant look. He took Dean's hand, as though he was far away in a drugged-out stupor. Linda, on the other hand, looked him up and down as if she was appraising a hunk of meat at the butcher shop.

He felt very uncomfortable with her as she grabbed his hand for a few minutes, gazing deeply into his eyes. He retracted it and politely commented on how nice it was to meet them all. Childs suggested that the family take a dinner break, that they would watch Aston until they returned.

Top sat down by his side and shook him awake. He greeted Aston as a friend, but Dean did not think that they were close. He could not see Aston's expression but by his one arm movement, Dean was surprised that he was happy to see Childs. Top did most of the talking. Aston would try to express himself, but Dean could not understand what he was trying to communicate. Childs would guess and when he hit the thought, Aston would nod.

Childs motioned for Dean to come over, he had been standing on Aston's right side, in his blind spot. Smoke turned slowly and Dean caught his expression as he came into view. It was one of surprise and confusion.

Dean came to stand next to Top and expressed how sorry he was to see him ill and apologized if he had put any undue stress on him. As Dean spoke, he could see Aston's expression change from surprise to anger. Dean could see that he still was not making any points with Aston, so he quickly forgave him for his abuse and left the room. Aston was so angry that he almost sat up in his bed. Dean took a seat down in the lobby and waited for Childs.

He eventually showed up, shaking his head. He told Dean that it took him about fifteen minutes to get Smoke to relax. Dean told Top that he had no intentions of seeing Aston ever again. Childs looked at him strangely and suggested that he thought Dean would touch Aston in a significant way. Dean's first thought was 'fat chance.'

In the middle of June, Dean received a letter with a check from his father's estate. The letter indicated that it was Bud's wish that Dean pay off any medical expenses for Melody and buy a new car for the family. He showed Natalie the letter and the check. They both laughed, remembering how Bud reacted to the Cornet. The letter also indicated that a large portion of Dean's inheritance went into a trust fund for his education when he got out of the service. This was another answer to prayer.

The old red beast, as Natalie called it, was not running well anymore. It was starting to smoke and even though Morton and Dean would tune it up, the engine no longer ran well. Morton was not sure, but he thought it might be a bad valve or it needed a ring job. Either way, the Larsons did not have the money to fix the problems. Now they did not have to, they could buy a fairly new vehicle. When the army doctors couldn't find out Melody's problems, they took her to a specialist. Doctor Johnson wanted his money and they would be able take care of all those bills.

The next day Thursday. Dean caught a ride with Porter and they stopped at the bank on the way home that evening. He put the money into their checking account, they informed him that it would take a couple of working days for the check to clear the bank, then he could use the full amount on whatever he wanted.

That evening, he took the family out for dinner to celebrate their new found fortune. On their way home, they stopped at a couple car lots to look at some of the vehicles. Dealing with the salesmen was like getting mugged by a thief, but it didn't matter, they didn't see anything they liked or they didn't like the feel of the man they were dealing with.

They went home and Dean told Morton about the money and asked him if he knew a good car dealer that they could buy a vehicle from. Morton held up a hand and told Dean that he was going to make a call to a friend of his. He came knocking on Dean's door a few minutes later.

"Hey man, I've got a friend that deals in bank repo and I guess he has a beauty sitting in his warehouse right now."

"What is it?"

"It's a 1976 Ford Mustang coupe. Only a year old."

"What kind of shape is it in and why was it repossessed?"

"He says it is cherry and with very few miles on it. His name is Albert Combs and he is willing to show you the car tomorrow if you're willing to take the time and look it over. It might be the best deal you will get around here for the money."

"Does he know that I don't have the money in hand Morton?"

"Yep, I told him your situation and he told me that he was willing to wait if you're willing to pay for the car in full. It was repo because of lack of payment on the former owner's part."

Morton offered to take Dean over to see Albert the next day. After work, Morton drove Dean to a warehouse at the edge of Hopkinsville. Morton led the way to an office where a large man sat looking over some paperwork. He instantly stood up and gave skinny little Morton a big bear hug.

Morton had met Albert while on maneuvers and they had become best friends. He was older and had retired from an infantry unit that Morton had been an observer for. Albert had sold Morton his vehicle and it was still running well. Introductions were made and Albert led the way to the repossessed items.

The first rows they came to were furniture, then appliances. Dean could see about ten cars off in the distance. The first few were trashed, but his eyes became fixed on a cherry blue and white Mustang with mag wheels. It was beautiful and very clean. He wouldn't allow Dean to drive it out of the building but they did start it up and the 351 V-8 engine hummed like a beautiful song. Dean was sold, but he looked it over closer and told Albert that Natalie was the real boss and that they would have to take it out for a good test drive. They agreed upon a date to meet again, one in which Dean thought he would have the money in hand. The nice part about the price is that they would have plenty of money left over since his father had given them enough to buy a new car.

When they were back in the car driving home, Dean asked Morton what he thought of the car. Morton had not heard anything that caused him to be concerned, but there might be problems with the undercarriage that they could not hear unless they were out on the road. The tires were brand new with very little wear. Morton suggested that he go with them when they tested the vehicle. Dean agreed. He was over the initial desire to purchase the car based on emotions and was considering any possible problems.

After hearing the engine, he asked Albert why the car had been repossessed. Albert had told him that the man that owned it had been a crew member on a C-130 Hercules airplane, so he did a lot of flying and that is why the car had low mileage. He got caught dealing drugs, was thrown in jail, and was no longer able to pay the payments. The drug sales were one of the reasons he could afford to buy a brand-new Mustang.

He told Natalie about the car, but she was less than enthusiastic about a fast sporty car. Dean reminded her of praying for another vehicle, that it would be in good condition, few miles on it, and that it would meet their needs. She nodded in agreement that they would buy it if Morton thought it was a good purchase.

It would be the best car Dean ever had if he bought it. He had learned to drive on the old Chevy pickup back home, they had owned the Opal in Germany, and now they were trying to get by with the Cornet, which was running out of steam quickly.

A couple days later they were informed by the bank that the check had cleared. The next day Dean, Morton, and Natalie went down to the warehouse to meet with Albert. He had the Mustang out in the parking area. Natalie was surprised by how clean and pretty it was. Albert let them go out alone because the back seat was not very big. Natalie did complain about that, it was not comfortable for her to sit in it but it was large enough for the two children. They drove it for a couple of miles and everything worked to perfection. Dean was pleased about how it would pick up speed and he knew the car could go a lot faster. Morton gave his approval after driving it himself. Natalie agreed to the purchase.

They made a deal with Albert and paid for the Mustang. It was the largest check Dean had ever signed his name to, but they had the title of the car in hand. They still had a large amount of money left from the inheritance. They hired Angela, Porter's daughter to watch the kids and they took Morton and Carrie out for dinner and a movie as a celebration. Of course, they had to use the new car. It was fast and the evening was enjoyable.

Around the first part of July, Melody stared crying at about one in the morning. Dean crawled out of bed and picked up his baby girl. Even when she was weeping, she looked like an angel to him. He felt the heat coming off her body and put his hand to her forehead. She was burning up and he called Natalie out of bed. She came running with great concern in her eyes. She kissed her head and confirmed Dean's assessment of his daughter's fever.

She ordered Dean to get John ready for a trip to the doctor's office. She went to the phone and called Dr. Johnson at home, telling the weary man about Melody. He told her to meet him at his office in fifteen minutes.

The doctor was there a few minutes later. He rushed Melody into his private office and did a battery of tests on her. At about three in the morning, he was handing the baby back to Natalie. The fever was gone and Melody was sleeping soundly. Johnson had become frustrated with Melody's health issues.

They would bring her in, and would catch the end of the fever, but when they did the tests, the results would indicate all was normal. That is why he had them call and met them at the office. He wanted to test her when she had the fever.

Johnson was an older man, tall with gray hair creeping up from the temples of his head. The gray was starting to pepper the rest of his scalp. He rarely smiled, but when he met with them a couple of days later, he gave them a big toothy grin. He had told them not to give her any water when she broke out in the fever next time. This time he had found a urinary tract infection. Somehow her system was flushing the infection out before they could find it. Finally, they had found the problem which gave them some peace.

A couple weeks later they took her to the hospital and they found that her kidney had two tubes going to the bladder. They would have to operate and fix the problem. Dean didn't like the idea of someone cutting on his little girl. He asked if she might grow out of it. They didn't think that was possible so they consented to the procedure. When they went in they not only found an extra tube but the flap was not working properly. They fixed both items and she never had the fevers after that.

When they brought her out, she looked dead, almost like a gutted fish. The doctors assured them that she was doing well. They suggested that because of her health problems she might be a little slow in school but that she would eventually catch up with the rest of the students. She spent several days in the hospital and Natalie was by her side most of the time. The Childs, Porter's, and Morton's visited her several times.

It was good that they had a lot of money left over after they bought the car. The government took care of most of medical expenses and Dean took care of the rest.

In the first part of August, Dean took his final on math and came out of the class with a B-. As he was getting into the Mustang, it was like God reminded him of the bargain that he had struck with him, that if He would take care of these four problems, that Dean would seek after Him.

Dean was determined to keep his end of the bargain.

Chapter 17

HELLO ALAN

With Aston gone, they brought in a new Chief of Smoke as soon as possible. His name was Jake Rose and he was not to be messed with. He informed the battery while in formation that he would kick anyone's rear end up between their ears if they made fun of his last name. Willie leaned over to Dean and suggested he thought the man could do it.

This was the first time Dean thought Willie was actually in awe of someone else and that he had deep respect for the man that stood before them. Willie respected most of the officers and sergeants because of their ranks, but in the case of Rose, he honored the man, which was a whole different attitude for Willie. Willie could live with things; he was about to get out at the end of July which gave him about a month to deal with Rose.

He was tough but fair and Dean grew to like the new Chief of Smoke quickly. The battery learned where he stood on issues and that if he called them young man, they were in big trouble but if he called them young soldier, they were okay. He never smiled, nor did his facial expressions change under any circumstance. When he called, them, they could never determine if the soldier was in trouble or if he was wanting to give them some instructions. He was always spit and polish and had airborne and air assault wings on his chest.

A story had followed him over to the unit that a big sergeant from his old unit had been giving him a hard time and he had put him in a head lock. He ran him up to the second floor of the building, pushed him out the window, grabbing ahold of his ankles, and holding him over the sidewalk until he agreed to behave himself. No one knew if the story was true or not, but they had no doubt that he could do it. If nothing else, it kept the trouble makers steering clear of Smoke.

It was a hot muggy day in July when they went out to the field to perform maneuvers and did some night shooting. Porter seemed on edge the whole time they were out there and had a hard time concentrating. Smoke took him off to the side and had a long talk with him. Porter had been promoted to staff sergeant and was in charge of the gun crew.

Arthur was acting assistant section chief because the buck sergeant had just transferred out. No one knew what was said, but Porter came back to the gun with head bowed. Dean asked him if he was alright but Porter just shook his head. He said very little and Garcia seemed to run the gun more than Porter.

They got back to Campbell around two pm the next day. Dean was informed that a sergeant had dropped by that morning wanting to see him. He was a part of a new battery that was being put together for the 101st Airbourne Division and he was going to drop by that evening around five, Dean asked Clark what his name was, but the sergeant would not leave it with Clark. Dean put it aside, even forgetting about the sergeant until that evening when they were called to formation.

There standing off to the side was an old familiar face from Baumholder, Germany; it was Alan Walker smiling broadly at him. Dean could hardly wait for his release so he could get over and give Al a handshake. Walker didn't just give Dean a handshake, but a half-hearted hug with a joyous greeting. "What are you doing here man?"

"I extended my enlistment by a year to get transferred to an 155 howitzer unit here at Campbell. Why don't you buy your old fearless leader a round at one of the local bars? I want to talk to you about an opportunity," Walker exclaimed excitedly.

"Can't do it tonight, I promised Natalie that I'd be home for some time with the family since I was away last night. Tomorrow is Thursday and I told Willie that I would take him out on the town since he's getting out of the army at the end of this month. It's a short timers party. Why don't you tag along? We can talk in between the times Willie is picking fights. We will have two other guys with us. If I say you're alright, it will be no big deal to them."

"I don't know, man. Are you sure it will be alright?"

Willie was walking to the mess hall. Dean grabbed his arm and turned him toward Walker. He introduced them and asked Willie if it was alright for Walker to tag along with him on his party.

"Hey, the more the merrier. If Larson says you're alright. You can come to any party we have," Willie said with his winning smile.

When Dean got home that night, he informed Natalie that Walker had transferred to Campbell. She instantly suggested that he come over for dinner some night soon. Unlike Baumholder, Natalie knew only a couple of the men he worked with. She had never met Willie or Garcia. On the other hand, she had a lot more lady friends at Fort Campbell than she ever had in Baumholder.

The next evening, all of them piled into Garcia's big car and drove to one of the local bars. He introduced Walker to Garcia and Clark. He bought the first round and everyone shared with Walker where they came from and some of their experiences in the army. After two beers, everyone seemed relaxed and got along with one another.

Walker talked about some of his adventures with Dean in Germany. Dean was in charge of getting everyone home, so he nursed his second beer for a long time. Clark and Willie asked two ladies to dance, so it gave Walker time to talk to Dean about the opportunity that he wanted to present to him.

"I'm in charge of one of the SW sections on a towed 155 unit. We don't have a full crew yet, so I talked to my first sergeant about you and if you want to be a part of the section you can have a job with the unit."

"I didn't know they had nuclear rounds for the 155," Dean said surprised.

"They just finished developing them recently, it is not like the 8-inch round at all. It is self-contained with a very low yield."

"Hey, man. What are you trying to do steal one of the best men off the gun grew? Besides that, he is my friend. Don't do it, Larson. Just think, you only have another month and you'll be leaving the army anyway," Garcia blurted out.

"There is one catch, you will have to extend for a year if you want into the SW section. I know that you have plans, but it will be better duty and it will be like old times, so think about it."

Dean looked down at his beer and rolled the glass of beer between his two hands. His first inclination was to say "Noo." He knew he would have to run it by Natalie first.

Since it was a week day, they all decided to go back to base about ten that evening. Dean had limited himself to two beers, but because it was obvious that the other four were drunk, the MPs made Dean get out of the car and walk a straight line. He had to recite the alphabet and do some coordination test before they allowed him to drive them back to their quarters.

The next morning, they gave Willie the honor of carrying the battery standard on the three-mile run. He would start processing out of the army on Monday. He looked good, like he could take on the whole battery in a fight. Dean asked him how he was doing after all the beer he drank. Willie told him that he was fine, but that he needed a shower.

Garcia and Clark fell out of the formation after about a mile an half and they soon had Rose chewing them out for lagging behind.

Willie was also starting to slow down. They finally relieved him of the flag and the four ranks parted around him like the Red Sea parted for Moses. When Dean double timed pass him he got the strange smell of ammonia coming from Willie; he was sweating the alcohol out of his pores.

A week later, Sergeant Randy Ellis from FDC started processing out of the army. He had always been helpful and kind to Dean. Dean would miss his friendship; Ellis was going home to Iowa to become an insurance salesman.

After the incident out on the field with Porter and Smoke, Top Childs ordered Dean to come to his office. He questioned him on several topics concerning his section chief.

"This is just between me and you Larson. I don't want you to talk to anyone about our conversation, not even Natalie. Do you understand?"

"Yes, Top, what is this all about?"

"It's about Porter. I need to know what is going on with him and I need you to be as honest with me as possible, not only for his sake but for the battery's sake. He is not going to get in trouble from what you say."

Dean felt very uncomfortable. He did not want to rat on Porter. He liked Top and, though Porter had been aloof many times, there were still times Porter acted friendly and helpful. Dean wasn't sure what was going on with him but the fact Top had assured him that Porter wouldn't get in trouble because of things said, gave him some peace of mind.

"Well, I don't know if I can help you Top, he is keeping me at arm's length a lot lately."

"He's doing the same with me and I have been hearing some rumors, so I'm asking you if you have heard the same or can verify them?"

Dean adjusted himself in the chair, feeling even more un-comfortable. He looked down at the floor and thought for a long time and then nodded his head.

"I've heard that he is smoking dope again and that he is into some very ugly pornography. Can you verify any of this?"

"Well Top," Dean took a deep breath. "I know that he has smoked dope. I have smelled it on him. I have no idea about the porno, but what does that have to do with being a section chief?"

"I can't have one of my section chiefs doing drugs. The porno and drugs open up doors emotionally causing demonic oppression. It can also affect his family. He should know better than mess with that stuff. He is in deep trouble; I want you to keep an eye on him. Dean I would suggest that you pray for him, that the Lord would set him free from that stuff."

"I don't pray much, usually just ask God to bless the food, and family. What should I ask the Lord to do in Porter's life?"

"Ask the Lord to have mercy on him and to get his heart right with Him."

Dean was released to go home; he was troubled by the conversation. He was wondering if he should have snitched on Porter. He didn't want to get him in trouble but Porter did act like he was in a fog at times and the last time was in the field which could cause safety issues in the future. What did Top mean about open doors.

Natalie knew that he was bothered by something the minute he walked in the door. He would not discuss with her the talk that he had with Top. He did ask her about open doors but she had no idea what Top was talking about. He suggested that they pray for Porter and the family. This surprised Natalie, he had never made a request like that of her before. She questioned him, but he stood his ground on not giving her any details. They prayed for the family that evening.

Chapter 18

A VISITATION

Dean was sitting near a floor vent that was blowing cool air out into the sanctuary. It was a hot July evening and he was in church waiting for the guest speaker who was to preach at some special meetings. Childs made a strong argument compelling him to attend. He had even come over and picked him up to make sure that he made the event. He had tried to get Porter to come. Dean and Suzan encouraged him, but he rejected the idea of attending.

Sally Jackson had just finished singing a special, it was a beautiful rendition of "Amazing Grace." She sat down by a large man that had piercing green eyes and features of a small lion. He looked fierce, yet loving, which was an odd combination. Dean had never seen him before.

The man did not sing the worship songs, but sat there with eyes closed. Suddenly, he would look up and gaze around the room, his head would stop at some point in the sanctuary, then he would close his eyes again. He did it once and those piercing green eyes fell on Dean. The man seemed to peer through Dean, then he closed them again, it unsettled Dean.

Pastor Jethro stood up after Sally's song and gave the guest speaker an introduction. His man was Pastor Shawn Button from Oklahoma City where he had been leading a church for twenty years. Pastor Button got up and told them all a joke, it got a good laugh, but it seemed foreign coming out of his mouth. He seemed too serious to be telling jokes.

He changed gears in a big way, talking about Heaven and hell. He spoke with such power and authority, that not a sound could be heard in the sanctuary but his voice. There were several toddlers in the building, but there was not a peep from them. He didn't use a mike, but roamed freely from side to side on the podium. He did not shout, but his voice carried to the farthest corner of the room. He was talking on hell, something about eternal torment, when he stopped in mid-sentence, pointed at Dean, and told him to come forward.

Dean was surprised, he felt the presence of God all around him. He couldn't describe it, something like goosebumps all over his body. Still, he pointed at himself, Button nodded yes and waved him forward. Dean gulped hard, stood up, and walked to the podium. The pastor stood right in front of him.

"Are you ready for this?" asked Button

"I don't know," responded Dean in a daze.

"It doesn't matter, here it comes."

Button laid his hand on Dean's head. It felt like electricity shooting up and down Dean's body and he collapsed on the floor in a heap. Button turned and started marching back and forth on the stage, preaching his message where he had left off. Dean regained enough of his motor skills to crawl back to his seat and pull himself up into a sitting position. He didn't hear any more of the message; he had never felt such freedom from the world. Joy, peace, love, hope engulfed him. All he could do was sit there and grin from ear to ear.

After an hour, the service ended and Button came over to him and laid hands on him again with Childs, and pastor Jethro. They all prayed for him. The presence of God became so intense that Dean slumped down on the pew. Childs held him in place until they were done. Jethro and Childs helped him to the car. This euphoric feeling did not subside until Dean got home it was like being drunk, only better. Childs saw him to the door and left him there. It was very late and both of them would be reporting for duty early in the morning.

"What happened to you," quizzed Natalie once Dean got into the light.

"I don't know for sure. I'm pretty sure it was God, whatever it was," Dean said with a big grin.

"Whatever it was, you look so at peace and it is good," Natalie said staring deeply into his face.

"Natalie, I feel so good and so free." He then explained what took place at the service. She suggested that he get back with Jethro and Childs as to what had been prayed over him. He couldn't remember any of it. She recommended that they get to bed, it was late and the morning was coming quickly. She grabbed him by the hand and led him to the bedroom. He crawled into bed next to her and gave her a good night kiss.   She rolled over and was quickly asleep, but Dean couldn't get to sleep. He finally got up, grabbed his Bible, and started reading in "Matthew."

The words jumped out at him, speaking to him in powerful ways. He fell asleep around 2 am that morning with the Bible still in his hands.

Natalie woke him up and he quickly got ready for the day. He still felt energized and never felt weary that day. Things seemed to fall in place all day without any problems. When he had a minute to think about the Lord, suddenly his presence would fall on Dean. He would fall to his knees under the power of the Spirit, it was like he was drunk again. He would crawl to the tail of the gun and sit on it until it passed. This would happen for the next few weeks, then it suddenly stopped.

A lot of the people closest to him noticed a big change in him. They would ask him what had happened to him and he would testify of how the Spirit of the Lord fell on him, giving him peace, joy, and rest. Dean became addicted to the Bible. He read through it four times in two years.

On the other hand, Porter seemed to distance himself more than ever from Dean. He tried to talk to Porter several times, but Porter would put up a hand and walk away. Porter even talked to Top about transferring him to another gun. This gave Childs a chance to discuss with Porter about his backsliding away from God, but Porter assured him that he was doing find.

Top brought out the rumors that he had heard about him and that if they were true, Porter better get it taken care of. Childs would bring, not only action in the church, he would deal with the drug problem the army way if Porter didn't get straightened up. He reminded him that death came with sin and that the pleasure would eventually end in pain and suffering. Dean was certain that Porter thought he had informed on him because of Natalie's and Suzan's relationship. Natalie had never said anything to him about the Porter's home life.

Every so often, Walker would invite Dean to the bar to have a couple of beers and play some pool. Dean ordered his first beer but down deep within he felt like something was wrong. He shook it off and took his first sip, it tasted flat. He beat the first game and finished the beer, and ordered another one, hoping that the next one would taste better. Again, he had that unsettling feeling. The second beer tasted worse.

He complained to the bar maid, she took some out the tap sampled it and reported to him that his taste buds must be out of whack because the beer was good. He decided that he would not come to the bar again. He asked Walker how his beer tasted. Walker thought the beer tasted fine. Walker decided to get him off the subject of beer and asked him several questions about his encounter with God.

Dean had already discussed it with Walker before, but he was glad to recount the visitation again. He told Walker about his need to read the Bible and that he was reading the letters of Paul for the first time. Some of the scriptures had really spoken to him. They left after two games, the last one Walker won. Dean was about to step into his car when he heard an audible voice say, "That's enough!" He looked around and saw no one but Walker but it had not been his voice.

He asked Walker if he had said anything or heard anything. Walker looked at him in a strange way and denied hearing or saying anything. He shook his head and drove Walker back to the barracks.

As he was driving home, he heard that voice again. "That's enough!"

"Enough of what?" Dean asked. He knew he was speaking to God now.

"No more drinking Dean."

From that day on Dean stopped drinking any alcoholic beverages. Alan and him continued to play pool but Dean would drink soft drinks. Walker asked him about it and he informed him that he thought it was time to stop partaking of alcohol.

Dean didn't know how he would take the thought that he had heard from God, if he would consider him insane. He rolled it over in his mind several times. It was the first time he had heard that voice. He was fairly sure it was God, after all, the devil would have suggested that he have a great time, not that he should have stopped drinking.

Natalie was concerned about him since the changes were so drastic. She insisted that he talk to Pastor Jethro about them. Besides that, he was curious about what they had prayed over him. Jethro had always been warm and loving towards Dean, even when he had sinned with Ann. He had not been judgmental, but always spoke of forgiveness and about God's mercy. He met Dean at the door with a strong handshake and a warm hug.

"What can I do for you Dean? I imagine you have a lot of questions about what is happening to you."

"Pastor, thank you for taking time to see me. You're right, I have a lot of questions. What happened to me that Sunday night? Natalie suggested that I was immersed in the Spirit, but she had never seen anyone change so much."

"She was right, but when the Spirit does that, it affects people in different ways. I have to say, I haven't seen very many people react the way you did. I imagine you needed a lot of forgiveness and a lot of healing in your life. I also believe you have a special calling and that when you go through the hard times, that special time with God will be an anchor for you."

"Does God speak audible to people now days? I mean, I thought I heard someone tell me to stop drinking Pastor. Am I just going crazy?"

"Usually, He speaks to me in the scriptures. It would not surprise me if He spoke to you verbally. He has given me dreams and an occasional vision to direct my path. I know through a vision that I'm going to be leaving this church soon for a church in Memphis. Before I act on such communications, I wait until it's confirmed.

"Recently I got a letter from a church in Memphis asking me to interview for a senior pastor position. I'll be going down there to speak to the board next week. Sally and I are excited because it will be closer to the grandchildren. See how that works? In your case, it is obvious that you should stop drinking, not only because it has gotten you in trouble in the past, but it will make you a better witness in the future."

"I'm going to miss you," Dean said thoughtfully. It was quiet for a long time.

"You still have something on your mind, Dean?"

"Yes, what were some of the things that you guys prayed over me at the meeting? I was so out of it that I didn't hear the message, nor did I hear the prayers."

Jethro laughed. "That's not surprising. You did look like you were somewhere else when we were speaking over you. Let's see, Button said that you would find great favor from the Lord and that you would come to know the true meaning of what the promised land is. The Lord gave me that you were born for such a time as this and that he had a great purpose for you, but many would not understand or want to go with you.

"Childs declared that you were a warrior for the kingdom and that war against the kingdom of darkness was in your heart and you would take ground back. You were to stay here in the army longer. I know that all of that was from the Lord, but you need to pray long and hard about staying in the army. That might be his desire, I know he loves you a bunch."

"What does all that mean? I'm starting to read the Bible, but I don't understand most of that."

"Relax, Dean the good Lord will reveal it all in due time. Go home and write down what you can remember. Look at it once in a while to see if it was from the Lord. The things you forget won't matter, but if the words were from the Lord, then you will see them being fulfilled."

Before Dean left, Jethro prayed with him and he felt a peace wash over him. He was at rest in his heart about the things that had happened in the last week, except the idea of staying in the army. He had no such plans and was going to speak with Childs about it the next day. He went home and told Natalie about his conversation with Jethro as he wrote down what had been prayed over him.

He asked Clark if Top had some free time after duty the next day. Clark informed him that he was having a meeting with the BC at the time, but if he wanted to wait, they should be done in a few minutes. Dean took a seat, and got the latest rumors flying around the battalion from Clark. It was nothing new or exciting.

Finally, Knight came out of the office, Dean stood at attention, showing respect to his commanding officer. Top invited him in. Dean asked him about the prayers that had been spoken over him. Childs basically confirmed what Jethro had already told him.

"What about this thought that I should stay in the army? You know that I plan on going home at the end of next month."

"You need to pray about it, Dean. I believe that the Lord has something He wants to teach you here at Campbell. I would like to mentor you if you don't mind."

"That would be great. I would like you to disciple me, but I'm afraid you'll have to move to Idaho to get the job done. I will take your advice and pray about it though."

"That's fine. If I'm wrong, please forgive me. If you still feel lead to go home, I will help you in any way I can."

Dean left the office, still wondering about all that had been exposed to him. As he rounded the hallway to the door, he bumped into Porter. Porter looked him in the eye for a second, then looked away to the floor. His eyes were sunken and a strange expression flooded his facial features.

Before he knew what was being said, Dean blurted, "You need to repent quickly, for you have opened a door to the enemy by which he will bring destruction on you and great harm to your family."

Porter looked surprised and fearful. Dean tried to apologize, but Porter ran off. He tried to talk to him a few times during the week, but he would walk off before Dean could say anything to him about it. Dean finally pinned Porter down, but he indicated that he didn't want to talk about it.

Chapter 19

THE PRICE OF SIN

Dean awoke out of a sound sleep. Natalie sat straight up in the bed as someone pounded on the door at about four in the morning. Dean turned on the light and crawled out of bed. He pulled on a pair of pants and a T-shirt. He went to the closet, pulled out the 30-30, levered a round in the chamber, and walked to the door. Natalie was close behind him. He looked through the peep hole in the door after turning on the outside light. It was Suzan Porter, and she looked frantic. He opened the door and she burst into his arms sobbing. He gave Natalie the rifle and towed Suzan over to the couch.

"You've got to stop him," she blurted out after she caught her breath!

"Stop who?" asked Dean.

"Ross, he's going to kill Jon Kelly."

"Why, what did Jon do?" questioned Natalie.

"We don't have time for that. Dean, please stop him before it's too late."

"Have you called the police?" demanded Natalie.

"No, he tore the phone out of the wall."

Natalie ran to the phone and called the police. Dean hesitated, considered if he should take the rifle or not. He decided to leave it and ran toward Jon's mobile home, hoping to intercept Porter before he got there. He didn't want a gun battle with Ross, he was going to try to talk him out of doing something stupid. It would have been nice if he knew why Porter was so upset with Jon. He would have to fish for the reason during his conversation with him. About halfway over to Kelly's place, he heard a weapon go off. His first thought was oh God, he shot Jon. Several lights came on and Dean slowed his pace toward the mobile home, he now reconsidered if leaving the rifle at home was a good idea.

Two more shots sounded off in the dark, they were very close together. He thought he had seen the muzzle flashes from the window. He approached the door cautiously and peeked through, it was slightly ajar. He saw Porter looking down at a mess that had been Jon Kelly.

Porter was saying something to the corpse, but Dean couldn't make it out. Dean quietly moved to the step but kept it at an angle so that he could quickly duck behind a wall if Ross pulled up on him. Dean was fairly certain that the two last rounds had gone into Jon's head because it was nothing but a bloody pulp. Dean stayed hidden in the shadows next to the steps. If Ross decided to come after him, there were many hiding spots.

"Hey Sarg, are you alright?"

Porter looked his way, but kept the .45 caliber down at his side. He looked back at the corpse and then down at the weapon again.

"Hey Sarg, my friend, it's me Larson. Are you alright?"

"Stay away from me, Larson."

"Ross, why don't you put the gun down and we can talk about things?" He could hear police sirens in the distance. Porter had messed up. He was going to jail but Dean did not want him killed. He was very concerned about a gun fight near so many homes. Morton suddenly appeared, peeking around the side of a mobile home. Dean waved him forward; he had a weapon in his hand. He stood a few feet away from Dean with his pistol at the ready.

"Hey, Ross. The police will be here soon, please put the gun down and come out. You know how they are. We don't want anyone else getting hurt," pleaded Dean.

Porter caressed the barrel of the .45 in his left hand looking at it for a few minutes. It was like he had come back to this very moment and that he realized what he had done. Dean could see a difference in his eyes and the way he looked around the room and back at the gun.

"Dean, I know that you tried to be a good friend and I'm sorry that I shunned you. Take good care of your family, keep them safe. Tell Suzan and the girls that I loved them and that I'm sorry."

He put the weapon up under his chin and pulled the trigger. Dean saw him raise the gun and rushed through the door but it was too late as the impact of the round lifted Porter's head upward, a spray of blood and matter. The body settled into a heap near Jon. Dean stopped in the middle of the living room, he just turned away. He knew Ross Porter was dead, no one could save him.

Two policemen appeared in the doorway with guns drawn. They ordered Dean to put his hands up, then they entered the room. Dean couldn't help it, the tears came. They were silent like his grief. They patted him down looked over the scene, they asked him what had happened.

Dean told them the story and Morton came in without his weapon and confirmed Dean's account of the events. One of the policemen had been involved with Dean's false arrest. He told the other one to let them go after getting their addresses. They would have the detectives look the scene over and do the follow up investigation. They escorted them away from the crime scene. Dean and Kevin walked back to their homes in silence.

Suzan was still at Dean's house and Natalie was holding her in her arms. With all the shooting, both of them knew it wasn't good news. Natalie's face lit up when Dean walked through the door. She had feared that Dean may have been one of Porter's targets.

When Suzan heard Dean come through the door, she looked up into Dean's eyes hoping for some good news. Dean looked down and then told her that Ross was dead. She collapsed on the floor and wept in anguish. No matter what Natalie did, she couldn't comfort the woman. Tears gushed from Suzan's eyes like a river flowing over a waterfall. Dean went to Morton's house and asked Carrie to get Suzan's daughters and bring them to their mother. He suggested that she inform the police as to where the family was.

With all the shooting and police sirens, the whole park was awake. People were either wandering toward the sirens or to see if neighbors were alright. Dean tried to help Natalie comfort Suzan. Melody started crying, so Dean grabbed up his little girl while Natalie sat hugging the distraught woman.

An investigator showed up with Carrie and the two girls. They kept asking what was going on, that's when Suzan seemed to get control of herself and took the two girls aside. She told them what had happened to their father. Angela collapsed while Darlene started weeping uncontrollably.

The police investigator took Dean aside and questioned him about the events, as he observed them at the mobile home. Dean described what he had seen when he arrived at the house and then the suicide of Ross Porter. The policeman asked him if he knew a motive for Ross killing Jon Kelly. Dean had never heard of any hard feelings between the two men. He also inquired as to what kind of relations Dean and Ross had.

He informed him that he was his section chief and all the other information as to where they worked and the unit they were attached to. Dean looked at his watch realized that he needed to call into the battery and inform them that he was not going to make it in today and why. He talked to NCO that was on duty and told him that he had to take care of some police business.

Natalie was the next one that he interviewed. He bypassed Suzan and the girls because Suzan was still comforting the two young ladies. Natalie confirmed the first part of Dean's story and the shots she had heard. He asked her if she could escort the two girls into another room so he could talk to Suzan. Natalie helped the girls into Melody's bedroom.

The policeman turned his attention to Suzan, asking all the pertinent questions about where they lived and their relationship. He asked her what had led up the events that caused her husband to murder Jon Kelly.

"Well, we caught our daughter, Angela, sneaking back into house this morning between two and three am. Ross and I questioned her for a long time and she finally confessed that she had been sleeping with Jon Kelly and she had done so several times. She is underage. I had never seen my husband so angry." She paused, finally looking up from the floor. She searched Dean and Detective Lonnie Byers face for their reaction.

Dean was shocked by the revelation. Byers on the other hand kept a poker face and asked her to continue with her story.

"Ross was so angry that he slapped Angela, knocking her to the floor. He has never hit either of the girls like that before. He grabbed her by the hair, dragged her into the bedroom, and told her to get to bed." Tears started flowing again. Suzan had to pause and get control of her emotions.

"He grabbed his gun and started for the door. I got in the way and calmed him a little, suggested that we talk it out. He got a beer out of the fridge and I thought maybe it would settle him down. I suggested that we could call the police and have Jon arrested for rape, since Angela is to young."

"How did he handle that suggestion Mrs. Porter?" asked Byers.

"I couldn't tell at first, he got up and started pacing, still drinking his beer. He finished his first beer and got another one. I thought that was good because he usually becomes more mellow the more he drinks. But I could tell by the look on his face that he was working himself into a rage. He picked up the gun again, checked the clip, he put it back into the weapon, and chambered a round. He pulled the phone out of the wall and left. That's when I ran to Dean's place."

Byers went into the bedroom and questioned Angela alone. He came out looked at his watch and made some notations on his note pad. He started to leave so Dean showed him to the door. Byers stopped, looked back at Suzan, and commented that he felt sorry, for her, she was going to be carrying a lot of baggage for a while.

Natalie started fixing breakfast for everyone. Morton had gone in to work, he had told the BC and Top what happened. Top gave Dean a call and gave him a phone number for grief counselling for everyone involved. He asked Dean to come in at some point that day. He wanted to talk to him to get more information on what had occurred. Dean told him that he would report sometime later that morning. No one ate much, nor was there much talking.

Dean did break the silence with the phone numbers to the counselling center and suggested that they make an appointment when they felt up to it. He pointed Angela out to Suzan. She just stared at her food, looking down, avoiding looking at anyone.

Dean left the table after having a few bites and went into the bedroom. John followed him in wanting to be held. The little boy sensed that something was wrong and needed to be assured that everything was okay. Natalie brought Melody in, giving her to Dean. She was going to help the three women back to their home. She dressed and went to the Porter home with Suzan and the girls.

Melody soon fell asleep, she had been awakened too early, leaving Dean alone with his son. He held him tightly thinking about the tragedy. At first all he felt was anger towards Angela and Jon for doing the things that they had done.

Then he felt frustration towards Ross, though not necessarily for killing Jon because he was not sure what he would have done if it had been his own daughter. The selfish act of committing suicide and not facing the consequences of his own actions seemed to be the cowardly way out. The more he thought about it, the more outrage he felt toward Ross.

Suddenly another idea took over, where was God in all this? Why didn't He stop in? After all a lot of people had been praying for Ross. What was God doing, sleeping on the job when it was so important for Him to be working in these circumstances?

He mulled it over in his mind and became angry with all of them and God was included in that package. He was all powerful, He could have stopped it. Dean could not come up with an answer as to why He was asleep at the helm. He got up and paced up and down with John in his arms, trying to think through it all. He finally set it aside, nothing made any sense to him, so he needed to run it by Top and Pastor Jethro, maybe they could shed some light on the subject.

Natalie still wasn't back by eleven in the morning, so Dean asked Carrie if she could watch the children for an hour or two. She readily agreed and Dean drove in to base. Top's door was open, he spotted Dean and waved him into the office. He called Captain Knight in to hear what had occurred with Porter.

Dean related the story for the tenth time, it seemed, if not by telling it to someone, but also by living it over in his mind. He wondered if he could have said something different or been faster at charging in and grabbing the gun from Ross.

Knight thanked him for coming to the battery and reporting the details. He stood and left, Dean was about to leave, but Top told him that he wanted to talk to him alone. Knight shut the door behind him, leaving the two staring hard at one another.

"You look troubled Dean. Do you need counselling?"

"Most likely. My question is, where was God in all this, Top? You told me to pray for him. Was I asking God all the wrong things?"

"The Lord was in the room with you, Dean. He never left Ross but Ross left Him when he would not turn from his sins. God will never take away your free will, the right to destroy yourself if you want. Ross set his face and the Lord let him have his way. I know Ross was warned at least two times to repent, once by me and once by Pastor Jethro. The wages of sin is death and he got paid Larson.

I'm not the judge Dean, I don't know what God did with Porter. I hope he made it, but lots of people go to hell every day. You go home, seek God, pray, and read your Bible. We will see you bright and early tomorrow."

Dean would go to counselling sessions with Pastor Jethro for two weeks. At the end of those weeks Jethro and Sally left the church for a position in Memphis.

Chapter 20

REUP

Dean woke up in a cold sweat, he was sitting up with the vivid memory of Porter putting the gun to his chin. He was having the nightmare often. He would wake up just about the time Ross pulled the trigger. He looked over to his wife who was still sleeping soundly, she always had peaceful restful slumber. He envied her, he had not slept soundly since Baumholder and the army putting him on the NROSS list.

He had always been concerned about missing one of their alerts and being counted AWOL. He rarely got a good night's sleep since then and he was never able to sleep in on Saturdays.

He quietly got up out of bed, retrieved his glasses and looked at the time. It was a little after two am. He was afraid to go back to sleep, so he put some PT shorts and a T-shirt on and went out to the living room. He was going to start processing out of the army in a couple of days. He was looking forward to getting home and out of this area for many reasons.

He had learned from Childs and Pastor Jethro that Porter was not only addicted to drugs, but was looking at a lot of pornography. Jethro had kept it confidential, and only told Dean that he had confronted Ross on some sin issues, but Childs had revealed to Dean what they had been. He continued to advise Dean that no matter how much we pray, God will never take free will from a person; He would not snatch the weapon from Porter's hand, that it was his choice and he had the right to take his own life.

Suzan had taken his remains home to be buried close to where his parents lived. She was coming back to make arrangements to move back there. The girls and Suzan needed the family support. Dean paced the living room for a little while. He had not read his Bible for a couple of days, nor had he prayed. Anger and frustration towards God had consumed most of his thought for over a week.

Even though Porter had almost cut him off, he was hoping that they could have worked things out. After all, he was still his section chief. He had suspected him of using drugs, but was completely surprised at the revelation that he was spending hours looking at pornography. Suzan was a beautiful woman, and he couldn't understand why he would look elsewhere.

He sat down in his chair, turned on the light and picked up his Bible flipping it to Isaiah 50:10. The scripture talked about fearing the Lord and obeying His voice, to trust Him even in the dark times. His King James version stated to 'trust in the name of the Lord, and stay upon his God,' the word 'stay' jumped out at him.

Childs had told him several times that the thought he should stay in the army and with the 101st. Walker advised him to reup and come to the 155 unit with him. Natalie felt impressed that the Lord wanted them to stay in the army. This was a big reversal to her desires for most of his army career. Captain Knight had called him into the office and given him a bunch of reasons for making the army a career.

Chief of Smoke had walked up behind him during formation and whispered in his ear, "Young soldier you should reup, you're a good man and the army needs more men like you."

"Smoke, I'm so short that I can't reach over my boots to sign the paper work," responded Dean with a smile.

It was the first time he had ever seen Rose grin. He patted Dean on the back, commenting that the army was going to miss him.

His brother, Jack had asked the renter of their father's house to find another place to live so that Dean and Natalie could move in. The plan was for Dean and Natalie to stay and help out on the farm until Dean could get enrolled at the college in Twin Falls with a part time job and a place to live. That wouldn't take place until next year. They had everything planned out and they had already set things in motion. How could he change things all of a sudden?

He paced back and forth in the living room and decided to put the word to the test. He silently prayed that the Lord would confirm his plan, by giving Natalie a dream either this very day or the next evening that indicated they were supposed to stay at Fort Cambell. He continued to pray and read the scriptures.

About the time he needed to get ready for the work day, he got another scripture that spoke to him. It was Psalms 46:10, 'be still and know that I am God.' This portion of the verse touched his heart in a big way. It was like God was beating him over the head, but he was going to wait and see if God spoke to Natalie.

Dean was dressed and drinking his first cup of coffee before Natalie emerged from the bedroom. It was going to be another hot humid day which to him was another good reason to leave for Idaho. He was tired of dripping sweat all night and day.

She gave him a kiss and moved into the kitchen to get breakfast started. He continued to drink his coffee and read his Bible which had been their routine. He was reading the book "James." It was a powerful epistle showing how a person should live their life.

She called him to the table and set before him a plate of eggs, toast, and ham. They sat in silence for a few minutes while he focused on the meal.

"How did you sleep?" asked Natalie.

"Not very well, I was up most of the night."

"I thought so, you look tired. What was bothering you?"

"Porter, I had that same nightmare, I've been having. He's about to pull the trigger and I wake up. I'm glad. I don't think I could handle watching the top of his head come apart again."

"Dean we will continue to pray and ask God to heal you of those nightmares. Is Childs counseling you still? How is that going?"

"I think I have a better understanding of Porter and the Lord in all that mess. I don't know why Porter fell into drugs and porno again. He came back from Nam with those things hanging on him, but got set free from them. I imagine once you fall into something like that you have to always guard your heart from it."

"By the way, Dean, I had a strange little dream this morning. We were in a car traveling at a good clip. We were coming to a stop light and it was green, just about the time we got to the intersection, it turned red. Maybe it was heartburn, but it seemed so real. What do you think?"

It was time to go, and Dean didn't have time to discuss it with her, all he could do is mutter the word "damn" under his breath.

He was on auto-pilot all the way into base. He couldn't even remember stopping at the gate and talking to the guards. All he could think about were the verses the Lord had given him and the dream that Natalie had gotten. He stood in formation and thought about his options and got in trouble for not paying attention by Smoke. What would God do if he disobeyed?

Garcia talked him into going to the mess hall and having coffee. He reminded Dean that he had seen Willie over the weekend and Dean had asked him how he was doing. Garcia attacked his food while Dean sipped his coffee.

"Hey man where are you? Remember, you asked me about Willie, but you're off in la-la land."

"Sorry Garcia, I have a lot on my mind. So how is our little trouble maker doing in Cleveland?"

"He has the life, man. He introduced me to his five girlfriends. Talk about some good-looking ladies. Two blondes, two brunettes, and one red head. He met them in college, but I think he is so busy trying to keep those ladies entertained that he has no time to do class work. He has a part time job unloading trucks. We sure had a good time together, he told me to invite you up some time."

Dean could only see trouble if he went to see Willie. He did miss him, that boyish face with the smirk on it. He did not miss the fights, but he longed for the adventures that came with being with Willie.

Still, he no longer drank, and girls were not an option, and Willie was not one to just sit down and shoot the breeze. He told Arthur that he would think about it, but he had no intentions to go unless Willie would marry one of those beautiful ladies and settle down.

Garcia was in charge of the gun section with Porter gone. Harvy Johnson had been a spec four when Dean had arrived at the battery, but had been promoted to a buck sergeant. He had been Porter's assistant gunner. He had transferred to another unit just before Porter took his life.

Garcia had gone to the promotion board to be considered for sergeant stripes but was denied the rank because he was going to get out of the army in a few months. Dean had gone through the same process but was denied the stripes for the same reason.

Garcia put them through their drills, marching, and parading around with their weapons for about an hour. Rose watched them carefully, knowing they had no NCO in charge, but Garcia was flawless in his orders and corrections if someone didn't do things right. They went to the motor pool afterwards and pulled maintenance on the weapon. Dean was released to get his paperwork taken care of so he could get out of the army.

He wandered around in the halls for a little while until he was sure that Childs had no one in his office. Dean went into the outer office and had a conversation with Clark. That's when Childs saw him and invited him in. Dean shut the door behind himself, and Childs picked up on the fact that they were about to have a serious conversation. He thought it would be about Porter, but Dean asked about being disobedient to God.

Top laughed, "You got orders from God that you're supposed to stay in the army, didn't you?"

"Yes, I'm pretty sure that the Lord has told me to reenlist. My question to you is, what would God do if I disobeyed?"

"It is hard to say, but He does not take rebellion lightly, Larson. You would be counted AWOL and he deals with that as hard as the army deals with it. I do believe that He wants to teach you some things and He is going to use you for some kind of purpose here. There is a story in the Bible in which a man rebelled and did the opposite of what the Lord told him to do."

"Who was that and what happened?"

"His name was Jonah and a fish swallowed him up. Do you remember that story?"

"Aw, yes. I remember that story from when I went to Sunday School and my mother was still alive. I guess I could stay away from any large body of water, but He would most likely have something else eat me."

"Well do you want me to get the reup papers together and what kind of terms do you want?"

"I don't know Top; can I reenlist for just a year? I have thirty days leave coming to me. I should take time off and go home. Our families are wanting to see Melody."

"It's done. We can swear you in on Friday. I can have the BC do it if you wish. When you get back, be ready, I'm going to send you up before the promotion board again."

"I need to go home and talk to Natalie; I didn't have time to discuss it with her this morning. I got these verses that indicated that I was supposed to stay, but I wanted to make sure, so I asked the Lord to confirm it through her. Well, He gave her this dream. Enough said. It would be hard for me to deny that He did not speak to me."

"Go ahead, get home and make your plans. Bring Natalie in Friday with you. We will have the ceremony before roll call. It will be just you, your family, the BC, and myself if that is all right with you?"

Dean just nodded. It was overwhelming to him. Why was Top pushing so hard for the promotion board? He really had mixed feelings about being a sergeant. He kept asking himself about the idea of leading men. He was content being a follower. The other thought that came to him was getting back into SW with Walker's unit. The duty would be a lot easier, but he just knew in his heart that he needed to stick close to Childs.

Something came back to him. It was the last prayer that Pastor Jethro had prayed over him just before he left the church. It had something to do with God promoting him spiritually and physically. The Lord was going to reveal His power to him in a way that he had never seen before.

Dean had just thought that the promotion indicated that he would get a job quickly. He had set his face to getting out of the service but now the word made much more sense.

Natalie was surprised to see him home so early. When he sat down to have a very serious conversation, an expression of concern dominated her features. Dean told her about the verses he had received that morning and the confirmation she had given him with her dream.

At the end of the discussion, she seemed relieved and gave him a big hug and kiss. She agreed with the decision and felt like they were supposed to stay. They prayed about it and felt like the Lord wanted Dean to reenlist for just one more year. He called

Childs and told him that he would reup for one more year.

He told her about the leave time and suggested they travel by car. That way they could see different places on the way there and on the way back. Natalie had mixed feelings about it because of the children. Dean suggested that they map out the route and make arrangements to stay on the way home and back. They would stop every so often to get some exercise.

He had a long-lost uncle that they could stay with in Missouri and Natalie had an aunt in Oklahoma that they could visit. They got the atlas out and mapped out their routes. Both of them became very excited about the trip.

On Friday morning, Dean showed up with his family at Knight's office. Like Top promised, it was a very private ceremony with one exception, Rose was standing in the corner. He had the same somber expression on his face as usual until the captain shook Dean's hand after swearing him in. He came over with a slight smile and held out his hand to congratulate him

"I thought you said you were too short to reup soldier?"

Dean pointed at Natalie. "She found a ladder which allowed me to get above my boot straps and use a pen on the paperwork." He said with a large grin and everyone chuckled, even Rose. He took Natalie home, worked on reversing the paper trail, checked out the equipment he needed from supply, and took his transcripts back to the college.

He signed up for another history course while he was there. He also found out that Ann Hunter had received orders to Fort Sill, Oklahoma. This made Dean feel better, he always felt a tinge of guilt whenever he saw her.

Just before they started their leave time to go home, Suzan came back to make arrangements to ship their personal items back home. Natalie and Suzan had been very close at one time, just as Dean had been with Ross. Suzan came over to have a long talk with Natalie and insisted that Dean be in on the conversation.

"Natalie, I want to tell you how sorry I am for cutting you and Dean off. I was so embarrassed and felt like a failure because of what I was going through. It was almost like the Ross that came home from Nam. He was all messed up. I was patient with him and he agreed to get some help. After a few years of counseling, he started acting like the Ross I married out of high school." She broke down weeping and Natalie took her hand.

"It's okay, Suzan. We love you and I am sorry that you are going through this."

After a long time of silence and sobbing Suzan finally gained control of her emotions. He got clean of the drugs, put aside the porn, and started going to church with me and the girls. I thought everything was going to be all right, but Ross seemed always restless even though we had a nice home and he was making good money.

The tears started to well up again and Natalie reached over to hug her. Dean was not even sure he wanted to hear this story. He was pacing in the living room with Melody in his arms, she was being little fussy. Suzan broke from Natalie's grasp and went to the window. Dean suspected that she did not want to face them while she told them the rest of the story.

"He talked me into going back in the army. It was good at first, but when he came back from Germany things went downhill fast. I could tell he was back into drugs and then he started looking at pornography. I suggested counseling again, but he insisted that he would stop.

I know he went out with other women and that's when I started talking to him about a divorce. He seemed to take notice of this and told me he would get help. A couple days later he found out about Jon Kelly. Now you know the whole story." She turned from the window and tears were rolling down her face like a torrent of rain coming down from the skies in Kentucky during the spring.

Natalie went to her and hugged her.

Dean went in the other room, he couldn't stand to watch her cry anymore, nor did he want to relive that awful day Porter took his life. He put Melody up in the air, she stopped fussing, hoping her father would feed her. She rarely cried, but would fuss when hungry. She was sweet and had already gone through a lot as a little girl. What would Dean have done if Jon had done the same thing to Melody? He would have most likely killed him.

Committing suicide was a selfish way out though. Ross had so much to live for; Suzan was a beautiful woman and they had two lovely daughters. What was he thinking? Dean would never know. Porter was dead and the story ended there for him except for the nightmares he was having.

Natalie called him out of the bedroom, announcing that Suzan was leaving. They exchanged addresses. Dean told her goodbye and that they would be praying for them. He gave Suzan an awkward hug and she left.

Chapter 21

HOME AGAIN

The first leg of their trip landed them in Milo, Missouri, a small farming community. The town was just a spot in the road. It was easy to find his uncle's farm from there. Carl Larson had been the youngest of four boys and one girl. He was still farming two hundred plus acres but confided in Dean while they were visiting that he was thinking about retiring.

Carl and Hanna, his wife, gave Dean and his family a warm welcome, setting a wonderful meal before them. It was a hot day and Carl didn't have AC. The mature trees provided shade and as the sun went down, the house became bearable to visit in. Carl was vocal about Dean missing his father's funeral, but after Dean explained the circumstances, Carl seemed to put it aside.

They stayed there that night and the next day. Carl and Hanna acted like grandparents to the two children, taking John out to the swing, and pulling him around on an old cardboard box in the grass. Hanna had a girlie outfit for Melody and dressed her up in it. Carl took Dean around the farm showing him the crops that they would harvest soon. He questioned Dean about his future plans and encouraged him to go to college.

The next morning, they started north, to South Dakota where they would take in Mount Rushmore. They planned on staying at

Rapid City for a day and see as many sites as possible, then they were moving on to Cody, Wyoming. They planned on going through a couple museums and travel through Yellowstone Park and look at as many animals as possible. After that they would travel as far as possible south to Rupert before staying at a motel for the night.

Mount Rushmore was an awe-inspiring site. As they stared at the four presidents that sacrificed so much for the nation, Dean noticed that Abe Lincoln, George Washington, and Roosevelt all looked tired and wore out from their time in office. Jefferson, the youthful visionary, was the only one that looked rested and relaxed.

The museums at Cody were great to go through and the town was western in every manner. Yellowstone was beautiful and they saw foxes, elk, deer, a moose, bald eagles, and bison but no bear. One of the bison reached in through Natalie's open window in an attempt to eat her hair. After that Natalie kept her window rolled up unless the animals were far away. They stayed in Idaho Falls and finished their journey home the next day.

Jack and Helen had lunch ready for them. The Bakers were in the guest list and it was a warm welcome. The kids were the main attraction, with Troy and Laura doting on Melody. Troy was still not married, but was dating. She had turned out to be a pretty woman. Last time Dean had seen her she was awkward and heavy, now everything fit together in a nice package.

John was having a great time. If grandpa was not tossing him up in the air and hugging him, he was playing with his cousin Bud, Jack's son. He had named him after his grandfather. They went exploring the farm, of course Jack would yell at Bud to stay out of certain areas and to behave. Dean would admonish John to be safe and follow the rules.

They caught the boys chasing the chickens which earned them a time out. Later they caught them playing in the hay stack and jumping into the loose hay. This was fine, in fact the two men joined them. All of them were laughing and having a great time until Helen, who was pregnant with their second child, reminded Jack that they had some chores to get done. The two men went off to finish some work, leaving the boys laughing and playing in the hay.

When they came back, the boys were missing and they found them throwing rocks in the irrigation canal. Jack jumped Bud right away and told him to get up to the house. Dean grabbed up John and told him to stay away from the water and that children drown in the canals every year. It was off limits to children and they were sent to the house. Bud was young but Jack had tried to instill in the child early that the canal was off limits.

When Jack got back to the house, he told Bud to go get a switch which the boy did. When Bud brought the willow back to his father, Jack looked it over and nodded approvingly. He then laid the switch on Bud four times on the butt and legs. It hurt but the boy didn't cry. Jack turned the boy around, looked him square in the eye, thanked him for getting a good switch, and asked him if he knew why he was being punished.

"Yes Daddy, I'm not supposed to play near the canal. I might drown."

"So, go in your room and think about things. Remember, I love you."

Bud walked a little funny as he proceeded to his room. He wanted John to come with him, but Dean knew that would not be punishment, so he took John to another room and made him sit in the corner.

Helen questioned Jack about Bud's spanking, and added no cake after dinner. Dean realized that John was older and had never had so much land to roam around in. He was free and probably leading Bud in places that were off limits to his young cousin. He went in and talked to John and informed him that he was limited to the yard unless he was tagging along with him or his Uncle Jack. There was no anger in what Helen said to Jack, just a little chewing out. That was the first day being home.

The next day Dean was up with Jack helping him with the chores. Bud and John were also up helping, no worse for wear after their punishment. In fact, they stayed very close to the men, helping with the chickens, milking the cows, and herding them out to the pastures.

Dean helped John onto one of the small ewes, which he rode on in the corral. It was a sight to see, the ewe just boulted running as fast as she could and John held on for dear life until the ewe took a sudden right turn, which sent John flying off forward. He got up dusting himself off. Dean and Jack laughed at the sight because it brought back fond memories of them riding the ewes.

"Hey, Dean. Do you remember that mean ram Dad use to have in this corral?"

"How could I forget. He was the meanest animal we ever had on the farm."

"Yeah, he would come out from under the shed, trying to butt one of us kids. Dad would yell at us to show the thing who' was boss."

"I remember that one time you tried to show it who was boss, Jack. You hit him with that stick and it ran you down. Dad had to rescue you. You had cuts, scrapes, and bruises. When Dad brought you in to Mom, she sure gave him the what for when she heard the story."

"But you were the one that put Dad straight, Dean. You told him the next day that ram knew who was boss and it wasn't us boys." They both laughed.

"Well, the best part of that little incident happened two weeks later when Dad walked across this corral. That ram butted him and we had mutton for dinner for a couple of months," Dean said laughing hard with his brother.

"Yes, best mutton I ever had," Jack chimed in.

They started for the house; it was time for breakfast. Bud Jr. and John were hungry, so they ran ahead of the two men. Jack became serious, looking down at the ground, he cleared his throat and Dean knew he had something on his mind. He could almost guess what it was, but he would allow Jack to bring up the subject. They stopped underneath the large cottonwood tree near the house.

"So, Dean. Why didn't you come back to Dad's funeral? I have to admit that I've had some hard feelings toward you about that. I also don't understand why you decided to stay in the army. You were so adamant about getting into school."

Dean looked his brother in the eyes. "I gave Natalie a lot of reasons for not coming back home. I know that she wanted to see the family and it might have been selfish on my part not to come. We were having some money problems.

"I was taking college classes at the time and the army was keeping me busy. All those reasons were side issues, Jack. When Dad came back to see us in Kentucky, we said our goodbyes. He was so happy being around the kids, laughing, so loving and alive. I just couldn't face him being dead. Do you understand, Jack?"

Jack nodded and gave Dean a hug. "I understand, you remember the best part of that time. I still struggle with the pain and suffering he went through, working out the details of the funeral. I hated it all. It brought back what Mom went through."

Dean then told the story of what happened when he was trying to leave the service. How God made it obvious that he wanted him to stay in. Jack shook his head and suggested that it was better to be obedient to God. Helen peeked out the door and ordered the two men to come in and have breakfast before it got cold. Jack put an arm around Dean's shoulders, dragging him toward the house.

The breakfast was large, it came with working on the farm. Dean helped his brother for most of the day. He would quit around two or three in the afternoon. He had to study the Code of Conduct manual for his NCO board. They went over to see the Bakers and friends several evenings. It was great getting connected again to those they loved.

Dean had to explain to Lawrance Baker why he had not come home to his father's funeral and why he decided to stay in the army. Lawrance seemed to grasp what God was doing with his son-in-law and, like Jack, gave him a big hug. He held on and prayed a blessing over him, that God would continue to direct his path, protect them all, and teach Dean the things that he wanted him to learn in this new season. Dean was so touched by it that he shed a few tears.

The time flew by and before they knew it, it was time to say goodbye. The Bakers came over early and Helen and Natalie fixed a big breakfast for everyone. They lingered at the table, telling stories about what they had gone through since they had been separated. Jack promised Dean they would have father's old house ready for them in about a year. The place would be vacant and fixed up. Dean swore that they would be ready to come back and put it to use, unless God suddenly came up with another plan.

They said their final farewells with a lot of tears from the women-folk. Dean loaded his family in the Mustang and drove it out of the driveway onto the paved road. They were soon on the freeway, heading toward Salt Lake City. They made good time skirting the cities and stopped at Fort Bridger in Wyoming.

They stayed at the fort for over an hour, reading about its history and Bridger, the explorer. It was good to get out of the car, stretch their legs and wander in and out of the buildings. They bought a book at the gift shop. They left feeling refreshed and ready to continue their journey. They stayed the night at Rawlins.

They took a southeastern approach back home cutting across the corner of Colorado into Kansas. They stopped in Dodge City for an hour. They looked over the town and Dean stopped in the Long Branch Saloon to watch the dancing girls and drink a bottle of sarsaparilla while Natalie and the kids explored some of the gift shops. As they drove through Kansas, Dean couldn't figure out why anyone would want to live there. All they could see was flat land with wheat everywhere and trees. The north wind had blown them to the point that they all sagged to the south.

They continued mostly south into Oklahoma where they stayed a couple of nights with Natalie's aunt Jan in a little store outside Norman. Her husband had passed away several years before, so she ran the store by herself. She spoiled the kids with sweets and bear hugs whenever she had a chance.

One of her children, Jerry, lived in Norman and brought his wife, Penny, and their three children to visit. They were treated well and Dean instantly loved them all. Jerry acted like he was a long-lost brother. It was the first time Natalie had met Penny and they were soon visiting like sisters. Dean and Natalie were sorry they couldn't stay longer, and promised to stop by next year on their way home.

From Norman, they shot northeast, ending up staying one night with his Uncle Carl. It was late when they pulled into the farm. Dean had called ahead, asking his uncle if they could visit. Carl and Hanna welcomed them with open arms and provided them with dinner that evening and breakfast the next morning. The children had been getting fussy and they were making a lot more stops, allowing them to run off their restless energy. They ran them around the yard for about an hour before saying farewell, loaded up the kids, and started the last leg of their journey.

It was late when they got near Campbell. They stopped by a fast-food place grabbing a quick meal in a bag. They drove home. Dean was hauling the gear out of the car and Natalie was already feeding the kids when Morton and Carrie came running over. Carrie was ecstatic, giving Dean a quick hug, and running in the house to talk to Natalie. Kevin was right behind her, he handed Dean a cigar. Dean was so weary that nothing was sinking in. He looked at the cigar, then he looked at Kevin.

"We're going to have a baby, man."

"Oh, congratulations," he said, grabbing Kevin's hand and shaking it. They had been trying ever since Melody had come into the world. Carrie had picked her up when Natalie brought her home and they could see that look in her eyes.

"So, what are you hoping for Kevin? I bet you want a little boy since you have a girl."

"You said it. We want a boy." Morton declared as he pulled items out of the car trunk. Dean filled his hands and entered the house which was filled with laughter and two women hugging. The Morton's didn't stay long because they noticed the kids eating. Kevin helped Dean get the rest of the things out of the car and back into the house.

As he left, he turned back to Dean and informed him that Sergeant Ellis had left the army. Dean knew that Ellis' time was about up. He had said good-by to him before going on leave. Dean knew that he had not measured up to his standards for working in FDC, they had remained friends.

He had invited Dean and his family over for barbecues and Dean had reciprocated the invites. What surprised him was that Captain Knight was being transferred out of the unit. They were about to get a new battery commander. He was too weary to be concerned about it at that point and sat down to eat his dinner.

Chapter 22

BIG CHANGES

They had gotten home on Saturday so they stayed home and rested up from their trip. Dean checked the car out, making sure that everything was in working order. Morton came over to help him. Kevin informed him that he had a new section chief. His name was Sergeant George Ramsey. Morton knew very little about the man since he didn't work around the guns. Kevin invited them over for lunch which they readily accepted since they were worn out from the trip.

At lunch, the girls talked about the baby that was on the way. Morton informed Dean that they were scheduled for the rifle range and the gas chamber at the end of the week. Dean loved to go to the range, he was always ready for that but he hated the chamber. They would always make sure that soldiers donned their gas masks before they went in. They had to fit it and make sure that it was working properly.

Soldiers went inside the chamber, the gas made their skin itch, then they would be forced to take the mask off, and take a good breath of the gas before they were allowed out of the building. They came out coughing and crying like a baby until the stuff wore off.

On Monday morning, the first thing Dean did, was report to Clark that he was back from leave. Rose was coming out of Child's office. He looked at Dean, he told him that he was glad that he had come back, told him, he would have hated reporting him AWOL this morning.

Larson smiled at him because what Rose was really saying was that he was glad he was back. Dean smarted back at him in a way that he thought would bring a smile to Rose, but with the respect that Smoke demanded.

"Smoke, I would not want you to have the pleasure of reporting me missing from the ranks. It would most likely bring a smile to your face and we couldn't let that happen."

He did see Rose's frown turn up just slightly. He liked Rose, he was tough and he sensed that Rose liked him even though the man acted like he hated them all. What's more, he had a feeling that Smoke liked Willie, but he had ridden Willie, making him toe the line. He had never let him get away with anything. He made Willie pay for everything he did wrong and got caught at. He even made Willie pay the price for things he had not done but it kept Willie on his toes.

Childs' called him into the office. He informed him that he had a new section chief and that his name was George Ramsey. He reiterated what Morton had told him about the weeks schedule and that they were going to get a new battery commander at the beginning of next week. He thought he was about done and was ready to turn and leave the office when Childs dropped two bombshells that took him by surprise.

Childs informed him as to when he was going up before the promotion board. It was sooner than Dean had really expected. He caught his breath and decided that he was going to make sure that he was ready for it. Top's next news was that there was a slot open for air assault school and he wanted Dean to go.

"Well, I don't know, Top. I mean I can't see any real reason for repelling out of a perfectly good helicopter," he said; taken completely by surprise. They had never breached the subject the entire time he had been in the outfit.

"Shut the door, Larson." Dean turned to the entrance and did what he was told.

Childs directed him to a chair. "I can't make you go, but I would highly recommend it. Morton will be going at the same time. He is also going up before the promotion board. Both of you have some excellent letters in your files that will help with those sergeant stripes. Going to this school will help your chances. I want all this paperwork in before we get the new BC. We don't know what kind of man we will be getting." He paused, looking Dean over from top to bottom.

Dean wiggled in his chair, feeling very uncomfortable for the first time in Childs' presence. He knew in his heart that Childs always had his best interest at heart. He loved to fly and felt comfortable being in a plane or chopper. The idea of dangling from a skinny little rope from a chopper fifty feet off the ground was not appealing to him, it was a little disturbing. Then he thought wow what an adventure to repel down a rope from a helicopter. Top is right, it can't hurt my chances at being promoted. He had been staring at the floor the whole time, thinking things through. He looked up into Top's eyes and agreed to go to the air assault school.

At roll call, he met his new section chief. Ramsey was nice, older than Dean had expected, close cropped hair and a uniform that fit loosely on his body, like he had lost a lot of weight. He also had a problem with his eyes. They always seemed to be moist and he was constantly wiping them with a handkerchief.

Ramsey had heard that Dean was going up before the promotion board so he would put him in charge of some aspect concerning the duties that the section had to perform. Dean did have a concern with him, he would pass him occasionally and he was sure he caught a whiff of alcohol, but he was never certain.

Dean got a hold of Walker during the week and asked him to check in on Natalie and the kids while he was at air assault school. He did it while they were playing pool and Dean was drinking a soft drink. When he asked Walker, he stared at Dean for a long while until he took his next shot.

"What is wrong with you, Larson? I thought you couldn't wait to get out of the service. Now, you're going to air assault school and trying to get sergeant stripes. I can see you reupping for a better job in the army, but to stay in a combat unit with your brains, it just seems like a waste. Especially when you could have come to my unit where the duty is a lot better."

"Well, see I'm not as smart as you think I am. Will you look in on Natalie and the kids, Walker? I would appreciate it."

"Yes, of course I will. You are my friend, but I have to tell you, you act so different from the guy I knew in Baumholder. You're getting religious has taken some of the fun out of you man."

"I'm kind of insulted by that comment. I am trying to work out a relationship with God. Religion is the act of trying to be good enough to go to Heaven. I plan on trying to get to know God good enough that He won't leave me in the grave. I have to admit staying in the army was His idea. I was on the fast track to leave."

"What do you mean? Did God speak to you?" Walker asked, eyeing him suspiciously.

Dean told him the whole story and how he came to the conclusion that God wanted him to stay at Campbell. There was a long period of silence before Walker looked up from a shot.

"Well, if I got all the signs you did from God, I would stay in Campbell also. You know, when I was a kid and my parents were still married, we used to go to church. I still remember the stories of David, Noah, Cain, and Jonah from Sunday School. Once my parents divorced, we just stopped going. Maybe after the assault school I will tag along with you and see how church is again."

The weekend was uneventful and was two days of relaxing. They went to church and met the new pastor and his wife. They introduced themselves as Ivan and Lacy Norman. They were both short, he was a little round but not fat, she was thin with hair to her shoulders, a pretty face but she looked sad. He wore glasses that would slip down to the end of his nose and he was constantly pushing them back on to the bridge of his nose. His hair was starting to thin on top. He was energetic and anointed. Dean liked him and when they shook hands, his grip was firm. They just exchanged a few words, but Ivan expressed the desire to get together.

Monday morning found Dean in formation, watching Knight handing over the battery to Captain Leon Bradberry. Once the flag ceremony was over and Bradberry had control of the battery, he gave a short speech on what he expected out of the men. Dean had seen this before, but he then walked down the ranks inspecting the men. He mentioned several gigs and demanded that they be taken care of before the day was over. He caught one of Ramsey's men needing a haircut, Dean was glad that it was not him.

After the formation was released, Ramsey marched his section down to the motor pool to perform maintenance on the equipment. Dean was just about to start working on the Gamma Goat when the BC's driver called him out and told him to get in the jeep. He was ordered to take him back to see Bradberry. All the way back to the barracks, Dean wondered what he had done to deserve an audience before the commanding officer already.

He found Morton sitting in Clark's office and so two things came to mind instantly, the promotion board or the air assault school. They waited only a few minutes before Top came out and ushered them before Bradberry. They saluted the captain and stayed at attention until he had them stand at ease. He never offered them a chair like Knight would have.

He got their names right and went quickly through their files indicating what each of them had done. He then asked them if they were both planning on going to air assault school. They both affirmed that they were, answering him as though they were talking to a drill sergeant in basic.

"Well, if you ask me neither one of you has done anything to suggest that you have earned another stripe. What do you say to that?" They both remained silent. He continued to wait but they would not answer him. This seemed to irritate him. "What? "Don't you have anything to say for yourselves?" he said raising his voice slightly.

"No sir, why should we? It's your opinion sir," answered Dean.

"But my opinion counts, doesn't it? I know a lot of units give their men special time to train for it during duty hours. In this case I will not. You will have to fulfill your regular duties and get ready for the school on your own time. Any questions?" Morton and Dean did not respond. "Then you two are dismissed." Dean and Morton saluted and after he saluted back, they turned and left the office.

After they left the building for the motor pool, Dean turned to Kevin. "Man, I suggest that we don't wait, I think we should start hating this guy right away."

"Get in line, Larson. I think I already do. He is a selfish ass and I doubt that he cares about anyone but himself. You know what. It means we are going to have to get in shape on our own. So where is your weakness, Larson?"

"Upper body is where I lack. How about you?"

"I could use work in both areas."

"I've been studying up and got some inside information from Sergeant Hover on both the promotion board and the school."

Hover was an assistant gunner on number two howitzer. He had just gotten his new stripes and gone through the school about six months ago. He informed Morton about a bunch of questions that the board had asked him. Current events, chain of command, Code of Conduct, future plans, the workings of the gun, and leadership ability.

After work, they did a three-mile run. Dean and Morton went home and did forty push-ups. They did as many pull-ups as possible. Morton got seven done while Dean could only do five. Morton had some weights; they ended the day pumping iron. Dean went home and had dinner with Natalie and the kids.

Kevin showed up a hour later and they discussed current events and the Code of Conduct. They made arrangements to meet the next day. Dean was glad he decided not to take college courses. All his spare time went into reading the Bible. He was not going to have any time to take classes.

Dean and Morton never marched or walked anywhere. They always did double time at least, if not faster. Ramsey was always helping Dean out by allowing him to either run to get something or by teaching him the hand signals to bring in the choppers. In the evening, Dean and Kevin would continue to work on getting stronger and then they would hit the books so they could impress the promotion board.

They took Hover out to one of the local bars for a couple of beers. They grilled him on both aspects, the school and the board. He gave them some good insight on both challenges that lay before them, especially the school. He described the obstacle course, it was formidable.

He emphasized that they had to have everything in the packs at inspection times or they would be sent home. They had to stay hydrated, if they got a cramp they would be sent home. They needed to follow the instructions concerning hooking up the loads to the choppers. They needed to get used to repelling out of the helicopter. The last day was a twelve-mile hike with a forty-pound ruck sack on your back. You had to do it in under three hours. Dean and Morton looked at each other, a doubt was starting to surface in Dean's thinking. Hover hit both of them in the head.

"You two have this. If you doubt that you can do it, you won't make it. A lot of it is mental, you have to work as a team, keep each other's backs and encourage one another. I believe you both can do it. The question is do you believe you can do it.?"

"Yes, we can do it." Both of them yelled at the same time.

They all took a swig of their drinks. They relaxed a little and he continue to give them insight as to how he got through the course. They both listened to every word he spoke. They were home before dark and did as many upper body exercises as they could get in. After showers and dinner, they grilled each other for the promotion board.

Early Saturday found them on one of the back roads. They used the car to map out their twelve-mile hike and then they were on their way. Morton was used to hiking, he often humped with a pack on his back all day long with the infantry as an observer. He was soon ahead of Dean and he came in a little over three hours. Dean was almost four hours and neither one of them had forty pounds on their backs.

Morton figured out a way to beat the game. They would have to keep a close eye on their watches and at certain points they would have to double time, quick march and then double time. He told Dean that he would stay with him as long as he could.

They went home and took showers, ate breakfast, and study-ed for the boards. After, that they did all kinds of weight training, mostly upper body. Both of them were starting to do more pull-ups and push-ups. They were going to start it all over again on Sunday, but both wives put their foot down and made their husbands rest. Dean used the time to do some special prayer on the two upcoming events. He prayed every morning but he came at the Lord from several angles.

He also got his Class A uniform ready for the meeting. He cleaned all the brass and produced a high shine on his jump boots.

He bought a brand-new blue beret for the occasion. He measured all his ribbons out to make sure they were in the right places. He sat down and thought for a while to see if he could think of anything that he might have missed. A couple of things came to mind so he looked them up and felt satisfied.

Morton and Dean sat in the room waiting for their turn to appear before the men that would decide if they got their stripes. They got a pep talk from Childs before they came. Dean looked over at Morton, who was fidgeting in his chair. Dean thought he should be doing the same, but he was completely at peace and knew that he had done all that he could do. Now the rest was in God's hands. He had asked the Lord to help him with the questions.

He was called in first. They first reviewed his record after they allowed him to sit down. They asked him several questions on the chain of command, then came several questions of the Code of Conduct. Dean was sure that he had the correct answers on all of them. They then quizzed him on a couple items concerning current events. They asked him about his thoughts on leadership and finished the interview with a few surprising questions.

"We see that you were taking college courses, do you plan on pursuing higher education?"

"Yes, I do sergeant."

"Good, we see you have taken math, English, literature, and history. What subject do you like the most?"

"I really enjoy history sir," Dean said emphatically.

"Any particular time or portion of history?"

"American history, very interested in the Civil War."

"Any favorite general or leader that you admire?"

"Yes, Chamberland, the hero of Little Roundtop and General Grant who I believe led the Union Forces into modern warfare."

Dean noticed that several eyebrows raised as several of them looked at each other. He was not sure if that was a good sign or a bad indication but it was too late. No way he could take back that opinion. He thought he was done, but one of the members brought up a few questions. "We noticed that you were within the nuclear program in Germany, do you know that we have a nuclear program here?"

"Yes, one of the guys I worked with in Germany came over to be a part of it. He invited me to be a member of his section."

"Why didn't you transfer? They would probably have sent you over."

"As you can see by the letters in my file, we had almost perfected putting the eight-inch round together. It was good duty, but I like to be challenged and pushing myself to do new things. I embrace the struggle and enjoy the victory."

Again, the members looked at one another and dismissed him from the room. Dean felt a little uneasy at those reactions, but it was all over and now he had to wait to see what they decided. He waited for Morton to go through the interview and then went back to check in with Top. Childs questioned them about how they had done.

Morton did have to admit that he had missed one question on current events. Dean confessed that he was not sure how he had done on the last two questions. The BC was gone to briefings for the day so Top sent them home.

They did the twelve-mile hike and lots of work on the upper body. Dean had gotten the hike down to under three and a half hours. Morton was already below three hours but they still were not carrying forty pounds on their backs.

A week later, Childs called them into his office. He looked them over and gave them the first big smile since Bradberry had come to the unit. They had noticed that the relationship between the two was always professional and strained.

"Well, I have very good news for you two. I had a friend on the board and I talked to him recently. They were all very impressed with your answers and I have a feeling that if you two become air assault, you will see those stripes."

Dean and Morton patted each other on the shoulders. They smiled and congratulated each other. They told each other they knew they could complete the school.

"Larson they were very impressed with you. They liked the fact that you were going to college and one of the guys on the board was a big General Grant fan. They also liked your answer on passing up the nuclear program here in Campbell. They are looking for educated leaders so you might think about taking some college classes at some point, Morton." Kevin nodded and he dismissed them.

Chapter 23

AIR ASSAULT SCHOOL

Dean was woken violently; it was still dark out and he was expecting a long day. It was early fall so it was cool, which was good for everyone in the school. He tried to look at his watch to see the time but his eyes would not focus on the task. He was yelled at to hurry and noticed Morton getting his gear together and dressing.

He hopped out of bed, put his fatigues on, and got his rucksack together. He put his area in order and was ready when they called them out in formation. He was given a roster number and his rucksack was inspected for all the items that were on the list before they came to the school. Ten men failed the inspection and were released back to their units.

It was zero day and there was zero tolerance for certain things. They had to have all their gear and if they didn't have it, they were out. Another item on the agenda was a two-mile run in which you had to be finished in less than eighteen minutes. Dean and Morton breezed through the run. The two of them had not ran with the battery formation but constantly ran three miles, getting their times better as the days grew closer to the school.

The Sabalanski Air Assault School's mission was to train soldiers in air assault operations. They were taught to sling-load equipment and vehicles under a chopper. The soldiers were supposed to help with medical evacuations, pathfinder operations, com-bat assaults, and repelling out of a helicopter. It was a ten-day course that tested physical and mental abilities. They demanded a meticulous attitude in everything because it could cost a life or the destruction of equipment if things were not done right.

Dean had the inside track when it came to being meticulous. Putting nuclear rounds together demanded the same disciplines. Morton was very cautious when it came to putting rounds on the target or shooting bullets down range, but most grunts were a little sloppy in other ways.

They did PT and ran everywhere they went and zero day was the beginning of it all. The next item on the agenda was the obstacle course, that separated more soldiers from the school. The first obstacle was called the Tough One, it was about thirty feet high. They had to climb up a rope walk on planks and then down a rope ladder. It was used to determine if they could look down and not get dizzy, or if they had a fear of height.

The next item was a high structure called the Confidence Climb, it was constructed like a large fat ladder in which you had to climb up each rung and down the other side. It was about thirty-five feet high and the rungs got wider at the top. It was easier for Dean than Morton because he was taller and used the sides of the ladder to climb over the next rung. He never looked down, just up or to the front until, he was back on the ground. These two obstacles had to be passed.

Dean and Morton overcame those two challenges. They cheered each other on as well as their fellow teammates. They could flunk one miner obstacle but if they failed two of them, they were gone. By the time they got to the last challenge, all of them were worn out. It had been a long day and the heat had settled in. Dean was drinking several sips of water between each obstacle.

They were warned not to drink too much nor to little. It was a balancing act. One of the other obstacles was called the Weaver. It was a structure built like a house with a peak and no walls. Dean guessed it was a forty-five-degree angle. They had to weave their bodies under one pole and over the next until it was completed.

Morton was like a monkey on the thing, finishing with the best time. Dean, with his longer body, seemed to be having problems making it under the logs. About five logs short of his goal, he lost his grip and fell to the ground. It hurt and he cussed for the first time in a long time. They were quickly by his side to see if he was alright. He got up and dusted himself off. He knew he could by pass it and he would still be in the school, but he did not want to quit now.

He got in the back of the line to allow aches to fade away. He rubbed his arm and flexed it. He also did a bunch of sit ups, trying to get the muscles to loosen up. By the time he got to the front, he was ready for it. He was not fast at it, but did get through the challenges. After each obstacle they had to yell "air assault" and he roared it out when he was done. Everyone was resting under a shelter, drinking water, and eating some food. Zero day was over and both Morton and Dean had passed.

The next day was filled with classes. It was good because everyone was feeling the soreness from the course. Dean was also glad he had taken the college math course because there were calculations to figure out. It was another long day with not much sleep, so Dean brought his canteen filled with cold water with him. He would drench his handkerchief with water and wipe his face and neck. He caught Morton starting to relax too much in his chair.

Dean leaned over and tapped him on the shoulder so he would focus on what was being said. Dean was used to these conditions; he had to fight weariness every time he was listening to an instructor teaching a college class. That evening, they found themselves studying the booklet and the study guide they had been given.

They were soon practicing sling loads under the belly of a CH47 or Chinook helicopter. It would hover about eight feet off the ground and a crew of three would hook up the equipment or cargo. There was always a man in front directing the pilot to the left or right, up or down. These men had to know those hand signals.

Ramsey had taught Dean those signals so he had that all figured out. They learned to put an A22 cargo bag together. They figured out how much a CH47 could carry and as to whether they were overloading it. The chopper was a real work horse and it could carry an amazing pay load.

They were taught where all the equipment was hooked up so the chopper wouldn't lose it. In fact, everything the 101st air borne had on could be relocated by a Chinook. He was surprised they had not hooked up to one of the buildings on the base. They had to be meticulous in all this because it was a matter of safety load distribution in the chopper and things under it.

Dean was right, it came easier for him, he caught straps not hooked up right or unsafe practices a lot faster than Morton. Kevin was quick to catch on and was doing as well as Dean by the time they moved to the next phase of the school. They drummed it into the soldiers and taught them in several different ways.

They were instructed as to how to exit the CH 47 under combat conditions. Then they learned about the job of being a pathfinder. The pathfinders were the first ones into a combat zone, marked out an area where the rest of the units would come in behind enemy lines, and secured the LZs [Landing Zones] either by repelling or by landing the choppers. It was all exciting and hard work.

On the evening of the eighth day, Dean woke suddenly out of a sound sleep. He went to the latrine, relieved himself, sat on a chair, and took a sip of water. He suddenly wondered how he had gotten so quickly from going home and into college to his present situation. Why was he in Air Assault School? Well, Top had recommended it and advised him that it would look good for a promotion.

He had never considered himself leadership material and didn't know if he really wanted to be a sergeant. He did like the challenge; it had showed him how tough he could be. He knew he couldn't take all the credit. Morton and others had cheered him on as he had encouraged them. He had also sensed God's presence during some difficult times. Suddenly a face popped into his mind, it was Captain Bradberry. Dean realized this man had inspired him above all others.

He had treated Morton and Dean like they were nothing and would never be anything if he had his say. Dean above all wanted to stand in front of him with his air assault wings on. In other words, he wanted to tell the BC to kiss his foot in a respectful way. This brought a smile to his face and he was able to lay down and catch some more Z's.

Repelling was the final subject the class had to deal with. They were given the equipment to do the job. Dean thought the thick leather gloves were the most important piece of equipment. If everything else gave out, he could hold on to the rope for dear life with the gloves. They had to master the hip seat or the Swiss rapped seat which were basically the same things.

His first repel was down a wall and then off of a platform, with feet dangling freely in the air. The final repel was out of a helicopter, dangling from a rope about sixty feet off the ground.

Dean and Morton found it exhilarating and enjoyed all the times they hooked up to the ropes and slid down. Dean still thought it was better to stay in the chopper rather than repel; it was much harder to shot a person in the chopper than it was a man dangling in the air from a rope. He thought of himself as bait on the end of a fishing pole.

They also had to take a fifty-question test on all they had learned. They had to get at least a seventy percent or they were sent home. The test was easy for Dean, he had been taking them with his college courses. Morton passed with an eighty-three while Dean came up with the score of ninety-one. They had been quizzing each other almost every evening.

It was the last day both Morton and Dean were feeling mentally and physically worn out. They had another ruck sack inspection. Morton's face became pale white when he was told that he was missing his ear plugs. The inspector told him he could retrace his steps to see if they had fallen out.

As he started walking off, Dean grabbed an extra pair that he had and tossed them to him. Dean had brought them along in case he had forgotten his. Morton nodded but retraced his steps as he had been told. He came back showing the instructor the ear plugs.

The final test for Dean was the twelve-mile hike with a forty-pound rucksack and M-16. When they were practicing, Dean had just barely made the march under three hours. A couple things were in Dean's favor; the day was cool and cloudy. He said a little prayer as he always did in the morning, but his thinking was much clearer and he suddenly felt better physically. When the hike started he stayed with Morton for a long distance, then he fell behind but kept Morton's back in sight until they had done between six and a half to seven miles.

After that, he lost Morton in the crowd. At about ten miles, his body was starting to hurt. Then, in his mind, he saw Bradberry laughing at him for failing with a smug look on his face. Dean picked up the pace out of shear will power. About a half mile out, he found a kicker and started double timing, beating the three hours by about fifteen minutes. He collapsed next to Morton who looked rested and was eating some food and slugging down water.

Dean joined him and could not express how elated he was. Morton finished his hike just a little over two hours, coming in third place. They both had passed Air Assault School. Out of 243 students, only 182 had passed the course.

The families were invited to the ceremony when they were given their wings for passing the school. The wings looked like a Huey helicopter flying straight at the viewer. They were pinned on the left side of the soldier's chest, offered a hand shake and a congratulations.

The best part was when Natalie threw her arms around his neck and told him how proud she was of him. He picked up John in his arms and the boy touched and played with the silver emblem on his chest. Dean saw Childs in the crowd, he gave Dean a thumbs up and a smile. He left the ceremony allowing the families to have a special time together.

At the battery formation, Bradberry called Morton and Dean out of formation to announce that they had passed the Air Assault School. He saluted them and shook their hands. He told each of them how proud he was that they had passed the course. When he came to Dean, Dean thanked him and that he appreciated him for spurring him on. Bradberry looked a little surprised.

"Well, I'm glad I could help, but in what way?"

"I just love to show people who think I can't that I can," Dean said with a smile.

Childs, who was standing by him, coughed a little. Bradberry looked down at the ground and then looked into Dean's eyes. "Well, I'm glad you both proved me wrong." Dean knew by the look that the BC gave him that he had not appreciated the comment or the reminder of what had been said in the office.

Chapter 24

SURPRISE VISITOR

The phone was ringing and Dean had just sat down after getting off work. He was starting to read his Bible and Natalie was in the kitchen fixing dinner, so he quickly launched himself out of the chair to answer it. Melody was still napping in the other room and he didn't want to wake her'

"Hello."

"What are you doing in Kentucky, man?"

Dean was so taken by surprise; he didn't know what to say. The voice sounded familiar but he couldn't place it.

"Well, I'm in the army and..." Then it came to him. "Reed what are you doing, man? Are you finally back in the world?"

"Yep, I got out a month ago. I've been staying with my parents, taking it easy. The question remains the same. Why are you still in Kentucky and not in Idaho farming or taking classes at the local college?"

"Well, it's a long story, but I decided to stay in the service one more year."

"I'm looking forward to hearing all about it. I called your father's number. I couldn't get anyone but finally got in touch with your brother. I'm sorry to hear about your dad. Anyway, I talked him into giving me your number with the promise that if I wasn't really a friend, he would get my first born."

Dean laughed, "That sounds like my brother Jack. He is kinda protective of me and the family. So, what do you mean that you're looking forward to hearing my story?"

"I have a sister living in Portland Oregon and she helped me find a job out there. I'm going by car and will see some of the country at the same time. Since you live in Kentucky, I'm heading south into Texas to visit Fletcher for a couple of days. Do you have room for an old pal?"

"Of course, man, you are always welcome. When do you think you'll be in this neck of the woods?"

"Just about the time Natalie is going to be throwing that turkey into the oven for Thanksgiving. Do you think you might have room at the table for me?"

"Of course, and we invited Walker to dinner also. It will be like old times," Dean said laughing.

"Good I want to see Walker and chew him out for abandoning me in Baumholder like he did just so he could be closer to you and home," Reed said laughing.

With that, they said their goodbye's and hung up. Natalie was waiting at the phone to hear about the whole conversation. She was ecstatic to hear that Reed was going to be visiting them. Walker and Reed had been the two men that she had grown most fond of while they were in Germany. The Morton's were also guest to the Thanksgiving meal. Carrie and Natalie had already decided on the menu and who was making what.

Ever since Dean and Kevin had gotten out of Air Assault School, the battery had slowly been getting ready for the battery test that was going to take place in January. The days were cold and rainy or snowy. It was miserable working on the guns in those conditions, but Rose constantly reminded them that if war broke out, it might not be fair and sunny all the time.

Dean found himself on the advance party more often because of his air assault training. He was also taking more responsibility for the gun crew because Ramsey was missing more often. Rose questioned him about the where abouts of his gunnery sergeant, but Dean didn't know where he was. When Ramsey did show up, Dean could detect the smell of booze on him. Garcia was getting out in December so Dean was going to be the man with the most experience in the section besides Ramsey. He was concerned how Ramsey was going to handle the battery test.

A few days before the holiday, Bradberry called Morton out from the formation and awarded him his sergeant stripes. Everyone congratulated him and Dean was especially happy for him, but had to fight off envy. He wondered where his stripes were and why he had not heard from anyone about them, not even Top. Still, he shook Kevin's hand and gave him a manly hug, telling him that he had earned them and he meant it. Morton thanked him and assured him that he would be a sergeant soon.

Unfortunately, there was a downside for Morton, since he was the low man when it came to the duty roster he was given duty Thanksgiving day. This pushed their celebration back to the evening instead of the afternoon.

The Wednesday before Thanksgiving, Reed came driving up. It was a cold blustery day and he beat Dean home from work. Natalie gave him a big hug at the door and welcomed him in. She gave him a cup of coffee and they sat down, visiting until Dean came through the door. He went out and helped Reed bring in his bag.

They had three bedrooms so they put Reed in the one that was furthest form the kids. The bed was about the size of an army cot and Reed made a comment about it with a laugh. Dean assured him that it was a lot more comfortable than sleeping in front of the five-ton or in the back of the van. They both laughed and agreed with one another.

They sat down at the table and started eating the dinner Natalie had prepared for them. Natalie came out with the first questions for Reed. "So, what have you been doing since you got out of the army?"

"I just took some time off; I went hiking in upper state New York during the fall to look at the trees while the leaves turned the different colors. I spent a lot of time with my family reconnecting. My parents are starting to look their age. My father is having a hard time getting around, so I helped him with their big yard and grooming some of the trees."

"So, what's in Portland?" asked Dean.

"My sister, her husband, and their two children. He works for a big manufacturing company and they got me a job in one of the departments. One of the guys is retiring and the position opens up starting January. My brother-in-law is high up in the company so he got it set aside for me. They are encouraging employers to hire us vets now-a-days."

"You're going to stop to see Fletcher. How is he doing?" Dean questioned.

"He is good, working on a big ranch. He might own it someday as I understand. He is dating one of the daughters of the owner. I don't know for sure but I think she is going to hog tie him, if you know what I mean." They all laughed. "What are you still doing in the army? I thought you had it all planned out to go to college."

Dean cleared his throat and looked down at his meal. He didn't know where to begin. He decided to start with Top and Natalie telling him that they thought that he should stay in the service. He then told him about how he thought the Lord was telling him that he should stay.

He could see by the look on Reed's face that he was filled with a little awe and a lot of disbelief. At the end of the tale, Reed asked him if he was sure that it was God. He had never heard of anyone being dealt with by God that way.

"Reed, you haven't read much of the Bible, have you? The good Lord has worked in a lot of people's lives exactly like that. I by no means think that I'm special. In fact, I still have no idea as to why He wants me to stay here. I'm air assault as you can see by the badge on my uniform, but I don't know if that was part of His plan and if I was expected to learn something from that."

"He's also on the promotion list to become a Sergeant," Natalie interjected.

"Wow, that is an interesting story. I will have to think about all of that. I have heard some of the Bible stories when I was a kid, but I just don't think God does those kinds of things anymore." Reed looked down in his plate and played with his food. There was silence and Dean could see that Reed was uncomfortable talking about the subject. He questioned Reed about what took place after Dean left the battery.

"I bet you know from Walker that Cain and I did the next inspection after you left. We got only two gigs. Everyone seemed happy with it except Cain. He wanted to have none, but one of the gigs was on him. I saw him and Walker leave the battery shortly after that. I just barely beat England out; he was retiring when I came home. Man, I did like that guy. He was sharp."

Dean agreed and they started reminiscing over some of the things they went through while they were in Germany. They were laughing because just about everything had a funny twist to it now. Reed was also making friends with Melody and John while they relived their adventures with the eighth infantry division in Violent Baumholder.

As was his custom, Dean was up early drinking a cup of coffee, reading his Bible, and praying. Reed joined him about an hour later and they discussed the things he had gone through since he came to Fort Campbell.

John came out and Dean had to rough up his son, it always took place when he was home in the morning. Natale soon followed with Melody in her arms. She fixed them breakfast, while Reed helped her and Dean took care of the children. Melody demanded her bottle and Dean loved feeding her, she would coo while sucking on the nipple.

Walker showed up around one with a six pack of beer. Reed and him nursed a beer while Dean sipped on a soda. They were laughing, talking about old times, and discussing what they hoped to do in the future.

Reed was going to Oregon for the job, but wanted to take night classes at a local college. He was still not sure what to become when he grew up. Walker was going back to Pennsylvania for full time schooling to study forestry.

Carrie and Joan showed up about three pm. She brought her dishes and helped Natalie with the rest of the meal. Morton showed up after his duty and everyone sat down for Thanksgiving dinner. Dean started off with a prayer and then everyone dug in. After dinner they played various games and talked late in the evening. It was a great time.

The next day, Reed took the Larson family out for breakfast. Walker met them there and they continued to talk about all kinds of things. They finally left the restaurant around ten am. Walker went back to the barracks.

Though it was cold, they took Reed to some lakes near Campbell to walk along the beaches. They stopped at several stores on the way back to pick up some souvenirs. Reed bought several gifts for the family and they stayed home the rest of the weekend because of the weather.

Reed left that Monday on his way to Texas. It had been a very enjoyable time. Dean was back at work and noticed Garcia and Clark laughing and talking near the office. He wandered over because he knew that Arthur had spent Thanksgiving with Willie. "You need to hear this Larson. Willie is going to get married."

"You're kidding me."

"No, this pretty little blonde got her hooks in him."

"Tell me about it, man."

"You know that he was chasing skirts and not doing his school work, so he was flunking out. His councilor suggested a tutor and he agreed. They sent Debbie, this blond beauty, over to do the tutoring. He hit on her, which comes as natural to Willie as fighting. She told him to pay attention to the books. He persisted, she slapped him good and hard, and got up and left," Garcia said laughing.

They joined in. Willie was rarely bested by a woman because of his boyish good looks and charm. "Well, what happened next, Garcia?" queried Dean.

"He hunted her down and apologized to her, telling her that he needed help badly. She made him swear that he would keep his focus on his studies and not on her. He agreed, then she informed him that she had heard of his reputation and she was not interested in being another trophy. She was looking for a meaningful relationship. He confessed to me that he had never met anyone like her and that he fell in love with her and eventually won her heart." Top came out of the office and told them to get to work.

They went to their various areas to perform their duties. Garcia put the crew through several fake fire missions helping the new members of the crew to make adjustments of the gun quickly. He also showed them some short cuts on doing things. Ramsey was close at hand during these occasions and it was good because Rose showed up several times to check on all the crews. At one point, he came near Ramsey and sniffed at his breath. Ramsey was clean and stayed that way all day long.

That Sunday, they had a special guest speaker at church. Pastor Ivan got up and announced that the speaker was an evangelist from California and he would be in town for a couple of days. His name was Anthony Davis and he was tall and thin like a ramrod. He had a deep baritone voice that demanded attention. Walker had started attending church with the Larsons. It was especially nice this day because the Morton's were sitting in the row with them.

Davis started off by introducing himself and some of the history of his walk with the Lord. He then got into his message, which was out of Romans ten. The verses dealt with repentance and believing in your heart that Jesus is the Son of God. That He died on the cross because all have sinned so that everyone could be saved.

The Spirit of the Lord fell in a powerful way; Dean could sense the presence of the Lord flowing through the church in waves. Walker fell to the floor and on his knees, weeping like a baby. Davis pointed to Carrie. "You have been betrayed and hurt, but not by the man next to you, for he has been like a rock to you, loving you and your daughter who is not his.

I want you to know, young lady, that the Lord is also a rock and He loves you more than you can ever know. If you were the only sinner in the world; He would have come down and died for you. He will never leave you or betray you if you will put your trust in Him."

Davis held out his hand toward her, inviting her to come and she slowly made her way to him mumbling, 'how did he know that?' She was also weeping uncontrollably. Kevin was following her with Joan in his arms. Dean noticed a few tears making their way down Kevin's checks.

Davis did not stop there, he pointed out others and gave them similar words. Dean leaned down to Walker and started praying for him. He asked the Lord to make Himself real to him that He would heal his hurts physically, mentally, and spiritually. Walker got up and went up front, giving his heart to the Lord as well as the Morton's. Dean could see a change in all of them when they came back to the pews.

After everyone was prayed for, people continued to tarry in the church, praising God and testifying of what He had done in their lives. The service did not end until two in the afternoon and it had started at ten thirty that morning. Still, people even lingered after that. As Dean and Natalie started toward the door, Childs and Eve came up to Dean with a very serious look on their faces.

"Hey, Top. Lighten up, the Lord really moved. Don't you think?"

He smiled, "Yes, He did an awesome work in a lot of lives. I need to tell you a few things Dean. I want you to know that I consider you like a son, something like Paul considered Timothy. Do you know what I'm talking about?"

"Yes, I've read the two books of Timothy. I'm honored that you would think of me in that way, but why?"

"I've seen something in you when we first met. Also, the Lord has told me something about you and told me that I need to mentor you. You are about to enter a great spiritual and physical conflict. It is why He kept you here. You will not be alone in this; I will be with you, but most of all God will be with you."

Eve reached over and put a hand on Natalie, "Be of good cheer daughter, the Lord says. Take courage, for I am your fortress and I will protect you through the days ahead." She patted Natalie on the arm and then gave her a hug.

Then Childs left. Dean turned to Natalie and told her that was a really weird conversation. They went home. The next day Dean and Morton had to work late, but Carrie and Natalie went to the Monday night meeting and mighty things took place again. The lesson had a deeper insight about who God was. More people were won to the Kingdom and some individuals received healing. Dean was sorry he missed it.

Chapter 25

SERGEANT LARSON

December came in cold and nasty and as the battery test got closer, there was more pressure to train on the guns and to act like a team. Garcia was exiting the army. He had enlisted in December and as an added bonus, he would be leaving for home before Christmas. They brought in another man who had come from the Bronx; he was as stout as a horse and broad through the chest.

Lyle Taylor usually had a grin on his face until Rose got done chewing him out for smiling in formation. The man was usually happy until he got really cold and then he started whining about things. Ramsey helped Dean get the members established in their positions within the crew. Often, he would disappear, leaving Dean in charge.

Clark pulled Dean off to the side one Tuesday and informed him that Bradberry was suggesting they get a new sergeant for the gun, since Dean's promotion had not come in. He was also thinking Ramsey was a little flaky. The captain wanted them to double their efforts to catch him with a drink in his hand during duty hours, if that is what he was doing.

Rose and Childs suggested they leave things as is until after the battery test, and that throwing a new person into the mix might disrupt the team effort on the gun. Clark informed him that Childs and Rose had won out, but Bradberry was insisting that they watch Ramsey closely. He didn't need a drunken gunnery sergeant killing someone down range. If the gun and crew didn't perform well, he would move people a-round.

As usual, when they got to the motor pool Ramsy left and Dean was left in charge. He put them to doing maintenance with Taylor watching over the crew. He went into the connex, a building where they stored their gear. They had a heater set up where they could warm up if the weather got to them. About a half hour after formation, Rose came by to check on everyone's progress.

He asked Dean where Ramsey was and Dean gave him the usual answer, which was that he didn't know. This time Rose grilled him for about twenty minutes on Ramsey's schedule and if Dean had ever seen him with alcohol in his possession. He wanted a straight answer and Dean did not lie about Ramsey in any way.

When they were out in the field shooting, Ramsey was all business and from what Dean could tell, he knew that he was doing. He had a way of instilling loyalty within the crew, and when something went wrong, it was usually a minor infraction. He didn't throw the man to the wolves, but took the blame on himself. Dean not only felt like Ramsey had earned his trust, he liked the man personally.

Once Rose left, he kept busy in the connex and tried to think of a way to fix the problems. He came up blank, then he decided that they were beyond his abilities any way. He should have thought of this first, but why not give it to God? The first thing he brought up was the fact that he was still a Spec four and that he wanted to stay with this crew. Dean thought he had done a good job with his answers at the promotion board. He asked the Lord to move in his behalf so that he might get his sergeant stripes.

He had no idea as to what to ask for concerning Ramsey, so he asked the Lord to make himself real to the man and to set him free from alcohol. He would help if the Lord would show him what to do. He was about to get up and check the crew when he felt like the Lord whispered one word to him. "Nam." He thought about it. He knew very little about Ramsey, not even where he came from.

The next couple of days, Ramsey stayed close to the battery area, at one point he was going to leave but Dean warned him that Rose was watching and suggested he stay nearby. Sure enough, Smoke showed up looking things over. He came close to Ramsey and sniffed him. Ramsey just laughed and asked Rose if he wanted the name of his aftershave. Rose looked at him and walked away. Dean could tell that Ramsey was hankering for a drink all day.

A couple of weeks before Christmas at the end of the day, the battery was in formation about to be released for the day. Instead of letting everyone go, they called the men to attention. Bradberry asked Larson to come to the front. He presented Dean with the paperwork and buck sergeant stripes; Dean had his promotion.

The captain informed him that there had been a problem with some of the information getting lost and he would be getting back pay for November. Dean couldn't help but grin. The Captain, Morton, Childs, and Ramsey came up to shake his hand plus others. The one that touched him the most was Rose.

"Soldier, wipe that smile off your face. I've seen you take care of that gun crew; you deserve those stripes." He turned and walked away.

The next day, he took Ramsey to dinner, as a celebration for his promotion, but it was camouflage for what he really wanted to do. They ordered food and Ramsey asked that they bring him a beer with it. They started with small talk and Dean found out that he was from South Carolina and that he had two brothers and two sisters still living in the small town they had all been born and raised in. He was the only one in the family that had left and had not come back to stay.

He had been married once and was making a living when he was drafted. Some years after he got out of the army, they got a divorce because he had changed so much. They were served their food and Ramsey had already had some long draws on his beer. Dean said a short silent prayer and jumped into it. "So, what happened in Nam, Serg?"

Ramsey was taking a bite, and choked a little. He caught his composure and chewed on his food. Dean could see him wrestling with the question. He was considering what he should say. "So, who told you that I had been in Nam?"

Dean hesitated, wondering how he would take his answer, but decided to wade into it because truth was the best policy. "God."

Ramsey's fork and food stopped midair. He looked at Dean for a few minutes and took in the bite. After chewing and swallowing he said. "So, you often hear from God?"

"No, usually when he speaks to me, it's his written word. So, this is kind of special, but Serg I want you to know that I like you and if you're around I enjoy working with you. Rose has orders from the BC to keep a close eye on you and if you're caught with a drink on you during duty hours, he wants to know, so that he can get rid of you. I don't want that to happen, so let's get down to the root of why you drink."

"I want to thank you for caring, no one seems to be concerned about me much except my mother, Top, and you. I know that you cover for me a lot, but I think I'm beyond repair."

"That's a bunch of hog wash. I believe that there is still hope for you. I believe you can pull your butt up out of the muck and mire that you're in with a lot of help from friends and God. I believe you need the good Lord in your life. God still loves you and he came to set the captive free and you are held in bondage by your past and liquor."

"You kinda sound like my mother. She told me the same things last time I was home. I know that Rose is watching me close. If I get kicked out of the army, I know that I will end up on the streets homeless. I can't bear the thought of living with my Mom as an alcoholic, yet she would take me in. I know that she prays for me every day. Well, what's your plan Sergeant Larson? He said with a hopeful smile. Ramsey calling Larson sergeant sounded so strange to Dean, almost surreal.

"For one thing, I'm going to hold you accountable for every minute of the day. Taylor and the rest of the section are going to keep tabs on you as much as possible. If you want to have a drink, you give me a call or get a hold of one of those guys and we will help you through the withdrawals. So, what happened in Nam Ramsey?"

"Nothing more than what happened to others. My buddy and I were drafted and ended up at Fort Sill training on the guns. We got shipped to Nam together and ended up in the same outfit, a fire base on a s-- t hill that no one wanted but the VC. We were not on the same gun crew but worked right next to each other. You had to be on the lookout all the time, they used to sneak through the wire and cause havoc at night.

"One night they didn't just slither through the wire, but they brought a bunch of their friends from north of the border. I don't know how many we were trying to hold off, but a lot more than what I wanted to see. We were shooting beehive rounds down on them for a while. Those rounds would leave big holes in the ranks but they got close enough that we could no longer suppress the tubes enough to fire for effect.

"We left the guns for the trenches. Albert and I jumped inside, shoulder to shoulder. One of them threw a grenade into our hole, Albert never flinched, he just fell on it and saved my worthless hide," Tears were rolling down Ramsey's check. He quickly wiped them away.

They had finished their meal and were just drinking coffee. Dean looked at Ramsey until the man looked back at him. "Apparently Albert didn't think you were worthless, George, he was willing to die for you. Don't you think that you should pay him back in some way by not only living for yourself, but for Albert also. Try to fulfill some of his dreams and his hopes. I'll tell you about another man that thought you were dying for.

Jesus Christ died on the cross for you to saved you from your sins. He has a purpose for your life and if you will give him your life, He will give you peace and help you accomplish that purpose. I doubt Albert would want you to grieve over him for the rest of your life. Jesus' plan had nothing to do with drinking yourself to death. He gives life, hope, and faith."

They sat there for a while and Dean could see Ramsey was sorting things out in his mind. They finished the coffee and Dean picked up the tab. Dean drove him back to his housing unit. The roads were slick, so it took him some time. He left George to his own thoughts until he pulled up to his quarters. "Well, what do you want George? You want to get off the sauce, or do you want to continue as is?"

"I'm tired of the same old, same old. Come into my place and I will give you my stash of liquor. I guess that beer at dinner was my last drink." Dean entered his quarters, it was obviously a bachelor's pad and by the time Ramsey had gone through things, Dean was packing out three and a half pints of hard liquor.

"Well, what about giving your life to Jesus, Ramsey?"

"I will have to think about that, Larson. I don't know if I'm ready for that."

"Can I at least pray for you before I leave?"

"I would like that."

Dean grabbed his hand, "Lord, I lift up my friend before You, knowing that You love him more than he can know. He has started a new journey and he is going to need Your help. I would ask You to set him free from the alcohol and that you would show Yourself strong on his behalf. May he sense Your presence when he is going through the hard times. In Jesus' name, amen." Ramsey also agreed.

Dean left, poured the bottles out on the ground, and threw the empties away. He went home and told Natalie what had happened. She suggested giving Pastor Ivan a call and ask him about a program Ramsey could become a part of that would help him kick the habit. The gun crew all agreed to keep watch over their sergeant. They would watch him closely and when they saw him start to wander, they would grab him up and find work for him. Ivan directed Natalie to a church that had a recovery program for alcoholics in the area. Dean took him to his first meeting and sat with him. Childs found out what was going on and took him a couple times.

Ramsey insisted that he needed to go home for Christmas. They were concerned that he might stumble if they were not there to help him, but they could not deny the fact that he seemed to set his face to overcome his problems. He caught a military flight back home most of the way. His sister picked him up at the base and took him the rest of the way.

Dean did not know what Ramsey had in mind when he went home, but it was to make amends and start the healing process with his family. He went to everyone that he had hurt after coming home from the war and asked for forgiveness. There were a lot of tears on both sides. He also went and saw his ex-wife and tried to make atonement, but she was less open to his confession. She did let him see his daughter. She would not come close, and stayed close to her mother. He gave her a Christmas present and she finally gave him a hug.

He had abused his wife on several occasions. He promised to do better on the child support. She admitted to him that she was about to be married to a very good man. He told her that he was going to send her money anyway and he would appreciate it if she would start a college fund for the child. This seemed to soften her a bit and she became a little more open to his apology. He also asked for more visitation rights and she agreed.

On Christmas day, Dean got a long-distance call. It was Ramsey. "Are you all right, George?"

"Yeah Larson. I'm great. In fact, I'm wonderful. My mama wants to talk to you. I know it's Christmas, but can you spare a couple of minutes?"

"Sure. Whatever you want."

"Sergeant Larson, I want to wish you and yours a very Merry Christmas and I want to thank you for giving me my son back. Thank you so much for helping him out. Here's George back."

At least that is what Dean thought she had said. Her southern drawl was so deep, Dean wasn't sure what she had spoken. Ramsey came back on the phone and translated.   He also confessed to Dean that while he was with his mother at church, he went up front and gave his life to Christ.

After getting off the phone, he told Natalie and they both danced around the room, praising the Lord. It was a very special Christmas for them. Ramsey came to salvation. Dean had his promotion and Melody opened her first present with a little help from her brother. They called family back home and found everyone doing well. On a sad note, and yet a happy one, Garcia was home with family. Dean had a feeling that he would never see him again.

Chapter 26

THE TEST

Dean watched as gun three got ready to send the first rounds down range to bracket the target. It was cold, but this time Dean was prepared better; he had store-bought thermo underwear, thick mittens that he used while he was not working the weapon, and a parka hidden in the gear that he would use after dark. He and Ramsey had advised the crew to do the same, most of them had listened and seemed to be weathering the frigid temperatures fairly well.

The first round left the tube and the light breeze brought the smell of gun powder down to gun six. Dean loved the aroma, and it made him focus more closely on what was about to happen. Adjustments were made and the next projectile was fired, more corrections were made and the third round was on target. Now it was fire for effect and the rest of the battery got involved, sending fire and destruction on a target they could not see.

Dean didn't notice the cold as they accomplished the mission. After it was done, Dean immediately got his hands warm because they would be almost numb. To make the fine adjustments you could wear only the wool inserts for your gloves. The cold metal would quickly seep through the material and fingers would demand attention.

He looked behind the gun and noticed that Bradberry and Top were watching them do their jobs. Ramsey seemed oblivious to them, directing the crew to get ready to do what came down next whether it be another fire mission or pack up and move. It didn't take them long to decide, it was another fire mission.

Dean's focus went back to the gun and his job. To him it seemed like the crew was working well together. The rounds were going down range at a good clip, he had no time to compare gun six to the other crews. Ramsey and the powder monkeys had the opportunity to look over at the other guns, but the rest of them had to focus on what they were doing. Yes, there was some friendly competition with the other guns, but to win they had to pay attention to what they were doing.

After that mission, Dean turned to see if the BC and Top were still behind them and noticed that they had gotten behind gun five. Top had a stop watch in his hands; they were seeing how many rounds a gun could fire down range in a certain amount of time. They had two more missions in that same spot with the BC and Top standing behind the next batteries to observe them.

Orders came down to pack up. They were moving to another firing position. Number six-gun crew was not the fastest crew to get ready for the road march, but they were not the slowest either. Dean was glad he was not the gunnery sergeant; poor Ramsey was stuck up front as the assistant driver standing on the seat watching the sky for enemy aircraft. At least, the driver of the Gamma Goat had the windshield in front of him. Dean got to sit in the back but the canvas cover on the back of the goat did little to shield them from the cold.

Taylor was a part of the advance party, so he directed them into the firing position. Again, the crew was not the fastest at setting up, but they were not the last gun to set up the camouflage. Being the NCO that he was, Ramsey went around to the crew asking them if they were all right and thanking them for doing a good job.

They did several more fire missions that day. They ate their meals close to the gun and Ramsey left the area with a couple of men to get coffee from the mess. Dean was the first to get his cup and Ramsey was the last to get the warm liquid. Dean drank the coffee slowly, keeping his hands cupped around the metal container. Before he could drink it all, a mission came down and he was busy at the gun. By the time he got back to his coffee, it was cold and some ice had formed.

They got several more fire missions, after dark they all had more coffee. Dean brought out his parka. He was cold, but he could tell by the way Ramsey acted that the cold had gotten to him. He covered him in the heavy coat. It came down to his knees, he made him sit and had one of the men rub him down.

He had to get blankets for Taylor and one of the other men, PFC Linus Struck, and they all drank the coffee, trying to get the blood flowing, Ramsey soon perked up and Top came around, checking on how everyone was doing.

He caught Ramsey under the parka, smiled, and mentioned the parka was a good idea. He enquired how everyone was handling the cold. He looked at Taylor and Struck, suggesting that they go into the FDC tent and get warmed up for a half hour. Ramsey was feeling much better. The parka was doing the job. He gave Dean his parka back and fifteen minutes later they had a fire missions come down. Taylor was back at his position before gun six went into action. Struck joined them about forty-five minutes later.

They had to stay at the gun all that night, getting several missions in the early hours of the morning. When Dean was on the gun, he played it smart; keeping the parka on, then his shelter half over that, and the wool blanket over his legs. Dean even got some sleep during the night. Ramsey stayed in FDC but came out often to check the men who stayed in their shelter halves.

There was hot coffee throughout most of the night.

In the morning they had set up a warm up tent, giving a couple members of each crew time to eat a hot meal and drink something warm. They got an hour respite and then were back out on the guns. During the day, Dean had to get used to being without his parka because it was not considered a part of the uniform. If they got a fire mission, everyone left the tent and rushed to the guns. Every morning, it was Rose's delightful duty to get everyone out of the tents. He would crawl out of his tent bare chested, declare how invigorating the air was, then roust everyone up to start the day.

On the last day of the test, it went late. There were arguments as to whether the convoy should return to the base or stay out one more night. As cold as it was, everyone decided that the men were exhausted and they thought some of them might fall asleep at the steering wheel. Ramsy and Dean put their shelter halves together, though some of them wanted to bunk with Dean because of the parka. They got into the mummy bags and Dean put the parka and wool blankets over both of them as much as possible. It grew warm fast and Dean was about to doze off when he heard this terrible noise next to him. It sounded like when his father took a chain saw to the trees out back of his house. He could not see Ramsey's face, but he knew that he was warm, happy, and sound asleep. He didn't know when it happened, but he finally fell into a deep sleep himself.

Dean was suddenly brought out of that sleep by Rose bellowing that it was time to get to work. He looked at his watch. It was nine hundred hours and the sun was peeking between some of the clouds. Ramsey was already gone, Dean hunted up his boots and field jacket. He crawled out from beneath his tent and spotted a mess truck with steaming food cooked and ready for the taking. He got in line, while Ramsey fell in behind him.

Smoke Rose was walking down the line and something came over Dean. "Hey Smoke, now I know why your last name is Rose."

Rose stopped in mid-step and everyone took a deep breath nearby. He turned and came near Larson. "And why is that soldier?" He got almost in Larson's face as he asked the question.

"It's because of your rosy personality on a cold winter morning," Dean said with a smile.

The statement took Rose by surprise. "Well, that is the first time anyone has said that to me soldier," he said with a slight smile creasing his chiseled features. He started walking away and Dean moved the conversation a little deeper. "It couldn't be about smell, none of us here smell like a Rose."

Rose came running back to him, "You're coming close Larson. If you weren't such a good soldier, I'd take you back in the woods and teach you about respect."

He grabbed Dean and Ramsey's jacket collars and looked them in the eyes. "You two did far better than what some thought you would on the test. You both are fine NCOs; you took care of your men. Kept those 'cruits' straight.

I know what you did, Larson. How you watched over everyone's back and got them through some hard times. I admire that. You are a good soldier, but if either one of you tell anyone that I said these things and ruin my reputation, I will kick your butts all over this base. I will kick them so much that you will be farting out your ears. Do you understand?" Others that were in line and heard the conversation showed astonished looks on their faces. They had never heard Rose say so much and it was a compliment.

"Out of all the men in the army that have complimented me for my service, I will remember what Smoke Rose said to me. But no doubt I will never get it in writing," Dean said loudly.

Rose turned once more and gave Dean a slight smile. Dean came to attention and saluted him out of respect and Rose returned it.

"You know, I wouldn't press it any further. I think he could kick our butts until we were farting out of our ears. The thought of gas being passed that close to my nose is kind of a disgusting though, so you behave Larson," whispered Ramsey.

"Yes, I know. I think I got away with one. You know what I think? You are right, he probably could do exactly what he threatened to do," Dean replied smiling

The hot breakfast and coffee were excellent. Dean rode up front with the driver as they convoyed back to base. It was a miserable ride, but Dean was hoping that it would be his last maneuver in the winter. Usually after the test, the battery focused on maintenance and other types of training. They had to store all the gear, the guns, and the Gamma Goats before they were released for the day. Morton had been out in the field, calling in the rounds, and he was already home. Once the last fire mission was done, they had brought him back in by chopper.

When he saw Dean pull up in the driveway, he came out and asked how gun six had done. Dean told him what Rose had said. He made Kevin swear that he would not reveal who had told him, repeating Smoke's threat. Morton nodded and confirmed that Rose could do it.

Dean rushed into the house and gave Natalie a big hug and kiss. He turned his attention to John, grabbing him up and wrestled him to the carpet. He sat down with both kids in his lap as Natalie poured him a hot cup of coffee. Melody gave Daddy a big sloppy kiss and was soon on the floor playing with her brother. Natalie came over with the coffee and a late Christmas card.

It was from Suzan Porter. The family had gotten settled and Suzan had found a job. The last sentence was sad and Dean couldn't hide the grief he felt. Angela had become pregnant by Jon, the child would never get to know his or her father or grandfather. It also stirred up that old memory when both men died. He had a nightmare about it that night.

A week later at formation, they were told that Charlie Battery had won the award for being best battery in the battalion. Bradberry, being who he was, declared they needed to do better and that he expected to win the award next year. Dean and Ramsey didn't care either way, they had gotten a complement from Rose and the word had gotten around. For about a month the rest of the battery treated gun six with great respect and awe. Dean and Ramsey bought the team a case of beer. They drank sodas themselves and played some card games with the men before going to their own quarters.

Chapter 27

LOU ANN

It was the second week in March and that Tuesday was decent, a breeze but not too cold yet chilly enough that everyone kept field jackets on. The weather was something that a soldier always kept his eye on. It determined what he was going to wear and how he was going to do things.

Even though Dean had gotten off the farm, the weather still ran his life. Monday, they had gone out to the rifle range. It was different for him, instead of sighting his weapon in, he was helping others to make sure their M-16s were accurate when they used them. It had been a long day; it had kept his mind occupied.

After he got home, he sat down to read his Bible, but his thoughts wandered to the Sunday service. They were in the Easter season, but Ivan had been preaching almost nonstop on faith and giving. He didn't believe that Easter required a certain type of service, but he did notice a lack of anointing on the messages lately. It seemed like Ivan was missing something.

Dean had read the Bible through once since his encounter with God and was now reading the book of James again. The word of God kept jumping out to him and directing him to make changes in his own attitude. He was praying a lot more and treating others differently. Fist fighting seemed out of place, but if it came to defending his family, he was sure it was an exception to the rule.

He was also a lot more forgiving than he had been with people.

Still, the Sunday message continued to bother him. Morton and he talked about it, and Kevin had seen no problem with it. He discussed it with Natalie later that evening and discovered that she was troubled by it as well, but could not pinpoint the reason why, other than there was no real Spirit in what he said. Dean rehashed the sermon in his mind again and what other had been said. Still, the pastor had scriptures to back up what he was preaching. Dean wrote all of them down and planned on looking them over again. He tried to refocus on the scriptures, but was interrupted by a knock on the door. It was Morton.

"Hey, Larson I'm taking Carrie to the hospital. She's having the baby. Can you watch Joan?"

"You bet, I will come and get her."

Natalie was soon at his side. He held Joan's hand and waved as Kevin and Carrie drove off.

"You want to bet on what the child will be?" asked Dean.

"You're on. I get to choose first. I know Kevin is hoping for a boy, so I'm going to bet on a boy," Natalie declared.

"Okay I'm going to put a week's worth of breakfast in bed on a girl." They both laughed. Natalie took Dean in to work leaving Joan with Natalie. Natalie was waiting for him out at the car when the day was over. She smiled and waved at him while he talked to someone about work. He excused himself from the other soldier and walked up to her. "Well?" he asked.

"A little girl. Eight pounds, six ounces. It's wonderful."

"The question is, how does Kevin feel about it?"

"He is ecstatic about that little girl. You men are all alike."

"Not quite, but we have to hold the line against you women. Besides that, I'm happy. I just won; you owe me breakfast in bed for a week because it's a little girl."

"I know better than to gamble, so breakfast it is," Natalie said smiling.

"I don't know why you shouldn't gamble. The good Lord is the biggest gambler in the universe. Every time He breathes life into a child, He's betting that we're going to love Him and do the right thing. I wonder how often He wins."

"Dean! That is sacrilege, you should repent."

"I'll think about it, but I'm wondering if He is having a good laugh over it."

"Come on, I'll take you to the hospital and you take a look at her yourself. She is a beautiful little girl."

"Question, darlin.' Does Kevin have cigars and does that little girl have hair, or does she look like Yule Brynner?" Dean said with a laugh.

He hopped into the car and she took him to the maternity ward. Kevin was holding the baby and cooing at her. He smiled at Dean, a big toothy grin and held her up so he could see her better

"So, what's her name?" asked Dean

"It's Betty Lynn Morton," Carrie announced.

"Well, with a name like that, she is going to be someone very special," Dean said laughing. Morton gave the baby to Dean so that he could get a close look. Sorry, he thought, she does look like Yule. Even though Natalie showed him some light blonde hair on her head. Dean thought she looked beautiful. She wasn't crying when he held her and that was a plus. Kevin produced a cigar and snatched his child back out of Dean's arms.

Dean noticed Joan sitting in a chair looking dejected. "So young lady, what do you think of your brand-new sister?" She just shrugged her shoulders.

Dean went over to her and kneeled down in front of her. "I bet you're going to have all kinds of fun playing with her and helping your mama raise her up to be special like you are."

Joan brightened instantly. "I'm special?" she asked with a big innocent smile.

"Older sisters are always special to younger sisters. Besides Mommy and Daddy love you like crazy. How could you think you're not special?" he said whisking her up in his arms. He took her over to Kevin who made room on his lap. He let Joan touch her new sister and look at her. It was a very special moment for the whole family.

They talked for a while, then Kevin gave the baby to Carrie and asked Dean to step out in the hallway. "I wanted you hear this first, Larson. We have been neighbors for a while and we went through air assault school together. When it comes to the battery, I feel closer to you than anyone else. I've decided to make the army a career. I spend so much time with the grunts, it's hard to get to know others in the battery.

"Top and Bradberry know of course but no one else. I talked to them about how I could further my chances of promotion and both of them suggested jump school and OCS [Officer's Candidate School]. I have a great deal of respect for you Dean, so what do you think?"

"Well, I think you're crazy wanting to jump out of a perfectly good plane. The idea of saluting you if you become an officer makes me want to get out of the army all that much faster." he said snickering. "To tell you the truth Kevin, I think you would make a fine officer and if the army is your choice, have at it. I have always considered you a friend but more than that, a good soldier."

"That means a lot to me. Promise me you won't get angry? My orders came in a couple of days ago. I will go to Fort Bragg for jump school, and then I will be assigned to one of the units over there."

"Man, you are a stinking traitor, going to the 82nd Airbourne division. The enemy? No wonder you're keeping it a secret." They both laughed. Dean turned serious, "Don't ever forget that Joan is your daughter also, don't forget to treat her special at times, okay?"

"I got the drift in there. I was just so excited about Betty. Thanks for reminding me that I already have a special little girl. You know, I'm really concerned about jump school. I won't have you around to cheer me on. Are you sure you don't want to come to jump school with me?"

"You must be kidding me. No way am I going to jump school. I am going to leave this man's army and go to college," he said laughing.

A month later, the Morton's were gone to Fort Bragg. Dean and Natalie missed them in a big way. They had all been through so much. He grew closer to Ramsey. He was a completely different man from the one that had first taken over the section. He was still going to the AA meetings, but was now attending the church that they were meeting in.

One of the hefty robust ladies, named Lou Ann that was also attending AA had grabbed him up in one of the meetings and told him they were going to get to know each other and if he stayed straight, he was going to marry her. Like a good soldier, Ramsey was toeing the line with her. He said that the way she came on to him, he didn't dare say no.

He insisted that Dean meet her so he made a date with her inviting the Larsons to go with them on their first excursion together. She was thrilled to meet Natalie and Dean. They both liked her instantly. She was all bubbly; laughing and praising the Lord about everything.

Dean could not figure out where she got all her energy, he got tired just watching her. She talked so fast it was like watching a locomotive rushing down the tracks. At times it was hard to understand her but she never seemed to mind repeating herself when asked to. She didn't apologize for it, just commented that she had always talked fast, had a lot to say, and needed all the time she could muster to get it out. Talking about opposites attracting, Dean thought.

Ramsey was so easy going, he said very little, but when you were in his section, he expected you to listen. He once told Dean that his father chewed tobacco, took him off to the side and said, "Son never spit in the wind more than three times. If they don't understand you by the third time you're talking to a fool and wasting your time." George was so easy going. Dean had never once seen him lose his cool while under fire, while Lou Ann seemed in constant motion, even when she was sitting.

As was a part of her nature she asked Ramsey to marry her in the spring of that year and in the early summer they tied the knot and she became Mrs. Lou Ann Ramsey. She said it was meant to be; the name seemed to flow off the tongue just right.

George asked Dean to be his best man and Dean was honored to do so. John became the ring bearer, and Natalie had the duty of getting the church ready for the nuptials. It was a small wedding and at the end of the dinner, everyone started laughing as Lou Ann dragged George out to the car for their honeymoon. She was a woman on a mission and for the first time since Dean had known Ramsey, he saw a hint of fear in his eyes.

Natalie had gotten a letter from Suzan Porter. Angela had a little baby boy, the child was a little premature, but healthy. She had sent a picture with the letter. Angela was holding the baby; it was a beautiful child with lots of dark hair. The mother looked worn out and very unhappy. Dean still saw that deep sadness and guilt in the girl's eyes.

Chapter 28

THE FIRST BATTLE

It was a beautiful April day and Dean was carrying Melody toward the church doors. Natalie had John's hand and was guiding him in the same direction. The greeter handed them a program and they quickly proceeded down the side passage to a seat near the middle.

They were cutting it close, so there was no visiting before the service. They got settled, with Natalie rushing the two children to the children's program. Dean looked around the room for the Childs. They were up front, close to the area they usually sat in. He looked down the pew toward the aisle and noticed a young lady staring at him, that he had never seen before.

She was looking at him and she looked slightly familiar, but he couldn't recall where he had seen her before. Pastor Ivan stood up and started announcements which drew Dean's attention forward. Natalie walked in front of him and as she sat down, Dean looked to the right and noticed the young lady had slid closer to the center of the pew.

He didn't think anything about it at first. He guessed she was just giving room for others to sit on the pew. The church had lost a lot of members because of various reasons, so the congregation was a little lean in numbers now days. A lot of the messages were on winning others to the Lord, faith, and tithe.

Dean did not feel they were maturing as they had been under Jethro. He had gotten saved in this church and felt some loyalty to it but still, he had heard enough messages on the subjects that Ivan was teaching on. The worship was great and then Ivan started on his message. He taught on faith again. Though he always had great scriptures to back up what he was saying, something did not sit right in Dean's heart. He couldn't put his finger on it, so he decided then and there that he would do a study on faith. He had read through the Bible once, had finished the New Testament a second time, and was now in the book of Numbers.

The sermon ended and, as always, everyone stood up and milled around, talking to old friends and the visitors. The young lady ignored everyone else and came straight towards Natalie and Dean. She held her hand out to Natalie and shook it quickly, then turned her attention to Dean. She also held her right hand toward Dean, saying at the same time, "Don't I know you?"

"You seem kind of familiar, but I can't place you," Dean said as he started reaching for her open palm. Something inside him told him not to respond to the hand, so he acted like he didn't see it and scratched his head instead. He put his arm around Natalie keeping her between him and the young woman. "Maybe your name will remind me of where we met before."

"Oh! My name is Matty Devin. You're Natalie and you're," she said holding out her hand towards Dean again.

"I'm Natalie's husband, Dean," he said reaching toward the hand.

Suddenly he felt strong arms grab both of his arms pulling him back slightly. Childs reached around, grabbed her hand and introduced himself to her. She giggled a strange little laugh and told him her name.

"It's nice meeting you sorry to interrupt, but can I borrow Dean for a few minutes? He's one of my NCOs and I would like to speak to him about a few Army related things." She just nodded. Childs steered Dean out to the aisle away from her hearing. He handed Dean a piece of paper. "You need to study these scriptures very carefully. One more word for you Dean, 'Ann.'

Dean looked at Matty, the woman was a brunette she had a pleasant face to look at and a modest body, but by no means did she look like Ann. Matty looked back at him, then he saw it. She looked at him like Ann did. It was like he was naked and hanging on a meat hook. Natalie also saw the look and there was a coolness that came over her and she instantly excused herself to get the children.

Matty turned and walked out the door shaking several hands plus Ivan's at the door. Natalie came back with the kids and grilled Dean about Matty as they left the church. "Where do you know her from, Dean?" He could sense a touch of mistrust arising in her voice and he couldn't blame her.

"I believe she may be why we are still here, Natalie. I've never met her in my life, but that is why Top came over to me and warned me to be smart about being around her. Natalie, you need to promise me to run interference with her and don't you ever leave me alone with her. Did you see how she looked at me?"

"Yes, I did, that is what bothers me."

"I know, but I swear to you that I don't know that woman, as far as I'm aware I have never met her. I don't think I've even seen her before," he said putting his right hand on the Bible.

She nodded and he knew that she was satisfied. All the way home he knew he had never met Matty but he knew what laid behind those dark brown eyes. He had seen it in Ann and he wanted no part of it. His first thought was to run to another church and bypass the problem.

When they got home, Natalie started dinner and Dean pulled out the paper that Childs had handed him and looked over the verses.

"What's that?" enquired Natalie.

"It's a bunch of verses that Top gave me and told me to study."

"What's the first one?"

"It's in Ephesians six, starting with verse ten and it talks about putting on the armor of God. The next one is in Matthew eighteen and speaks of binding and loosening. The last one is Revelation twelve, verse eleven where it speaks about the blood of the Lamb." He stopped and pondered what he had just read.

Dean also thought about who had given him the verses and how he had deflected Matty's handshake. Childs always seemed to be ahead of the curve, knowing things before they occurred. Dean always thought that Childs had a prophetic gifting.

Childs had asked him out of the blue how he liked basic training. Dean confessed to him that he had not been fond of it, his freedom was stripped from him and all the yelling. Childs looked him in the eyes and stated that he would not like what was coming, but that God would equip him with what he needed.

"Did he write any others?" Natalie asked, bringing him back to the present.

"Let's see. Yes, one more. Matthew eight, verse twenty-eight about the man possessed by the devils. Wow do you understand all these and why he gave them to me?"

"Yes, I think I do, but I think you should study them and try to figure out things for yourself and then it will stick with you a lot better."

He gave her his pleading look to see if she would at least give him some kind of clue, but all she did was point to the Bible and told him to study. He put the Bible down and suggested some lunch first. Since he was in the studying mode, he would look into faith more closely. Even while he ate, he thought about what he would look into first.

The warrior verses were intriguing, he had never liked the idea of being a sheep. His father had a herd of sheep on the farm and they were such stupid animals, causing more trouble than they were worth. That is probably why his dad had gotten rid of them.

After lunch, he launched into the study of the verses with Bible in hand and a pen and paper on the end table near his chair. John came running around him, wanting to play, but he would not stop the study. When he couldn't figure something out, he would pray and wait on the Lord until he got some kind of answer. Natalie called him to dinner but he informed her that he would eat later, she eventually put the food in the refrigerator. Finally at three in the morning, he laid down on the couch to sleep not wanting to wake Natalie.

Natalie had waited to the last minute before waking him up. He didn't shower but threw on fatigues, shaved, ate breakfast, and flew out the door. Natalie did question him about what he had learned but he told her that he would talk to her that night. He just didn't have time to tell her what he had found. He gave her a kiss as he opened the door and told her that he would be late.

As he stood at attention in formation, he felt energized, like he had gotten a great night's sleep. They ran three miles that day with PT and close order drill. He was alert and never missed a beat in all of it. He performed all his duties and caught Top at noon to set a time that night so that they could talk.

Childs rarely mingled with the lower rank NCOs, so when they got together it was always at a little dive on the Kentucky side of the border. Most troopers from Fort Campbell did business in Clarksville, so it was unlikely they would run into someone they would know. They said very few words. Top knew why he wanted to see him, and gave the name of the place where they had met before.

After that, the day seemed to drag on until everyone was released for the night. Walker showed up out of the blue suggesting that they play a few games of pool, but Dean had to beg off, telling him that he had a meeting to attend.

Childs met him at the diner. It was dark and dingy with one of the bar stools missing at the counter. They did serve great pie and a wonderful cup of coffee and they ordered one of each. The waitress was older, friendly, and very efficient. She never let the cups go dry.

"Well, what did you learn?" questioned Childs.

"I'm taking from the scriptures you gave me that Matty is possessed by some kind of spirit."

"In her case, it's more like she is oppressed, giving a lot of control to unclean spirits. Can you tell me what kind of spirits?"

"I know for sure that she has a spirit of lust. It was the same thing that Ann had."

"Good, but one of the secrets to the kingdom of darkness is that they try to mimic the Godhead, so they usually travel in at least threes. Got a clue as to the other two?"

"No, not at all."

"She has a rebellious spirit, or a spirit of witchcraft, and a mocking spirit."

"How do you know these things, Top?"

"Long story. Someday I will tell you about it, but the short version is that the Lord has given me the gift of discernment. I can tell sometimes when people have evil spirits. By the way, I met Ann one time and knew what she had." At the mention of that name, Dean looked away feeling embarrassed and guilty.

"Don't feel guilty Dean, that is of the devil and he will use that against you to make you feel unworthy. You have to remind yourself every day that you are forgiven and free of sin. That is a part of your testimony on overcoming the enemy. Remember the verse in Revelation?"

"Yes. So that is what you wanted to show me. What about the blood, how can that be used to overcome the devil?"

"Have you ever seen sci-fi shows with the space ships and

they have an invisible shield around them? Well, that is the blood. Ask the Lord to cover you and your property in the blood and the devils can't penetrate that shield. That does not mean that evil men can't come through, it just means that devils can't harass you unless God gives them permission."

"I don't know, Top. This sounds so weird and well I...I mean my family and all."

"Listen carefully, one of the purposes that God brought you into the kingdom is for this time. I saw it on you the first time I laid eyes on you in formation. You will never be at peace in your heart until you get into the fight. Don't retreat from this battle. Hold your ground and know that the Lord will take care of you and your family. You just be as obedient as you can.

"Remember this, the warfare that takes place in the spirit realm is similar to what takes place in the natural. Study to show yourself approved to be his soldier. Know your enemy, how he does things so that you can overcome his strategies.   Reach your hand towards me." Dean did as he was told. "You just reached into the spirit realm. It is all around us. We just don't see it. Well Larson, what are you going to do? Turn tail or fulfill God's perfect will in your life?"

Dean picked at the top of the coconut cream pie that sat in front of him. He put down the fork and took a sip of his coffee as he considered all the information that Top had just shared with him. This was one time he felt the decision was going to have to be made by him without Natalie's input.

The thought that God would take care of his family was a comfort but still, taking on devils was something that he had never bargained for. He could only see himself as the reluctant soldier in God's army. David taking on Goliath, the giant and winning had been one of his favorite Bible stories as a child. If David could pull it off maybe, he could find the courage to get some kind of victory with the Lord's help. He took a bite of his pie, it was excellent. He looked Childs in the eyes and told him that he was on board.

"Good, I always knew you had it in you."

"Okay, what about the verses in Matthew, this binding and loosening?"

"Take Matty for example, you could release angels to bind those three spirits that hang around her. That would give them limited access to the people she comes in contact with. You have to be specific with the names of the devils otherwise they will not respond. It's like when you shoot your rifle on the range. You have to hit the mark or it doesn't count. The other thing you need to do is study what angels do, because they are your allies and will fight for you if you're on God's side."

Dean digested this as he ate his pie. The waitress came over and filled their cups up and they sipped the hot brew as he thought about some of the questions he might have. This was the time to ask Childs. He struggled with the next question, wrestling with whether he should ask it at all.

"What's bothering you Larson?"

"Well, it's Pastor Ivan's messages on faith. Maybe I shouldn't bring them up but they seem to me to be out of balance and I want your opinion on the subject."

"Go on, what do you mean out of balance?"

"Well, he is not considering God's will in the matter. Jesus said that he did what he saw the Father do and He said what the Father said. Wouldn't He also pray what the Father wanted Him to pray? What makes us think that we would know better than God in any situation? I don't know maybe I'm out of line."

Childs gave him a big toothy grin, "You are growing up quickly, my young recruit. You have not stepped out of line; you have discerned correctly. That doctrine is what I refer to as hyper faith and is a perversion of the scriptures. Our pastor has some real flaws and we need to pray for him."

"I have to confess that I haven't been doing well when it comes to praying. I love the Bible and I'm still reading large portions of it at a time."

"Now is the time to start praying, and a lot. Just get off by yourself and talk to God. At some point, it will become natural to you like talking to Natalie, only with a lot more reverence. After all He is a King." Childs said with a smile. That ended the conversation about what was happening in the church. They talked about family and about what was happening at work.

Dean was met at home with John grabbing his leg and Natalie grilling him on where he had been and learning of his meeting with Childs. First things first, he grabbed up John and wrestled him to the floor, tickling him. After a little while, John became satisfied and sat on Dean's lap while he ate a warm supper.

Natalie sat across from him with a cup of coffee, waiting for Dean to talk to her. He started off easy, telling her about what he had discovered about Ivan's messages on faith. She thought for a few minutes and then complimented him on figuring that out. This did not deter her from wanting to know what Childs had said.

Dean took a deep breath and dove into their conversation. When he told her about the decision, he had made she took a deep breath. She took a sip of coffee. Dean could see the wheels turning, her mind weighing all that she had heard.

"Of course, I would have liked being in on this discussion, but I can see where there really was no other choice for you Dean. We are in this for better or worse. I love you, so I'm on board." Dean let the air out that he was holding in and sighed in relief.

They fortified their home by claiming the blood of Jesus on the building and the property. Dean had read something about anointing oil and purchased some olive oil from the store. They placed some on the door post of the home and sprinkled some over the four corners of the property. They added this little ceremony to their efforts after watching so many people being anointed for healing.

The next Sunday, they were ready for battle. They picked up Walker for church. He had been on duty the week before. They sat in a pew and a few minutes later, Matty came and sat at the other end. Walker was closest to her but Dean kept a close eye on her. She started to make a move towards Walker. He stood to shake her hand but Dean stood up next to him and prayed quietly to the Lord to bind those spirits that were in her. Her eyes got big and she shrunk away from them, going to another pew.

"What was that all about?" asked Walker sitting back down.

Dean leaned over and told him. It was Walker's turn to have big eyes. He looked at Matty and stayed away from her the rest of the service. He would not attend the church with them after that. He started going with Ramsey to his church. It was an eye-opening moment for Dean and Natalie, they decided to focus on praying against Matty.

Chapter 29

AMBUSHES AND ALLIES

The next Sunday, Dean and Natalie were a little late for service on purpose. They surveyed the congregation and spotted Matty. They sat two pews behind her and started praying against the spirits that were in her. In the beginning of the sermon, Matty suddenly laughed out loud. It caused Ivan to stop in midsentence and everyone looked her way. She grabbed her mouth and acted like she suddenly wasn't feeling well and left the building.

The Childs family came up afterwards, Isaiah, their son slapped Dean on the back and commented on the weird moment in the service. Dean looked around the sanctuary and noticed a lot more talk going on than average. Jason Childs held out his hand and Dean took it. Top used it to lead him away from the others.

"Nice shot Dean. I'm going to use that outburst to talk to Pastor Ivan about her."

"Natalie and I are going to focus on coming against her every time she comes through the doors."

"Listen, I told you that warfare in the spiritual is like warfare in the natural, so be cautious and don't become a casualty. You took a shot. It can open you up to an attack. Listen to your commander, Jesus, and He will see you through every situation. Do you understand?"

"I told you that it occurs around us and above us. That is why one of the names for the devil is the prince of the air. It does not take place in Heaven, where God has His throne. Your faith and prayers stir God to release His angels in this area to battle in your behalf. When there is any kind of victory on the behalf of either side it will manifest itself in some way. You won a small victory today when she laughed out load. It exposed her, but the battle for this body of believers has just begun. We all need to do some heavy praying."

Dean looked down, considered what he had heard. "Thanks, Top," he mumbled as he escorted his family to the door. Dean just nodded at Ivan and Lacy as they left the church.

They went home and Natalie fixed dinner. He usually played with the children, then did some Bible reading. This time, he went into their bedroom and used his concordance to look up every reference the devil appeared in scriptures. It made sense to know your enemy.

While he had been in Germany, they often had classes on the Soviet military. What they wore, what the equipment looked like, and their tactics. He studied every incursion that the devil made into the natural he could find. He only stopped for lunch and then found himself reading more scriptures about his enemy, the weapons he used, and his tactics.

At six in the evening, it all started running together, so he stopped and played with John before he had to go to bed. He helped feed Melody her last meal before she landed in the cradle. He sat with Natalie until nine.

Discussing what he had learned, she was able to shed some light on the subject. Much of his understanding came through the Spirit that gave him enlightenment on what he read in the Bible. He didn't get much sleep that night, as he would wake, thinking over every scripture that he had read that day.

He still felt alert at work and was getting things done when Ramsey interrupted him. George looked concern, asking him if he was alright. Walker had told him what was going on in the church. Ramsey wanted to know if it was alright to have their Bible group pray for the church and the Larson family. Dean thought about it for a little while before he answered.

"George, I don't want you to give the name of the church. In fact, I would like you to make it two separate situations. Make the prayer for the church very general in terms of some major problems facing the staff and congregation.

"I would like you to get very specific about the Larson family facing demonic opposition. I would prefer that you do not give our last names so they don't know exactly who we are. Do you think you can do that without giving things away?"

"You've got it, man. Lou and I are there for you," he said with a big smile.

"I can't tell you how much we appreciate you all taking time to do that. You all be wise and pray for protection for yourselves and your church also."

The next Sunday, they tried to ambush Matty again but she had brought a friend along. Whenever Dean and Natalie would pray against those demons, Matty would grab her friend. She would giggle out loud but would not leave the church. People would look at her but Ivan would continue the service, ignoring the outburst.

Dean noticed two other new people in the midst of the congregation. One woman had long hair, and a lean physique. She sat ahead of them on the right side of the building. The other visitor was a medium built lady in her mid-forties.

The Childs family did something that Dean had never seen them do before. Eve and Isaiah sat behind one of the new ladies while Jason and Esther took a pew behind the lean lady. You could tell that both of them felt uncomfortable during the service.

They would fidget and squirm in their seats but stayed. They then came over and shook Matty's and her friend's hand. This seemed to calm them and they left the church.

Dean was disappointed that Matty was able to stay through the whole service. He was able to look into the younger lady's face and nothing seemed to catch his attention until he saw her eyes, which seemed to be little black orbs with no life in them. It was unsettling and Natalie grabbed his arm and asked him what had just happened.

Dean had no answers for her. They wandered over to the Childs family to question them, but instead they got an invitation to a barbecue that evening.

At dinner, Childs not only cooked up some great hamburgers, but gave them some other food to digest. He wasn't sure, but thought that Matty was a member of a witch's coven and she had come in to scout out the church and see if it was open to demonic incursion of some kind. Apparently, they felt like they could cause some real problems because now there were three of them.

"Don't you mean four of them, Top?" suggested Dean.

"No, just three witches and a walking cauldron. Whenever the devils in them feel threatened, they will go to the woman that sat near Matty to be revived like we go to the Spirit of the Lord to be refreshed. We could see more of them; a coven usually has a least thirteen witches in it."

"Have you brought up these concerns to Ivan?" enquired Natalie.

"I uh well..." "He is part of the problem," interrupted Eve. She looked at her husband. "My husband is too much of a military man to bad mouth someone that is over him. I, on the other hand, don't mind calling a spade a spade and a heart a heart. When Jason told Ivan his concerns, all Ivan said was that she paid a large tithe and that he didn't believe in demon possession."

"How does he explain the giggling, the facial contortion like she is about give birth to a child?" remarked Dean. He was incredulous at what he had just heard.

"He believes that she has a real spiritual problem and that she needs to stay in church and get the help she needs. I did get him to call a board meeting, so we can discuss the problem in front of the elders. I'm supposed to present my arguments before them on Tuesday night. You might spend some extra time in prayer that evening."

"I just have to ask you, what is a walking cauldron?"

"Well, Natalie, I don't know if I can explain it very well myself. As I understand it, it's a brew of demons and incantations dwelling in a human chalice. Don't shake hands with that woman, she will drain you spiritually. Just continue to come against the witches."

It became very quiet. Dean considered what he had heard, but the thing that continued to come to his mind was, how did Jason Childs know all this? The final thought before they left to go home was, is he reading more into the circumstances than was really there? Still, he had seen that look in Matty eyes and how she had reacted when they had bound those spirits. The new woman's lifeless eyes told Dean all that he needed to know for now.

He took time out to play with the kids but after they went to sleep, Natalie and he discussed their visit with the Childs' family. Natalie was concerned that they had gotten in over their heads. She had never experienced any of this her whole time as a Christian.

Dean informed her they couldn't just back out now. He was not willing to run from this fight. He had not won every fight he had been in but he had never run from any. After she went to bed, he prayed for a while but never felt like he got anything from the Lord.

That week, Childs met with the board of elders and Jason, spoke openly about what he perceived was going on in the church. He said they were all polite and listened carefully. There were a lot of questions and then Ivan got up and suggested that a possessed person could not possibly sit under the preaching of the word or sit among the saints. There was a lot of discussion and at the end a vote was taken. Half of them sided with Childs suggestion that they confront the individuals and half of them agreed with Ivan to allow them to sit under the preaching in the hopes that it would change them. Ivan casted the tie breaker so they continued to let them remain in the church.

At the end of April, Dean took Walker out to a private going-away party.   He was getting out of the army at the end of May. They went out to Walker's favorite restaurant and then to one of the local bars so Walker could have a couple of beers and play some games of pool.

They stayed away from the subject of the church. They focused on the fun times they had in Baumholder and some of the times they had at Campbell. They talked about the dust of Grafenwöhr, the wild boars in the woods, and the men that they had served with. It was about ten p.m. when they decided to call it a night. It was not like the parties of old, it was a lot quieter.

Dean pulled out his keys to unlock the front door of the Mustang. He felt a cold breeze pass by him and silence fall like a blanket on them. The hair on the back of his neck stood up and fear knifed into his heart like a steel blade. He could see Walker look at him over the top of the car. His eyes were like small saucers.

"What the h- -l was that?"

"I think you just said it, Alan. I think hell has come a-calling."

The silence that engulfed them drowned out the juke box from the bar, the heavy traffic on the street about a hundred feet away, the sounds of the night, the crickets, and the birds.

Dean quickly pushed aside the fear and prayed the blood of Jesus over both of them and the car. He started to open the door slowly, but heard a small still voice tell him to stop. He was to stand still and see the salvation of the Lord. He suddenly saw a human form moving toward Walker. "Don't be afraid, Alan but something is about to happen," he said softly. He had to maintain his faith in what God had just whispered to him.

Al did not see the form; his back was towards it. He was still in expectation that Dean was going to quickly open the door and they were going to fly out of the area. The form got within a few feet of Walker when suddenly the man like creature jumped back as if in pain and there was an unearthly scream. The figure looked like a man without human features, it seemed to be holding its arm. Walker and Dean just about jumped out of their skins. Neither one of them had ever heard a shriek like that. Walker's eyes were no longer the size of saucers but they could have held a full dinner of food on them.

"Let's get out of here, now! You weren't kidding when you said something was about to happen." He tried to pull the door of the car open and looked frantically at Dean when he realized that it was still locked. The form was still visible to Dean and it was starting to circle his way."

"Don't be afraid Alan. Remember that the Lord is with us. Take a look to your left."

"My God, Dean. What is that thing?"

"Well, I'm assuming that is a demon sent to scare me. But watch, God is going to scare it back to where he belongs. Devil I command you to leave this place in the name of Jesus Christ of Nazareth." The form suddenly disappeared and the silence went with it.

"Man, let's get out of here. I've had enough excitement for one night. I thought this was going to be a quiet celebration, but you go and invite some ugly guest."

"Sorry, I didn't know we were going to have someone crash the party."

They both got into the car and Dean drove him back to base. Walker had several questions and Dean answered them as best as he knew.

"Who do you think sent the demon and what was it supposed to scare you into doing?"

"I think it was those witches at church. They are trying to drive Natalie and me away from our Christian family."

"I don't know. I'd be tempted to find a new bunch of believers to fellowship with."

"What do you mean. You did find a new church, you whimp."

"You're right, and I'm glad I did after that encounter of the worse kind. Why did it scream, was that just to scare us?"

"Not necessarily, I think it came in contact with the blood of Jesus and it got burnt badly, if you know what I mean.?"

"No, I am not sure what you mean by that?"

"You need to do a study on the blood of Jesus and then it will become real to you."

There was silence for most of the rest of the trip. Dean let Walker out at his barracks and Alan left with a comment that the next time they got together, it would be in the daylight hours.

When he got home, he told Natalie about his encounter with the demon. She was wide eyed and very attentive. He gave God the glory and the victory over his enemy.

The next Sunday, they were late as usual hoping to sit near Matty but when they came in, she was sitting in the last pew against the wall. She was sitting on one end of the seat and a young man was on the other end. Dean had never seen the young man, not knowing his name he prayed for him.

They took seats in front of them. They tried to focus on the service and yet keep tabs on what Matty was doing. Dean looked back at one point, and the young man and Matty were gone. The

Larsons later learned from Childs that Matty had talked the young man into taking her out for breakfast. She then seduced him into taking her to a motel room.

The young man later came into the office and confessed what had happened. They prayed over him. He told them that he was ashamed about the sin and didn't want to be a part of the church with Matty in it. They never saw the him again.

Once that came out in the open, the board met and they called Childs in to inform him about what had occurred and to ask his advice. He again suggested that they throw the four individuals out, inform the church what they were and that if anyone felt like they needed special prayer because of these individuals, they would do it behind closed doors. Again, the board was divided on the issue at hand.

They finally settled on confronting Matty and telling her to stay away from the men in the church. She would also be ordered to start counseling sessions from the pastor and his wife on a weekly time frame. After much discussion, the rest of the board members agreed to the compromise. They did not ask Jason what he thought of the plan, but he confided in Dean that he thought it was a bad idea and that they were opening themselves up to more problems.

Childs was hoping that this would drive her off, but she agreed to the board's requirements. She started meeting with Ivan and Lacy every Tuesday evening at seven p.m. She told them that she was sorry and shed a few tears over what she had done with the young man.

One beautiful Sunday morning after the service was over, they opened up the alters for prayer. Another young man by the name of Jeremiah Smith went up to the alter to seek the Lord. The witches never participated in this but Darla Bidwell, the one with the shorter woman, went up to lay hands on him. Childs started to get out of his seat, but Dean beat him to the altar.

Dean laid his hands on Jeremiah's other side and started praying. Darla looked up and gave him a dirty scowl, but Dean just smiled at her and kept praying. Dean could sense the battle that was going on in the young man. His tall thin frame would jerk slightly and his head would bob sideways until he suddenly threw off both sets of hands. He stood and turned to the back of the church and started running for the door. As he fled, he yelled "I choose Jesus!" The whole congregation watched as he exited, laughing and cheering him on. Most of them had no idea the battle that had just occurred for his soul.

Darla turned to Dean and snarled at him. Dean smiled back and gave her a small wave with his right hand. Indicating that she was dismissed. They both went back to their seats. Dean looked over to Jason and he gave him a thumbs up. Smith came back and professed that Christ was his savior. Isaiah quickly befriended him and they sat together every Sunday and became very close friends.

Chapter 30

DISTRACTIONS

The doctor looked at some things on his desk and turned to Dean who was still on the examination table. This was his second visit in a week. The doctor smiled at him and stood up. He was an older man with graying temples and thinning hair on top. His brown eyes were framed by black rimmed glasses and he was thin.

"Well young man, I have some good news and some bad news. You have given birth to an ugly little ulcer. You need to get rid of some of the stress in your life. The good news is I can prescribe some medicine that will clear up the problem but you need to look at your diet and eat more bland foods. Stay away from the Mexican restaurants. I'm betting that you are going to deploy down to Bragg for war games. You need to relax and keep your stress to a minimum."

"That's easier said than done," remarked Dean.

"I know, but you need to release that stress somehow. You might go to the gym and blow off some steam on one of the punching bags. Here's the prescription, you can fill it at the pharmacy here in the facilities."

He thanked the doctor and picked up his medicine. It was late morning so he went back to the office and reported back in. Rose was at the motor pool so Childs called him into his office and questioned him about his health. Dean had been having problems with his stomach since the middle of April. If he kept it fed or drank milk the pain seemed to subside and was manageable. He thought it would just go away but it kept getting worse.

He was not a real fan of doctors or hospitals because of his experience with them during the death of his mother. By the time they had figured out that she had cancer, it was too late. It had ended with a lot of heart-breaking visits to a sterile room and seeing her decline very quickly. Dean was able to say goodbye to her and two days later she was gone from his life forever.

He had asked several people to pray for him, but the Lord had found it fit not to heal him. When he told Childs about his health issues, Top had prayed over him and had suggested that it might be an ulcer.

His little problem seemed to badger him mostly at night. He would go to bed, start thinking about what was going on in the church and try to solve the problems in his own mind. If it wasn't that, it was what they needed to do for the deployment and on the maneuvers. He would fall asleep only to be painfully reminded of his stomach problems. He would get up drink some milk and pray for a while and eventually fall asleep again.

"So, I was right. It was an ulcer?"

"Yes Top, you were right," Dean said slightly irritated. In some ways he blamed Childs for pain in the 'As-' stomach. No, he thought, Top just confirmed what he felt like the Lord had told him. Here, he was doing what he thought God wanted him to do and He wouldn't heal him of his current problem.

"Larson, you are out of focus. You are concentrating on the problems instead of on the answer. Take those problems to Jesus and let him handle them, even the army stuff. Do what you can, then let Him do the rest. His shoulders are big enough to carry the load, nothing is too big for Him."

"I do, I've been praying about it all. I try not to stress about any of it."

"I have no doubt that you do Larson, but the Lord says you're picking it back up at night and you have no peace of mind. I want you to repent of your anxieties tonight and ask Him to put your thoughts at rest before you climb in bed. Don't forget to take your meds. Now get to work. We all have a lot to do before we go to Bragg."

Dean took his advice and that evening he slept well and felt rested the next morning. He was focused on God until things came up that demanded his undivided attention. Before he started them, he said a little pray and things seemed to go better throughout the day.

Two days before Walker left for home, they had him over for dinner. Dean was going to miss him. The army tried to get him to reup but Walker had a dream and a vision as to what he wanted to do with his life now and the army didn't have any place in it. He wanted to go to college for forestry and get a job in helping the environment.

At dinner, he told them about all the information he had gotten at one of the colleges back home. He loved John and left him a gift, a stuffed dinosaur before he went back to his quarters. John always called him Uncle Alan. It had melted his heart and he always played with John when he came to visit. Melody always scared him because she was so small. They ended the evening by discussing what was happening at church.

Walker went home two days later to family and college. He was a faithful friend, calling them once in a while and writing notes or short letters often. Even after they left Kentucky, he kept in contact with them as did Reed.

Dean and Natalie decided that they needed to get away from everything for a little while, so they planned on taking some kind of leave soon after the war games. They chose to go to Nashville and see as much as they could of the sites in between. Then they would go to Chattanooga and look over the Civil War battle sites and explore that city. Dean was excited about the trip and was looking forward to having some time off from everything.

The first Sunday in June, the church found six more witches coming and sitting among the congregation. This time four of the elders of the church sat behind the visitors and started praying against them. Natalie continued to focus on seeking the Lord about Matty.

Dean went and sat down behind a woman that was in her forties. He took note of her, that she not only looked ugly physically but the very spirits that moved in her repulsed the people around her. The people near her moved away from the woman. Dean started asking the Lord to bind those evil entities that resided in her and that He would send warring angels to drive them out of the church. It worked, the woman got up and left the church. Several others did the same and they never came back.

The four that had been there persisted. Matty caught another young man on the back bench. Dean tried to make friends with him and invited him to sit with them. He even offered the young man lunch. His name was Adam, but he indicated that he felt more comfortable sitting where he was. Matty had already talked to him. About a hour into the service Matty and Adam were missing from the rest of the congregation. They never saw Adam again.

At the service, Childs told them all that they needed to start praying that every lying, deceptive spirit would be bound and that the Spirit of Truth would prevail over the church. That all the things that were being done in darkness would be brought out in the light.

Some of the elders were stepping up and doing their part against the three witches, giving the Childs family and the Larsons a break. Four of the elders were getting more persistent about getting the four women to leave. Ivan continued to insist that Matty was starting to come around and was about to repent for her sins.

One of the elders spoke up stating that he saw no fruit of them turning from their transgressions, that they were being even more bold when doing evil. He indicated that the Spirit was not moving like it once did in the midst of the congregation and they were starting to lose members. Ivan countered by suggesting that if they could win Matty to the Lord, the others might repent also.

It became another stand off and things stayed the way they had been. Dean was very concerned about what was going on. The church was starting to become divided. He was reminded of a verse he had read where a little leaven thrown into the dough of the bread affected the whole loaf. It was starting to happen in the church.

He shifted his fucus to getting the gun and crew ready for deployment to Bragg. Having air assault training found him over-seeing getting some of the equipment ready to be loaded on to the C-130s. This kept him late at work. He hated the fact that they were going through this spiritual conflict and he being away from the family so much. He told himself that it was what it was and that he could only do what he could do.

He had read the Bible through one time and was about to finish it again, he was now in the book of Daniel, he just had to finish the minor prophets. It was helping him through the times he found himself in. Sometimes, he would come home from church and take two showers because of how he felt dealing with the spirits. He hated it and was looking forward to getting home, out of the army and away from witches.

Before they deployed, he took Natalie shopping to make sure that they had enough food while he was away. He wanted her to stay close to the home or visit Eve Childs, but he didn't want her out after dark. He didn't want her caught in the same situation that he had gone through with Walker at the bar. She made sure that they had plenty of provisions and assured him that they would be alright, that God would watch over them.

The Sunday before going to Bragg he spent most of the day loading the 3rd of the 319th on to the big planes so they could take off bright and early Monday morning. It was hot and humid like always and though he had plenty of help, it seemed like it took forever. The loads resisted them at every turn.

Finally, they took a little break and Dean sat down by himself with a cup of coffee in his hand. He took out a pocket size Bible that a Gideon had given him some years back and read a couple of passages. The verses didn't really speak to him, but he did find some peace in them. He prayed a little prayer asking for a little divine help and direction concerning the work at hand.

Things went better and the loads seem to fit in the big bays like pieces of a puzzle. They had to make sure that the weight of the equipment was evenly dispersed for logistic purposes and so that it could be unloaded quickly. The crew also needed to leave room for the troopers to get to the mesh seats along the walls of the plane.

Dean hated the seats, they had the ability to cut off the blood flow from portions of your body, putting things to sleep and making it very difficult to exit anything in a hurry. They finally finished up about six that evening.

Dean was so worn out he didn't even have the energy to wrestle with John. He ate dinner, read a chapter in Daniel, took a shower, and was in bed by nine thirty. He awoke from the angry clanging of the alarm clock.

Natalie had the kids up, feed, and dressed. He ate breakfast and quickly got his uniform on. She took him to the barracks gave him a big kiss and left him. He met Ramsey and they both went to check the section to make sure they had all their gear.

This deployment would be a new experience to most of them. Dean warned them about the seats and that they needed to hold on to their gear tight when exiting the plane or they could be chasing after it through the fields near the landing strip.

They loaded up and Dean immediately took out his earplugs, yelled at his men, lifted the plugs in the air, and placed them in his ears. They did the same, once the big turbo props started up, they all knew why. You could lose your hearing real quick with even a short trip from the sound of the big engines. Dean spent time reading his Bible and praying. Ramsey sat right next to him but it was a waste of time trying to talk.

A couple of hours later, they found themselves on the ground once again and, as Dean had warned them, things started flying once they emerged out the back of the plane. The turbo wash from the engines blew helmets off heads and items out of hands. Ramsey and Dean laughed as two of their PFCs chased a helmet and some personal items amongst the trees near the field.

Dean was looking forward to three things when it came to Bragg: It would be his last trip there, he would be going on leave soon after they got back, and he was hoping to connect with Morton and family while he was at the base. Natalie and Carrie had been exchanging letters ever since they had left. They all moved into the wooded area away from the strip so the next plane could taxi.

Chapter 31

THE RIGHT TIME
THE RIGHT WEAPON

They had already zeroed in to a certain area. Ramsey was told to fire the star cluster which he quickly ordered the rest of the crew to do. The round flew out of the tube and traveled quickly down range. The projectile burst high in the air, lighting up the ground below. Troops from the 82nd Airbourne were caught in the open. A bunch of imaginary rounds were put on the area, causing a large amount of imaginary casualties. The battery put out about ten rounds a piece from six guns into the area before a cease fire was ordered. A road march was ordered and the guns were convoyed to another location.

Ramsey asked Dean to go with the advance party. He climbed into the Chinook helicopter with the rest of the men and sat back in the seat. It only took them about fifteen minutes to get to their next destination. The men quickly exited the chopper and formed a defensive perimeter.

Once the area was secured, Top and Captain Bradberry laid out the positions for the different sections. Dean had to admit that Bradberry was very good at his job. That didn't mean Dean liked him, he didn't, but he had to admire the way Bradberry handled the battery. Dean was stomping down grass and getting the area

473

ready for the gun when he felt something welling up inside of him. He had never felt it before.

He sensed that it was a warning of danger. He looked around closely but saw nothing. He knew he didn't have to worry about wild boars, but he had been told that there were Water Moccasins, Copper Heads, and Rattle Snakes in the area. He turned on a small light, took the butt of the rifle, and swept the grassy area with it like sweeping the floor with a broom. Suddenly the head of a Copper Head raised out of the blades of grass. He started beating the area with the butt of the rifle catching a portion of the body. He spotted it slithering thought the grass and struck at it again but it escaped back into some bushes. Top came over to see what was going on. Dean informed him about the reptile.

"Is the warning over?" asked Childs.

Dean stood there, searching for what was going on inside him. It had subsided, but now it was back stronger than ever before. "No, it is still with me. What is this? I have never felt it before."

Top looked around. Everyone was taking it easy, waiting for the convoy to appear. It would take time to take things down, line up for the road march cover the distance to this area. "It is a warning that someone is in trouble. Who comes to mind when you sense it?"

"Natallie, but she should be home safe and sound."

"It doesn't matter what you think. You need to pray for her Larson."

"I don't even know what to say."

"You need to let it flow; the Spirit knows what to pray." He touched Dean's stomach and Dean started praying in a language that he had never spoken before. He could feel anger and knew it was against some kind of spirit. He went about his business and continued to praying at the same time. All of a sudden, he could feel it break and the danger warning in his heart lifted. He knew the battle was over.

Top came over and questioned him if it was done yet. Dean nodded that it was over. Childs informed him that he had to pray the same way for Eve and that it was also finished. Both of them wanted to call their wives badly to see what had transpired, but they would have to wait until they got to a phone.

While this was taking place, Natalie spilled the baby formula as she was trying to fix Melody's evening bottle. It was her last can and it was almost full. She debated whether she should scrape the top portion that was on the floor back into the can and use it anyway. Melody wasn't complaining too much.

John was getting ready for bed and she would have to take him out in the night air. Carrie was no longer around to baby sit. John was tired and a little fussy. She missed Carrie. The new neighbors were a young married couple that partied a lot and weren't very interested in getting to know the Larsons. She swept up the mess and rocked Melody in the chair. This quieted her for a little while, but as the evening wore on the little girl started getting more demanding about food.

Finally, Natalie gave in. She got John out of bed, dressed him in a jacket, and wrapped Melody in a blanket, and loaded them in the car. She drove quickly to the nearest store which was a pharmacy. It wasn't busy, just a few cars in the parking lot. There were two clerks, a man and a woman, and the woman was dealing with two customers at the cash register.

Natalie found the formula and rushed up to the checkout stand. She was feeling uneasy, as if someone was watching her. She was in a hurry, but the clerk knew the guy in front of her and was taking her time visiting with the customer. They were flirting with one another.

Melody started crying and this hurried the transaction along, neither one of them wanted to listen to a baby screaming. Natalie paid for the item and rushed out to the car, she wanted to get back home as soon as possible.

She was about fifteen yards from the car when the door suddenly flew open. The form of a man appeared in the back seat. Even though the car light shined brightly, she couldn't see any features, just a black silhouette. What's more, it was fighting with some unseen force. It was trying to maintain its position, but was losing the battle. It was like an unseen leg kicked it out of the seat, the form landed on the pavement and slowly got up. Again, there was no sound, even Melody had stopped fussing and John was hanging on for dear life to his mother's leg. There were no birds, crickets, or traffic noise, just deathly silence. Fear fell on her like a blanket. She wanted to run for the entrance to the store.

Just as suddenly as fear took hold of her emotions, a peace fell on her, driving the feeling away. A small still voice told her to turn to the store and walk slowly inside. The Lord told her to get the male clerk and ask him to escort her to her car, that she had seen an intruder in it.

Natalie did exactly that.   When they came out, the door to the car was still open, but no one was in sight. They checked the inside and found no one. He asked if she wanted the police to come out and investigate it, but she was sure that they would never find the intruder.

She speeded home, making it safe and sound. Melody was soon fed and John back in his bed sleeping. Natalie could only sit on the couch for a long period of time, thinking about what had just occurred. Once in a while, the hairs on her arms and the back of her neck would stand on end as she relived the experience.

Two miles away during the same time frame Eve and Esther were enjoying watching Isaiah play a baseball game. He was up to bat and had one ball and one strike. The pitcher threw a fast ball to the outside corner of the home plate. It was the kind of pitch Isaiah loved. He leaned into it and swung the bat with all his might. He connected, hitting it to left center field. The outfielders were out of position, the ball hit the ground and bounced off the fence. Isaiah had a stand up double.

The team needed one run to tie the game and two to win, it was the last inning and they either got the hits here or they went home with a loss. They had one out and Isaiah was hoping one of the batters would get enough of a hit so that he could score.

The next player that came up to the home plate was an average hitter. His first two swings were a foul ball and a strike. The next pitch was a ball. Isaiah kept cheering him on, encouraging him to pick a good pitch. His teammate swung again and fouled it off into the stands. "That's it, only this time get the whole thing." shouted Isaiah. He did.

The ball went zipping by Isaiah's head, a hardline drive landing in the outfield and rolling all the way to the fence. Isaiah took off running, the third base coach gave him the go ahead, so he rounded third base in full stride. He looked to his left and saw the second baseman catch the ball. The infielder hesitated just for a moment, deciding to try to throw Isaiah out at home. This gave Isaiah some extra steps and he took advantage. The man threw it home and Isaiah slid under the throw. He was safe and the go ahead run was secure on second.

He had hurt himself on the slide, injuring his ankle. He got up and hobbled to the bench. One of his teammates came out to help him to the dugout, but Isaiah would not sit. He insisted on watching the next batter and leaned up against the fence. The coach offered to tape his ankle up, but he would not sit down; he wanted to cheer on his teammate. The next batter went to the plate, his first pitch was a ball but the next one was a hard fast ball and he connected, knocking it over the fence. The game was over and Isaiah's team had won. As the two players made it around the bases, Isaiah sat down and one of the coaches started working on his foot.

Eve and Esther made their way through the crowd and sat down by his side. They were ecstatic over the win and talked about it while the coach checked out the ankle, trying to determine if it was broken or not. The other ball players came by, asking him how he was doing and giving him high fives.

After the examination, the coach felt it was a sprain and not a brake. He wrapped it and ran to a nearby shed to get a pair of crutches they kept around for such cases. By the time he had finally found them, everyone had cleared out except for the four of them. The coach gathered up his equipment, threw it in the back of the pickup and disappeared into the night.

They slowly made their way to the car. The night had turned eerie and the shout of the crowds had faded away, being replaced by a deafening silence. Eve was reaching for the door handle when the hairs on the back of her neck stood up. She stepped back and looked around. She saw nothing but sensed that something or someone was watching them.

"Do you feel what I'm feeling?" She asked both kids.

"Yes, what is it?" asked Esther.

"Well, it ain't no Santa Claus," stated Isaiah.

"It's demonic, so let's pray." Eve took their hands and they started praying in the Spirit, and demanding that the evil spirit be gone in the name of Jesus Christ. After ten minutes, it lifted and they started hearing the birds chirping and frogs croaking again. They took a deep breath at the same time. Being married to Jason, she had run into similar situations so she knew that Jesus was the answer to this problem. They quickly got into the car and went home.

It was morning and a crowd gathered near a line of trees that skirted the meadow where they set up the guns. It was early but Dean had a fresh cup of coffee and was waiting on breakfast. He wandered over to the area with Taylor following him.

"What's going on?" enquired Taylor.

"Don't know, let's go find out."

The men had made a wide circle and kept hitting something that was on the ground. As they got closer, they could see something slithering in the grass. It was a copper head and he was highly agitated

"It's a d- -n snake, what are they doing playing with a snake? Is it poisonous?"

"Taylor, you need to know what can bite you and make you sick or dead. That is a copper head and it will make you sick, if not kill ya."

"Then what are they doing playing with it? They trying to make it a pet or something?"

"No man, they're just keeping it corralled, setting it up for a final goodbye.

One of the other gunnery sergeants always carried a machete with him for such occasions and he suddenly appeared with it. He allowed the serpent to raise its ugly head, then there was a quick swipe with the big knife from the sergeant. The head went one way while the main body wiggled in every direction. Dean started moving closer, while Taylor was slowly backing away. Dean turned to him to wave him closer. He wanted Taylor to know what it looked like so if he ever saw another one, he would stay clear.

"Come on Taylor, get a closer look so you know what this rascal looks like."

"Naw, I'm close enough," the broad smile that was always creasing his face was now a very large scowl.

"Hey man, the thing is dead, it can't hurt you now."

"I doubt that it is dead enough for me. I don't like snakes or, for that matter, any creepy thing so I will pass on coming closer."

The mistake Taylor had made was he had declared that loud enough for the rest of them to hear. The sergeant picked up the wiggling body and came toward Taylor with a mischievous grin. "Here Taylor, it is going to get you," he yelled.

Taylor turned and started running. Dean estimated that he was at a full gallop within about four steps. He didn't look back, he just ran. If he had looked back, he would have found the sergeant had only taken four or five steps and had stopped. It would have not mattered; he would never have caught up to Taylor. Taylor's travels took him to the closest gun near them, he jumped up on the tire, over the breach, on to the other wheel, and down to the ground. He ducked under the tube of the next gun and quickly passed through the rest of the meadow. He finally stopped, hiding behind a tree at the edge of the field. Everyone was laughing so hard that no one would have been able to pick up the chase. Most of the battery saw the fleet-of-foot Taylor make the mad dash to save himself from a dead snake.

Breakfast was finally ready, most everyone gathered around the mess tent. About fifteen minutes later, Taylor wandered in to eat. He received a lot of ribbing from everyone before he got his food. The best one was that he should not eat anything that look-ed like chicken, it was actually snake. Taylor took it well; he had regained that big smile and gave some smart remarks back.

They had several fire missions that day, moved one more time, and spent the evening at the last position. The next day they road marched back into base and the war game was over. They were told not to go anywhere alone and to stay out of trouble. Ramsey's gun crew stayed together for the most part. One of the men and Ramsey were assigned to help load up the equipment. Dean talked most of them into going to the PX with him. He immediately called Natalie and she told him what had happened. He told her how the Lord had moved him to pray for her.

He then called the Morton Residence and got ahold of Carrie. She was glad to hear from him. They had been told by Natalie that Dean was going to get in touch with them. Carrie got in touch with Kevin and he took the rest of the day off. Morton picked him up at the PX, so the rest of the section left Dean and went to one of the bars to get a few beers. Dean warned Taylor to make them be on their best behavior and to stay away from trouble.

Morton showed up after about a fifteen-minute wait. He had not changed much and he still loved the army. Dean looked at the base while Kevin drove, he noticed that they had the emblem back on top of the headquarters building. He laughed to himself knowing the truth about what had happened to it. Kevin took him to a small house off base that had two bedrooms. Carrie had made it very homey and the two girls were growing up fast. Betty was the perfect image of her mother and sister. She seemed to have a more outgoing personality and was a little more aggressive like her father. Dean played with the girls and visited at the same time. They had lunch and talked about what was going on in each of their units. Dean stayed away from a conversation about the church, but was glad to hear that they had found a good body of believers to fellowship with. Morton had not gone to jump school yet, but he was scheduled for the next session.

"I guess Rose and Bradberry are going up this afternoon to make a jump."

"What, didn't you want to go up with them?" snickered Morton.

"No, I have no desire to rub elbows with Bradberry, I think he's a big jerk. Besides I do not want to float down to the ground hanging on to a bedsheet from ten thousand feet up."

"Ah, yes but you got to love them. Now, that's what the good book says," Morton said with a broad smile.

"Yeah, that's what it says, but I remember you complaining about him enough. Besides, the Bible says we have to love them, but it doesn't say we have to like them. I don't like the man or how he treats others.

"I just think he has this superior attitude. He's Airbourne. I get that all the time when they look at my air assault badge. Then they ask me why I'm not Airbourne and when I tell them that I'm going to the school, they say 'good' and leave me alone. So, I can't talk you into reupping and going to jump school with me? I would put off going if you would come along for the ride. We had so much fun at air assault."

"No way, I want to be assaulting books in a year. You are a lifer, man. Poor Carrie, she is going to be lugging the luggage while you chase tanks for twenty years."

"Yes, but I'll be retired in twenty years while you're still trying to teach kids what the Revolution was all about."

"After being in the army for all those years, you deserve to retire in twenty years."

Carrie got up to refill the coffee mugs, patting Kevin on the shoulder. "He's worth following around, he's a good man and I love him," she said smiling.

"Well, you must see more than I see in him," laughed Dean. They all laughed and made fun of each other for the next few minutes. The Morton's started wading into what was going on in the church, but Dean would not discuss the problems.

Kevin took Dean back to base and escorted him over to the area where the unit was spending time before they left the next morning. Morton wanted to see some of his friends in the unit. Childs and him had always gotten along as well as some of the rest of the men. The camp seemed to be in some turmoil as they approached. Taylor came running out to meet them. He was a little out of breath, so it took him a few minutes to spit the word out.

"The BC had an accident when he jumped out of the plane. I guess his static lines got tangled up and he landed hard, they think he broke his back. He's in bad condition, they do figure he's going to live but he's not going back home with us.

"How's smoke?" asked Dean.

"Oh, he's fine, he saw it all happen. You know I don't think he liked Bradberry, I wonder if he messed with his chute?"

"Taylor, that's how rumors get started so stow that thought in that tiny little brain of yours," Dean said in an angry manner. He knew Rose well enough that he would not put another soldier in a place they might be killed. Yes, hurt them, but not murder them. They went to the CP and found Top, Rose, and the XO, Lieutenant Patton, discussing the situation. They stopped for a few minutes to say hello to Kevin, but asked all of them to leave so they could talk about the BC in private.

Kevin went to the different gun sections visiting with old friends while Dean talked to the men of his section about what they had heard.   He put a stop to any rumors, especially about Rose. He gave them the facts as he knew them and told them to wait for the official word from Top or Rose. Kevin came over to Dean and hung out with them, waiting for a report from the hospital.

"Hey man, do you want to still go to jump school?" Dean said with a very serious look on his face."

"Yes. It's sad that he got hurt, but it is what I want to do."

"Next, you will want to go to ranger school."

"Now that's a thought." Kevin said grinning.

The time seemed to drag and though most of the men didn't like Bradberry, they respected him and didn't want to see anyone get hurt. Finally, Patton came out and commanded everyone to get into formation. He called them all to attention and then ordered them to be at ease.

He informed them that the BC was conscious and breathing on his own. That he had motor skills in his upper body but that he was paralyzed from his waist down. He told them they would be deploying back to Campbell as scheduled. He dismissed them and searched Morton out. They went into the CP and they had a good visit with Childs and Rose. Dean would be the last to say farewell to his good friend and a tough trooper. As Morton left, he turned one last time to wave at Dean. They would never see each other again. Carrie kept in touch with Natalie, writing her about their many adventures. Eventually, the letters would get fewer as time passed until the Larsons heard from them no more.

The flight back to Campbell couldn't be fast enough. Natalie was waiting for him at the airfield. The first thing that they discussed in the car was Bradberry's accident. She was shocked and glad that Dean had not gone to Airbourne school. They were up late in the evening discussing the events that occurred during their separation.

Chapter 32

TIME OF REST

The Grand Old Opry. Dean didn't think he would ever see it, but there he was listening to Johnny Cash and having a great time. Cash was singing a lot of his best hits and Dean was enjoying all of them. The problems were far away from his thoughts, Natalie and he were relaxing. They were resting in what Childs had told them just before they went on leave. The battle was over and when they came back, things would be different.

Natalie and the kids were back at the hotel resting from the trip. She had insisted that he go see the show by himself. They knew the kids would not like all the noise and Dean loved listening to Johnny. The performance was everything that he had hoped for, Cash was a wonderful artist, keeping the audience entertained. Natalie was still up reading a book, but she was worried about him because he was about an hour and half late getting back.

She gave him a hard time about losing his way. They settled down and went to bed. They both slept soundly. Melody woke them up in the morning wanting to be fed and John attacked his father, who was still lying in bed. Natalie fed Melody while Dean got dressed and took care of John. Dean finished taking care of Melody while Natalie got dressed. They went out to breakfast, went back to the hotel, and lounged around the pool for several hours. They wanted to see several things pertaining to the Civil War, but they just wanted to take it easy the first day.

The next day they visited Fort Negley, it was built by the Union Army after they took Nashville. It never saw much action, but was a sound fortification. It was constructed out of stone and John loved running free around the grounds. They also went to Fort Nashboro which was where Nashville started and covered two acres of ground. It was constructed to keep the wild animals and Indians out. Again, John took the lead and directed the exploration of the facilities. Dean took a lot of pictures of the family and the area they explored. He wanted to use them when he was teaching.

They traveled to the Jackson Hermitage where President Andrew Jackson lived. The brochures they were reading showed how he had added to the home over the years while he lived there. It was a beautiful building. This time, Dean led the way in searching out the grounds and home. They kept John close to them. John had worn down somewhat. Dean was carrying him a lot of places. It was time to go back to their room and get some rest.

After a good night sleep, they visited the Country Hall of Fame and Museum, getting a look at the lives of the rich and the famous men and women that made it big in the music business. John and Melody were starting to complain about all the travel and walking. After the Hall of Fame, they visited some of the neighborhoods traveling slowly, and looking at the old mansions and the well-manicured properties. From there, they went to the State Capitol Building which was a unique building. There was a lot of history recorded inside. Then it was back to the hotel where they spent time around the pool.

They spent some time in the hotel room and near the pool the next day. After lunch they went to Opry Land. The kids were too young to ride most of the attractions. Dean and Natalie would take turns entertaining the kids and experiencing the thrill of the rides.

Dean would have enjoyed being with his wife on some of them, but that was a part of being a parent.

John was in the midst of a growth spurt, so if you fed him some food, he seemed to be happy. Melody was mellow as long as she had her bottle when she was hungry and they paid attention to her, she seemed content. They spent most of the rest of the day in the park, then back to the room and resting.

They left for Chattanooga the next day. On the way, they took a detour to a nearby lake, renting a small cabin. They spent a night and a day there, resting up and swimming in the lake. John loved it, playing in the sand and getting his feet wet in the lake. Melody finally got the hang of the sand, as she kept trying to eat it. Natalie had to keep running over to her and scooping the dirt out with her fingers.

It was a very pleasant time and it reminded Dean of the Snake River, his father would take Jack and him to the river once in a while and they would just fish or wade in the water. Now he was making good memories with his family and he felt blessed. The last few months had been filled with conflict in one way or another. It was good to be free of it for a little while.

Natalie had made all the arrangements and their first night in Chattanooga was spent in the Read House which had been constructed in 1926. They got a room in the Tower which gave them a view of the city and the mountains that surrounded it.

When it came to the Civil War in Tennessee, this is the city that Dean wanted to visit. The Confederate Army had the Union troopers besieged in the city while they held the high ground. Eventually the northern armies would break the siege and it was a large victory for them in the war in the west.

They spent most of the day in their room looking at the mountains and watching the city going about its business. Finally, night fell and the city seemed to reach up to the sky and become a part of it; it's light and darkness blending with the night.

They went to another hotel the next day, one that was not so expensive and spent the rest of the day visiting the sites in the city. They went to the Southside Railroad Baggage Building that was built in 1870. While they were in the area, they went to the Railroad Museum. They went down the streets visiting some of the old homes that had been constructed at the turn of the century. In this area they found some more of those beautiful old mansions. They finished the day by visiting Ruby Falls, the nation's tallest underground water falls. They had never seen anything like it and Natalie was spellbound by it. The water was crystal clear in the pool that it formed. The greens and blues in the cave were wonderful. That particular sight ended the day and it was good since the kids were getting fussy.

Early the next morning, they took the train up to Look Out Mountain. This was one of the high points that the Confederate Army held while they observed the Union Army in the city. A Civil War cannon still marked the spot.

Again, Dean took a lot of pictures, hoping to use them some day in his classroom. He could almost picture the battle that broke the siege, imagining the Union blue charging up the hill toward the Confederate lines, breaking through, and causing the rebel army to retreat. He turned away, but a thought suddenly struck him so he looked the battlefield over again. He wondered what spiritual entities fought a long side the soldiers and who was praying. He put that thought aside and once again focused on his family.

John was fascinated with the cannon, but what kept his attention the most was going up and down on the train. It also kept Natalie's focus, since she did not like how steep it was. The budget demanded that they start for home the next morning, so they stayed close to the hotel room and the pool for the rest of the day. Melody and John loved playing in the water.

They took a long scenic route home; the state reminded him a lot of Germany. It had a lot of forest with beautiful green rolling hills.   Germany was less humid, but Tennessee had a lot more sunshine. They stopped at a couple places to stretch their legs or to read something about the local history. It was late when they got home and everyone went to bed early.

Dean slept in to seven am, but was soon up reading his Bible and drinking a cup of coffee. Melody was awake at nine which stirred the rest of the household to the kitchen. They had breakfast and lounged around until the latter part of the afternoon. They went to the store to fill the cupboards and the fridge. It was a Thursday and they relaxed at home the rest of the day.

Friday, Dean went into the battery to see how things were going. It was in the afternoon and most of the men were at the motor pool. Top was busy talking to Ramsey, so Dean sat down and talked with Clark.

The clerk informed him that Bradberry was doing better, but he still had no feeling in his legs. The captain had informed everyone that at some point he would walk again. Patton was doing a good job of running the battery and everyone was hoping that he would be promoted and take charge, but that was doubtful. Clark had gone to Willie's wedding, which occurred when the unit had been down to Bragg. Clark had taken leave and was an usher at the nuptials. Arthur had showed up as best man. They talked about it once when Dean was back from Bragg, but now he had time to discuss the wedding in more detail.

Clark said that she was a real bomb shell, a beautiful blonde, and she had Willie right where she wanted him. She demanded they call him by his rightful name, which was Willian and they could also forget about the word 'wild' with his name. "I can't believe she had roped him, tamed him, and branded him,' Clark said laughing. "I didn't think that could ever happen to him."

About that time, Top's door opened and Rose and Ramsey walked out.

"It's about time you came back to work Larson. I was about to declare you AWOL," announced Rose.

"Now, you know I would never go AWOL while you're my Chief of Smoke. You have put the fear of God in me. I would never give you a reason to smile by reporting me missing." Smoke turned quickly to hide a little smile as he left. Rumors were still being circulated that Smoke had something to do with Bradberry's static lines.

Ramsey grabbed a hold of Dean's arm to talk to him, but Childs called him into the office. Dean told Ramsey that he would catch up with him later. He was glad that Top stopped him, he was hoping he would have news about the church. Childs told him to sit down looked at him with a very somber expression. He then gave him a slight smile.

"It's over, Matty is gone and I'm afraid the Normans have also left."

"What happened Top?"

"Well, I guess Ivan was spending a lot of late nights at church. Lacy decided to investigate her husband's new work ethics. She caught him and Matty, let's just say, in a very compromising position. She took a broom that was nearby and started beating both of them. She left after Ivan took the broom from her, but she wasn't done.

"She went storming over to two of the board members and informed them that Ivan had talked her into doing some underhanded things with the money. They checked things out and found that she was right. It didn't matter, his infidelity would have been enough for correction or dismissal. The elders that had been supporting him also stepped down. They're going to repent before the congregation this Sunday."

Silence filled the room and they just stared at each other. Dean didn't know what to think. He was relieved, it was over but who else was a casualty of this ugly little battle. Matty was still a witch, the Normans had been caught up in some of the snares of the enemy. He wondered if all the people who had left the church had found another church or if they gave up on Christianity all together.

"Victory, Larson. We have ourselves victory on many fronts."

"Yes, but at what cost Top. How many did we lose in all this?"

Childs shook his head and looked down at his desk. Dean left quietly.

Dean caught up with Ramsey and they discussed some things but a few seconds after he left him, he couldn't remember their conversation. He rushed home and gave Natalie the news. They put a Christian record on the stereo and worshiped the Lord for the victory He got over the witches and the powers of darkness.

Chapter 33

SAYING GOOD-BYE

Dean looked at the ugly gas mask in his hand. A week before he was to start the process of getting out of the army and he was at the gas chamber, about to enter, and take the mask off so he could get a good dose of tear gas. He tried to talk his way out of it, but Rose seemed to enjoy messing with him lately.

"Hey short timer! Put the mask on and lead those three others into the chamber," said Rose with his stony expression.

"Yes, Smoke."

Dean donned his face mask, cleared it, and led the other three men into the building. As they entered, four men were exiting. Their masks were in their hands, they were coughing, choking and wiping tears from their eyes. The room was foggy, indicating that it was filled with gas and the fumes pricked at their skin, making them want to leave.

It was an odd sensation that Dean couldn't really describe. A few of the NCOs would come up to the four soldiers and tap them on the shoulders, and then the men would take their mask off and breath in the gas. After they were tortured sufficiently, they were released toward the door to gulp in fresh air.

Dean felt the tap on his shoulder and removed his mask. His nose instantly started running and his eyes were burning. It was a nasty sensation and he was glad to finally get that second tap that allowed him to move toward the exit. They had to guide him to the wall, which allowed him to feel his way out the door. The humidity seemed to add to the crawling feeling on his skin, but the air smelled good. He gulped in a couple of large breaths between coughs to clear his lungs and nasal passages. After a little while, he started feeling normal again. He was glad it was over with; the rest of the week was filled with routine things on the schedule.

"Well, Larson are you going to forget us?"

It was Rose and he was staring at him. Dean stared back at him and smiled. "How could I ever forget my time with the 101st Airbourne Division and you're smiling face."

Smoke grunted and left. The rest of the day was spent in the motor pool doing maintenance on the equipment. The morning plunge into the chamber added to the misery of the hot July day. When they had the late afternoon formation, Dean felt a tap on his shoulder. It was Smoke, and he was holding a pen toward him.

"Here's a pen, Larson. I know that you're so short that you can't reach over your boots, so I will carry you to the office so you can sign those reup papers."

The whole section had stopped in their tracks to hear Dean's response. Dean smiled and turned to Rose. Dean suspected that Rose had very few friends but almost everyone respected him. "Now, Smoke, I'm almost tempted, but I'm going to pass. I have to confess I'm going to miss that smiling face of yours and the kind way you treat me."

Rose broke down laughing and everyone joined in. Dean had never heard him laugh and it was a great outburst that came way up from the belly. He finally gained control and everyone stopped giggling.

"Larson, you're the only one that I have ever met that can say that kind of s- -t to me and get away with it. I don't know what it is about you, but I am going to miss you. Take care of yourself and the family. Hope to run into you some day." He held out his hand and Dean shook it.

Rose turned to leave, but Larson called him and when he turned, Dean came to attention and saluted him to show respect for the last time. Rose returned it and that was how they said good-bye.

On Friday, Ramsey had Lou invite the Larsons over to a farewell barbecue. The section was invited to attend. All of them came and Natalie jumped in to help Lou fix the food. Ramsey brought out the beer, but Dean and Ramsey drank lemonade.

The men sipped at their beers and everyone stayed fairly sobber. They talked over the various adventures that they had participated in. Dean questioned them about some of their future plans. Taylor admitted that he liked the army and that he was thinking about staying in.

They all reminded him of his fear of snakes and that if he was going to survive Campbell, he would have to get past that little flaw in his character. They laughed as they recounted the story and this time, Taylor could laugh with them.

Ramsey got up and started cooking the hamburgers and hotdogs. It was a very relaxing occasion. They recounted the way Rose treated Ramsey and Dean. They were amazed at how they were able to joke with Rose and no one else was. Someone brought up the rumor that Rose had gotten rid of Bradberry by messing with his static lines.

Dean was about to correct that rumor, but stopped when he was reminded of a conversation that he had with Smoke. He had come straight out and asked Rose if he had tampered with the captain's parachute lines. He expected Rose to jump all over him. Smoke looked at him in a very hard way and then asked him if he thought he would have done that to the BC. Dean looked right back at him and told him "No."

"Soldier you are correct in your assumption. Even if you don't like the guy, you look out after each other. Just as you watched over Ramsey during his hard times. You take care of one another, because in combat that can mean your life."

"Why don't you deal with these rumors that are flying around?"

"The people that need to know, know it was an accident. Even if I stood before the battery and denied any wrongdoing, some would think it was a lie. I allow the rumors to spread because those people don't know if I won't do it to them." he said with a slight smile. He turned to leave and stopped, turned back, and pointed a finger at Dean. "Don't think for a minute I won't throw you off the top of the barracks if you tell anyone."

The food was great and the men seemed to enjoy the home cooked meal. Lou dominated the conversation once she sat down to eat. She had learned to relax around the Larsons, but with new faces at the table she was always in motion. Natalie would try to get her to settle down, but she was always saying something or serving food to one of the guests. George just sat there, would say something to one of the soldiers, or smile at his wife. You could tell that they adored one another by the smiles that they would exchange or the gentle touches.

At the end of the meal, Ramsey presented a toast to the Larsons with apple cider. He wanted to thank them for being the best kind of friends. Caring loving people that stuck with everyone in times of trouble. He lifted his glass to Dean and toasted him for being one of the best soldiers that he had ever served with while being in the army.

Taylor then stood with a small plaque in his hand, it had the artillery emblem on it with Dean's name. It read, "Our Soldier of the Year" on it. It also had all their names on it. Dean was touched and was at a loss of words. He wiped away a couple of tears and thanked them.

Soon after that, the men slowly disappeared after saying goodbye and shaking Dean's hand. They all told him that it had been a privilege serving with him. Taylor seemed to linger, as though he wanted to do or say something. He wandered over to the food and picked out a small desert and slowly ate it. Both Dean and Ramsey watched him for a few minutes while he hovered in the area.

"What's up Taylor?" asked Ramsey.

Taylor came over to them and sat down. "I just wanted to thank both of you for being there for me. My old man went missing on me years ago and you two have been like a father to me. I've learned so much from you. Well, Sergeant Larson, I'm going to miss you like crazy. I'm going to stay in the army, but if I ever get out Idaho way, can I come see you?" He said it with a shaky voice and wiped a tear from his eyes.

Dean was so touched; he gave Taylor a manly hug. Taylor, you are always welcome at my home. I'm betting you're going to make sergeant someday soon, just watch after your men and take care of Ramsey here. Oh, and stay away from those snakes." He said with a laugh and it lightened the mood.

Taylor just grinned. Thanks, Sarg, I'll keep all that in mind. I'm not a writer, so keep in touch with Ramsey, I want to know how you are doing." He held out his hand, Dean stood took it and shook it vigorously. "I'll see you Monday in formation," Dean said smiling.

With all the guests gone Lou and Natalie finally sat down and all of them had a final cup of coffee. They talked about future plans. Dean reiterated his hope of going to college next fall. Natalie was excited about getting back home to her family and reconnecting. Ramsey was talking about retiring in a couple of years. He was going to try for a promotion to E-7 before he left the service. For once, Lou was quiet but she could not keep her hands calm. She was either getting more coffee or playing with her hair.

"Are you going to continue working at the Addiction Center, Lou?" asked Natalie.

"Yes, I love to help people, to see them set free from drugs or alcohol. Most of all I love to see people come to know the Lord." She looked Natalie in the eye and a tear ran down her check. "Natalie, you have been such a good friend and so kind, and Dean. I just love ya both. I am going to miss you like I would miss my own sister and brother."

She fell on Natalie who was sitting next to her and hugged her while weeping. She hugged her so hard that Dean saw his wife's eyes bulge a little. When she embraced him, Dean was sure that all the kinks in his back were put back in place. Lou was a big lady in every way. She loved big and the Ramseys were a couple that they would never forget.

At church the next day, Pastor Jethro was at the pulpit preaching. It was a good service, he would show up every once in a while, allowing one of the elders at his regular church to take over the service. Healing was taking place in the building and the congregation. Childs had led the elders and the people in spiritual cleaning of the building. Now when he went to church, it felt right.

At the potluck after the service, many of the families came over to say goodbye to the Larsons. Jethro and some of the elders anointed them and blessed them before they left.   They would leave the church in less than a month. It was a special time. They asked the Lord for traveling mercies as they went west, and that God would meet all their needs, and He would raise them up to be the people they needed to be. Dean felt refreshed after they were done. Jethro and the elders thanked the Larsons and the Childs for being faithful throughout the fight with the witches.

Monday morning found Dean in formation, answering roll call. He went on the run with battery but fell out afterwards to take care of the business of leaving the army. He had to turn in all his equipment and the supply sergeant made sure that it was all there and it was in good working condition.

Dean and Natalie had to arrange for shippers to come and haul the items that they packed up and send them back home. Jack would be waiting for them. They would go into Dad's old house. Jack had gone into the old home after the renters left and got it ready for the other Larson family to occupy. Dean had to get his college transcripts so he could use them when he got home. There was a ton of paperwork that had to be taken care of before he left the service.

The weekend before they left for home, the Childs family invited them over to dinner. Dean knew they would and he was looking forward to it. It was a hot muggy evening, so they were glad it was indoors. The dinner was another farewell and Eve promised that they would keep in touch. They all started wandering out to the living room after eating, but Top urged Dean to stay in the dining room.

"After any major conflict, the officers get together for a debriefing. I think we should have that Larson."

"Sounds good to me. I have a lot of questions for you, Top."

"Well young man, I believe the Lord is pleased with you on how you handled yourself during this little battle. You kept your eye on the problems in front of you and never wavered from seeking Him in the midst of everything that was going on. In the spirit realm, the enemy will throw curves at you, but you must keep your eye on the ball. Don't let the side issues distract you. You must also focus on the Lord at all times.

"How do you know all this stuff, Top?"

"My mother was a witch. My father stole me away from her at an early age. He took me to his parent's place and gave me into their care. I never saw either of my parents after that. My grandparents were very strong Christians. I remember them getting me up late at night. You could feel the evil in the air. We would pray until it lifted. They told me several times that the battle was over me, that the devil had come to claim what was owed him. I don't know if that was true, but I do believe my mother had given me to him. At some point, I felt free from the curse and the devils stopped bothering us."

"Wow, so you have had some first-hand experiences. I was never so glad to hear that it was over. I hope that I never get into another situation like the one we just went through."

Childs laughed, "You are a little naïve my young friend. The Lord didn't train you up for one battle. You will be facing a lot more in the future."

"I doubt that there are witches in Idaho. What will I be battling against?"

"Again, you are a little naïve. Idaho has its own evil, it is everywhere and we will be in spiritual foxholes together again and sooner than you think.

"What, are you coming to Idaho to live after you retire?"

"Yes, so I'm still going to be your spiritual father and I'm to disciple you for a season."

"I don't like spiritual warfare. I always feel dirty when I'm done for the day. I have no desire to be a pastor, but I don't see myself as a prayer warrior either."

"You have it all backwards Dean, it's not how you see yourself, it's how God sees you and the calling that he has put on your life. I can confirm that you are not a pastor, but you are a warrior and at some point, you will embrace it. Remember the blood of Jesus cleanses everything, so you might not feel clean, but you are."

Dean tapped his fingers on the table, thinking about what Childs had just told him. He picked up the cup of coffee in front of him and took a long sip. It was cool now, but he didn't mind it. He finally looked Childs in the face.

"What could we have done better in all this?'

"I messed up, we should have started praying against deception right away. You can always tell when the devil is lying and he always starts the fight with a lie. You can tell he's lying by the fact that he opened his mouth. It is in his nature to lie. We should have bound the lies and loosened truth right away. Maybe the Normans and some of the elders would have seen through Matty's fibs before it was too late.

"Remember, you take no ground from him unless you loosen the opposite of what you are binding. It's sad because Ivan and Lacy were the focal point of this battle, then the elders and the rest of the congregation."

"They made their choices and I am sorry to see what happened to them, but you talked to him many times, what more could we have done?" questioned Dean.

"Like Porter, Ivan opened up a spiritual door by not believing in possession and by stealing from the church. Judas was a thief and the devil used him to betray Jesus. Keep as many doors closed as you can Dean.

"In the future you will be caught in several snares, learn from them and call on the Lord and He will rescue you. These traps will teach you to have more compassion for others who sin. The final thing I want to remind you of is that you are an ambassador for the King of Kings. You represent His government; you offer peace between Him and humanity. On the other hand, you declare war on His enemies under His direction."

He gathered the Larson family together and blessed them and prayed for a safe trip home. They stayed for a while longer but Dean didn't hear much of the conversation. He was wondering about all that Childs said, about falling into the snares of the enemy. It troubled him all that night, he tossed and turned until Natalie awoke. She finally comforted him with the thought that he could take it to the Lord in prayer and God would help him through it or around it.

His first day as a civilian, he went early to the battery and shook hands and said good-bye to his friends. After the final farewells,

Dean went back home and they packed up the car. All they were carrying were the clothes they needed while on the road and their trusty atlas. The landlord came in and checked out the mobile home. She went back to the office to cut a check for the cleaning deposit. They took one last look at the place. He started the Mustang and they pulled out on the road, heading for his uncle's place in Missouri.

EPILOGUE

The 8-inch howitzer was phased out of the U.S. Army's arsenal in the 1990s.

The 3rd of the 319th became a part of the 82nd Airbourne during a period of reorganization in October of 1986. Since the 82nd couldn't beat them, they made the unit join them.

Sergeant Lawrance Cassidy made First Sergeant before retiring after twenty-four years in the service.

Brian Clark finished his three-year obligation in the army. He went to college for business and became an accountant for a large firm in Ohio.

William Clinton, [Wild Willie] finished college with the help of his wife. They have three children and have a nice home in Cleveland. He is managing a small grocery chain.

Randy Ellis took his family home to Nebraska. He became an insurance salesman and eventually ran his own brokerage firm.

Top Henry England retired after thirty years in the army. His wife Nancy and he settled in a small town near Fort Hood, Texas. He had saw action in three different wars and was highly decorated. Four years after he retired, he was diagnosed with brain cancer. He died less than a year later. They believed his death was associated with agent orange.

Arthur Garcia was killed in a car accident by a drunk driver in 1983. He was engaged and was to marry a young lady and died two weeks before the wedding.

Pastor Jethro and Sally Jackson continued to pastor in Memphis, Tennessee. He had a massive heart attack at the age of sixty-eight while preaching before his congregation. He went home to be with the Lord two days later, never waking from a coma. They said Sally followed him six months later, dying of a broken heart.

Captain Harold Knight distinguished himself in "Desert Storm." He was a part of the 2nd battery 41st field artillery. He eventually retired from the army as a full bird colonel and settled down in South Dakota.

Kevin Morton became Airbourne qualified. After his time in Fort Bragg, he decided to become a Ranger and in 1983 was one of the first to land in Granada during "Urgent Fury" with the 75th Rangers. He was caught in several fire fights and came out without a scratch. He went to OCS and became an officer. In 1990 he found himself a part of the 7th Infantry. One year later he was involved in "Desert Storm." He was wounded but survived his injuries and was sent home. Kevin obtains the rank of major. Carrie and he were still devoted to one another and she gave him a son.

Sergeant Joshua Marks married a young German woman. They had four children. He quickly advanced in rank and found himself as a senior drill instructor at Fort Sill, Oklahoma. While instructing a group of recruits on the 155-Howitzer he was involved in an accident. His right leg was severely injured, giving him a permanent limp. He was honorably discharged from the army with pension. He took his family back to Germany.

Ivan and Lacy Norman divorced and went their separate ways. Ivan never preached again. He got a job building houses. The church never prosecuted them because the money was returned. The church became a lot stronger because of what it went through.

Suzan Porter remarried after being single for five years. The Larsons lost contact with her and the girls.

Eddie and Maria Perez stayed in the army for four years. They returned to California. The couple have a son and another daughter. At last report, Eddie was working for a seed company, managing one of its departments.

George and Lou Ann Ramsey continued to love and honor one another. He made Chief of Smoke after twenty-one years of military life. He started to have health issues because of the many years of alcohol abuse. His physical health continued to decline until he succumbed to total liver failure. Lou Ann and his daughter were at his side as he passed away.

Chief of Smoke Jake Rose saw action in Grenada. He was highly decorated and ended his career as E-8 or Top after twenty-eight years of service. He settled in Nashville and invested in a gym where he taught young men the fine art of boxing. He never married

Lyle Taylor worked his way up through the ranks retiring as a Top. He saw action in Granada and "Desert Storm," receiving several decorations. He married a young lady from the south and they raised two children. He continued to keep his smile through his thirty years of service but never got over his fear of snakes.

PRAYER

Lord, forgive us, your people, for becoming apathetic and lethargic at this point in history. Stir us to action, to be about your business fulfilling your purposes. May the cry of a warrior arise in our hearts and may we take the land back that the enemy has stolen from us.

In Jesus Christ's name Amen, Amen.

CONTACT INFORMATION

If you desire to obtain copies of this book other than through Amazon or the publisher, or have any questions about it or any other information contained within it, you can contact the author through messenger on his Facebook page or email at dav.kelley@hotmail.com. You can also write him at the following address:

David Kelley
632 Teton Dr.
Nampa, ID. 83686